Loving Me For Me

by Naleighna Kai

Macro Publishing Group
Chicago, Illinois

Loving Me For Me by Naleighna Kai
Copyright 2017

Cover designed by: J. L. Woodson www.jlwoodson.com
Interior design by: Lissa Woodson www.naleighnakai.com
Cover Image: www.vikkaszone.com
Models: Vikkas Bhardwaj and Ashley Carter
www.vikkaszone.com

Printed in the United States of America

Acknowledgements:

All praise and honor is due to the Creator always. A special love and respect to my guardian angels, ancestors, teachers, and guides.

To my spiritual mothers: Sandy Spears and Bettye Mason Odom; to my son, Jeremy "J. L." Woodson, just when I think you can't up your game, you prove me wrong. I am so proud of you, Number One Son. Much success to you in your graphic design and consulting business. Oh, and I have to add, you put your foot in the cover of this novel!

To the people who continuously have my front and my back: Renee Sesvalah Cobb-Dishman, Debra Mitchell, Martha Kennerson, Marilyn Gill, Liz Hill, Shannan Harper, DeMarco Suggs, Jennifer Addison Cole, Aisha Lusk, Jamyi Joy, and Ehryck F. Gilmore; to Janine Ingram who helped me come up with the title for this book; to Janice Pernell (my developmental editor who also has the best ear and doesn't mind giving it to me straight, no chaser); to my wonderful Beta Raders (who expanded this book from the novella it was intended to be to a BAB (big a$$ book): Martha Kennerson, Priscilla (Lady PBJ) Jackson, Royce Slade Morton, Anita Roseboro-Wade, Martha Kennerson, Latisha Dewalt, Lu McCoy, Michelle Wright, Marze Scott, Christine Pauls, E. N. Joy, Shannan Harper, Joylynn Jossel Ross, and Brynn Weimer. Many thanks to Vikkas Bhardwaj for the Hindi translations, information on East Indian culture, and that hot cover image; to Suresh Bhasin for his hospitality and insight into East Indian Festivals; to M. Sheena Khatwani for always looking out for me when I come to Tiffin's. To Sanjay, Kim, and Leo and everyone at India House Chicago who have shown me so much love.

To the book clubs and avid readers who support my work—I love and appreciate each one of you.

To everyone I mentioned (and those that I may have forgotten to type), thank you for everything you are to me.

Wishing you all—peace and love, light and joy.
—Naleighna Kai

Dedication:

My mother, Jean Woodson
My grandmother, Mildred E. Williams
My brother, Eric Harold Spears
My niece, LaKecia Janise Woodson,
a rising star who left us much too soon

To Leslie Esdaile Banks (L.A. Banks)
Octavia M. Butler,
two of the best storytellers the planet had to offer.

To Anthony "Green Eyes" Johnson,
to Derek V. Fields (a fallen Cavalier angel)

About the Author

Naleighna Kai is a national bestselling and award-winning author of several controversial novels, contributor to a New York Times bestseller, and the E. Lynn Harris Author of Distinction. She has penned *Every Woman Needs a Wife, Loving Me for Me, Was it Good For You Too?, Open Door Marriage, She Touched My Soul, Rich Woman's Fetish* and other contemporary fiction novels that plumb the depth of unique love triangles and women's issues.

In addition to successfully cracking the code of getting published and landing a deal with a major publishing house, she continues to "pay it forward" by organizing the annual Cavalcade of Authors which gives readers intimate access to the most accomplished writing talent today. She also serves as CEO of Macro Marketing & Promotions Group which offers aspiring authors help with editing, publishing, marketing, and other services to jump start their writing ambition. Additionally she is Editor-in-Chief for Naleighna Kai's Literary Café Magazine and Acquisitions editor for NK Recommends—a mail order book service that caters to a select audience. She was born and raised on the Southeast side of Chicago, the setting for most of her novels and where she is currently working on her next books: *Slaves of Heaven* and *Mercury Sunrise.*

Find her on the web at
www.naleighnakai.com,
www.thecavalcadeofauthors.com,
www.facebook.com/naleighnakai
twitter.com/NaleighnaKai

chapter 1

"My God they look like us."

Reign's heart took a quantum leap into her throat. The deep timbre of that voice belonged to the one man she never wanted to lay eyes on again. Before she could catch up to the hostess and make it to the nearest exit instead of the reserved table, he spoke again.

"Reign?" Her name carried across Tiffin Restaurant, causing a few heads to turn in his direction.

She nodded slowly, unable to get her vocal cords to produce any sound.

Devesh rose from the table where a group dressed in vibrant East Indian garments had gathered, and sauntered along the path to Reign and the two children he, up to this point, knew nothing about.

One night with him a little more than five years ago had changed her life. Reign had left her soul in that luxury hotel room and walked away with a broken heart—and a pregnancy—neither of which any woman with a grown son would have ever desired.

She had blocked all communication with Devesh that next day and made it her business to stop traveling in circles where they would come in close contact. She had managed to avoid him for so long; yet, a trip with the twins to Disneyland had placed them directly in his path.

Her children, Leena and Kamran, were unaware of the turmoil warring within her. They released their hold on her hands and ran to Devesh, offering an embrace. Though Reign had kept knowledge of their existence from Devesh, she'd made sure Leena and Kamran knew about him. For some reason, they'd been asking about him more and more lately. She showed them current images of him so that in the case of her untimely or accidental death, they would know exactly who their father was. She had even braced herself for the possibility that they might seek him out when they became teenagers if not before. She certainly wasn't prepared for a chance meeting like this. How could fate be so cruel?

Devesh lowered to his knees so he was at their eye level before glancing over Leena's shoulder as he asked, "Are these your children?"

Reign nodded, her voice still failing. She'd never imagined seeing her twins with Devesh, but in this moment, their resemblance to him was nothing short of astounding. Leena and Kamran carried Devesh's olive skin, raven hair, well-defined cheekbones—a combination that made him a highly sought after spokesperson in media and print advertising. They even had dimples on the right cheek. The same almond-shaped eyes. The same pert nose. Only the slight fullness of their lips, the curliness of their hair, and eyes the color of emeralds hinted that Reign gave them half of their DNA.

"They are absolutely beautiful." Devesh said, tweaking Leena's nose and ruffling Kamran's hair. The twins' hearty giggles caused Devesh to laugh in kind.

His family and the other patrons of Tiffin suddenly became more interested in this unlikely reunion than in the fine cuisine the place offered.

"So, you're married?" he asked, picking the children up as he stood, with absolute no protest from the twins. If the gleam in their eyes told anything—they were elated to be near him.

"No," Reign whispered. She closed the distance between them, intent on extracting her babies from his hold. "I've never been married."

"I didn't realize you were dating back when we …"

Reign witnessed a range of expressions flitter across his face, signaling that he was trying to sync up timelines and possibilities. He glanced at the children in his arms, inspecting their features before he frowned. No doubt he was recalling the night the two of them had shared a little over five years ago. Her mind followed suit.

A week before the Advertising Age Convention, Devesh had injured his leg during an accident caused by another member during a workout at a fitness center. He was ordered to stay off his feet for at least two weeks. Devesh had a commitment to the companies that sponsored his appearance. Backing out at the last minute wasn't something he would do. Friends and acquaintances, including Reign, banded together to assist him during that week. She arrived at the convention with the Intellectual Property attorneys from the law firm where she worked, but managed to inform the woman putting Devesh's schedule together that she could help at night. All of the friends took turns, whenever time permitted, to make sure Devesh let his body heal from the day's efforts and strengthen enough so he could carry out his duties for the next day.

Reign pulled the "night shift" and brought him some meds, several ice packs for his leg, then massaged those aches when needed. Devesh had asked her to stay a while so they could talk about the things that transpired over the two years after Vegas when they hadn't been in contact. Getting reacquainted led to a host of conversations that lasted well into the night. Time slipped away from them, and when the clock struck midnight, Devesh said, "Why don't you stay here with me." He gestured to the opposite side of his bed.

"Oh, that's pretty slick trying to get me in the sack," she replied with a laugh. "Are we doing that one leg on top of the covers thing?"

"Woman, I don't have to play games when it comes to my feelings for you," Devesh countered and his tone was dead serious. "I want you in the best and worst way. But I have control and so do you. It's late. Having someone see you tip out of here might cause a few tongues to make something out of nothing. The lawyers you work for are here."

She hesitated a long moment. Truthfully, it wasn't him she was worried about. She had fallen for him before because he had shown her more love, compassion, and consideration than any man before. Finally, he ended her confusion and misgivings by saying, "Go on, Reign. I'll call you if I need anything. I promise." She knew he wouldn't. The others had already let her know he was stubborn, overexerting himself and not taking the injury seriously. She opted to stay.

On night two, when he asked her to stay again, she woke when he touched her, beckoning for her to move toward him. He slept with his arms around her, spooning her in an intimate embrace that made her feel safer and more loved than she had ever been. She also watched him as he slept, noticing he was resting better than he had the night before.

Night three and four were more of the same. Night five was a mind-blowing, next-level sensual experience neither one of them could have foreseen, but Reign welcomed it with everything she had to give. Yet, the next morning Devesh's expression was solid and purposeful as not a word passed between them about that love-making or how close they'd become. Actually, he seemed to forget everything that had happened. She laid her head on the pillow and closed her eyes for a moment. When she opened her eyes again, he was gone. The rejection was so profound, she vowed no one would ever have that power over her again.

"You have to come back to the house," Devesh said, snapping her back to the present. "We need to talk."

The children had a vice grip on his neck. Two identical pairs of green eyes pleaded with her to say yes, then Leena, the more talkative of the twins took things a step further. "Please, Mommy. Please ..." while Kamran nodded his support of that request.

"I'll see if I can make time to come," she whispered.

The twins' joy spilled over in the form of chuckles that brought smiles to the lips of the few family members who circled Devesh, fascinated by the children. Especially delighted was Devesh's twin Anaya, whose beauty matched his handsomeness measure for measure.

Reign remembered the family member's faces as Devesh consistently posted photos of all Indian holiday celebrations, birthdays, and family gatherings on social media. She also remembered that each of them had been extremely vocal in their opposition to Devesh's desire to pursue a relationship with her.

"How is Jay?" Devesh asked, referring to her older son.

"He just graduated from Columbia," she replied, trying to keep her voice steady. "He's building his portfolio."

Devesh and Jay had become close during those first two years of Reign's and Devesh's friendship. Though her son was loyal to her, she told Jay that she didn't see a reason for his relationship with Devesh to end simply because she wasn't having anything to do with him. Her son was careful to keep any information about Devesh to himself, although there were many times when she wanted to ask. The twins were a huge secret for Jay to keep, which said more about her son's need to keep the relationship with Reign intact, than to jeopardize it by breaking his promise to her.

Now she would be unable to take the coward's way out. And if the pointed looks Devesh's family shot their way were any indication, the members of the Maharaj family were going to give voice to the main question long before Devesh could demand answers he was fast becoming aware he should ask.

The twins had inherited Reign's uncanny sense of observation early on. They now eyed her with keen interest, as though they sensed that her present anxiety was related to Devesh.

"Can I put you down for a moment?" he asked the children.

The twins shook their heads and tightened their hold, causing Devesh to put an intense focus on Reign, blinking as though still trying to get an understanding. His lips parted to speak and Reign braced herself. Then Devesh grimaced, clamped his mouth shut and shook his head.

Devesh's mother, Jasinder, had an eagle-eyed gaze locked on Reign. She lifted her left eyebrow, posing a question of sorts or giving Reign the opportunity to confess.

She knows. My God, she knows.

Reign transferred her focus to Anaya, who peered at the children, apparently summing up things on her own.

Devesh's father, Suresh, leaned in to his wife, eyebrows drawn in, his face registering his concern at the intensity of the unspoken exchanges taking place around them.

Jasinder formed the sounds slowly enough for Reign to make out five distinct words, "They belong to our son."

Suresh blanched, eyes flashing with fire before a scowl descended on his wide mouth. Then he shook his head as though to rid himself of what those words meant. Both Jasinder and Suresh focused on the children again, who were now holding an animated conversation with Devesh about their day at the amusement park. The accusation behind the curious glances from Jasinder, Suresh, and Anaya galloped Reign's way.

"I'll text you my address," Devesh said to Reign.

Her children. No—*his* children gave Reign a look so intense her knees almost gave out.

Kamran tilted his head as he studied her, probably taking in the tense lines of her face. Leena's lips pursed into a thin line, but it was her eyes that said everything. They knew Reign had no intention of showing up, even at Devesh's insistence.

Devesh leaned down with Kamran in his arm and said, "Hand that to me, little guy."

Kamran quickly plucked the cell from Reign's hand before she could protest. He passed it to Devesh, who manuevered to use the pad of his thumb to scroll down the contact list. "My number's not in your phone?"

Reign parted her lips to defend herself, but shut it because he wasn't done.

"And you blocked me on Facebook too? I don't understand any of that. We definitely need to talk." He looked down at the children, who were so comfortable they still wouldn't let him go. "I thought we were friends, Reign," he whispered so his family wouldn't hear. "That we were close. How could you disappear on me like that? How could you ..."

The unspoken words *"not tell me that you had my children"* hung in the air.

Reign reached for Leena, and her daughter shrank back, and laid her head on Devesh's chest instead.

An unexpected pain seared Reign's heart. "I had my reasons."

"You should ride with them, Devesh," a voice behind them encouraged. "Make sure they arrive safely."

Reign turned, upset that Jasinder would try to box her in by voicing such a suggestion. A petite woman with a salt-and-pepper braid flowing down her back, came forward to stand next to Jasinder. The woman gave Reign a calming smile and a slight bow of her head as if Reign was royalty; the only one standing with Devesh's family who wasn't glaring at Reign as though she had committed a crime.

"Would you like for me to ride with you?" Devesh asked the children. They approved vehemently.

"Looks like they agree," he said with a victorious lift of his chin as he studied Reign's face.

"Papa."

Oh, sweet Jesus. No. No. No.

Devesh's attention snapped to Leena with that one word before he peered at Reign. "Wow, I must look a lot like their father for her to say that."

"Imagine that," his mother said, and her tone was every bit sarcastic as Devesh's had been. "He definitely must be East Indian, yes?"

Reign paused, tamping down a weary sigh. "Yes, he is."

"They look like they might have some Maharaj blood somewhere along the line," she mused, stroking a weathered finger across Leena's cheek.

Reign saw the seed taking root deeper in Devesh's mind. He was silent as he put his focus on the children.

"Reign," Devesh said, taking her attention from his mother's hard glare. "Come. Let's go."

"I won't be able to stay long."

Devesh exchanged a speaking glance with his mother, possibly alarmed by the change in her demeanor. Jasinder's stony expression was a sure sign of displeasure. Whether it was in response to Reign's statement or because she was well aware that some major deception was going on remained to be seen.

The smile didn't reach Jasinder's eyes as she said in thickly accented English, "I am certain that a short while is all it will take."

Reign recognized those words for the threat they were designed to be.

chapter 2

An hour later, the family settled Devesh down on one of the many sofas scattered about in several adjoining rooms. His parents and aunt pulled out the baby photos of him and his twin. Then other family members gave Reign a tour of the nearly eleven thousand square foot oceanfront mansion.

After nearly every family album had been placed before Devesh and Reign in an attempt to get her to acknowledge the obvious, he finally looked over to Reign, gestured to the albums and said, "I am their father."

Reign closed her eyes, trying to calm the fear that had been tap-dancing in her gut since the near silent drive to the place, then walking into a home—actually, mansion—that took her breath away. Evidently, the Maharaj family was wealthy, though Devesh had been so humble that she would never have guessed that was the case.

"Leena is a mirror image of my sister, and Kamran is a reflection of me," Devesh explained with a pointed glare at Reign. "That can't be a coincidence. And they are how old?"

She parted her lips to give a non-answer but nearly choked on the ball of pain lodged squarely in her throat.

"We're four years, six months, two weeks …" Leena offered cheerily as she glanced at Kamran who looked up from his Disney watch and finished with, "five days and …." Leena frowned at Kamran, nudging him as she whispered, "You're supposed to say the hours and minutes, too."

"It keeps changing," Kamran said, scowling at his twin. "I have the hard part."

Reign's lips tightened when Devesh leaned back in his place on the sofa and continued to study her, eyes widened by the undeniable truth. She'd always encouraged the twins to keep up this way because it made them more aware of the importance of numbers. Now they'd given him the exact coordinates needed to map out the answer on his own, without her confession.

"What made you check out on me back then," he whispered, frowning as though trying to make sense of the whys of it all. "And why would you keep my children from me? Did I hurt you in some way?"

"No." She shook her head, alarmed that he would jump to that conclusion. "No, you didn't."

"I thought our night together was so beautiful," he said in a voice that only she could hear. He moved closer to where she stood—a spot that was not too far from the front door. "When I woke that next morning there wasn't one ache or pain in my body anywhere. Everything was right in my world." He cupped her face in his hands. "I was determined to go home and let my family know that I would have you in my life no matter how they felt. And then you weren't there anymore. You didn't say a word. Left me thinking that I was wrong about us—that you didn't love me."

Every word was a stab of pain in her heart.

The tears streaming down Reign's face almost touched him. Almost. She had kept his children from him all this time and never once considered how much they— or she—would mean to him.

He sucked in a deep breath to calm his anger. Instead, he felt his body go rigid with remembered pleasure of being with her, and quickly decided it would be best to keep a little distance between them for the time being.

Devesh cast his glance over to the twins. Leena was now in Anaya's arms, and Kamran was on Mumma's lap. The years when he could not reach Reign had been hard on him. And none of it seemed to faze her— not his pain, not the fact that he was hurt even more by her insistence on keeping this secret. This beautiful, but heart-wrenching secret.

"I demand to have equal time with my children," he said when no answers were forthcoming from Reign. His eyes held tightly to hers. "You have had them all to yourself for four, nearly five, years. And I have had none. I demand some time to get to know them. For my family to get to as well."

Reign placed her focus on the twins, who were taking a pointed interested in the private conversation being held between their parents on the opposite side of the room.

"You have done them and me a great injustice, Reign," he said, his voice holding a gravity that mirrored how he felt. "And I demand that you make it right. Give me some time with them—alone." He placed his hands on her upper arms. "Four years would work. Four years, six months, two weeks and five days to be exact, but I'll settle for a couple of hours until we can work things out."

She vehemently argued her point against leaving the children with people they didn't know. This went on for nearly half an hour, and he countered each and every one of her objections before she finally gave up, stared up at him, then snatched from his hold.

"Two hours. Is that too much to ask?"

Reign went to her children, gathered them from his mother's and sister's arms. She held them to her for several moments, then whispered something to each of them. They embraced her and nodded their acceptance of what she had said, but did not look happy.

She gave Mumma an intense look, and when the salt-and-pepper haired woman slowly nodded to the unspoken request, only then did Reign release a resigned breath. She left the house without giving him or anyone else so much as a goodbye. And as much as he wanted to run after her, the anger holding him hostage would not let him. He continued to watch through the foyer's windows as the rental car she slid into drove off and disappeared.

Children. He actually had children. For so long, he thought maybe he was sterile because none of the few women he'd been with had ended up pregnant. Not that he'd been trying to sire a child, but he hadn't exactly been careful about doing what it took to prevent a pregnancy either. But that one majestic night with Reign had been the most powerful and explosive love-making he'd ever experienced. Somehow, it resulted in giving him the one thing that had alluded him for far too long. And it happened with the woman he had fallen for from the first time they'd held a conversation in Vegas.

Though he had witnessed the love that his parents had for each other, marriage had not been something Devesh had wanted early on—until he met Reign. Given his family's rejection of her, before she had even graced their presence, he thought that the union would never be possible. By the time he was prepared to defy them, his ambition had taken a front seat. Travel to other countries and charity work for the orphanages in India helped keep him from obsessing over his family's rejection of Reign. But when he thought about a family, he wanted it with a woman who had it together, who knew how to establish goals and reach them. A woman who was done playing games. He wanted a woman that he could learn from, that he could love, and who would love him not for the way he looked or for his body. Someone who would complement the parts of him that needed it most.

Devesh knew from day one that Reign was that woman, but his family was not hearing him. Especially when Tiya had taken it upon herself to extract a few images of Reign from a social media page. When his mother and father took a look, saw that she wasn't his age and that she wasn't East Indian, they were adamant about Devesh cutting off all ties with her. The argument went on for months before he'd allowed his friendship with Reign to diminish, and he had hated to give in to their wishes. Nothing filled the void that the loss of her had created—not work, not travel, not family. Nothing.

Then they reconnected almost two years later in Atlanta. It felt as if no time had separated them between Vegas and Atlanta whatsoever. This time, he was ready to take on every one of his family's objections—and he had, vehemently, and won. He called to share the news with Reign, fully prepared to forge ahead with a relationship if she would have him. Silence on her end. Now he wondered if he should have expressed his feelings to her *before* they left Atlanta. Maybe then she would have accepted his calls. Maybe then she would have responded to his emails. Maybe then she wouldn't have disappeared as if he hadn't mattered to her as much as she had to him.

On his birthday, fate had brought them together in a way that neither Reign nor his family had any choice but to accept. And his brutal words had sent her running from his parents' home, hurting in a way he never intended.

Leena looked up at him, a single damning tear streaming down her face, soon followed by several more. She did not look away, and the searing pain in her eyes was not hard to miss.

She had a weary expression that no child should ever wear. Devesh could practically hear her thoughts.

Losing my mother is the price of having a father?

Yes, he had every right to be angry with Reign, but to separate his children from the only parent they had known was downright cruel. Even for a small amount of time.

Leena tugged on her brother's arm, and Kamran followed her to the northeast corner of the house—the wealth corner—where an altar, a Puja, a brightly lit lamp, the scent of sweet incense, and other sacred pieces and scriptures held space.

The two of them settled on the white marble floor, sitting Indian style—lotus position—as though preparing for a private meditation all their own. Kamran placed his arm about Leena's little shoulders in a protective gesture. Devesh had done that same thing with his own twin when they were growing up—two East Indian children transported from a place filled with culture, music, literature and familiar faces and dropped into the busy and fast-paced urban landscape of the Bronx.

His children had their backs to the adults, who all looked on, amazed at their silent solidarity. Leena and Kamran somehow recognized the Puja room, a place where Devesh gave reverence to the Creator every day, as the safest place in the Maharaj home. The twins were very much aware of the purpose of this space, and that touched him. In his culture, God the Creator is considered the true owner of the home, and the people within are simply the caretakers. Puja is a daily reminder that God is supposed to have the most important place in everyone's life, heart, and mind. Evidently, Reign had at least exposed them to some aspects of his culture.

The air was tense, filled with the silent condemnation the twins were too young to speak. He had done them a disservice, and now his children were making their displeasure known. Devesh could only wonder what kind of prayers his children were sending up at the moment. Especially since he, a man who he wanted them to love and trust, had already hurt them. The fact that the twins felt the need for God's assistance caused a sliver of anguish to run through him. He would make this right.

Devesh crossed the distance from the family room and into the living room, lowered to his knees and settled in the space behind his children at the Puja, who did not bother to turn around and acknowledge his presence.

"I will go and find your mother," he whispered.

Only then did Leena look over her shoulder, slowly, as though considering those words and the person who said them. She gave a single nod then put her focus back to the Puja. Kamran, obviously the more stubborn of the two, did not acknowledge him at all. The firm set of his shoulders was saying everything that needed to be said. He did not appreciate the way his father had treated his mother, and he would not be swayed as quickly as his sister.

"I promise to bring her back," Devesh vowed. "Kamran, will you look after your sister for me?"

Seconds passed before Kamran's body angled to face him, but only slightly. He peered upward into Devesh's eyes as he said, "I take care of Leena." He nodded then as though that was the end of the subject.

So serious for someone so young. What had they been through? What did he really know about Reign?

"Thank you."

Kamran took his sister's hand before putting his focus on the altar again.

Devesh stood, thoughts whirling of what he would say to Reign when he laid eyes on her again. Without another thought, he snatched up his keys and marched to the door. His youngest sister's voice rang out loud and clear. "So already we have to take care of your little half-breed bastards?"

He froze with one foot halfway over the threshold. Anger rippled through him so quickly he couldn't send a message to his brain that he should keep marching toward his mission and ignore that taunt. He was in Tiya's face within ten strides that ate up the carpet.

"Don't you *ever* insult them that way," he snarled, while Anaya tried to put a solid grip on his arms and hold him back.

"Well, that's what they are," Tiya countered, putting a few inches of space between them. She almost tripped over the long, flowing strands of dark hair that touched past her ankles.

Aunt Kavya turned an icy glare to Tiya, then looked to Devesh before placing a calming hand on his arm.

"Yes, they are of mixed parentage," he agreed. "But you meant it as an insult beyond that, and I'm taking it as one. Keep a civil tongue when you have anything to say about my children."

She blew him off with a shrug. He realized that if Tiya could give voice to this kind of anger, then leaving his children there would not be a good thing.

"Leena. Kamran. With me," Devesh said, extending his hand toward them.

The children were by his side in the time it took to blink. Each flanked him and took hold of one of his hands. Both of them glared at Tiya as though they understood that she had said something improper about them and it was the reason Devesh was not pleased.

"Son, go," his mother encouraged, leaving her position next to his father and moving into a place in front of Devesh. "I will look to their well-being. Go to her." She placed a hand on his cheek. "They need her. And *you* need her. They should not hear the conversation you will have with their mother."

"Mumma …" he began, using an East Indian endearing word for mother, before sweeping a look across the silent members of his family who donned expressions that ranged from indifference to curiosity to slightly hostile. Except Aunt Kavya, who smiled.

As though sensing the reason for his concern, Mumma added, "I will take care of them myself. I promise you."

Devesh lowered until he was eye level with his children. "I'm going to your mother, and I'd like for you to stay with my Mumma. Alright?"

The twins took a searching glance at Mumma, whose smile wavered a bit as she tried to be reassuring. Then they scanned the faces of everyone else in the room who stared back at them. The twins tightened their grips on his hands, then released them as they moved forward and reclaimed their positions in front of the Puja.

Evidently, they had a survival instinct that was more intact than his own. And they trusted each other more than they trusted anyone else. Hopefully, that would change over time.

With one last warning look at his youngest sister and a reassuring nod from Mumma, Aunt Kavya, and Anaya, Devesh was out the door and on his way to an uncertain future.

chapter 3

Reign's heart was so broken she didn't know if it could ever be mended. He hated her for what she'd done. She was certain of that one thing. And he had every right to feel that way.

She had taken the easy way out, all because she feared that Devesh would reject the children as he had rejected her—just like Jay's father had done.

Reign never realized Devesh came from a wealthy family. All this time she believed him to be a struggling aspiring actor who welcomed her help to get his career moving in the right direction. The minute she set foot in the Maharaj home, any myth she'd bought into about him had disappeared so fast it was as if it had never been there.

Though Devesh was loaded, he had the humility and compassion of a man who had grown up on the poorer side of life and didn't hold the world responsible for any shortcomings.

She thought she'd been so clever by setting up an estate plan that contained explicit details for the children's care into the age of majority and a letter explaining their existence to a father who would be blindsided by the news. The letter also explained why she felt it necessary to withhold the information that he was the father of two precious children. No need for such a letter or to keep putting money in those trust funds now.

The Maharaj home exuded an unforgettable ambiance from the moment she crossed the threshold. The display of wealth was extremely unsettling, as it brought the reality they had enough money to give her a serious custody battle. That thought was the only reason she had given in to leaving the twins with him for those two hours. Denying him would have made the situation worse.

She dropped down on the bed and rummaged through the tote bag until her cell was in her hand.

First, she tried to reach her friend Renee, but she was in the middle of counseling a client. Then she tried for Debra who said, "Let me call you back later, love. The massage therapist is here." Deb's efforts at regaining full range of motion after a hip replacement was definitely more important than Reign's unburdening of her soul.

Reign then dialed Janice, who informed her that she was in the lawyer's office finalizing the details of gaining her freedom from a man who had not seen her value for nearly two decades.

She held the phone for several minutes before making a call to the one person who knew almost as much about her situation with Devesh as she did.

"Jay, I messed up so bad," she admitted.

"Mama?" he said, and she could tell she had woken him from a daytime nap. He worked on design projects mostly at night, as there weren't so many distractions. "Mama, what's wrong?"

"I ran into Devesh today," she said, her voice barely a whisper. "He … he's going to take them from me."

"Mama, calm down," he admonished, and she heard a rustle of what had to be bed linens in the background. "He wouldn't do that."

"You didn't see him. You didn't *hear* him," she cried, gripping the edge of the bed. "He's so angry with me, it's not even funny."

"Where are the munchkins right now?"

"With his family. He asked—no, he demanded—that they spend time with them today." She mentally flipped through the images of the Maharaj mansion including the billiards room, pub-style bar, temperature-controlled wine room; and her worries intensified. "The man is rich, Jay. He has the kind of money that could tie me up in court for years. I don't have the kind of funds it'll take to fight him."

The majority of her money had been dropped into their college and trust funds. Basically, for the first time in a long time, she was living paycheck to paycheck in a job that was merely helping her make ends meet before she met the end. And though his house and family would benefit her children on a number of levels, and it seemed Devesh could give the twins things she couldn't afford, splitting their time between California and Chicago was not going to be the best thing for them.

"Mama, I think you're buying a problem before it's even been sold," Jay said in a voice that irritated her because it was so calm and rational. He was always the voice of reason, and she could swear she didn't know where he came by that trait. Jay was so unlike her in many ways. And definitely unlike the father who had abandoned him early on in life. All the hurt and pain her oldest son had endured from his absentee father was heartbreaking enough. Reign was determined that the twins would not be subjected to that kind of hatred.

"You're not going to say I told you so."

Jay was silent for a moment before he answered, "I don't need to. You did what you thought was best, but now you'll have to get used to doing something different. You'll need to share them with him. You'll just have to find out how it can be done in a way you can live with. They are his children too, Mama," he said in a low tone. "I never understood your stance on this because you definitely weren't like this when it came to me. You told my father straight out of the gate. Anytime I wanted to see him, you would drop whatever you were doing and take me to his mother's place where he's been living since Hector was a pup— and Hector's a big dog right about now and Dad is *still* living with his mama. If I was on punishment, you took me off long enough to spend time with him." Again he didn't say anything for a second, and then, "I appreciate the fact that you never kept me from him. You never said a negative word about him. I found out what a deadbeat he was on my own."

Reign had tried her best not to put his father's trifling ways on blast and to make sure that Jay had some positive male presence in his life. She'd put him in martial arts because it had a multitude of strong men as mentors, and she'd even landed a big brother for him through the Big Brothers Big Sisters of Metropolitan Chicago. She had grown up with a father who went out for a Pepsi and some smokes and he didn't return until twelve years later—with another set of children and a mistress in tow. The family had been devastated by his absence when it first happened. With the breadwinner missing in action, the family went so far down, they didn't know there had ever been an up. Their mother, Thelma, a housewife who didn't have a high school diploma or skills that could hold a job that would support six children, never knew what would happen from one day to the next.

The Latino family next door, were in the same state as Reign's family. The father had left the seven of them. They were poor but not quite on the level of Reign's family. So the two mothers began to share resources and survived that way. That is, until Roberto, the oldest son of the Madera family, fell for fourteen-year-old Reign, and she became pregnant.

Thelma put a suitcase filled with only a few of Reign's things outside the front door and said she couldn't come back unless she agreed to have an abortion. When Reign picked up that suitcase and made it halfway up the concrete pathway to the sidewalk, Thelma quickly amended her stance. "Since you're so hell-bent on keeping the baby, you can return under *one* condition."

Maria was forced to intervene and give Reign a place to stay right after that "condition" placed by her mother went in a direction Thelma never intended. She had to stand in front of the members of the congregation— and apologize for her sin. The process didn't go well for Reign's mother or the pastor.

Thelma, still upset about being ostracized from the church she had been a member of for most of her life, unleashed her rage on Maria for helping Reign. She called her a *spic*. Maria saw Thelma for what she really was—a hypocrite—and told her straight to her face. She hadn't been a *spic* when she put groceries on the table of a house whose cupboards were bare. She wasn't a *spic* when she shelled out money to keep the lights and gas on for Reign's family. Maria wasn't a *spic* when it suited Thelma's needs, but after Maria saw fit to have compassion on a fourteen-year-old who was pregnant by her twenty-one-year old son, she was every name but a child of God.

Roberto turned out to be more like his father than anyone realized. He had been a grown man, seven years older than Reign, yet he blamed *her* for getting pregnant. Not only did he float in and out, making "guest appearances" in Jay's life, but he would also get upset when he finally offered the crumbs of his life and Jay showed him that he wasn't all that hungry. Roberto also had forced Reign into an ugly child support battle that waged all the way up until Jay started college. Over the years, he avoided paying child support—switching jobs, taking menial positions, collecting unemployment, becoming a "professional" student, and attempting to terminate his parental rights, to name a few.

Finally, after an experience where Roberto ducked into the bathroom right before a court appearance to avoid having to see his son, Jay told Reign, "Enough! I'll make it on my own. Stop going to court for this. I'm going to be married with my own children, and you'll still be up in this place trying to get what you feel he owes you. Enough, Mama. Let it go. Let *him* go. I'm certainly going to."

And he was right. The minute she simply left the situation with Roberto having to pay the twenty grand in arrears and nothing more for college, the doors opened for her son to attend Fisk University in Nashville on a presidential scholarship, then South Carolina State before finishing up years later with a graphic design degree from Columbia College in Chicago.

"I know that my father not being in my life was his choice, not yours," Jay explained. "You didn't give Devesh a chance to do right by his children. You made it *your* choice, not his," he warned, and the truth was a little hard to bear. "Somehow, it seems like the Universe wants you to do something about that."

Yes, her oldest child was right about that, too.

chapter 4

Anaya Singh Bakshi watched her twin rush from the living room. Her focus went to the two children who were suddenly thrust into a world that had more questions than answers. They were positioned in the same place their father chose for meditation and answers each day. Anaya had a feeling that the entire family needed to go to the Puja and join the two little ones in whatever quest they were on at the moment.

This situation, though, had the entire family shaken. No one in the Maharaj family had married outside of their culture. And for Devesh to want someone like Reign—a woman who wasn't as young as he was, and who was Black—her parents were holding it together pretty well.

"Well that was intense," her older brother, Bhavin, said. His petite wife, Sana, nodded from her position on the family room sofa.

Conversation among the family resumed, most of it speculation about Devesh's relationship with Reign or lack thereof. The rest was centered around what they believed would come from this new development.

A lot of things had happened in the Maharaj family over the years, but Devesh's desire for Reign, and now the discovery that they have children together, had to be the most scandalous. Things would be different if the more immediate family had been left alone to wrap their minds around the situation before the extended part of the family became involved.

Unfortunately, the Shoreview Mansion was the center of all social activities for the Maharaj family. All of the family, extended family, some of their friends and co-workers paid into a pot that purchased the groceries for dinners that were prepared for everyone on a nightly basis. Mumma, Aunts Kavya, Prisha, and Neerav kept everyone's babies, toddlers, and preschool aged children during the day so that the women in the family could pursue their careers. The nightly dinners also served as a safe haven to discuss many things or for everyone to pitch in to watch the children if a couple wanted to go out on a date or vacations.

When Devesh landed a major role in a Bollywood film, he had used every dime of that money to purchase this home in the warmer climate of California. Then he expanded it according to Mumma and Papa's wishes. That was before moving the immediate family from New York to California—his parents, Anaya and her husband Pranav, his brother Bhavin and wife Sana, sister Tiya and her husband Hiran, uncles Samar and Mitul and their wives Prisha and Kavya, along with cousins Neerav and Meenu. Soon, a few others followed and settled in homes in nearby suburbs. All of them were in the house at the moment, as they had come to celebrate Devesh and Anaya's birthday. The day started at Disney Land, Devesh called it the "happiest place in the world." The party at the house would normally continue well into the next morning, but no one was in a festive mood at the moment.

"I have never seen Devesh so angry," Papa said, concern etched in his tawny face.

Papa was wrong. Devesh had been livid several years ago after the ugly things some of the family members said about Reign when he told them he had every intention of marrying her. Tiya had taken the liberty of stalking Reign's social media pages and printing pictures for all of the family to see. She deliberately pulled ones that were not the professional images that Anaya had seen, when she too, had sought to find out more about the woman who had captured her brother's heart. No other woman had made Devesh want to take that trip into holy matrimony. Not even the blonde "starlet" he'd had an on again-off again relationship over the years.

Anaya extracted herself from the flurry of people holding multiple conversations, wound her way into the kitchen to pour two small glasses of fresh mango juice. She placed them on a tray then journeyed through the series of open rooms the family called the four corners—a den that led into a family room which led into the living room and parlor—before sliding it toward Devesh's children.

"No, thank you," Kamran said, looking up at her with green eyes so expressive that Anaya wanted to take him in her arms and make up for all the hugs she hadn't been able to give him.

"You must have something, little one," Anaya whispered, stroking a hand through his hair.

"No thank you, ma'am," Leena said, her eyes glazed with tears. "We'll wait for Mama and Papa."

"She said drink," Uncle Mitul roared all the way from the den, causing the children to flinch. His face was a mask of unconcealed fury. He had always been loud and brash, but never to the many Maharaj children when they were sitting on his lap as he told them stories or gave them treats and gifts.

"They are children," Tiya snapped, her fist shaking in the air.

"Why are we deferring to what they want?" Uncle Mitul asked. "They should do as we say."

"No thank you," Kamran said more forcefully, moving to be in front of his sister as though to protect her with his little body. "We will wait."

Silence descended over the room again. These children had commanded the attention of everyone. They were beautiful and had a strength about them that belied their tender ages.

"Leave them be," Papa said in a tone that caused everyone to turn toward him. "They are my grandchildren. If they do not want to be bothered—Leave. Them. Be."

Leena used Kamran's shoulder to pull herself up from her spot in front of the Puja. She made a beeline through the parlor and living room, then went straight for Papa and wrapped her arms around his legs. Kamran was right on her heels, but he went to Mumma instead.

Papa's dark brown eyes widened with shock, then he melted with an expression; something so pure that it touched Anaya's heart. Papa's hand reached out to stroke the silky hair that was so like Anaya's had been as a child. The little girl looked up at him with eyes filled with gratitude and love.

The fact that the twins were well aware of which people in the house were in their corner spoke volumes. Papa, normally the more talkative of Anaya's parents, had not said much. Until now.

Everyone had been elated when the passion Devesh felt for that woman died down. Now she was back, and if the anger rippling through her brother was any clear sign, he was still in love with her. Angry, but the love was still there.

When Devesh made the transition to product spokesperson, Reign had helped him in minor ways that brought him a small amount of success. Anaya hadn't envisioned that Reign could be in her brother's life in any capacity, except as a friend. But as Devesh talked about her more and more, in ways he never had with any other woman, his tone was so enthused and inspired, that for a minute, Anaya became alarmed.

Then she took a peek on Reign's Facebook page and quickly dismissed her as a threat to any plans their family had for him. Reign was an exotic beauty in her own way, but plain in comparison to the model types her brother was used to dating. Even the Maharaj women were beautiful enough to participate in pageants, and almost all of them had trophies and landed scholarships that furthered their college education as part of the prizes. Reign was more the motherly, nurturing kind of woman. So yes, friendship was the only thing there could ever be between her and Devesh.

The tide turned when the family voiced their concerns over the fact that Devesh was spending too much time on the phone with her, texting, calling, video chatting—all innocent; mostly business. So they thought. But there was something about the vibe Devesh had after speaking with her that Anaya recognized as something she'd only seen in one other person. Herself, when she fell in love with Pranav.

But Devesh was intensely steeped in their culture. He knew what was expected of him. He could "play" with foreigners all day long, take them for a test drive if need be, but even he understood that he'd better ride home with an Indian woman for that life-long marital journey.

Though he had dated women of other ethnic backgrounds, none of them had been Black. None of them had been older. None of them had been so … thick. That was the word—the woman was curvy. What were they calling it these days? Plus size. How could he be attracted to her? So the blonde aspiring actress didn't hold his interest anymore? He had to sleep with a grown woman with some years on him? And she managed to get pregnant? How irresponsible!

Anaya swept a look to the twins, who were listening to a story that Papa was sharing to keep them entertained. All the other family members had gone back to eating and gossiping but were sending looks at the children, watching how Papa, Aunt Kavya, and Mumma seemed to be at ease. Even her husband, Pranav, was smitten by them.

She could swear it took everything inside of her not to scream "DNA test." Honestly, there wasn't a need for one. Those children didn't look like they took any genes from Reign other than her green eyes and a little fullness about the lips. They did seem to take her determination, strength, and intelligence, though.

Leena scrambled down from Papa's lap, cornered one of the coffee tables and stopped in front of Anaya. She tilted her head back until she could look her directly in the eyes. A small smile played about her little lips. Whatever Anaya's misgivings, they didn't matter at this point.

Anaya brushed aside all thoughts and reached down to take Leena in her arms.

"I'm your Aunt Anaya."

"Anaya," Leena repeated, placing a hand on her aunt's cheek. "Anaya is pretty. Like my Papa."

"That's because your Papa is my brother."

Leena blinked twice, absorbing that tidbit of information. She flickered a look to her brother and then back to Anaya. "Like Kamran …"

"Yes," Anaya said, smiling at her niece's perception. "Like Kamran is your twin brother, Devesh is mine."

Leena returned that smile and Anaya's heart swelled with love. Devesh had said he'd wanted marriage and a family, but it wasn't high on his list of things to accomplish. Now she was looking down at his child, and the family had not been silent since he ran out the door, all voicing their opinions on his choice for a mate.

If she, who loved her brother dearly, couldn't accept Reign, how on earth would they?

chapter 5

Devesh activated his blue tooth the moment he was about to exit the expressway. He placed a much-needed call to someone who he spoke to every week, but had never let on about the twins. He had to wonder what their friendship was based on if he, too, could keep them a secret.

"Jay?"

"Devesh," was the one-word reply. Almost as if he knew the reason for the call.

"Why?"

"You know why," he replied. "Lovers come and go, but I only have one Mama. And whatever reason she had for not telling you, I had to respect that. Even though I didn't agree. Loyalty is a big thing with my mother. I've seen her cut off family members who are still trying to figure out how she peeped their games."

Devesh tried to wrap his mind around Jay's reasoning. People didn't disown family. That's not how things were done.

"I try to stay out of grown folks business," Jay continued. "But I did give you an opportunity quite a few times."

Devesh rubbed his temple, trying to figure out what the heck Jay was talking about.

"How many times did I ask you to come to Chicago?" Jay asked. "How many times did I *insist* that you slide through here?"

Realization slammed into Devesh. That he did. Evidently, if the new information Devesh had gathered, those invites came on dates right before birthdays belonging to Jay, Reign, Devesh, and the twins—along with Christmas and New Years. Even one that had come a few days ago. And Devesh had ignored them all. He wasn't sure he could be in the same city without seeking Reign out and pressuring her for a relationship she obviously didn't want.

"All it would have taken was having you—and them—in the same space," Jay confessed. "And you would've figured it out without me having to say anything. And that was a little white lie that I could tell, and she would believe."

Devesh glanced at the towering structure of the hotel, taking in the families making their way inside the glass doors. "Well, it took a lot more than that when I ran into your mother and the twins in Cali. I just couldn't fathom that Reign would do such a thing. My family probably thought I was a little … slow."

Jay chuckled. "Yeah? Well, I'm not going to tell you what I thought."

"So what would've happened if I came to Chicago?"

"Oh, an accidental appearance of you at the same place as the twins," he replied in a nonchalant tone. "You know, something like that."

"So much for not getting in grown folks business," Devesh said sourly.

"I said accidentally, didn't I?" Jay defended with a laugh. "I've been encouraging Mom to tell you for years. That's been the only issue that brings us to a straight up argument."

Devesh was saddened to hear that news. That the issue had driven a wedge between mother and son.

"I haven't been in a whole lot of relationships myself," Jay continued.

"But I'm going to say this—you have the upper hand here. Use it. You love her. Use that to drive your efforts in doing what's best for both of you. Even if she doesn't agree. At first, you were the one backing away; now she'll be the one trying to do the same. Buy yourself some time to let her see how you two can work."

Jay was right. Devesh had let other things get in the way. Minor things. "Did you ever consider that your telling me would be about the children, and not about her—or me?"

Jay didn't have a response to that question.

"So why are you helping me now?" Devesh asked, glancing at the Marriott's towering glass structure as he pulled into valet.

"I know what it's like to grow up without a father," he confessed. "I never wanted that for my brother and sister. When she came back from Atlanta, I thought things would be different. But she was so sad, so quiet. I wasn't sure what happened. Truthfully, I didn't want to ask."

"I apologize for not listening to you," Devesh said, sliding from behind the wheel and dropping the keys in the portly valet's hand. "For not honoring your request. I let family issues cloud my judgment. It won't happen again."

"It's alright. Weren't you the one who said everything in its time?"

"Yes," Devesh answered with a laugh. "There is that. It is definitely time."

❦ ❦ ❦

Devesh had the red-haired woman at Marriott's front desk announce he was on the way up to Reign's suite. The lobby seemed to stretch a mile wide before he reached the glass elevators that would take him to the 19th floor.

So many thoughts were running track in his mind. He had loved Reign from the first moment he laid eyes on her at the advertising convention in Vegas. A few exchanges became long talks about things they both loved—Indian foods, Indian movies, and novels. If there was such a thing as instant, mind-blowing, life-altering attraction, he had experienced it right then and there. All of that later transformed into him opening up to tell her about experiences that weighed heavily on his soul. She gave him encouragement and inspiration at his lowest moments. Just saying her name brought him an immense pleasure that he couldn't explain. He wanted more, so much more, despite the difference in their ages and the fact that they came from different worlds.

The only problem was that his family had not understood his choice when he had first brought it before them seven years ago when he first met Reign, then again two years later after coming back from Atlanta and rekindling the friendship, this time hoping for more. They still wanted him with an Indian woman. Hell, even a White woman was acceptable in their eyes and given the tumultuous history between the British and East Indians, that was truly a stretch. Admitting that he loved a Black woman who was older than him became such an intense issue when he broached the subject that he eventually backed down. Then when they reconnected in Atlanta after not being in contact for those two years, he was fired up and was ready to give anyone hell who didn't see things his way. What he hadn't been prepared for was the fact that fate wasn't seeing things his way. This time, after Atlanta, Reign was the one to disappear.

Now that he had the opportunity to have the unconventional love and family in a way that the Maharajs had no choice but to accept, he'd let his ego screw it up.

Standing in front of the door to Reign's room, he took a deep breath to collect himself before knocking. The door swung open, and he said, "Reign."

"Why are you here?" she practically growled, peering behind him, and frowning when she didn't see the children.

"My mother's watching them for a short while," he said to her unspoken question. "Because we need to talk where their little ears can't overhear," he assured her, stepping over the threshold when she moved aside. "I went about this all wrong."

"Ya think?" She left the space in front of him and slammed one of the children's garments into the suitcase that had been tossed across the bed. She was leaving California? The twins had mentioned some type of starlight train trip that should have kept them in the area for a few more days.

"I'm sorry," he said, reaching for her hand and extracting her from the task of packing their things. "I'm sorry for making the demand of you in that way."

Reign put some instant distance between them. He felt the loss immediately.

"I missed out on so much," he said, perching on the end of the bed. "First words. First steps. First smiles."

She put her back to him in a defiant move that was so much like the children had done earlier, it pained him. "Why didn't you tell me?"

Reign turned to focus on him a moment; then she broke eye contact with him to study the muted figures on television screen.

He tried to resist the pull that her obvious pain had on him, and the need to comfort her.

"The morning after we were together, you didn't seem to remember anything," she said, dropping the cosmetic case into one of the side pockets of the suitcase. "How was I going to get you to believe I was pregnant with your child? What conversation would that have been?"

"A DNA test would've solved everything."

"And exactly how would I have gotten to that point?" she said with a bitter laugh. "You would've thought I was crazy." She folded a tiny shirt and tucked it into the suitcase. "I don't know what hurts worse. That I enjoyed being with you so much or that it meant so little to you."

"That's not true," Devesh said, standing so he could take her in his arms. "I remembered *everything*. But you seemed so distant that next morning. For a minute, I thought I had dreamed the whole thing. But I definitely remembered how good it felt to lay next to you; to hold you; to be inside you, connected that way." He pressed a kiss to her temple. "With everything I was going through back then, nothing made me feel as good as being with you." Devesh stroked his fingers along the smooth expanse of her caramel skin, down her cheek and to the soft curves of her neck. "Reign, I have always loved you."

She moved out of his reach.

"We had a deep affection for one another. Can't we…" He moved until he blocked her path to the closet. "Can't we build something from that?"

"What are you saying?"

Devesh moved in, took her in his arms. "We should marry."

Reign nearly slipped out of his grip and straight to the floor. Was the idea of being with him so repulsive?

"What did you just say?"

"The children," he said, grasping at a reasonable counter to any misgivings she may have. "Our children should grow up in a household where their parents are together. We should be as one."

She hesitated a moment before moving to one side, a nice little distance away from him. "You have lost your ever-loving mind. Marriage was never part of my plans—ever. To you or anyone."

"Marriage provides them with some protections," he shot back, stung that she could say such a thing. "And you too."

"How so?" she asked, almost shrugging as if what he said was of no consequence. "You don't even have a job, just hopes of reviving your acting career, and that always comes first."

"I'll be putting my career aside," he replied, sharing the decision he'd come into as he drove the several miles to the hotel. He'd already placed a few calls on the way and had some serious leads. "I'll have something before the end of this week. Trust me. I have a family to support now. No time for dreams that only halfway came true. I'm done with that part of my life."

Several emotions flickered across her face, and he wasn't sure what any of them meant. "So from wanting me to leave my children with you and disappear to wanting me to marry you and live with you in Chicago."

"Actually, it's best that you move here."

She stumbled backward. "What?! You expect me to uproot from everything I have in Chicago and move to—"

"California. With me," he chimed in.

Reign lifted her chin and glared at him. "Now I know you've lost touch with reality," she countered. "No way am I giving up a stable job, a house that's nearly paid for, and my family."

"What family, Reign?" he demanded. "Your only family is Jay, and he's a grown man."

"And how will it look for me to marry a man who's the same age as my son?"

"What does that have to do with anything?" he shot back, trying to keep his anger in check. "This is about the children, Reign. Our children. They don't care how old we are. We are their parents."

She looked away, closing her eyes as though summoning some type of strength before opening them again.

"Parents who will make decisions together," he continued, noticing her gaze had shifted from his eyes to his lips. "Eat together, grow together, and give them a stable home. We'll be a family. More family than they'll have in Chicago."

"A family that does not accept me—or them."

"They will," he said, taking her in his arms again, relishing the feel of her next to him.

"Your people are not that evolved and you know it."

"This isn't about them. It's about us."

Reign shook her head, tried to push him away. Devesh stood his ground. Finally, her shoulders relaxed and all of the fight seemed to ease out of her body. She allowed him to lead her to the bed, and when she sat down beside him, he pulled her closer.

His eyes returned to her mouth, and he rested there for several moments before finally reaching out and cupping her face in his hands.

Speaking of us," she began, placing a hand on his chest to stop any further movement. "How much of myself am I supposed to sacrifice for this belief of yours? This idea of marital bliss you're offering?"

"What do you mean?" he said, almost insulted by the disdain in her tone.

"I'm a woman," she replied. "I have needs. I've been dating a guy for several months now, and I just told him I'm ready to take things to the next level. I was supposed to be with him, fully commit, when I return to Chicago."

Something akin to jealousy flared in Devesh's heart. So there was someone else? Why didn't he think to ask? And why had she only mentioned it now?

"The only kind of marriage that would work for me is an open one," she admitted.

Where did that come from? Devesh had no words to respond to those hurtful terms. She hadn't considered—not even once—that he could be all the things she'd need?

"That way, it's a marriage in name only," she said, driving a stake through his heart. "And we both still have options."

"Open … marriage?" The two damning words practically stuck in his throat.

"That way both of us can find happiness at some point," she offered. "I'll stay married to you for eight years."

"Why only eight?"

"The twins will have reached the age of accountability by then. They'll have enough of a foundation where they can understand how things work."

Devesh stared into her eyes, saw the determination within and realized he could argue the point and lose her altogether or he could concede and that would give him time to win her trust and her heart. Because evidently, she didn't love him as much as he loved her. "These are your terms?"

"Yes. Open marriage. Eight years in bondage."

"Bondage," he spat.

"Marriage has never been fair to women," she confessed. "*Ever.* And I never understood why so many of them race through life to get down the aisle or the ones who feel incomplete without a husband. I have married friends, and I was on the receiving end of hearing all the crap they put up with. Why would I sign up for that program when the only one who benefits is the man? She cooks, cleans, takes care of the kids, runs the household and still has to work a 9-to-5, and he wears the crown of head of household? All so I won't have an empty bed or get a little pickle tickle now and then? No, thank you."

Marriage did not have to be the bondage that she believed it would be. The kind he desired was two people who were compatible in a number of areas, soul mates.

Devesh had his work cut out for him on so many levels.

"We'll get married right away," he said, trying to release the pain in his heart. "And you don't have to worry about our financial situation. I'll break my trust fund."

Her head tilted and she blinked her surprise. "Trust fund? Your family has *that* kind of money?"

"I wish." Devesh laughed. "I put most of the money toward something else, but a little of what I've made over the years in a trust just in case something happened to me while I was working overseas. Something you mentioned that I should do several years ago."

She studied the rest of the clothes strewn about the bed awaiting their trip into the suitcases. "I guess I'll unpack."

"No, continue. I own a building not too far from where my parents live. It's being gutted and rehabbed over the next few months. Until the contractors are done, we'll stay with my parents."

"Absolutely not," she said as her entire body tensed. "I'm a grown woman. I don't live with anyone's parents. Since I was fourteen, I haven't lived with my own."

Inhaling a calming breath, he said, "Reign, they need time to get to know Leena and Kamran."

"I can bring them over every day."

"That's foolishness," he said, taking the hanger from her hands, guiding her until she was in front of him once again. "It's only temporary. Think of the children."

"I am," she replied. "Your parents will get to see the children. And I'll get to keep my sanity."

Devesh vowed in his mind that he would find a way to change her stance. Having the woman he loved and his children close to him would be better for everyone involved.

❦ ❦ ❦

Reign mulled over what had transpired and wondered if she should have done things differently. She was tired of working at a job that showed at every turn how disposable the employees were. Like the time she'd been forced to transcribe tapes for an attorney who had a severe flatulence problem, and her complaints were blown off. Or the fact that the company had a no-asshole rule when it came to attorneys, but they let two employees bully the legal assistants and paralegals. Only when one of the bullies pissed off an attorney, was any action taken. The other one was still on a campaign of making Reign's life miserable.

Reign had thought of retiring early, moving to Atlanta or Texas, maybe. Now that she had two young ones, she needed the benefits and was preparing to buy a bigger place to accommodate their growing needs. Retirement was going to be a long time coming. So were the dreams she had of taking that Starlight Amtrak trip, the EuroRail through London, France, Spain, Italy, and Switzerland, and a tour of Northern and Southern India.

Marrying Devesh meant the children would have a two-parent home, which is something neither she, nor Jay, had growing up. Also, it would prevent a custody battle for the moment. If she left years later, one would probably be in the offing, but she could tough it out if the conditions were even slightly bearable.

Marry him for her children's sake? She could do a lot worse. She already knew he adored his nieces and nephews. Maybe loving his own would not be the problem she feared it would be. Roberto had blatantly told her that he "wasn't raising no mixed kids." To which she had shot back, "Even a child knows that when you put chocolate and vanilla ice cream on the same cone, that there's going to be a swirl of coloring. What did you think would happen?" He had replied, "That you were smart enough not to get yourself knocked up." In tears, she responded, "Right. I'm fourteen. You're twenty-one. Which one of us was supposed to be the grown-up here?"

Roberto rarely saw his son after he was born. Most times, it was better if he didn't because the pain caused by his appearance was worse than his absence. She never wanted that for her son. And definitely didn't want that for her twins whose father was from a family who tightly held to Indian customs and culture.

Loving her had never factored into the equation, so keeping Devesh at arm's length shouldn't be a problem, either.

She would never give him a chance to reject her again.

chapter 6

When Devesh returned to the Shoreview Drive home, the children immediately ran to him and Reign. The delight of holding them was second only to having their mother in that same space. His children. His beautiful children. And the woman who held his heart in her hands.

Only after a few moments did he put them down, and they ran off to his parents, who welcomed them with open arms. Anaya moved close to Mumma, and Leena leaned in for Anaya to take her from Mumma's arms. Aunt Kavya stroked a hand across Leena's face, bringing a smile to the little girl's face. The sight of his family bonding with his children did his heart a world of good.

Aunt Kavya left the sofa and held out a package for Devesh. An East Indian movie was inside, one that was so old that people had forgotten it existed. His petite aunt gestured to Reign and then tapped the package, signaling that she wanted him and Reign to have it. Watch it, maybe? But why? "I'll see what we can do," he said to his aunt in Hindi since she did not speak English. "But I'm going to need you to hold onto it for a moment."

She nodded, tucked the package under her arm and stepped away.

Devesh gauged the temperature of the room. Everyone seemed to be relieved that he had returned with a reluctant Reign in tow.

All except the pretty strawberry blonde with bluish-gray eyes whose expression was now the saddest he'd ever seen. The fact that he was the reason for such sadness was not lost on him. In all the chaos of becoming an instant father and soon-to-be husband, Amy Seran had become lost in the equation. Tiya must have called her when he left to get Reign. Amy was supposed to be in the middle of a cover model shoot in San Francisco that happened to be on the same day as his birthday.

Children. A new wife. Time to take on a new set of responsibilities. *Put away childish things* as the Good Book said. And that included a relationship that was never going anywhere. He had known Amy was a placeholder for a while and had planned to break things off with her for good because it wasn't fair to him or her. But he'd become comfortable with having a buffer to his family's constant pestering about marriage and children. Those questions all ended when he brought Amy into the picture. Not that they still didn't want him to marry and have a family; they just didn't want to encourage it happening with Amy.

"We need to talk," he said.

"Yes, I guess we do." She didn't bother to hide her sarcasm.

Amy had every right to be angry. They had been dating off and on for a few years and had appeared in many photo shoots and videos. All things that were designed to bolster his modeling career, and hers—still an undiscovered actress. But neither of them had caught their big break yet.

"I was not expecting Reign and my children today," he said guiding her to the far corner of the parlor.

Anaya and Mumma whisked a reluctant Tiya, her husband Hiran, sister-in-law Sana, and cousin Neerav out of the living room to give them some privacy.

"I asked her to marry me," he said, sliding into the seat next to Amy on the parlor sofa. "It's only fair that you and I break this off."

"It would be fair to send her packing," she said, glaring at him.

"Not going to happen," he replied. "She is the mother of my children."

"Yes, but that doesn't mean you have to marry her." Amy flipped her blonde tresses over her shoulder. "You barely know her."

That wasn't necessarily true. He had deeper conversations with Reign than he ever had with Amy.

Devesh knew some of the things that drove Reign, her past, her fears—one that had been so tragic at times that what she shared with him brought a fresh ache to his heart. He could discuss anything with her—better ways of handling his finances, the discrimination he'd experienced when paired against blue-eyed males who dominated the field; being blackballed in India by actors who felt threatened by a rising star. Reign understood. She would give him pointers on how to be better prepared when it happened again.

Amy had no such depth and insight. She was more interested in dancing, movies, travel and fun times than she was in the things that Devesh was aware would sustain a dynamic relationship for years to come.

"I always thought you would marry me," she said, wringing her hands on her lap.

"I've never led you to believe that we would marry," Devesh responded. "That was not the direction I ever saw our relationship moving."

Her lashes lowered, red lips thinned out in an effort to hold in her emotions.

"We were friends, lovers sometimes," he continued. "We have a lot in common when it comes to our careers. But I told you early on and never led you to believe otherwise. Every time you pushed for marriage, we took a little break. When you'd push to get back together, I thought you understood that nothing had changed."

"Yet you slept with her and had children by her while you were with me," Amy accused, flattening her hands against his chest. "I thought you were an honorable man."

"Let's be honest," he snapped, tiring of the conversation because her skewed take on their relationship was beyond selective. "You gave me an ultimatum before I left to go to the convention that year. I said we needed to take a break because your insecurity was driving me up the wall. I'd had enough."

"I was right to be concerned about you going down there and being near her," she shot back, ivory skin flushing crimson. "Tiya had warned me to step up because some thirsty Black chick was sniffing around you like a bitch in heat." She shook her head. "I didn't believe her at first, because she showed me pictures. No way would you choose her over someone like me. But whenever you talk about her or someone mentions her, your expression clouds over like … you're missing something." She reached out to touch his face. "I tried to be everything that you needed. I can't believe that I'm not enough for you."

"That's where you went wrong, trying to be something that you're not," he said, removing her hand and placing it back on her lap. "We were friends. I hope we still can be, but I never saw this going the distance. You saw it being long-term. I lived in the present. Right now my present demands that I do right by Reign and my children."

"She didn't do right by you and tell you about them in the first place," she taunted, not bothering to keep the ugliness at bay. "Yet now you want to break things off with me to be with her. How fair is it that you're going to break my heart for a woman who didn't consider you important enough that you needed to be in your children's lives? And if you hadn't run into her today at the restaurant, you would've never known about them."

Now *that* stung because it was the absolute truth. Come to think of it, he still didn't have a clear understanding of Reign's actions. But it didn't change anything that he would do.

"You're going to marry her on the spot," Amy said, practically snarling, which was not a becoming look on her. "No courting. No engagement period. Just—" She arched her hand in a dramatic flourish. "Right down the aisle and to the preacher man. I've been with you the longest and didn't get that kind of consideration. What's right about that picture?" She put her focus on Tiya, who had tipped back in and was eyeing them with mild suspicion from her spot near the living room threshold. "I took all of those pictures, let you sell my stock photos and I didn't charge you a dime."

Devesh put a pointed glare on Tiya and waved her away before focusing on Amy again. "It helped your career, too. So don't make it seem like it was only for my own benefit."

Amy stared at Devesh with eyes as sharp as daggers. "What career? Mine hasn't gone anywhere. Neither has yours. And if you marry her, what little chance you have at a career will circle the drain and go down for a royal flush."

"I don't think that's true," he challenged, noticing Reign slide from the den into the living room both of which had an open view of the parlor. She captured Leena before the little girl made it to Devesh, who said, "Give me a minute, Leena. Alright?"

Leena nodded and only then did she allow her mother to take her hand and lead her away.

"Try showing up to a photo shoot with her." Amy left the sofa and moved to plop down on a wingback chair that gave her a better vantage point to see Reign who halted at hearing those last words.

Amy laughed, the sound of it bitter and brash. "Oh, definitely won't be strolling down the red carpet with that. Love to see you explain *her* to the public." She raised her voice so Reign could hear. "You'd bypass me and all those beautiful models to marry a troll."

Reign flinched. He could tell that it was taking everything in her not to say something that would put Amy on notice.

"Amy, there are a lot of things I'll tolerate," Devesh warned. "But talking about the woman who's going to be my wife is not one of them," he said, taking in her sour expression. "I can't believe I didn't recognize that there's such an ugliness in your soul." He stood, towering over her because he couldn't bear to sit next to her any longer. "I'm marrying Reign because she has *always* had my heart. From day one. I was just too afraid of my family's disapproval to move forward in having a relationship with her."

"So what was I?" Amy asked, getting to her feet. "The second runner-up in the Devesh Maharaj pageant?"

"No, I never saw you that way," Devesh confessed, though the truth of the matter was somewhere laced in between. "We took it day by day. It's just that on this day we have to end things."

Amy inched forward so they were closer than he would like. "She doesn't want you the way that you want her," she said, shifting her blue eyes to Reign, who was eyeing them with interest. "She doesn't want you. Otherwise, she would've come to you long before now. Are you willing to lose your career for her?"

"She told me early on that small-minded people in the industry would try to use my relationship with her to negatively impact my career," he confessed with an intense glare at her. "None of it mattered to me."

Amy's tears seemed to dry up instantly. "I can still be there for you," she whispered, reaching up to touch his face.

Devesh extracted her hand and placed it back down to her side.

"I will be there for you," she said, her eyes filled with unbridled pain. "I love you. Don't let me go."

Amy's pleading seemed to suck all of the air out of the room. Reign shook her head and finally walked away.

"You're not hearing me," he said, quirking a confused brow. "*I love her.* I'm sorry that saying this hurts you, but you wanted the truth and I'm telling you the way things are."

Amy's ivory face darkened to an unrecognizable shade. "You're going to regret this," she said through her teeth, and there was a fire in those blue eyes that he'd never seen before. "You used me. All this time. You used me. And if there's ever a day where I can let the world know just how much, you better believe that I will."

Amy snatched away from him, ran out of the parlor and struggled to open and run out of the front door.

Devesh turned in time to see the sly smile that lit Tiya's features, and he wasn't all that pleased that it was coming at his expense.

chapter 5

The next day, Devesh perched on the edge of the king-sized bed in Reign's master bedroom in Chicago, watching as she placed some of the last of the items she was taking back with her to California. The rest of her things were packed in a series of boxes that would be shipped via freight and would arrive a week later. He had insisted on coming to help her with the transition. What he really wanted was to make sure she actually returned to Newport Coast. To be honest, he also wanted to lay eyes on the man who had somehow become important to Reign in recent months. He also hoped coming to Chicago would help him better understand the woman he would marry in a small ceremony in the place that would become her home. Devesh was set to fly her son, two nieces, two nephews and three friends as her witnesses and to offer support so she wouldn't be overwhelmed by the sheer size of the extended Maharaj family.

He found it amazing that the reason she had so little family was because she had spoken out against something that happened to the female children of the family at the hands of a male relative. Later, being pregnant with Jay caused a wider separation with her family. He still wondered about what transpired, but never pressed for more. It amazed him more that she had no desire to have any input in her own wedding. When Mumma called to inquire, Devesh could only state what he believed to be her wishes. If he didn't know any better, he would swear she was ready to bolt with the children and disappear altogether.

Couldn't she see how much he wanted her? Wanted his children and her—a true family? Could she come to love him again? And whether she had told him or not, he knew so long ago that she had. Fear on both sides had kept them apart for far too long.

The first day they'd arrived in the Windy City, Jay slid by the house and scooped up Leena and Kamran, so Reign was able to drive Devesh to see a few of the sites since he'd never been to Chicago before. They took in a breakfast meal at the Grand Lux Café on the Magnificent Mile, visited the Baha'i's Temple in Wilmette, then the Museum Campus and later had an eye-opening experience at dinner which further served to put Devesh on notice.

When they walked into the place with its warm décor of reds and purples with glass and silver accents; the host, the waiters, even the bartender came to greet Reign as if she was a long-lost relative. But it was the owner who moseyed from his office and put a lust-filled gaze on Reign that made the hairs on the back of Devesh's neck stand at full attention. Reign went into the man's arms willingly, and the embrace they shared was unsettling. The smile on the man's lips at having her so close to him was nothing short of an unspoken challenge. He was of medium height, olive skin, a layered haircut that gave him a well-lived lifestyle look further complemented by the European tailored suit draping his slightly muscular frame. The man was well aware of his sensual power and evidently had hoped it would work with Reign.

"And who might this be?" he asked over Reign's shoulder.

Devesh met the man's look measure for measure as he said. "The man she's going to marry in three days time. And you are …?"

"Samir," he said simply, with a curious glance in Reign's direction as he stroked a hand down the small curve of her back, dangerously close to her shapely rear end.

"You can release my woman now," Devesh edged, moving forward to extract her from his hold if necessary. "I'm sure you've said enough of a hello right about now."

Samir ignored that not-so-subtle warning and said to a wide-eyed Reign, "I wish I had known that you'd taken an interest in more than East Indian cuisine. I would have—"

"Been able to show us to a table a little faster, maybe," Devesh supplied drily though he didn't miss the alarm in Reign's expression. "We're famished with all the packing and everything."

The disappointment etched in Samir's face was rewarding. Message received.

"I didn't know," she whispered to Samir, and there was a slight sound of regret in her tone. "I truly didn't know."

So much for all that charm. Gratefully, it had gone right over Reign's head.

"Best wishes on your upcoming nuptials," Samir said, flickering a look between Reign and Devesh. "You will be my guest tonight, as is always the case when you come to me."

"No, I will take care of her meal. I can handle *everything* when it comes to my woman," Devesh said, clasping a hand on the man's shoulder in a gesture that was not at all friendly. "Wouldn't want you to think I'd let her starve ... on *any* level."

Samir's low throaty chuckle rankled Devesh's nerves, but he said, "As you wish. Right this way."

"That was uncalled for," Reign said when they were seated at one of the best tables in the place.

"No more than the fact he insisted on keeping his hands on another man's fiancée," Devesh countered. "I just wanted him to understand there was no need for any consideration on that level where you're involved," Devesh whispered and she averted her gaze. "Seems like the only person who doesn't know how beautiful, intelligent, amazing, and desirable you are ... is you."

They left the restaurant with no further incident from Samir other than a lingering look of longing when he laid eyes on Reign. And that's all the man had better do—is look. Devesh would do whatever it took to transition their marriage into something more than just friends sharing the same space and time; even if it took her a while to truly embrace the idea.

After dinner, they took a stroll along the path of Lake Michigan. Devesh had a special love for large bodies of water, but Lake Michigan was nothing like his beloved Pacific Ocean and the beautiful beaches of California. The lake's murky waters did not move him the way the California waves and sunlight did. Chicago seemed to be a nice place to visit, but the sun and ocean shore would be good for his children. And his wife to be, if she could release the anxiety she felt when it came to him and his family. Everything in its time.

Reign's row house in the heart of Historic Pullman was perfect for a small family. Two bedrooms, eat-in kitchen, and moderate living room. This place would fit into the Maharaj home seven or eight times over. The home was simply furnished with a cuddling chair and sofa, television, sofa table, and some vibrantly colored Jackson Junge artwork. The kitchen held a dining table that could seat six, but it was pushed against the far wall so that it only accommodated three instead. The appliances were stainless steel and looked as if they had been recently purchased, and the natural wood floors had been polished to a shine. The place smelled of citrus and freshly washed linen, which gave it a warm, inviting feel. Though clean and well-organized, he would never want his children so sparsely attended. It made him wonder if Reign was struggling financially.

Earlier, he had stood outside, taking in the area. Reign told him the homes had been built for workers of the Pullman Car company and had later been taken over by the State when Pullman cut wages for the men who built the train cars. Unfortunately, Pullman did not lower rent payments for the workers which started a riot that cost several lives.

Now over a hundred years later, a blend of freshly rehabbed houses intermingled with ones that were so dilapidated it was a miracle they were still standing. A group of young men was posted up on a porch three doors down from Reign's place, another trio was on the sidewalk, and other small groups were sprinkled on front porches and lawns all the way down Champlain Avenue. Three of them on the porch nearest him were passing some cannabis between them. The pungent and unwelcome smell floated down to where Devesh was standing. Children were on the sidewalk not far from them, playing with a water hose, trying to cool off. Did those men have no decency or shame? Children should not inhale such a thing or be subjected to behavior that was disrespectful not only to them, but to women and elders as well.

Further down the block, at least five different cars were blasting music that was so obscene that it wasn't fit for adults to hear it, let alone anyone under twelve. He couldn't get Reign and his children out of this place fast enough. Now he was even more alarmed that she would turn this house over to Jay, who could not be any safer here than she and his children had been.

"Wait," he said to Reign, snapped from his musings by the strange object in her hand that had been placed in a clear box as though it was a treasure. "What is that?"

She blinked, glancing down at her hand. "Something that provides personal pleasure."

"You're going to be married," he said, placing his focus on that "thing" again. "You won't be needing that."

"Oh?" Her left eyebrow winged upward. "A married woman *in name only*," she stressed.

A little anger stirred within him. Her words filtered through his mind and interrupted any rational thought. He was giving her a chance to change her mind, to reconsider his concern about this. But that hard gleam in her eye was a telltale sign that she wouldn't.

"You insist on bringing something like that with you?" Devesh stretched his body out on the bed, then leaned up on his elbow to inspect the clock on her nightstand. They had four hours before leaving. "Reign, you can't have something like this in my parent's home."

She froze, blinked a few times as though hit by an unpleasant thought. "Your mother isn't the type that'll go through my things, is she?"

Heaven forbid. No telling what else she would find.

"We need to talk about this," he said, unable to take his eyes off her *possession*.

"There's no discussion," she snapped, placing one hand on her hip. "I have to give up my house, my job, my city, so you can't expect for me to give up something that brings me pleasure, too."

"You will have a husband," he said through his teeth.

"In. Name. Only," she shot back. "We are getting married for the children's sake and no other reason."

Devesh fumed, tried to find words to put a voice to what he wanted to say.

"Would marriage be on the table if Leena and Kamran didn't exist? No?" She dropped that—whatever it was called—into the suitcase. "Then let's not pretend this is a love match."

Was that all that mattered to her, having something "there" to fill the void? What about passion? What about touching, tasting, teasing, doing the things that brought on her breathy moans and pleasure-filled sighs. That night between them was the best it had ever been for him; the perfect climax to years that transcended friendship that was more akin to unconditional love.

"Reign," he said in a patient tone. "If you would stop being so angry and listen, you'd know that I wanted this marriage because it's not only the right thing for the children, it's the right thing for us. We've always had an affection for each other. I care deeply for you. I've always wanted you."

"I can't tell," she said, zipping the suitcase and putting an end to that part of the conversation. "Last I checked, Southwest has flights to Chicago every day. So you didn't want me *that* bad, lover boy." She winked, giving him a sly smile. "But nice try."

How could he get her to see that his love for her was a real thing? That he had felt that way all along. Now he regretted not being so open with her the next morning after they had made love. His focus on getting his family to accept her first had definitely been the wrong strategy.

"You are making things more difficult than they need to be."

"No, I'm keeping it real," she said, and began pacing until she came to a stop in front of him. "I have no intention of going into this with any false illusions. Neither should you."

chapter 8

"How can you be so cool with this?" Anaya asked her husband, Pranav, who paused in the middle of putting his gun into the safety box, locking it, then sliding it toward the top shelf of the bedroom closet. Only then did she breathe a sigh of relief. She understood that his job as a detective required the use of a firearm, but having a gun in the house always made her uneasy. Almost as much as this turn of events with her twin brother. "He could do so much better than her."

While the family had all wanted Devesh to settle down for years, they had been more worried when it took so long for Anaya to snag a husband. Being raised in America for the majority of her life, meant she definitely wasn't a *traditional* Indian and the same went for Pranav Bakshi.

"Why do you think your brother did not want me to marry you?" Pranav asked, sliding the holster from his body and placing it in the closet near the locked box. "There are some things that I've done that I'm not proud of. He's well aware of it because I did my dirt when I was around him." He switched off a television and dropped the remote on the bed. "But you and I did what we wanted to do and eloped. Of course, we had to have a separate ceremony to marry in front of the entire family. But we lived through his anger and your family's disapproval and proved them wrong."

"But this is different," she said, lifting the pearls from her neck and placing them in the jewelry tray.

"How? Because she's Black?"

"Because she's *old*," she said shuddering,

"Forties isn't old."

Then she saw that he wasn't buying that simple explanation and added, "And Black. And also kind of plain. You know, not as beautiful as a woman he should be with."

Pranav stared at her for a few moments, and she became a little unnerved. "Never thought I'd see a day when you were this shallow," he whispered, dark brown eyes wide with alarm.

She winced as though he had struck her.

"What does any of that have to do with what he feels for her?" he demanded. "Devesh loves that woman, and nothing you all have said or done has changed that fact." Pranav rounded the bedroom, passing the sleigh bed and stopping at the window that overlooked the tree-lined street of the home they moved into after they were married for the "second" time. "I'm going to need you to give him the same consideration that he finally gave us. She could actually be good for him."

Anaya shook her head, pulled a silky night gown from the hanger and asked, "How?"

"He's already made changes in his life for the better," Pranav explained, putting his back against the wall. "As much as your parents were after him to let this modeling thing fall by the wayside, it wasn't until he realized that he had to man up and take responsibility for his wife and children that he let it go. He made the decision with absolutely no regrets, no vacillating. *Nothing* has made him give up his career before now. This woman and the children she bore seem to be more important to him than everything else. That should tell you something right there." Then he smiled. "He has children, Anaya. Children that already love him and you too."

Pranav was so right. The love that Leena and Kamran had for each other reminded Anaya of Devesh and how close they'd always been. But not close enough for Anaya to mention to him the childhood experiences that had haunted her for so long. She could never tell anyone, as it would completely destroy the family.

Even through the period when Devesh had a hard time with their move from New Dehli to New York, she was the one person he could turn to. When he was traveling and working in some of the most dangerous places in the world, she could always feel that he was alright. And there were many months he lived in places where phone or email contact wasn't possible. At the points she despaired the most, Devesh would reach out to her in some way. He would tell of exploits in places where poverty was so rampant that people ate some unmentionable things and did some unspeakable things to survive. He experienced things that disturbed him to this day. Something that he didn't realize they had in common.

Anaya tipped to the threshold, peered out and flickered a look toward her children's rooms, grateful that the day had worn them out so much that they fell asleep the moment their heads hit the pillow. She was so tired she wasn't looking forward to going into the real estate office tomorrow, but she had three closings to attend. And even two days later, her concern for this unfortunate turn of events with Devesh was wearing on her.

Her brother had always looked out for her, a lot more than their older brother ever did. Bhavin was equally as handsome as Devesh, had tried for a modeling career, but didn't do half as well as Devesh. And the difference between the two brothers was that Devesh was more than willing to share his wealth. Her house, purchased with a wedding gift from him, was in an amount that allowed them to buy it at a steal—just like the Maharaj house. She only knew the details because she had been the real estate agent that put the deal together and for other members of the family as well. A lot of rich people in the area were experiencing a severe downturn in their finances. So much so, they were releasing their

beloved homes for far less than market value. It was the main reason
so many of the Maharaj family, with careers that spanned technology
fields, franchises, and pharmaceutical research, had managed to snag
upscale houses nearby and it kept them close.

"I thought Amy was going to at least go the distance."

"But you didn't want him to marry her, either," Pranav reminded,
picking up the remote and clicking on the nightly news. "You mentioned
that she was too flighty. Amy was a *fun* thing for him."

"But she kept his mind off Reign," she said, hating the defensive tone
that crept into her voice. "I was so glad when she wised up and left him
alone." She thought back to that period in Devesh's life. "But I'd never
seen him so sad. My brother has been a lot of things, but sad was never
part of his vocabulary."

Devesh had changed after separating from Reign. He withdrew, like
nothing interested him as much anymore. Then he started writing. Her
brother, who didn't care for it at all and who struggled in English class
growing up, was suddenly penning poems and putting words in a journal.
It hurt Anaya's heart when she snuck into his room and read a few of
the things he'd written. The love he felt for Reign was deep. Maybe too
deep to understand. But would a woman like that make him happy?

The move from New Delhi to the Bronx had been filled with adventure.
While Anaya had embraced the Hip-Hop and Rap scene breaking out in
the Bronx and had made friends easily, Devesh had been bullied because
he was so scrawny and different, with an accent that set him apart from
boys his age. No one could imagine that he would become the heartthrob
that would return to take the runway and Bollywood by storm.

The storm fizzled when jealousy set in and A-List actors, who had
been in the business much longer than Devesh, put the word out that
they didn't want to work with him. Opportunities dried up faster than
a Solapur raisin. All the music videos, commercials, and runway gigs
became a thing of the past. Then some shady producers had lured
Devesh with false promises and nothing had come of those efforts.
But her brother, ever the optimist, had not given up. Until something
happened in India and he returned to America then washed his hands

of Bollywood altogether. For some reason, success at breaking into the American market was not happening. He'd been sorely discouraged, but still kept at it day after day.

Now, thanks to this woman, he would never become the Bollywood or American film star he was meant to be. Another reason to resent her intrusion in their lives.

She stilled her movements noticing that Pranav watched her closely, almost as though he could sense Anaya's unpleasant thoughts. She would have to tread carefully where Reign was concerned or she was going to have trouble, not only with Devesh, but with her own husband as well.

chapter 5

Devesh absorbed the implications behind Reign's need to assert her sexuality in this manner. Not once had she considered that maybe they could have a marriage that was more than "in name only"? Not once did she believe that he still valued her for what she had been to him and what he knew she could be?

He reached for a manila envelope that was right next to her passport. "May I?"

She slowly nodded.

Devesh slipped the contents from the envelope and found two birth certificates. One for Kamran Javesh Maharaj-King and another for Leena Devanee Maharaj-King.

Reign placed a finger to her son's birth certificate and spoke the meanings of the names she had chosen—"Success related to God," then she touched the other document and said, "Devoted to the Divine."

Reign had selected their children's names carefully. Maharaj meant royalty and the fact that Reign's last name was King was telling. She had given the children his last name along with hers, but the space for where his name as father belonged on the birth certificates was empty. That saddened him in no small measure. Like he hadn't mattered enough to fill even that space.

"Reign ..."

She stared at the space he touched, thought about it for a long moment and said, "We'll have to go downtown to make that happen. Shouldn't take long."

Why did it feel like he would never be ahead of the curve when it came to this scenario? "May I ask you a question?"

Reign extracted the documents from his hands and returned them to the envelope. "Shoot."

"I know from our conversations years ago that you didn't want children."

She lowered onto the bed, pushing the suitcase aside, waiting.

"What compelled you to give birth to Jay?"

Reign grimaced, inhaled and let out a long slow breath. "You misunderstand. I enjoyed motherhood; I did not enjoy pregnancy. Even at fourteen, being pregnant with Jay took such wear and tear on my body that I lost all of my hair, a substantial amount of weight, and I couldn't even keep water down. The doctor was going to take him because I became so sick." She adjusted to a more comfortable position on the bed. "Truthfully, I think I didn't want to be pregnant, and my body was trying to accommodate what was in my mind. Then I had the dream."

Drawing in a deep breath, she took a moment to pull herself together before looking up from her clasped hands to acknowledge him. "That night before I was supposed to go to the hospital for them to take him out of my body, I had a dream, and it was so vivid, so real, that the reason and meaning were clear."

Devesh shifted on the bed, keeping his focus on her eyes. "Will you tell me what it was?"

She looked at him for a few moments. "I was an Asian woman who had two little girls and I'd just given birth to a son. We lived in a palace, and I was an emperor's wife, third wife, concubine or whatever. But I had a boy child, and as soon as I'd weaned him off my breast, they put me—and the girls—out of the palace. They kept my son. They ... took him from me."

The wavering in her voice showed there was an emotional tie to the experience. Devesh remained silent, waiting for her to continue.

"Every day for an entire year, I would come to the palace gates and plead for the return of my son. No matter the weather, I was out there with my daughters, who cried with me; cried for my son and their brother. Finally, the guards or someone inside the palace must've grown weary of our voices because they brought him out to me." Reign smiled then, as if feeling everything the dream had to offer. "We were so happy; jubilant about his return."

Then the smile disappeared, and she closed her eyes while recanting the rest. "We walked away from the palace and somehow ended up in a dark tunnel. So dark that I couldn't see anything ahead of me. The little girls disappeared along the way, but I was still carrying my son. The further I went inside, I saw faces of people that I knew in this current lifetime." She shook her head, trying to bring her emotions under control. Then she opened her eyes. "They were bringing me things, Devesh. Presents, all kinds of gifts that would help me with my son. Their actions let me know that I should not be afraid because everything I needed would be there."

Devesh leaned in to wipe away the tears making tracks down her cheek.

"When I woke up from that dream," she whispered, adjusting so that her back was against the headboard. "I wanted my child. I *wanted* him. I sat down at the kitchen table, and for the first time in two months, I had a meal. A real meal. Not crackers or ginger ale. Salisbury steak, mashed potatoes and gravy, green peas and carrots and an ice cold glass of lemonade. Oh, and a biscuit," she said, smiling. "Don't forget the biscuit."

Devesh laughed because he was well aware of her love for freshly baked bread—especially Indian naan.

"For the first time in weeks, my food stayed where it was supposed to.

Instead of being frightened about the pregnancy, I was looking forward to holding my son and letting God send me the help that I needed. I was so afraid. I felt so alone without my family and the baby's father. Roberto had wanted me for a good time, and that was all. Maria could only do so much, but even she couldn't make her son take responsibility for his actions. The courts forced him to, at least on a financial level. But he didn't give a damn about his son."

If Roberto had been standing in front of him, Devesh would've smacked him upside the head. Thank God that Jay had everything that was wonderful about Reign inside of him. His determination, his drive, and generosity matched his mother. But he also had a peaceful vibe that was unlike Reign, a calming nature that was a balance to her fiery nature. She had raised a wonderful young man and Devesh was grateful that their relationship hadn't ended at the same time Reign had disappeared from his life.

"Having my son was the best thing that could've happened to me. I took risks because of him that I would not have taken if I were on my own."

"Risks?"

"When Jay turned three, and I realized that Maria was going to spoil him to the point he turned out as rotten as his father, brothers, and my brothers as well, I made a move that I would never have done on my own. There was a house in foreclosure down the street from Maria's place. The family had abandoned it, and a week later, I broke a window, climbed in, changed the locks and put the gas, lights, and telephone into my name." She smiled at his shocked expression. "I was eighteen. The VA gave me the time to get a job and opportunity to buy it for the amount remaining on the mortgage, using the down payment I saved from having teens sell fundraiser candy at their high schools."

She picked up the keepsake book that she planned to take with her as well. Flipping it open revealed photos of Jay as a toddler in a bright blue and white shirt and shorts, wearing a wide smile and sparkling brown eyes that spoke of his happiness.

"He was such a wonderful child. He truly was," she whispered, touching a finger to the image of Jay's smile. "I really thought I had this motherhood thing on lock." She laughed, and the sound of it snatched Devesh away from the other images of Jay. "I was about to adopt more children, went to classes and everything. Then Jay hit puberty, and it cured me of any ideas of wanting more children."

Devesh joined in her laughter as he remembered his own preteen years. It was no joke for him, either. He couldn't understand what was going on with his body or his mind. Thankfully, Jay and Reign made it through in one piece, as they were closer than ever.

"The lady from the agency called me and said, 'Ms. King, we haven't seen you in a while.' I replied, 'Let me tell you something. I don't want the little heathen I have, and I don't want your little heathens either.' She asked me how old Jay was and I reminded her that he was twelve. She laughed and understood. She said she'd hopefully hear from me soon. They're still waiting."

She traced her fingertips along the leather piping of her suitcase before touching the silken edges of the keepsake book.

Devesh placed his hand over hers to keep her from turning that next page. "Then why did you have *my* children?"

Reign sighed softly, adjusting her position on the bed before saying, "When I found out I was pregnant—that was before I learned I was carrying twins—I was going to have an abortion. I was too old to be having a child. I'm ready to kick back and travel and do all the things on the list that I've been keeping for years. This house is almost paid off, my finances were set, and raising children in this day and age isn't cheap … or safe."

Devesh tightened his hold on her hand, offering a silent support. He would find out what was on that list and make it happen. She should experience them because she'd sacrificed so much in her life to give the best to others.

"Then I had that dream again. But this time, only Jay was in the tunnel with me, about the same age he is now. We walked side-by-side into the darkness. Two children appeared, in this dream, a boy and girl who looked so much alike it was uncanny. I stayed back while Jay left my side, moved forward and reached for them. They ran to him, embraced him, and Jay asked, "What took you so long?"

"They said"—Reign locked gazes with Devesh—"We were waiting ... *on them.*"

Reign let that meaning sink in for a minute. Then she placed a hand over his, and he stroked his fingers on hers. "To me, that meant Leena and Kamran were supposed to come through us that one time we were together. I felt it all the way down to my soul."

He wiped the tears from her face and smiled. The message was so deep and profound.

"Unlike with Jay, where I had spent the first part of my pregnancy not wanting him, I immediately sent thoughts to them that they were wanted, loved, and welcomed. Oh, and to please work with me on the pregnancy thing. I didn't want to be miserable." She smiled, and it seemed the room brightened just from that small action. "They listened, or my angels and ancestors did, because that pregnancy was so much easier than it had been with Jay. I worried that so much in my body could fail—my heart, my kidneys—and so much could go wrong, like gestational diabetes. But they came through alright.

"Raising a child is not easy, especially when you have to do it alone." She extracted her hand from his and placed it on his cheek. "Devesh, I'm so sorry. Please forgive me. I let my fears keep me from doing what was right for my children. *Your* children. And I'm so very sorry."

Devesh reached out and pushed a few strands of hair away from her face. "We will work through this, all of this, until this relationship makes sense and it's something you are comfortable with, alright?"

"Alright."

Her answer sounded like more of a question than an answer.

Devesh leaned forward and kissed the pulse that was beating at the base of her throat and smiled when he heard her sharp intake breath and felt the trembling in her body.

As much as she tried to remind him that their marriage was "in name only," he had to wonder if she was saying it more for her own benefit than his.

chapter 10

Devesh thought a wonderful way to bond with his wife would be to have a little fun in the sun. The twelve-bedroom home on Shoreview had a private backyard oasis with pool, spa, dining areas, barbecue center and lush tropical landscaping. Unfortunately, when they made it out of the master suite, down the long hallway to the front stairs, they found the house was overflowing with strangers his family had invited. Quite a few of them Tiya's female friends.

Contrary to what Devesh believed, only a few of the people who came for nightly dinners at the Maharaj place, showed up for their wedding and reception a few weeks earlier. Reign had not realized how much they had been slighted, but Devesh was well aware and tucked that information in the back of his mind. That day, Reign had never looked as regal as she did in her Anarkali Salwar royal purple lengha choli set—tunic with matching pants. Devesh had worn a kurta of the same color, with gold accents. Anaya had done Reign's make-up along with an upswept look for her hair. Reign had always been beautiful, but on the day she became his wife, she was the picture of royalty she had been named for.

When she had glided toward him, his heart swelled with pride. Finally, he would have the woman who was meant for him. He knew it, even if it would take her some convincing. They had years now, and he would use every minute wisely. She said until the children were twelve—the age of accountability. He would find a way to extend that to many more years.

Devesh had turned to where the twins sat with his parents wearing colors and garments that matched the bride and groom. From his place in front of the Pandit, Devesh winked at them. They giggled, and Leena gestured for them to hurry up and get on with things. There was a food spread for the wedding reception that awaited which would satisfy everyone's soul, even if Devesh's choice of bride did not.

Weeks later, his family—and now their friends, were still reeling from the aftermath of his decision. Somehow, they had gotten over their reservations enough to spread out all over the Maharaj home.

The place, especially outdoors, was perfectly designed for the type of entertaining that was such a central part of Indian family life. But Tiya's friends weren't there simply to enjoy a beautiful day of socializing.

Every one of them seemed to have one motive—baiting Devesh into doing something no married man should be caught doing. No respect for the fact that he had a gold band that matched Reign's on his wedding finger.

Finally fed up with the women's antics, Devesh left the pool, and sauntered over to the place where Reign was stretched out on a lounger enjoying a novel. She'd taken to reading now that she had more time on her hands since Mumma and Aunt Kavya were insisting on keeping the children. And the twins loved Mumma, Aunt Kavya, Pranav, Anaya, and Papa something fierce. The bond and interaction often had them laughing like children themselves.

Devesh leaned in, kissed Reign passionately on the lips.

"Hey," she managed when there was a slight break and she could breathe.

He silenced her protest swiftly with the expert use of his tongue;

moisture from his massive chest was steadily dripping on the pages that were suddenly abandoned on her lap. His kiss deepened and intensified before blossoming into a world of exploration, and his senses reeled with the pleasurable onslaught. The taste of her, the feel of her, the scent of her—all combined to make him open to her in a way that had him on the brink of losing control.

Then he was gone, running back toward the Olympic-sized pool, feet slapping noisily on the stones before diving into the deep end, slicing through the water in smooth strides as if that damning kiss hadn't just dismantled his entire world.

❀ ❀ ❀

Devesh had kissed her. In plain view of everyone. And it wasn't tame by any stretch of the imagination. East Indian culture wasn't too keen on public displays of affection. The silence that descended around them was nothing short of earth-shattering. Everyone who had eyes had somehow focused her way, even the pets.

Soon, whispers of disbelief carried across the expanse of the area. The family members who were riding the fence about their marriage chimed in to answer questions they were hit with all of a sudden …

Wait a minute; he's with her?

Yes, he married her a few weeks ago.

Her?

That's what we said. Isn't it horrible?

Oh my God, really?

I know, right?

Where'd he get her from?

We're still trying to figure that out.

I thought he was with the blonde one.

Yes, we did too.

What ghetto did she crawl out of?

Only Shiva knows.

Reign shifted her gaze just in time to see Tiya's face flush with a color too red to give a name. Tiya's husband, Hiran, gave his wife's hand a reassuring pat while throwing an angry glare at Reign, who struggled under its intensity.

"Never knew Devesh to fall for a woman who was so ... you know," goaded one of Tiya's friends.

"That's what makes this so strange," Tiya answered, keeping a steady focus on Devesh's movements in the pool. "She's a little thick, I mean she's much smaller now than I remember in her pics, but still her whole vibe is so serious, so deep, a little edgy." Tiya didn't even bother to lower her voice. "We tried to separate them before, and you see how that worked out."

Basically, Reign understood that "Her?" was the resounding question.

Well, why not her? Maybe the man wanted a woman of substance. Something more than skinny, pretentious types like Amy Seran.

Reign almost felt sorry for the petite woman with bluish-grey eyes and sun-streaked blonde hair who had been Devesh's "sometime" companion for years. She'd been more like a sister than a love interest. The only time any sparks seemed to fly was when they were in front of the camera. When Devesh first mentioned her years ago, he'd merely said, "She's someone who takes pictures for free."

From that moment, though, they were seen in photograph after photograph, then videos showcasing how close they were as friends and hinting at a little something more between them. None of it was believable to people who actually knew the difference between real love and people who were just going through the motions. Devesh was with Amy because she was fun and she was eye candy that helped connect him to the market that was the foundation of his stock photo business. *She takes pictures for free.* Practical, because he didn't have to pay her with anything except the illusion of the possibility of a greater love ahead. Nothing more. She had the nerve to be present today even though Devesh had clearly told her he no longer wanted a relationship.

But he had claimed Reign. In front of his family and now in front of other strangers who couldn't make heads or tails of how their relationship worked. But the looks they sent her way brought to mind an experience that had always tap danced on the corner of her memories and was the very reason she had given up on relationships altogether.

She'd been with a man years ago who had waited too late to express that he had feelings for her. She had made a pledge to join the Nation of Islam—NOI—and Reign was always serious about her commitments. No fornication. No drinking. No pork. She had needed the discipline as well as the understanding of her people that came with accepting a religion that was vastly different from her Baptist upbringing. Especially since she hadn't set foot in a church after the day when she put everyone in the congregation on notice of their sins when they were taking her to task for hers. Pulled in by the words: *A nation can rise no higher than its woman*; the NOI also provided a base for making her think outside of the misconceptions from Christian doctrines she'd been spoon-fed since birth; ones that were not favorable to women.

Five years into it, Sister Reign understood that the NOI's stance that *a nation can rise no higher than its woman* was nothing more than empty words. As she had experienced in the Christian church, the high standards that applied to women in the Nation were swept aside when it came to the men. Far too many of the men thought a woman's worth could only be found in her supporting a man with her money or spreading them wide and hanging them high so he could sample that hidden part of her body.

The first thing Reign did upon leaving the NOI was to buy a bottle of Moscato. The second act was to place a call to Shawn Newsome, a former classmate who had expressed interest before she ventured into that religion. She informed him of her new status. He was more than happy to help break her five-year sexual fast. Their "relationship" lasted a full year and Reign was so focused on getting acclimated to her new life outside of the NOI, that she missed the signs that she was the only one who was in said "relationship." They never went out on dates like a regular couple. Everything between them happened under the cover of darkness—late night calls and late night sex. Those terms were fine by her at first because she didn't want her son to run into Shawn until they were taking things to a different place—but for some reason, discussions never led in that direction. Then one night changed everything.

Shawn had shown up, and he was three sheets to the wind and another five knots under the table. Unfortunately, he was sober enough to say, "You know, Black men don't really like fat women. You'll have to pay me for sex from now on."

Her world had crumbled. He believed that her self-esteem was so low that she would accept his new terms. Unfortunately, he was wrong. She put a vaginal grip on his erection so tight that he experienced a painful muscle cramp that wouldn't go away. She watched him roll around on her freshly shampooed carpet, screaming in pain for an hour before she finally called 9-1-1.

When two women rolled in to scoop him off her bedroom floor, take him down the stairs and into the waiting ambulance, Reign filled them in on what Shawn had said. Patty and Sandi—Reign would never forget their names—shared a speaking glance between them. They were about Reign's size. Raven-haired Sandi said to her fellow blonde paramedic, "Looks like we'll be taking the *scenic* route."

Shawn showed up two months later, begging for forgiveness and a second chance. Reign didn't allow him or any other man to touch her for years after that experience. She had already soured on relationships at fourteen after landing a lemon named Roberto Madera off the showroom floor. She didn't trust her instincts when it came to men and eventually lost the need to be with one. Hence, the entrance of her *little friend*—the one that Devesh had been trying to get rid of since she brought it from Chicago. She couldn't count the times she ended up hunting for it since they had been in California. Not that she needed to use it, but still … he would hide it in the most unlikely places. Made her feel like she was on an Easter Egg hunt. Every day.

Reign was sure Devesh would be alarmed to know that she failed to disclose information about some rather interesting experiences before he dropped back into her life. When her personal pleasure device didn't prove to be enough, and she was driven by the need for human contact, she took an exploration journey into Cuddle Parties that eventually led to Bliss Parties. Those social events led to meeting Ali Khan and followed with a series of dates that she thought would end her multi-year drought. Things with Ali hadn't progressed to a sexual level, but it was so close—practically supposed to happen when she brought the twins home from this spring break trip. Thankfully, she'd left the door open to continue that avenue and also allowed Devesh to maintain the relationship with that woman he'd been with all these years. Everyone could be happy, right?

Now Devesh, one of the most handsome, talented, and wonderful men in the world, had claimed her in plain view of everyone who mattered. She, who had been abandoned by her father, two boyfriends, and two religions, was being completely accepted by a man who had no qualms about anyone knowing how he felt. The little corner of her mind that screamed that she wasn't good enough was trying to override common sense. The wedding ring on her finger seemed to tighten a little in response, reminding her Devesh had married her strictly because of the children.

Reign made an attempt to block out the curious looks still focused in her direction and tried to put her eyes on the novel she held. Two things made it nearly impossible. The pages were too wet to read and she couldn't keep from following Devesh's movements in the water—smooth, purposeful, and beautiful. He made it to the other end of the pool and put his attention her way. His gaze held hers and he smiled.

Still affected by his kiss, she tried to smile back. She placed the novel face up on the patio end table so the sun could dry the pages.

Everyone who was giving her the side-eye could take a flying leap off a tall building in a single bound. With or without the cape.

Her?

Indeed.

chapter II

Reign had finally taken all she could. Laying next to Devesh every night, unable to make love because she wanted to hold fast to the groundwork they agreed upon for the type of marriage they would have. She was unable to explore this unleashed passion that was driving her absolutely nuts. And if she didn't know any better, she would swear he was courting her.

Early morning strolls along the beach. Bringing her a delicious and healthy protein shake or fresh fruit and grains for breakfast in bed every morning. He even managed, after some time, to get her on his motorcycle, despite her fears that came as a result of her brother dying in a tragic motorcycle accident at twenty-one years of age. At first, Devesh simply walked his Harley down the street with her on it, getting her used to the feel. Then he slowly transitioned to riding for a block and back to the house each day, adding another block until they finally reached a point where she could comfortably ride with him all the way to the beach.

He also had a standing Friday appointment for a spa team to come to the house and provide Reign with services that ranged from brown sugar scrubs to massages, facials, manicures, and pedicures. Not to mention that he took Aunt Kavya up on her offer to make clothing for Reign and the twins. They now had an array of beautiful Indian garments that far outmatched anything others in the family had.

The man was so attentive to her needs that she felt her heart opening to him again, and it frightened her to no end. This marriage, one that she never thought she would be a part of, was perfect in most ways except one. And she would not let it go down that path. She needed to move forward with keeping some distance between them. None of the married women in her circle had anything good to say about marriage. Fifty percent of them were divorcing. Good women. Same result.

Ali was in Los Angeles for a few days on the final stages of a merger and acquisition deal for one of his companies. When she explained the abrupt change in her status the morning she was to walk down the aisle, Ali spent hours on a call to her explaining why a marriage *for the children's sake* never panned out. He had left her several messages over the past few weeks. She ignored them. Now, hoping to put a barrier between herself and Devesh that would keep their marriage on the track they said it would stay on, she reached out to Ali earlier today. He was disappointed to learn that she had moved forward with those sudden plans to marry Devesh, but he was also intrigued when she explained that her relationship was of the "open" variety.

She dressed in a Rene Boyd-Goldstein original poncho top, a silky pair of leggings and heels. Earlier she had asked if Mumma and Aunt Kavya could look after the children for a while. Only a slither of a thought crossed her mind that maybe, just maybe, she should have discussed this with Devesh before undertaking this part of the journey. But what exactly would she say? "Gee, Devesh, I'm so hot for you that I need to sleep with someone else?" That would go over real well, but that was the terms of their marriage. An open marriage that allowed either one of them to explore avenues that would officially be closed in any other kind of marriage.

Reign had learned in her research on open marriages, that a good majority of the additional relationships were not sexual. People, like her, were under the assumption that those kind of relationships were all about swapping mates and having a wicked good time in bed. Not so. Swinging and open marriages were two totally different beasts— one was about sexual pleasure, the other was all about fulfillment in much more than just the physical sense. She found that men brought their wives into the concept kicking and screaming, only to get upset in a major way when the wives began to enjoy themselves by having fulfilling relationships and companionships that their husbands did not provide. The husbands tended to be the ones to demand that the marriages go back to being monogamous. As if they were the only ones who were supposed to enjoy the fruits of that kind of labor. Go figure.

The same way that Devesh had given her a hard time about her *personal pleasure device*—one that had them in Midway Airport's security for an extra half hour. The woman checking the bag did not want to pull such a unique and custom-made piece out for all to see. She finally asked the grey-haired TSA officer watching the screen to come over and take a gander into Reign's carry on for himself. His eyes widened, then he looked up a Reign, but put a much longer questioning and accusatory look at Devesh who fumed to the point that he didn't speak to Reign again until they'd landed in California.

Reign stepped out of Devesh's master suite that had a fireplace and full spa-centered bath as well as a separate workout room which connected to an office that served as his studio. She tipped down the hallway, then the front staircase and paused long enough to have an internal argument about whether to say goodbye or simply slide out the door with no fanfare whatsoever.

Come to think of it, that whole *no fanfare* thing was definitely the better option. She tipped soundlessly toward the door, grateful that no one was in the parlor or the living room this time.

"Mama," Leena squealed, scrambling from Aunt Kavya's side and rushing toward Reign. Kamran slowly ambled from the chair where he sat playing checkers with Pranav.

"Where are you going?" Devesh's voice boomed from the family room through the den and carried all the way to the parlor.

Conversations trickled to a halt. Leena froze several feet from Reign. Kamran nearly crashed into her. Both of them snapped their attention to Devesh whose tone was sharper than even she could recall.

"I have a date."

The silence and shock that rippled through the people in the den, family room and dining room, nearly tilted the universe on its axis.

His expression darkened as he covered some of the distance between them. "Come again?"

"A date," she repeated with a lot less energy than when she said it a few moments ago. "I'll only be out for a little while."

Murmurs of discontent echoed from everywhere, and soon the entire front areas of the four corners were overflowing with family who had come in to witness this strange turn of events.

Mumma moved from behind Anaya to watch, her eyes pleading with Reign not to break her son's heart. Reign knew that look all too well. The same one she'd had when Cassie, the girlfriend that came after Jay's relationship with his high school sweetheart had ended, had fallen prey to her own insecurities and had hurt him in the worst possible way. Then the young woman came running to Reign to help make things right. Reign schooled Cassie on the fact that what she had done would serve as a life lesson; Cassie would have to "woman up" and deal with the consequences.

Evidently, that was going to be Reign's lesson here as well. She should have communicated with her husband. Truthfully, she was still not used to having to work out her plans and progress with someone else. Before now she only answered to God and the IRS, exactly in that order. She was also not used to sharing her children with someone other than Jay.

"Absolutely not."

"You have the option to be with Amy," she offered, flickering a gaze toward his ex who for some unknown reason was still a fixture around the house every evening for dinner. "That's what an open marriage is."

"I gave her up when I married you," he shot back.

"I didn't ask you to do that," she countered, slipping the black clutch under her arm.

"You didn't have to," he yelled. "That's what a man does when he has every intention of being faithful to the woman he marries."

Amy's pale skin reddened with embarrassment.

"I didn't ask for that either."

"No, you didn't. *This* is who I am." Devesh hooked his arm under hers and guided her past the curious onlookers. "Come, we will not speak of such things in front of my family," he said.

"Why not? They're always around to hear everything else," she responded as he ushered her up the stairs, down the hall, and into the master suite.

Now, she was the one feeling some kind of way. "Devesh, we have an *open* marriage. That means I get to date."

"You should've talked to me about this first," he admonished, and was in her face in the five seconds it took to move closer.

"You tell me how to start *that* conversation."

"Devesh, I'd like to talk about maybe taking our marriage to the next level," he countered, and his expression was intense. "Maybe you would have understood that I was waiting for you to get comfortable with the fact that you're married now. I wanted you to make the first move toward becoming intimate."

She grimaced, stepping a few feet away, taking a deep breath before launching into, "You knew how much I wanted children. Knew that I thought I couldn't have any. You kept them from me. I can *never* forgive you for that."

The words, his hurtful words flung at her when he first learned of the twins, hung between them for several moments.

"If you can't forgive me," she replied, tilting her head to look into his eyes. "How am I supposed to believe that you love me?"

Devesh closed his eyes, shuttering any emotion that she could read there. When he opened them, he said, "I regret those hateful words." He crossed the remaining distance between them. "I thought by taking my time, you'd learn my feelings. You'd know that we belong together."

Every day she felt like she was going through the motions, doing what she thought was supposed to be right in a marriage. Taking care of him, anticipating his needs, giving him the benefit of her knowledge and experience. The fact that he appreciated it and listened gave her a heady feeling. Every day it was becoming so hard to hold her feelings at bay. Deep down she knew that he still hated her for the time he missed with his children. And she was also aware that his family had always proved to be more important than her. She could never let her guard down.

Devesh stroked his fingers through his hair. "I know what you sacrificed to bring my children into the world," he whispered. "And I am forever grateful for that. I know I agreed that if we married, it would be an open one, but ..." He lowered his hands, placed them on her arms. "Honey, I can't. The thought of you with another man tears my heart in a way I can't even explain.

He sighed, and the sound was weary and sad. She pulled him close; letting the emotions ripple through, trying to calm him so he would not break down. This issue went deep for him. And she never understood how much before now.

Devesh pulled away to look into her eyes. What she saw in those dark brown orbs nearly knocked her to her knees.

"I know what I said, but I can't do this open marriage thing," he admitted.

"So you were lying when you—"

"No, honey. I thought I could handle it but ... my wife, the woman who lays next to me every night, who shares my life? The mother of my children?" He dragged his hands down his face. "I can't do it, honey. Another man between your thighs can find his way into your heart. I'm not here for it."

She almost smiled at his use of common slang, but she also couldn't help feeling a little bit cornered. Did he really think that their marriage could go the distance? That there would ever be a time when his family wasn't looking down their nose at her and the twins?

"Why don't you at least give *us* a try instead of automatically believing that we will fail?"

Reign's cell vibrated. She was certain that her date was past impatient at this point.

Ali would be sorely disappointed at yet another obstacle in their blossoming relationship. He had wanted a more exclusive intimate connection and made no bones about it when he pursued her all this time. When he realized that she was going to stay the course for the next eight years, only then was he willing to explore the other side of the open marriage deal. Probably more in hopes that he could convince her to leave Devesh altogether than mere acceptance of her marriage alone. Now she had to wonder if sexual gratification would outweigh everything else that Devesh put on the table? Family. Trust. Love. Safety. Companionship. And now ... intimacy.

"Give us a try first, and if ..." His gaze slid to the plush carpet. He couldn't even voice the words. *If I'm not enough for you.* "Then we'll revisit this whole"—He shuddered—"open marriage issue."

Devesh cupped her face in his hands, kissed her lips and led her out of the room and down into the place where some of the guests had abandoned dinner and were having hushed discussions. All conversation came to a halt when they appeared.

Tiya's scowl showed exactly how she felt about things. Mumma's hand fluttered and landed over her heart. She was obviously feeling her son's pain and anxiety. For a woman who was so hell-bent on not wanting her son to marry a woman outside of their culture, she had made a complete one-eighty and was actually rooting for them to make it. That moved Reign.

She regarded Pranav a moment, before he nodded vehemently, evidently sensing that Devesh had set things right.

"I'll go out and tell Ali that—"

"I'll talk with him," Devesh said, stepping around her and aiming for the door.

Reign halted her movements. "Devesh, either you trust me, or you don't."

"Woman, a minute ago you were ready to be with him," he responded, eyes filled with heat. "And a man who's willing to sleep with a woman who took vows with another man. Him, I don't trust as far as I can throw him."

Devesh didn't give her a chance to respond. He was out the door in a flash.

Reign focused on Mumma, who breathed a sigh of relief that mirrored Anaya's expression exactly.

"What did you say to him?" she demanded when Devesh walked back in fifteen minutes later. A whole world of time seemed to pass for that conversation with Ali to have been a simple, *"She's not coming with you tonight."*

"I said what needed to be said." Devesh leveled a fiery gaze on her. "You belong to me."

The silence that expanded between them was telling.

"Care to dispute that," he challenged, and his dark brown eyes were intense.

Ali would not take highly to that claim. Especially since he had been the one to put in work all these months of dating, worthwhile conversations, intimate dinners, and excursions—almost the same foundation she'd had with Devesh. Well, except the cuddle and Bliss parties.

"You waited until I was here." She inhaled, struggling to contain her anger. "No job, no place to go, totally dependent on you. And now you want to have an issue with this." She shook her head. "You lied to me."

Devesh inhaled and clamped down on his response, but a few unspoken words hung between them. *And so have you.*

"To be honest, I didn't fully understand what you were asking," he admitted threading his fingers through his hair. "I thought it meant I had time to show you …" He exhaled slowly, closing his eyes as though to get his bearings. "To get you to a place where you could love me. Again."

Reign's jaw dropped, but she quickly recovered and stiffened her shoulders.

"I thought I could court you properly."

"Like flowers and dinners?" she scoffed, almost laughed at that notion. "That's not you."

"Woman, you don't know what I'm capable of," he shot back.

That wiped the smile from her face.

"We've waited nearly five years; a little while longer will be alright." Devesh pressed a kissed to her temple. "But only a little while, Reign. I can only be patient for so long. Then I'm going to start playing dirty."

"Oh, and you've been above board all this time?" she said putting some space between them.

"He warned me," Devesh explained, putting a halting grip on her upper arms. "Warned me that if there was a sliver of a chance with you, he would take it. That man wants you in the worst way." Devesh moved closer, effectively trapping her by invading her space. "What he fails to understand is … I. Want. You. *More*."

Her mouth went instantly dry. She'd never seen this side of him, almost feral, dominating, possessive. "You're not playing fair."

"Question though …" Then he smiled. It wasn't nearly as pleasant as she remembered. "Do you really want me to?"

❀ ❀ ❀

That kiss. That damnable kiss came to mind, along with her response to him.

"I'm hard-pressed to know how you love him," Devesh said so only she could hear. "When it's obvious that deep in this place right here." He gently placed a hand over her heart. "You love me."

Reign averted her eyes. Her breathing came in uneven measures, when she looked back he smiled and finished with, "I'm just waiting for the rest of you to get that memo."

She trembled, and he had to wonder if it was from fear? No, it was need. He recognized that because his was so strong, it took every ounce of strength for him to sleep next to her night after night and not have her. It was creating a pain so physical it sent him to work out, take a cold shower, and straight to the Puja. Not exactly in that order.

"I will wait for you," he whispered, directly in her ear.

"You don't have to do that," she confessed as though nothing he had said made any difference. "You can still be with Amy."

"Why? So you won't feel guilty about being with him?" He waved away that thought with a dismissive hand. "I take my vows to you seriously. I will not be with any woman *but* you. You know how I feel, you will have to make the first move, Reign."

She looked away for a split second, trying to collect herself.

"I love you, Reign," he whispered. "You are enough. You. Are. Enough."

Devesh saw the moment her eyes glazed over with unshed tears. Then she steeled herself, lifted her chin while an icy resolve shuttered her expression.

She did not believe him? Even now?

Patience, Devesh, patience. She is your wife now.

Sweeping her down the aisle and getting her to say "I do" was the first obstacle. Keeping her in that position of happily being his wife was going to be the challenge.

"Everything in its time," he said.

"You believe that?"

"I most certainly do," he replied, extending his hand to her. "Come, my love.

Reign hesitated only a brief moment before placing her hand within his and joining his family for dinner.

chapter 12

Devesh noticed that Reign had been a little distant ever since the night her date with Ali had come to an abrupt end. Maybe she was angry that he had interfered. The man was about Reign's age, seemingly wealthy, of middle eastern descent, handsome in a way that he could also be a model—enough that Devesh could see what appealed to Reign, but not so much that Ali Khan deserved to hold a place in his wife's life.

Devesh may have had the home court advantage, but he felt himself losing ground in Reign's life. She and the children were settling into his parent's home, but the first bone of contention came with the fact that Reign did not like having the children too far away from them at night. Though the house was massive, she preferred that he create the twins' sleeping space in the studio that was directly adjacent to his master bedroom. She wanted to keep a watchful eye over them—especially at night.

The place had a number of aunts, uncles, cousins, and siblings who looked out for all of the children, so Devesh did not understand her concern. He tried to talk her out of it, but she was adamant, or she threatened to sleep in the space that had been originally designated for the twins.

Devesh replaced some furniture and rearranged the rest in his master suite, then did his own brand of remodeling to make it a place that he and Reign could share comfortably with the children. He still managed to have a portion of the space sectioned off perfectly for the couple's privacy. With the children sleeping in what was now essentially a separate room connected to theirs, only then did Reign began to relax.

He had her meet with the architect and contractors working on his building—two upper-level condos being combined into a state-of-the-art penthouse. It would add more time to the completion deadline, but in the meantime, they changed his master suite in the Maharaj layout to satisfy her need to be near Leena and Kamran. Better to have her close and get used to sleeping next to him, than for her to be on the other side of the house, and the divide between them become wider. Though there was some privacy afforded between the master bedroom and studio, it wasn't enough. So much for seducing his wife over the next few weeks. That would be pretty hard to manage with two young ones nearby—and ones who were a little more aware of things than he would prefer.

Reign meant the world to him, and he was grateful that God had given him the opportunity to do what he should have done long ago. He could be patient. For a time.

Marriage was not something he—or his twin—had set in their sights. When Anaya had unexpectedly married his best friend, Pranav, Devesh had not been elated by the news. They waited until Devesh was out of the country filming a commercial. By the time he came back, they were married. For three weeks he didn't speak to either one of them.

Devesh's twin had relationships before, but they never seemed as solid or had a propensity to be as long-lasting as the man who finally convinced her to slide down the aisle. Then he watched them, witnessed a change in Pranav that was so profound that it didn't take long for Devesh to realize that there was no better mate for Anaya. His sister was glowing like a shiny rupee, and he'd never seen her so happy. Or Pranav for that matter. Then the children came. Seeing Pranav as a father was a wonder to behold. Anaya had become a mirror image of their loving, caring mother when it came to her children and husband.

Now Devesh was having his own time of it. Maybe he should call in some reinforcements.

🪷 🪷 🪷

Devesh was sitting next to Jay at his home office in Chicago putting the finishing touches on some images that would go on Devesh's website.

"Mom's been sad so long I don't think she knows how to be happy," Jay confessed, clicking the keys and brightening the onscreen photo of Devesh wearing a dark designer suit and tie, looking more like Bond— James Bond. "I mean, she has had her moments but ... she taught you how to play Spades, right?

"Yes, she's also teaching Anaya and some of the others who want to learn," Devesh said. "I think I'm getting pretty good, but Pranav learned from some sisters in college, so we get a little challenge on the board."

"Have you all ever been so low in points that you've gone below zero?"

"When I was first learning," he began, gesturing for Jay to slide to the next image. "We had to bid a blind six or seven just to get back on board."

"And that's what I mean," Jay explained, taking his eyes off the screen and putting it squarely on Devesh. "Some women experience things in their world that makes them spend their entire lives just trying to get to zero. Being molested or abused early in life puts them below zero and they struggle just to get on board." Jay put his focus on Devesh.

"Are you saying ...?"

"No, because that would be her story to tell," Jay said, and then he focused on the image of a family portrait next to his Mac taken when the twins turned four. "But I can tell you this, since it made local and national news; her sister was thrown down a flight of stairs by an uncle who wanted her to remain silent. The only thing that kept him from killing mom, too, was that she grabbed a butcher knife to keep him away. Then she ran out in the hallway of the apartment building and yelled fire—and everyone came running.

"Fire?'

"Yes," he answered. "She thought yelling *help* or *rape* wouldn't get the same response."

Devesh shook his head.

"The emergency team was barely able to save his life. They found him with the knife embedded so deep in his thigh it required surgery to remove it."

Devesh's heart slammed against his chest. Reign had mentioned some tragic experience had happened to her growing up, but had been vague about the details. So much so that he'd thought she had been molested. But nearly killing a man to protect yourself from harm and witnessing a sibling meet her death, and the horrible things that proceeded that act, that had to have a lasting impact.

"I think mom blames herself for Tasha's death because she didn't tell sooner."

So much loss and death surrounding their family. "So how do I help get her past all this, Jay? I'm sure it's still weighing on her."

"You just have to find a way to make her comfortable with being happy. It always seems as if she feels that happiness is about to float away."

"That sounds wonderful in theory," Devesh countered, still trying to absorb what Jay had shared. "But putting it into action—"

"Is not as hard as it seems. I was in the shower one day, and she came home early. I didn't know she was there and I came strutting out of the bathroom butt naked. She got a glimpse of what she hadn't seen since I was able to wash my own parts."

Devesh chuckled, realizing Jay was trying to lighten things with a little humor.

"I ran to the bedroom and put some clothes on. When I came out, she said 'one thing', then she pointed to my groin and said, "You got *that* from your Mama 'cause your daddy wasn't hung like that."

Devesh was too choked up to laugh. "She actually said that?"

"Yep. I was so busy cracking up. I didn't have time to feel embarrassed," he said laughing. "Laughter eases so much. Put Mom at ease, maybe that will work."

"Speaking of putting your mother at ease, let's revisit that plan to get you to move to California."

Jay laughed, but at least he didn't brush it off this time. Devesh had taken a step outside of the Pullman home and found the same issues existed as when he helped Reign pack up her life and move to California.

"I'm thinking about it more and more," Jay said, sweeping a gaze across several boxes from his apartment that he hadn't bothered to unpack. "I might have my cousins Shogun and Demarco to move in here.

"Cousins? Shogun?"

"He's a tattoo artist. Those two are some of the few family members that my mother actually keeps up with." Jay clicked and moved on to more family photos and the few friends that Reign had sent his way. "Mom's a little calculated with keeping her circle small. When she wants a family member to leave, she loans them money. She doesn't bother to call them and ask about it, because she knows they have no intentions of giving it back. That way, they can't be mad at her—it's a mutual parting."

"Damn."

"And you haven't heard the half of it," Jay said, grinning. "When my grandmother forced her to choose between having a roof over her head and being out on the street, my mother, who was fourteen at the time, didn't have any problem showing just how unfair that was."

❀ ❀ ❀

Fourteen-year-old Reign was forced to get up in front of the church and apologize for shaming her mother by getting pregnant. She complied, but was angry the entire time. Especially since she was fully aware of things going on behind the scenes. While she still held the microphone, she paused and then ended her apology with, "But I have a question, though. Is it only the girls you want to apologize just because you can see what we've done?" She rubbed her hand over her extended belly as the question drew murmurs of discontent. "Dawn got pregnant. No one asked Mason to come up here and apologize. Alexa got knocked up. No one made Eric say he was sorry. My brothers weren't made to get up here either."

The congregation roared with disapproval aimed directly at her. Some of them stood, raising their voices in contempt.

"Now, I know it does not excuse what I did," Reign continued, holding up a hand to signal they should quiet down because she wasn't done. "But I'm just saying Brother Harold's been sleeping with Sister Odessa's husband for the past two years. Everybody knows it." She focused on the golden man whose face turned a magnificent red. "Oh, and I don't see Sister Justine and Brother Martin up here apologizing for getting busy in the choir room during rehearsal when the pastor's wife caught 'em a few months ago."

"Now, wait a minute," Brother Martin stood, shaking his fist at Reign. His wife yanked him back down in the pew, then slapped her purse on top of his head nearly knocking him unconscious. Sister Justine left her husband's side and tried to run from the church. Her exit was blocked by the ushers who seemed to be having a grand old time with all of the skeletons creaking out of the closet and running up the church aisle as if the devil was on their heels. One of them, Sister Dorothy, even managed to give Reign the thumbs up sign, so she'd keep the party going.

"I'm just saying let's keep it fair," she said, ducking out of the reach of Deacon Jones who was making an attempt to snatch the microphone from her. "A sin's a sin. I think everybody should take a turn up here." She gestured toward Deacon Byrne as she slid up the aisle, managing to still be heard over all the chaos. "That is a *whole bottle* of Dr. Tichenor's in your pocket 'cause you need a little nip of that eighty-proof every now. Nobody needs fresh breath that bad." She winked at him, and even his wife laughed. "My mama told me that one."

The entire congregation was now on their feet, in heated conversations, some arguing about the truth she let spill. Choir members hastily left their seats. A few of them managed to tip out of the back door to the lower level before she let loose on them, too. The usher board had closed the rear doors so no one could run out that way. One of them sprinted down the right side aisle to get to the choir entrance to block that as well.

Reign slid a sly look to her fuming mother, who was dressed in the pristine white uniform of the pastor's personal nurse and was sitting in a special seat near the pulpit. "And the only reason my mother's on the nurse's board," Reign said, keeping a steely glare on her mother. "Taking care of the pastor, getting his water and handkerchiefs, fixing all that good food and baking those sweet potato pies especially for him, is 'cause she's hoping for a little … *sin* of her own."

"I knew it," the First Lady said, waggling a finger at Thelma, wide brim hat tipping almost off her head. She nearly climbed over the pew, aiming to get to Reign's mother. Two women nearest her, held the stout woman back.

Reign looked toward the red-faced Pastor who was fit to be tied. "And doesn't look like he's turning down nothing but his collar, so maybe I should pass the mic to him. Come to think of it, Brother Jimmy, Brother Patrick, and Brother Russell need some time up here, too." She moved up the middle aisle and back toward the pulpit ignoring the three men in question. "Each one of them offered me some money—for the baby's sake. That's what they said. But they wanted a *little something* in return. They seemed really happy that I was pregnant 'cause that meant I couldn't get knocked up again." She swept a gaze across the congregation as Sister Delores yanked the microphone from her hand. Reign dashed toward the choir stand to snatch another one from where the organist played. "And they're not the only ones up in here who did that. I've got nine offers from church men alone and close to $9,536.50." She waggled an index finger. "And don't forget the fifty cents. That's a lot of dough, especially for a sinner like me." She shrugged as if she hadn't set the church on holy fire. "So let's be fair about this sin thing."

"That's enough, young lady," the pastor said from the pulpit, gesturing for someone to grab her. Reign faked left, then moved until she was in the far left aisle blocked in by a few folks who were grinning at her efforts and didn't let the deacons near her.

"Oh, so I'm a *young lady* now?" Reign shot back, glowering angrily at him. "When you told my mother that she needed to bring her *little whore* before the church to apologize."

"No he didn't," Sister Mabel shouted.

"But you didn't make your nieces get up here when *they* got pregnant. Or any of the boys right here in this church who made them that way. I count about twelve so far. And that's not including the ones who had abortions." Reign snapped her fingers as realization hit. "But wait a minute, that counts as sin, too, right? But it's not one that you can see."

Gasps echoed throughout the congregation.

"So which is it? Whore or young lady?" she taunted, stretching out her hands as if in supplication. "Either way, I'm just saying—a sin is a sin. Let the church say 'Amen'."

Needless to say, Reign and her mother were immediately escorted from the church's main sanctuary, out the door, and told never to return.

Thelma was angered at not only losing her church home, but also the pastor, who—unknown to Reign—had become the main source of income for their family.

That day, Thelma said she never wanted to lay eyes on Reign again. She kept that promise until her dying day.

What she couldn't know was that Reign had already made her peace with whatever consequences would come with her brutal uncovering of church hypocrisy, long before she opened her mouth that Sunday.

chapter 13

"And you thought I was going to go against her wishes and let you in on that secret?" Jay shook his head. "No, no, my brother. I wasn't going to take that chance and have her cut me out of her life, too."

"She wouldn't dare."

Jay shrugged and put his focus on the notes he'd written to share with Devesh about branding and to create a more dynamic outreach.

"You haven't unpacked?" He gestured to all the boxes stacked up against the wall.

"No time, I've been hella busy."

Devesh shifted the keyboard and pulled up the Southwest Airlines website. "That means moving to Cali won't be much of an issue." He typed in a date for a week away. "Come on, Jay. Let's make it happen."

❁ ❁ ❁

"You have a commercial taping tomorrow."

Devesh shook away the last remnants of the power nap he'd taken. He was grateful to be home in Cali and that nothing unpleasant had transpired between Reign and his family while he was gone. He was also grateful that Jay had made strides to take him up on the offer. They weren't going to let Reign in on that little piece of information; not until everything was set in stone.

"What?" he said to Reign, rewinding his brain to what she had just said. "What are you talking about?"

Reign slid a set of documents his way. He sat up, swept through each one of them, trying to understand what she'd done. "I didn't send in anything to land this kind of work."

"I did," she confessed, looking a little concerned. "I sent in that media kit I created for you several years ago. Then they checked out the first stages of a website that Jay put up for you a few days ago. They liked what they saw."

Devesh studied the contracts she'd negotiated again and the amount of money the company was shelling out. "This is sweet, honey, but I can't do this. I'm out of that life now. I can't do both."

She extracted the contract from his hand and placed it on the nightstand. "Why don't you talk to the job and see if there's a night position or a way to work around your filming schedule?"

He thought that over for a moment. "I'll do that," he said, warily.

She fingered the fresh haircut that a stylist gave him before his first day out to work. Long hair was all the rage for product ads; not so much for conservative employers. "Having a family doesn't mean giving up on your dreams."

Devesh smiled up at her, pulled her to him, then held her in his arms, feeling it was too soon for another kiss like the one he'd planted on her that day out by the pool.

"Thank you for holding my vision," he whispered.

While Reign waited to hear from the headhunters who believed they could land her a job in the paralegal field, she enrolled the children into a Montessori school and also volunteered to work there to get a feel for their style of education and whether it was the best fit for the children. At night, she put her time and energy into something else—her husband.

"Do you trust me?" she asked Devesh.

"If I didn't trust you, honey, there'd be no way you'd have access to all of my accounts."

"And I appreciate that trust," she said slowly, as though weighing her next words carefully. "But I'm talking about something else."

Devesh put his full attention on Reign as he waited.

"Your poetry."

Those words were written to express what he felt for her since he hadn't had the courage to tell her back then. "What about it?"

"It's beautiful," she said, and the compliment made him hone in on her face. The expression was one he recognized when she was putting some serious consideration into things.

"Have you ever thought about putting your words to music?"

"What? No!" He waved her off, wondering how much she had actually read. "They're just my thoughts."

"I've heard you sing in the shower," she countered, giving him a megawatt smile. "I don't understand anything you're saying, but I recognize a man who can carry a tune."

Devesh's gaze lowered. Her robe had opened to allow a smooth curve of her thighs to show through.

She followed his line of vision and whipped it closed. "Do you trust me?"

"Of course, honey," he said, trying to ignore the furious pounding of his heart and the fact that his erection was making an untimely visit—again. Lord, he wanted this woman so bad.

"Then give me permission to use this one," she whispered and held up a piece from his journal.

"What are you thinking?"

"You'll see."

She placed the page gently on the coffee table. "Devesh, if you don't mind me asking, what actually happened in Bollywood? You never gave me any details and it seems like some dark hole in your life."

Devesh crossed one leg over the other. "I did something that no Indian actor had done before," he answered. "I saw all the poverty around me, and I wanted to help. Mostly, I wanted to understand. So I took some time away from the glitz and glamor of Bollywood and moved to the poorest part of India. I lived as they lived. Depended on the kindness of strangers. Never knew how people could be so mean to other human beings."

Devesh adjusted himself on the sofa until his thighs were closely touching hers. Reign laid her head on his chest as he said, "Someone took pictures, and word got around that Devesh Maharaj, the Bollywood star, was homeless and living on the street." He grimaced and the fury he felt at how the media and fellow actors he once admired had ripped him apart, still simmered under the surface. "No one would hire me after that. No one wants to be associated with poverty. It's cool to say you're helping the homeless and the less fortunate, but to actually get in the trenches to understand? Not the right move to make. But I … How can I know how to help unless I understand what help is needed? Throwing money at people only lasts so long. It's temporary. That's the main reason I take an interest in charities that help children."

Reign placed a hand on his cheek. "Let's see where this new direction will take you. Alright?"

"Alright."

⚜ ⚜ ⚜

Reign sent the poetry to a friend in Chicago. Percy, a former classmate, was one of the best underground musicians and producers in the Windy City. He had given up his dream of working with some of the big names in the industry when the politics of it all proved to be too much. But the man's skills were unlike anything she'd ever heard. She gave him a little of Devesh's background and sent him links to a couple of music videos

Devesh shot in India. Then she sang the melody that came to her mind, using the poem that Devesh had written as lyrics.

Twenty-four hours later, she received a track from Percy that was so beautiful it nearly gave her a heart attack. The sound incorporated some of the instrumentation that was used in Devesh's one hit that had landed on the music charts in India. She rushed home from the Montessori school with the children and played the music for Devesh. At one point he closed his eyes, tapped his feet before his body swayed to the beat.

"I love it," he said, smiling. The music had a blend of everything that was summer; that was him; that was a little of India, a little R&B, a little of what was mellow and could remind people of enjoying life.

Then she parted her lips to let the words come forth—his poem, his way of pouring his heart out to a woman he wanted, but wasn't sure if she wanted him. Devesh's jaw lowered, and it took a few seconds before he closed his mouth again.

He dropped down on the sofa. "Honey, I can't sing like that," he whispered as his smile disappeared.

"Mr. Woods, my high school music teacher, is going to Facetime with you every day to work on your vocals." She gestured to the iMac, then clicked a few keys, pulling up the application. "You'll be able to sing this song and others in your own way." She removed her hand from the keyboard and cupped his face in her hands. "You said you trust me. Now I'm going to need you to prove it."

"Why?" he asked, sitting on the edge of the desk, putting his focus on the screen that became filled with images of him in different poses. They were in slideshow mode so the images would shift to a new one every three seconds, but then it morphed into a brand new interactive website.

"You've had your image, face, and body in front of Bollywood and the advertising community for years. You need to do something different. Something to make the industry you've been trying to break into come to you instead of the other way around. You've gone to them hat in hand all these years and haven't been given a chance. You have to switch gears, Devesh. Take a risk and do something different." She saw the way his jaw tensed and said, "People *see* you all the time. Now they need to *hear* you. Hear those beautiful words. *Your* words."

Devesh pondered that for a minute. "Are you sure this is the way to go?"

"Trust me."

And he did.

While he didn't regret taking the job of a credentialing agent; checking backgrounds on people applying for passports or government jobs, wasn't the kind of work that he wanted to do for the rest of his life. Charities were where he wanted to put his focus and heart, but none of the places he'd applied paid the kind of salary that would afford him the best opportunity to take care of a wife and two children.

But singing? Really?

❀ ❀ ❀

Thanks to Mr. Woods and Percy, Devesh learned how to do his own backing vocals. Reign added her touch by having him listen to her singing and Devesh imitated the vocal acrobatics until they became second nature for him. And it worked, mostly because she was able to get him to hear how close some of the runs that R&B singers were known for sounded to East Indian chants and inflections.

At her insistence, they kept his family in the dark about these new developments so no one could throw salt or negativity on their plans. But Anaya and some of the others were curious because Devesh was humming all the time, had headphones on and was singing in a way that made his parents and even the twins smile.

Meanwhile, Percy was working on more of the poems and her melodies, bringing them to life for them to have an entire lead album of ten unique songs that would hit the world music scene, not just the States.

"Now, I'm going to need to get you into the studio to record it and a few others," she said to Devesh.

"This has never been my thing," he protested, one night after they had a scrumptious dinner with his family. "It sounds good, though."

"Think of this as one loooooooooong commercial," she said, grinning. "You're telling the world who you are through your words. You're opening your heart to them. Let's put one song out, gauge the response, but let's be ready to release an entire album when it does well, and there's a huge buzz."

Devesh had worked hard to deliver the songs in a sound that was true to himself, his culture, and his upbringing in America.

"Honey, I think it sounds amazing," he said, listening to the final tracks a month later. "But do you think other people will think so?"

"I know they will," she replied, with enough confidence for them both. "I asked Percy not to over-mix the songs, to make sure it sounds as close to how you would perform live as possible."

They recorded the first song in English, Hindi, Spanish, and French. They also had a version with a smoother beat geared toward the mature Steppers crowd in Chicago. Then the track was put to a faster rhythm—a dance version—to appeal to the younger audience. The song ended with a musical prayer/chant that blended in subtly with whatever version was created.

On the back end, Reign had Jay totally dismantle the last remnants of Devesh's current website—mostly stock photos that he had for sale, images he'd taken with too many women to count—Black, White, Asian, Latina, petite ladies and big mamas. A good majority of the front line images were of him and Amy. Those were the first to go. New images from Pete Stenberg arrived, taken on one of those weekend trips to Chicago for recording sessions with Percy. Devesh stayed with Jay who was finalizing the details of Devesh's new brand.

Jay's Columbia College skill set and experience in graphic design and brand marketing, helped create a whole new website with social media pages that had a consistent theme; as well as promo material, promotional clips, and print material that focused on Devesh in a more simple and streamlined manner than he was used to.

She had Pete make a trip to California with his wife, Kay, so he and his son, Erik, along with Jay, could shoot a video at Devesh's favorite place—the ocean. The video was simple, majestic, and put the focus squarely on where it needed to be—Devesh, his voice, and the words. No half-naked women. No flash or bling. Just the basic elements—earth, wind, fire, water—and Devesh.

One song—seven versions. One simple video.

All released at the same time. Twitter. Facebook. iTunes. Amazon.

The song hit number one on the American music charts within that first week and hit a heavy radio rotation right after—driven by listeners, and not from any additional efforts of Reign or anyone on Devesh's team.

The album uploaded two weeks later, and the sales were off the meter.

Devesh had placed his ultimate trust in his wife. She had spun his bricks into pure gold. Platinum. Multi-platinum. His family was every bit of shocked, amazed and proud.

The money flowed into his bank accounts and rolled into ones that belonged to the people who helped with his new brand imaging and the music. So no need to work that 9-to-5 any longer. All of a sudden, an industry that hadn't taken an interest in Devesh Maharaj before was ringing his phone.

Devesh became well-versed in another set of words. "You'll need to talk to my manager."

Then passed the phone to his wife.

Reign and Devesh, reeling from his sudden onslaught of success, also became aware of a completely new issue that a famous rapper once pointed out—Mo' money, mo' problems.

chapter 14

"Why does she keep pressuring us to watch that old movie?" Anaya asked, taking the old recording of *Prem Granth* from Reign and pressing it back into Aunt Kavya's hands. "No one watches it anymore," she said in Hindi since her aunt did not speak much English.

"It's so outdated. Let me get her something new, something with subtitles," Devesh offered, also in Hindi, but translated for Reign, who seemed confused by the exchange.

Aunt Kavya shook her head, thrusting the package back at Reign, then patting her on the shoulder before ambling away toward her room in the first level sleeping quarters.

"Do you have something we can play this on?" Reign asked Devesh, with a lingering gaze on the disappearing view of the older woman draped in a fuchsia and silver sari.

"No, but I'll check online and see if there's something on eBay."

"Or maybe a pawn shop?" Reign suggested, taking the old VHS tape out of its beat-up box. "There has to be one of those around here somewhere."

"What's that?"

"You really don't know?" Reign said, tilting her head at him. "And I thought you grew up in New York." She tapped a finger on the cassette. "There's a message in here for us. She's been pushing for us to watch this since the first day I came."

"Pawn shop?" Devesh asked, frowning as he took a glimpse of the cover.

"It's our best shot."

"I'm on it." He kissed her lips and was out the door.

❀ ❀ ❀

Anaya extended an invitation to Reign to join her in the kitchen to experiment with new recipes. Pranav followed both of them through the house and took a seat in the solarium, almost as if he didn't trust his wife to be alone with her sister-in-law. That action put Reign on notice.

"May I ask you a question?" Anaya said, leaning on the center island.

Pranav perked up, snatched from the newspaper he was pretending to read. His warning look focused in on Anaya who bristled under his scrutiny. At least he didn't say anything.

"I guess," Reign hedged, her green-eyed gaze taking in Pranav's body language and that entire silent exchange.

"What made you so interested in East Indian Culture? I mean, you do have a culture of your own, but …"

Reign blinked for a moment, possibly trying to gauge Anaya's reason for asking. "I took a trip up north to Devon Street in Chicago. That's the place where a great deal of the East Indian population resides. A lot of restaurants there; electronics, fabric stores, places like that." She inhaled and let out a long, slow breath before she smiled. "I went into this one place, Gandhi Indian Restaurant, and for the first time, I tried something different. The owner and his wife, treated me like royalty. They had never seen me before, but I noticed that the way they interacted with me was a little different than other patrons. They encouraged me to try so many things—put tastings on small plates in front of me and took the time to explain what they were and how they were made. This was my first introduction to East Indian culture and cuisine, and they made it so pleasurable that I came back week after week. Later, I branched out to Tiffin, another restaurant on Devon, and India House, yet another one in the downtown area and the exact same thing happened." She peered up from the glass she held and put her focus on Anaya. "Being treated well can be addictive. I enjoyed the food, the people, the music, and soon went into wearing the garments. I thought all East Indians were like the wonderful ones I met—and like Devesh who proved to be as warm and welcoming as they were." She scoffed at that sentiment and added, "And then I came here and learned something entirely different."

Reign kept her focus on Anaya for a moment before going to the fridge to select a few items to prepare for the meal.

"I'm going to set up the theatre," Pranav said with a parting look to Anaya.

The moment Pranav cleared the threshold, Anaya whispered. "Why my brother?"

Reign stiffened and glared at her, as though she expected that there was some ulterior motive behind Anaya's initial request.

"I'm not saying this to insult you," Anaya confessed over the rim of her coffee cup. "I'm just trying to understand."

Reign shelved the cookbook that Mumma had given her and turned to face Anaya. "I didn't want to love him. But from the very beginning, he did everything a kind, compassionate, and loving man would do. He showed up in my life every day, through voicemails, texts, private messages, and emails. Sometimes three times a day or more. He would ask my advice on anything and everything. I looked forward to talking to him, seeing him at the conventions. He made sure I knew I was important to him, that he appreciated me and valued our friendship. I didn't see it as anything more than that—friendship."

Anaya placed the seasonings on the center island in the kitchen, processing Reign's explanation.

"We are so different," Reign confessed. "He believes the best of everyone. I see the worst." She abandoned the meal prep, went back to the fridge and poured herself a glass of juice. "He's trying to get me to have some balance when it comes to that. I'm trying to get him to understand that telling people *no* when something is not in his best interest is a good thing. He's so free with his *yes* that he doesn't realize that the only thing people remember is when he doesn't give them what they want. He gets so hurt by their reactions."

Anaya absorbed that and realized Reign really did have a handle on how things were with Devesh. "I've tried to get him to see that for so long. It's one of the reasons I stopped helping him with his career. I was frustrated by the fact that he trusts everyone." She poured herself another cup of masala tea. "People he helped get started in the industry stepped on him on the way up and forgot all about what he did for them."

"Loyalty is important to him," Reign said, over the rim of her glass. "But he keeps attracting those who aren't loyal in any way."

Anaya's penciled eyebrows drew in. "You really love him."

Reign looked away. When she focused on Anaya again, she said, "I love him, but I'm not *in love* with him," she replied, placing her glass on the center island. "Amy was in love with him."

"Don't be fooled," Anaya corrected. "She was in love with what she believed he could do for her, nothing more."

Reign locked a gaze on Anaya who moved until she was next to Reign.

"Don't break his heart," she pleaded in a voice just above a whisper.

Reign scoffed and said, "I hate to break it to you but the fact that I'm only giving him eight years of my life means that there's a great possibility that I will do just that."

"Why only eight years?"

"It'll give the children a good foundation," she said, then leveled a stony look at Anaya that sent chills up her spine. "And also by that time, he'll find an East Indian woman that will be more to your family's liking."

Reign turned away, giving Anaya her back to ponder.

Anaya looked up in time to see Pranav glaring at her and knew a full-blown discussion was on tap the moment she got home.

Pranav crooked his finger, and Anaya's heart slipped to her toes. Evidently, he wasn't in the mood to wait until later. Bummer.

He hooked his arm under hers and quickly escorted her out to the solarium and further onto the patio. The late evening sun had splayed the last of its rays across the California sky. None of its beauty swept away the chill coming from Pranav. "Anaya I'm seeing the worst side of you since Reign has come here. It's like I don't even know who you are."

Anaya scanned the padded lounger where Reign had stretched out that day when she returned from Chicago. "Did you see the way he kissed her? That day by the pool?"

"Yes," Pranav said, and his lips lifted in a wide smile that irritated her.

"It was ... I don't know how to describe it," she said eyeing him closely and giving a weary shake of her head.

"It was sensual," Pranav explained. "That man has a hunger only that woman can feed. You all keep trying to come between that, and you will lose him, point-blank-period. I've been friends with him since you all came to America. And I've never seen him this way with *any* of the women he's been with. And trust me, you all don't know the half of the stuff he's been into. You've seen one side of your brother. I saw the rest." Pranav scratched his forehead. "To be honest, back then, I wouldn't have wanted him to marry my sister the same way he didn't want me to marry you. We knew too much, did too much."

"That was a blatant display of sex," Anaya reminded, unable to keep the disdain from her voice.

"That wasn't sex," he countered, moving until he was standing directly in front of her. "That was foreplay. Devesh is trying to seduce his wife."

"But right before our very eyes?"

Pranav placed his hands on her arms, forcing her to look directly at him. "She's fighting him. For whatever reason, probably because of her own issues and because you all are making her keep him at arm's length."

He grinned. For some reason, it didn't sit right with Anaya. "But did you see her open to him? Well, started to, before she caught herself and tried to scale it back. Now he's close to having her."

Anaya felt her face flush with anger. "You sound like you want her."

"You want to know the truth?" Pranav leaned in as though ready to share a secret. "Just watching them gave me a woody."

Anaya blanched, tossed her curls over her shoulders. "Family is more important to him than someone like her. She doesn't deserve him."

"What? Anaya? Really?" Pranav whispered, peering at her as if he didn't recognize the woman standing before him. "Let some people tell the story, I don't deserve you. I don't look anywhere as handsome as Devesh. To be honest, I'm a little round in the belly and kinda on the average side. So I should not have wanted a woman as beautiful as you because of that?" He paused, waiting for a dispute to kick in. "I wanted you for all the other qualities you had. I knew you before the pageants. I knew you when we snuck off to those underground clubs in New York when Hip Hop was just becoming a thing. I married a woman who was my friend, who knew how to enjoy life. That is what is beautiful to me about you."

She took a minute to let that sink in. "Please don't think less of me because of how I feel," she implored him.

"I don't think less of you for that," he admitted, stroking a hand through her hair. "But you and the family have to stop busting his chops. He's given you all thirty-one years of his life. He deserves the chance to live the rest of his years doing what's best for himself."

Anaya felt a tear slide down her cheek, and the guilt racked her so bad she wanted to run away and not see the recrimination in her husband's eyes. He was right. She was denying her brother the same happiness that she had found with his best friend.

Pranav tilted her head so their gazes met. "That man has not been with a woman in five years."

She stepped back, unable to believe a word. "He's had Amy."

"Then either you're not as close to your brother as you think, or you're just not that observant," he challenged and his voice was pure steel. "Their relationship has been purely platonic ever since he came back from Atlanta. He's just been too kind to put her out to pasture. Why do you think Amy's been more clingy, more possessive these last five years? She lost him the minute Reign came back in the picture."

Anaya waved him off. "My brother is much too sexual to go without."

"Why the heck do you think he spends so much time in Puja?" Pranav said, tweaking her nose. "He turned to God rather than using Amy to slake his lust."

Pranav waited a moment to let her absorb those words and said, "God answered his prayer by giving him the two things he desired most—Reign and children. The fact that they came as one package means Devesh made it to the bonus round." Pranav tightened his hold around her. "Devesh recognizes that his devotion to God paid off with a reward you all could never give him." He kissed the tip of her nose. "Think on that."

Then he left Anaya out on the patio, went into the house and didn't give her a backward glance.

❀ ❀ ❀

Two hours later, the entire family switched off the Cricket game airing from India. They had settled into the theater to watch *Prem Granth*. Since there were no subtitles, Devesh translated portions of it for Reign.

He put his head near hers and whispered, "That's a rich young man named Somen, and the woman is Kariji."

"She's breathtaking," Reign replied in a breathy whisper.

"Like you, my love." He picked up her hand and kissed it. "The problem," he explained is that she's poor and from a lower caste."

Reign put her focus on the movie, gathering some ideas of what was happening strictly from the acting—and over acting—of the people on the screen. The two had clearly fallen in love, but Somen's father, a wealthy politician, was against it.

The undertones of the movie had a great deal to do with her relationship with Devesh.

Somen makes plans to defy his politician father to be with her. By the time Somen leaves home and begins the search for Kariji, she had been raped by a wealthy stranger on the way home from the festival where Somen first met her. Though it was no fault of her own, the act and the results forced her to become cast away from her family without a dime to her name and a baby that was conceived during that horrific act. Kariji was too poor to feed her child. She had to bury it and grieve on her own.

When Kariji's baby died, the screen became blurry as Reign's eyes filled with tears.

Somen appeared on screen again. Devesh whispered, "A year has passed and he has been unable to get Kariji off of his mind."

Somen found her a year later working on his uncle's farm, and he loves her still. Kariji, brokenhearted by life and all the things that happened to her, turns him away even though she loves him too. All of these tragic experiences made her undesirable in society's eyes. Finally, because Somen wouldn't give up, she confesses her darkest secrets.

Reign knew exactly how it felt to have love climbing out the back door of your heart because fear was slipping through the front door, taking it off the hinges.

"Somen wants to marry her and he sets out to find the man who violated her," Devesh explained. "The rich man who stole her innocence was also the same man who had also raped Kariji's aunt. Somen hunts the man down and burns him alive while Kariji watches."

"Then the two lovebirds get married and live happily ever after," Anaya said in a cheery voice. "The end."

"What a tragic movie," Reign said, shaking off the imagery.

"No more than Romeo and Juliet," Anaya defended, taking in another handful of buttered popcorn.

Reign was still sorting through the scenario that the movie provided, filtering through scene after scene, also trying to ascertain what Aunt Kavya wanted her to know; wanted Devesh to know.

"*Jab pyaar hona chahiye, tab ho jayega. Chahe kuch bhi ho jaye,*" Aunt Kavya said in Hindi, grasping Devesh's hand and then Reign's before placing their hands on top of each other.

"When love is supposed to happen, it will, no matter what," Mumma said with a pointed look at Reign, translating Aunt Kavya's words.

"*Jab bhi do log ek saath hone chahiye, chahe woh alag hi kyun na ho, unka dharam ya samaj kuch bhi ho, aur chahe unke past main kuch bhi hua ho, pyaar raasta nikaal hi lega.*"

"Whenever people are supposed to be together," Anaya explained. "No matter that they are different, no matter their background, no matter what happened in their past—"

"Love will find a way," Devesh finished and his voice was filled with such wonder and hope that it brought a tear to Mumma's eye.

Reign thought over those words and returned Aunt Kavya's smile.

chapter 15

Devesh returned from New York after appearing on The Tonight Show with Jimmy Fallon and the family was set to hold a little celebration. The Maharaj family found any old reason to celebrate. Birthday. Celebration. Break a toe. Celebration.

"Well, at least the children don't look anything like her," Tiya said, causing Anaya to bristle. The women were in the kitchen as dinner preparations were underway and the uncles were settled around the breakfast nook watching a game of cricket on the television mounted on the far wall.

The children and all of the cousins were in the corner on the floor playing a game of Sorry—something the twins had taught them. But at the sound of Tiya's voice, Leena's head snapped in her direction. Green eyes were flashing with something that resembled anger. Kamran glanced at his sister, then frowned as he followed her gaze to Tiya, who gave them both an evil grin.

"We should be grateful for that," Aunt Prisha said over the rim of her owl-rimmed glasses as Bhavin's wavy-haired wife, Sana nodded.

"My God, imagine having to explain that nose," Hiran said, causing a few family members to laugh. All except Mumma, Papa, Anaya and Aunt Kavya who, unknown to everyone else, had wandered in from the solarium on the tail end of the conversation.

"Large enough to smell the cows taking a crap in Jaipur," Uncle Mitul said and almost choked on the words. "All the way from here."

Mumma and Anaya shared an uncomfortable glance as realization dawned in Papa's eyes.

Papa glared at his brother-in-law, but Mitul pretended to ignore him, causing him to say, "Mitul, this is my house. You will not disrespect my daughter-in-law this way."

The trickle of laughter and conversation came to an abrupt halt. A tenseness settled over the kitchen.

Anaya felt a stirring of anxiety in her mind. She looked toward the solarium's entryway only to find Reign standing there with a thunderous expression.

She had heard every word.

A slow smile crept across Tiya's lips, a sure sign that she had known Reign was nearby when she let that vitriol come from her mouth.

"Leena and Kamran," Reign said, causing their attention to snap to their mother. "Come this way."

They quickly left their cousins, who loudly protested their removal, and did as she bid them.

"Reign."

She cast her eyes on Anaya, the expression on Reign's face a warning to say the least.

"Mama?" Leena said, and there was a nervousness in her tone.

"Get your things, baby," Reign said in a calm tone that did not match her expression. "Your brother's too."

"Yes, ma'am."

Reign waited until the twins cleared the room before she put her focus on Tiya, then Uncle Mitul. "You said all those ugly things within full hearing range of my children."

No one disputed it.

"If I were a different type of woman, my husband would need bail money right about now." She circled the center floor island until she was a few feet from Tiya. "You always want to throw the words *hood* and *ghetto* around when it comes to me." She tilted her head as though studying a science specimen. "Honey, you have no idea." She flickered a brief look at the knife that was on the counter halfway between them. "You can come for me all you want, but you start messing with my children, and I will cut you too short to shit."

Nearly everyone in the room gasped.

Reign's smile was alarming. "You can be big and bold because your people are around. But when I come for you, they won't be able to help you."

Mumma brushed her way past Aunt Prisha and Neerav. "Reign, please do not go. Do not take Tiya's words to heart. Or Mitul's. We do not all feel the way they do."

"Really?" Reign tilted her head, scanning Mumma's flushed face before flickering a pointed look at each of the people staring back at her. "Yet none of you spoke up to say anything different. They laughed. I heard it. So enough of them do feel that way. And the truth of the matter is, I don't have the bandwidth to figure out which ones of you are friends and which ones are foes."

Leena and Kamran had their backpacks, and Leena held up her mother's purse that must have been retrieved from Devesh's bedroom.

"Thank you, baby." She stood and faced the people in the room. "I never go where I'm not invited. And I never stay where I'm not wanted." Over her shoulder, she said, "Tell my husband he'll find us at the condo. Permanently."

With that being said, Reign and the twins exited stage left.

"You foolish woman," Mumma roared at Tiya.

"I only said what everyone's thinking," she countered with no remorse whatsoever. "It wasn't an issue until she said something." She released a dismissive wave. "You and Anaya are trying to be her friend and all, but let her leave. We don't want her or her little half-breed bastards to be here. Even the White girl he was playing around with was a better choice, once she learned to put some clothes on."

Well, there had been some truth in that. Amy had shown up to their house that first time with her entire cleavage spilling out, shorts cut so far up her tail everyone could see the beginnings of places they shouldn't. Even their grandmother—God rest her soul—took one look, pulled her headscarf over her head and tipped out of the room. And it happened several more times before Amy finally got the message that showing so much of her body was not appropriate around the Maharaj family. Reign, at least, did not have such issues. The color of her skin and the fact that she was older than him, was the crux of the issue. On what planet did a woman her age pair up with a man Devesh's age, and it becomes a love match?

"This woman is his wife," Mumma said, first looking at everyone and giving them an eye-to-eye before settling her gaze on Tiya. "You might not like it but she is his family now."

"His family, not mine," Tiya said, tucking the strands of her long hair behind her ear.

"In a minute, you're going to realize they are one and the same," Anaya warned, hoping that her hard-hearted sister would get the message. "She manages his bank accounts and investments now. Aren't you and your husband always hitting Devesh up for money these days? Seems like you've been in his pocket ever since his singing career took off." She took a bite of an apple. "I'd be careful if I were you."

"He'd never deny us," Tiya said with a sweeping look across the people listening in. "Unlike the hood queen, *we* are actually family."

"Let's hope you never have to find out."

chapter 16

Devesh was incensed when he arrived at Maharaj house and Aunt Kavya filled him in on what transpired while he was away. Minutes after he stepped over the threshold, his mother, aunts, and twin came into his suite to pack up his things, and those belonging to his wife and twins. Pranav, Bhavin, and his cousins piled everything into their cars and drove the fifteen minutes to his building on Milano Drive in Newport Beach. The furniture in the master suite would remain intact, as Reign had already picked out what she wanted for the penthouse. Everything was set to be delivered a few days after the contractors put the final touches on the condos which had been combined and reconfigured to make a penthouse comprised of four bedrooms, four bathrooms, a massive kitchen, living room, dining room, spa center, office, and entertainment parlor with bar, and a separate elevator that bypassed the other eight floors and let out directly into their foyer.

Now that there wasn't a cushion of people and activity constantly floating around them, Devesh could clearly see the signs that Reign missed her older son dearly—and so did the twins who made it their business to video chat with him at least twice a day.

Loyalty was definitely something to be admired, and Devesh had been pleasantly surprised that Jay didn't end all contact because his mother's heart was broken. He surprised her by bringing Jay out for a visit in hopes that they could deepen the bond they had.

Devesh and Jay were lounging outside in the backyard with a kidney-shaped pool that was still being serviced, a game area for volleyball and a few other outside pursuits. A gazebo shielded them from the blazing sun and the insects trying to extract a pint of their blood. Finally, the conversation circled in on the heart of things.

"I dated an older woman once," Jay admitted, taking a swig from a shot of Fireball, grimacing as the cinnamon whiskey burned its way down his throat. "And I broke it off when I realized that it was not going to work for a number of reasons." Jay used a napkin to wipe the sweat from his brown. "Sharon actually had the nerve to call my mother to talk about it, not realizing that my mother does not interfere with my relationships. But she made an exception that one time."

Jay's focus shifted from Devesh to the garden materials piled up against the wooden fencing, awaiting the landscaping service that was set to come within the next few days.

"The call was on speaker, and I heard when Mom said to Sharon, 'Sweetheart, you have three children, a house, a good-paying job and a complete life. He's a full-time college student. You need a little more man than he can be for you right now. When he gets out of school and has a career—a *career*, not a job—and some life experiences of his own, *then* he can afford to be more than just an ear and emotional support to you. He can actually back up that romance with some finance.'"

Devesh knew firsthand how much of a realist Reign could be, so that advice was solid.

"I'm single right now," Jay explained, putting his focus on the cedar wood ceiling of the gazebo. "I'm trying to get my thing together before I bring a woman into my life again. When I do, I'm coming for my high school sweetheart. We were both too immature back then to appreciate what being together was all about." Jay whipped out his cell and showed pictures of the woman he loved. She was a honey-skinned beauty with hazel eyes and a curvy figure. "But I've done some growing and so has she. So I'm hoping that in a few months from now, since my business has taken off, I can step to her as a grown man and handle that relationship business the right way this time."

Devesh put his fist out for a pound and Jay obliged by tapping his fist to Devesh's.

"I'd like for you to come to my family's house for dinner while you're here," Devesh suggested.

"I'm going to pass," Jay said, stretching his long limbs. "I hear how some of them have been treating my Mama and the twins. Trust me, you don't want me to be around when they come at her sideways. She has to hold her tongue to keep the peace." Jay regarded Devesh intensely. "I don't have to. They come for my Mama and I'm going to set them straight. *Real* straight. Y'all don't want none of this."

"Fair enough," Devesh replied, studying Jay's face. "So when are you going to finalize that move to California?"

"You don't give up, do you," Jay replied, chuckling. "I've thought about leaving Chicago ever since I lived in Nashville and South Carolina when I was in school, but I didn't have the funds to relocate. But I do miss mom and the munchkins, though." Then he grinned. "Oh, and you too."

"Of course," Devesh said, returning his smile. "If you think about it, there's something to be gained by having you move here. Every time there's a shooting in Chicago she sends you a text."

Jay settled the empty shot glass on the patio table. "She doesn't ask me about anything like that."

"No, but she's actually checking on you, making sure you're still alive. I'm the one watching her freak out. I'd like to make sure you're safe—here in California."

Jay thought that over for a moment. "You want to know what's interesting?"

Devesh quirked a curious brow.

"Before I went to Fisk, we were living in Princeton Park, and the gunshots were nonstop at night. We would sleep on the floor to avoid getting hit." Jay sighed and took a sip, squinting up into the sunlight. "I found us a spot in South Shore, a more upscale area. And you know what happened?"

Devesh shook his head.

"I got robbed at gunpoint twice, in an area that supposedly had less crime than the place we'd left." Jay put his focus to Devesh. "Safety isn't promised anywhere. I learned that the hard way. At least both times I walked away with my life."

Devesh let that bit of wisdom settle for a moment. "You have a point," he said, crossing one jeans-clad leg over the other. "But I'm thinking of easing your mother's mind. One condo hasn't been leased yet. As I said, it's yours if you want it. Rent-free for an entire year so you can get settled. She needs you, and I know the children miss you as well."

"I wouldn't be hearing or seeing you and mom getting your freak on, would I?" Jay asked, his expression sour.

Devesh laughed. Jay actually had no worries on that score, because Reign *still* hadn't made a move to get physical, much to Devesh's chagrin. But he wouldn't share that with her son. Let him believe they were a complete couple. "That won't be a problem. It's on the first floor. There are children in the house."

"Hey, children have ears."

Devesh roared with laughter. "You know, I have a whole slew of people waiting to get to you. They've been impressed by the work you've done for me."

"Word?"

Devesh slid down in his chair, proud of all the recent accomplishments that stemmed from Reign's belief in both of them. "So I guess I can't keep my secret weapon all to myself."

"That's what's up," Jay said with a brisk nod. "You do know that you were supposed to ask me first before asking her to marry you?"

"I did, five years ago," Devesh protested.

"That permission expired after a year."

"Seriously? That's what you're rolling with right now?"

Jay laughed and polished the last of his shot of the cinnamon whiskey, peering at a man who was more friend than anything. "Did you just say—"

"I guess you're growing on me."

Devesh grinned. "Ditto."

"Does the age thing bother you?"

"Well, Elise is older than me," Jay hedged with a grin.

"By a year," Devesh shot back. "Seriously?"

And to answer your question. Yeah, a little," Jay confessed. "Can't very well call you dad if we're going to be stroking thirty-two at the same time." He shrugged, and Devesh grinned. "As long as she's happy and you're taking care of her." Jay stood, stretched out the kinks in his neck before reclaiming his seat again. "But I'm going to warn you of two things. First, my mother has no filter."

"Oh, really? Do tell," Devesh teased, causing Jay to give a megawatt smile.

"Black women have to be strong because they have no choice. They catch it from all sides. Mom's a little tired of that, so her filter's off."

"And the second thing?" Devesh asked.

"Her temper has hit a point that I've had to keep track of her menstrual cycles. Word to the wise?"

Devesh nodded and poured them both another shot.

"You'd better too," he warned. "Things that she'll let fly on other days will damn near get your head taken off during that time." He waggled a finger at Devesh. "Trust me; you want to have peace, you'd better be aware of when those hormones are about to spike, or you'll be taking stuff personally for a while." Jay tilted his head at Devesh. "Ask me how I know."

Devesh held up his glass and said, "Good looking out."

chapter 17

Devesh tipped into the spa room in the condo, one of the fully finished areas of the place. He put a finger to his lips to keep the spa team quiet as he slid onto the massage bench beside Reign's. She was so into the hot stone massage the buxom red-haired woman was giving her that she wasn't aware that he had come home early from a fashion photo shoot, simply to surprise her.

Minutes later, Reign moaned, then her head turned to the left. She opened her eyes and squarely focused on … Devesh.

She inhaled sharply, scrambled off the massage bench and almost slipped onto the marble tiles. She yanked the sheet from the bench and struggled to wrap it around her body.

"You! You can't be in here."

"Why not?"

"Because I'm naked," she cried, pulling the sheet up to her neck.

"So am I, under this towel," he said, amused at her modesty. "And you're my wife. I've seen it all before."

Reign shook her head vehemently. "Not ... not like this."

Devesh stared at her for a moment and all humor left. He didn't take his eyes off Reign as he sat up and said to the spa team, "Can we have the room for a moment?"

The three women soundlessly left the area sharing curious glances between them. He waited until the door closed before he said, "Honey, we need to talk about this."

"It was dark that night," she said. "You didn't see me in the raw and—"

"I am your husband."

"Yes, for the next eight years," she stated simply.

Devesh tamped down on his anger.

"Do you realize how much it pains me when you remind me that this marriage is only temporary?" Devesh whispered, moving toward her. "You never consider that I might want to be with you far longer than that."

Reign found a pointed interest in her bright pink pedicured toes. She inched back, keeping some distance between them.

He halted for a moment.

"Why would you?" she asked. "You only married me because of the children."

"I married you because I love you," he shot back.

"That's not what you said," she countered. "It was an ultimatum, a thinly veiled one, but one all the same."

Devesh closed his eyes, inhaled and let it out slowly. "I never meant it that way. Never meant for you to feel forced to marry me. If I had known—"

"If you had known what?" she challenged, her green eyes flashing fire. "That I married you because I feared losing my children? What difference would that have made?"

She only married him because she felt cornered? There wasn't some small part of her that married him because she loved him, too?

Reign was so filled with emotion that her trembling hands let the sheet slip down. She quickly yanked it back in place, scowling at him.

"I'll speak with an attorney tomorrow," Devesh said, snatching up the clothes he'd draped over the chaise on the way in. "You will have your freedom as soon as the courts allow."

Devesh wrapped the towel tighter around his naked body, tucked his clothes under his arm, and stormed from the room.

⚜ ⚜ ⚜

The absence of him was so profound it felt as though everything was about to collapse and take Reign along for the ride.

You will have your freedom as soon as the courts allow.

Those words had knocked the wind out of her.

Devesh said he loved her. He *loved* her. That's why he married her. Why was it so hard to believe?

She pulled on the robe hanging on the back of the closet door and went to the living room, aiming to ask the team to come back another time.

"What's wrong?" Shannan, the tallest of the team asked, her face a mask of concern.

"I think I messed up," Reign confessed, dropping down on the nearest chair.

Royce, the more petite woman on the team, uncrossed her legs and leaned forward. "You were that way with us at first," she said, and the others nodded. "You didn't want us to see you *in the raw*. Even though we've got the same thing you've got."

"Maybe a little less of it," Reign admitted, causing the others to laugh.

"But over time, you got used to it," the loc-wearing nail technician said. "Go to him. There aren't too many men who accept a woman for who she is—*all* of who she is. And it's so obvious that he loves you. Let him."

"How?" She looked toward the door expecting to see him walk in at any moment and say goodbye for good.

"First by showing him you trust him."

"We are the second step," Royce said, shooing Reign in the direction of threshold and toward the bedroom. "By letting him have this spa time with you will show a lot."

"You go in there and handle that first one," the manicurist said. "We'll be waiting."

Reign trudged past the twins' room, all of the contractor's tools stretched out against the wall, then toward the master bedroom. Devesh took his focus from the overnight bag he had on the bed. He paused, waiting for her to speak.

"I apologize for hurting you," she said, perching on the edge of the bed. "I apologize for not trusting you. For not believing you."

Devesh released the shirt he held and rounded the bed until he was in front of her. "Honey, I already know what your body looks like. You're the only one who has issues with it—well, you and the idiot who said such ugly, untrue things. You let *his* issues become *your* issues. And that's not fair to you or to me. He still has a hold on you, and I can't fight that. Unless you let me."

She looked at the carpeting, twisting her hands and barely speaking above a whisper when she said, "You're a handsome man. He was too. I learned that pretty boys choose the plain girls because it makes them look better. And the girls are supposed to be so grateful that the cute, popular guy is with them that they'll do anything for them."

Devesh threw his hands up in surrender. "Seriously? How messed up is it in your world?"

"Don't make like it's just Americans who do that," she countered. "Even with your culture's arranged marriages, don't think that the men aren't hoping to roll the dice and at least get someone who isn't damn unpleasant to look at."

He placed his hands on her arms and guided her from the bed and into his arms. "Let me in, honey. Let me in. Let me love you in my way." Devesh lowered his voice as he said, "You know what love is. I see it when you look at Jay. I see it when you look at Kamran and Leena. I see it when you look at me, but I also see the pain in your eyes, honey. As if a veil of fear covers it. That makes me sad."

Devesh placed his forehead on hers, then pressed a kiss to her skin.

"That man stole something from you. He took your ability to trust someone with your heart. Because of what he did, true love that actually belongs to you is within your reach, and you're turning it away at every chance." Devesh held her close. "I miss my friend. I don't know who this woman is who fights me on everything—as if I'm the enemy. I miss my friend, Reign. You were that before you were anything else. Please let my friend out of here"—he touched a finger to her temple—"So my wife can love me the way I know she wants to love."

Devesh stepped away, extended his hand to her. "Will you try to take a step toward accepting my love instead of running from it?"

She lowered her eyes to his hand. "I'll try."

"That's all I ask," he said, tucking the edges of her robe securely so they'd stay in place. "I'm not trying to check up under the hood. I'm just trying to play with the toys on the dashboard."

Reign trembled as he ran his hand along the smooth skin of her thighs.

"You know what?"

She shook her head.

"I can't wait for the day you get to that 'I don't give a damn' place in your life," he confessed. "Then you'll walk around the house butt naked in high heels, making a few unladylike noises."

"I would not do that," she said, eyes widening with shock as he grinned.

"What I'm saying is that I'm the one person you should be able to keep it real with."

He moved so only a few inches were between them. "I missed your voice, how soothing and sexy it sounded. How husky and sensual it became when I said something a little wicked, and you responded." Devesh threaded his hands in her hair. "I missed you, honey, and I don't care how God brought you back into my life, I am grateful for every day I get to be with you."

"Don't make me cry. I'm not wearing the good mascara today." She closed her eyes to hold back the tears, then felt him place soft kisses along the trail left by the one teardrop that escaped. She nodded toward the living room. "They're still out there waiting for us to finish."

"You're afraid?" he asked.

She nodded and shrugged.

"Let's take it a little at a time, alright? There was a time I didn't make a move without talking with you first, weighing my options, getting your advice," he said, stroking a soothing hand across her cheek. "I'm asking for that same trust. Talk to me about what you feel. We're not enemies. We are a team. A power packed house."

"You mean a *powerhouse*?"

"You know what I'm trying to say," he countered.

She smiled a little.

"We know how to get things done on a business level," he continued. "We're slipping on a personal level, but that doesn't have to be the case. I love it that people are insecure about us, maybe a little jealous. Let that be their problem, not ours. Alright?"

The look she gave him was so filled with longing for him; the need to believe that what he was offering was real. He wanted to lay her on the bed and have his way with her; show her how much he wanted only her.

"Alright," she whispered.

"I'll have them teach me how to give you a massage, and then it won't feel so strange for me to have my hands on your body—again."

Reign looked up at him, trying to gauge his sincerity level.

"It's going to be alright, honey. Trust me."

She followed him from the bedroom, and the moment they stepped into the living room where the team awaited, the three women broke into wide smiles and applause.

chapter 18

The evening of July 4th, Devesh sailed through the front door of the Maharaj place with a bottle of Stella Rosa, Reign's favorite Moscato d'asti. Reign saw it for what it was—a peace offering. She had become miffed with him because of an earlier conversation at the condo. She was seeking out a dojo—a karate school—for the children to continue their martial arts training.

"Sweet Jesus," he had said, dragging a hand down his face. "Can they just be little children for a while longer?"

"It's good for them. They love it. They should know how to protect themselves."

"*We* will protect them, honey," he had countered, leaning on the granite counter. "Let's give them some time to acclimate to things here. Then we'll revisit this karate thing."

She fumed.

"I'm not taking you to task for your parenting skills," he said. "I mean, Jay made it out alive."

Her eyes widened to the size of platters, and he could swear she was ready to go upside his head.

"Alright," he said, holding up his hands in surrender. "Bad joke. His words not mine, though."

Now as he wound his way through the parlor, living room, family room, and into the den, a blur of reddish-blond hair sailed through the air and landed in his arms.

"I've missed you so much," Amy said, pinning him with an embrace so tight it was almost hard to breathe.

Tiya rounded the corner and paused at the threshold, quickly beckoning for the family to come and witness what she thought would be a happy reunion—one that would hurt her brother's wife.

Reign hung back, watching while Kamran placed his hands in hers, frowning at the scene before them.

Leena evaded Reign's reach, brushed past everyone and ran straight to her father.

Devesh extracted himself from Amy's spider-like grasp and took several steps back. "I'm going to need you to keep your hands to yourself," he said firmly. "Do not insult my wife by doing this. You are Tiya's guest here, not mine. You can't do what you just did again. I will not stand for it."

"But I understand that you all have an *open marriage*, so that means …"

Leena yanked on his pants leg, demanding to be picked up. Devesh complied. Leena put a steady look on Amy that seemed to unsettle his ex.

"No, that was something that *she* wanted. I never did. And now it is totally off the table. We have a monogamous relationship." His voice was loud enough for everyone to hear. "I know that she is the only woman for me. I will not be seeking someone outside of my marriage for *any* reason." He settled Leena more comfortably in his arms. "So if you came over here hoping to become the side-piece, outside woman or whatever they're calling it these days, that's never going to happen."

Leena laid her head on his chest, studying Amy as though she was an experiment gone wrong. "Papa, she has a major malfunction?"

Devesh looked down at his little girl, realizing she had picked up the term from her big brother, and said, "Something like that. More like a misunderstanding."

"Oh, okay," she said and put her focus back on Amy so the blonde would get that memo.

"If you disrespect my wife like that again," Devesh warned in the hardest tone he could manage, "I will personally escort you from this house." He slid over so he had Tiya in his line of sight. "And I won't care who invited you."

Reign smiled inwardly. Amy was sad. Pathetic really. Devesh hadn't shown the least bit of interest, yet she hung on, hoping he'd throw her a bone. But Reign knew his *bone* belonged only to her, and he would keep it under wraps until the day she was ready to be intimate with him.

🪷 🪷 🪷

"Well that was interesting," Reign said, plopping down on the sofa next to him in their Maharaj suite.

"Tiya's only trying to stir up trouble," Devesh said, taking his eyes from the screenplay in his hands and putting them squarely on Reign. "If we ignore her, she'll cut it out."

Reign wasn't so sure. The woman was cruisin' for a bruisin' and Reign was in the market to give her exactly what she wanted.

"Speaking of outside influences," she began, then she paused, weighing her thoughts. "I just wanted you to know that I need to file a restraining order against Shawn Newsome."

"Why?" Devesh's whole body tensed. "Has he—"

"No, he hasn't come near me, but he's getting bolder," she admitted. "I blocked him on all my social media, from my phone and email, but he keeps trying to contact me through different numbers and different email addresses."

Devesh's gaze narrowed to slits. "What does he want?

"Me. He wants me to leave you and be with him," she answered, taking the script from his hands and placing it on the coffee table. "He's fixated on us becoming a couple again. He's really bought into the whole pro-Black thing, when it was never supposed to be anti-anything or mean that Black women couldn't date men who weren't Black."

"Do you want me to speak with him?"

"That'll just make it worse," she said. "Seems like we both attracted possessive people."

"How?"

"Amy's still hanging around giving you those puppy dog looks."

Devesh shook his head. "I straightened that out."

"Well, she doesn't seem like the type who likes to lose."

And Devesh had to call things as he saw it. Amy wasn't the only one who didn't like to be on the losing end.

Dr. Shawn Newsome was a prime example.

❦ ❦ ❦

"Devesh, may I make a suggestion without you getting ticked off?" Reign asked later when they were in their condo's master bedroom with the twins sound asleep in their own rooms.

He looked up from the schedule that Jay sent him earlier and raised an eyebrow. "Well, when you ask it like that …"

"Never mind."

His hand snaked out to latch onto her arm, holding her in place. "No, you don't get off that easy. Talk to me, honey."

She settled back onto the Palladian steel and wood bed. "I'd like to sign you up for salsa and stepping lessons."

"Dance?"

"Yes."

"Why?

Her focus shifted to the Junge floral artwork that she brought with her from Chicago. "You might want to think about putting together a music tour to promote yourself as a recording artist, and you'll need to captivate the audience with your moves, as well as with your good looks and sexy voice."

Devesh studied her for a long while, and when she wouldn't look at him, he asked, "Are you saying I'm stiff?"

She put her focus everywhere except him. "You might be a little stiff in the places you don't need to be."

Devesh frowned, unable to get her meaning.

"Your walk is smooth," she said, stroking a hand along his thighs. "Panther-like. You move like you own the joint. That's the first thing that caught my attention."

Then another thought hit him. "Are you saying that I'm also stiff in—"

"Oh no! Baby, you let loose when you made love to me that night." Her body trembled with the memories. "Good Lord."

She took a long, slow breath, pressed her thighs together and he tried not to laugh because he realized that memories were hitting her just as hard as they hit him. "What I'm saying is that with everything else, you tend to hold yourself tightly coiled. I just need you to flex and flow. It'll impact your stance, your movements, and your delivery. You already have a heady confidence, and that is more attractive than your handsome face and gorgeous body."

The concern he heard in her voice belied how serious she felt this issue was. "I'll take the lessons, honey." His gaze narrowed on her. "Is there anything else you suggest?"

She grimaced and quickly shook her head. Too quickly.

"No lies between us," he edged, using an index finger to tip her chin so their eyes met.

"Acting lessons."

Devesh closed his eyes, absorbing that idea and trying—although not so successfully—not to be insulted. But he was a little. He'd been acting for years. Acting was his thing.

"Your acting style is dated and one-dimensional, love," she admitted, and her expression spoke to the fact that it pained her to admit it because she knew it would sting. "I know you admire Arnold Schwarzenegger and Sylvester Stallone. That kind of macho imagery might work in

Bollywood action films, but you're trying to break into an American market. American women have moved away from that whole" — she changed the timbre of her voice to a lower range— "Manly-man persona." She shook her shoulders and straightened them to illustrate her point. "What makes them women want to spread 'em wide and hang 'em high is a man who shows them love and makes them feel safe and desired." She gestured sharply toward the kitchen. "And Lord knows, when I see you stirring a pot on the stove, or putting in the laundry, or maybe even making the bed." She shivered playfully. "Now, that's some sexy stuff right there." She nodded, giving him a playful smile.

Devesh laughed, and it lightened the mood. "So I need to be *softer*?"

"Not soft, love. Sensual. Attentive. Compassionate. Caring. Loving. The way you are with me." She looked away for a moment. When she focused on him again, she said, "It's almost like you're trying to right every wrong that was done to me."

"For every man who didn't see your beauty—I will." He stroked a finger across her cheek. "For every man who didn't value the most wonderful parts of who you are—I will."

"It's not your responsibility to make up for the choices that I made," she whispered, but her voice wavered a little.

Devesh had broken down her defenses once, and he hoped that her feeling free enough to talk with him like this meant he was making progress in doing it again.

"I wasn't there to protect you when all those other men hurt you, but I'm here now. And I hope that with me in your life, God blesses you with years of jubilee for every year of famine you experienced."

She nodded, and within seconds he had her in his arms. "You deserve this." He pressed a kiss to her temple. "And I deserve you."

chapter 15

Devesh sat next to Whoopi, who was in the lead chair for *The View*. The interview segment was going well. He bantered with Joy, Paula, Sara, Jedediah, and Sunny about his new movie projects for a short while. Then he saw Whoopi pull up an index card. "You know, I wasn't going here, but this seems to trend quite often."

Devesh took a deep breath, bracing himself for a subject which, though well outside of the talking points sent in by Reign, was bound to come up. He silently thanked his wife for prepping him to be ready for anything when it came to live interviews.

"It seems that Twitter—especially something called *Black Twitter*— is all up in their feelings about you."

"I can't see why that would be," he said smoothly, though he realized exactly what she was getting at: His wife. His music. His success. All three were intertwined, and he didn't care who had a problem with it, and evidently, a lot of people did.

"The brothers, especially one of your wife's exes, are gunning for you, the Bollywood actor who got the Black woman, career, and achievements they feel was rightfully theirs."

Bingo.

"Dr. Newsome is doing a speaking tour, blogs, magazine articles, and supposedly writing about the phenomenon that is Devesh and Reign," she said, pursing her lips as she read from the notes. "He has the Black community up in arms."

Devesh chuckled a little. "The Brothers can be upset with me all they want. Especially the ones who refuse to live up to even half of what is expected of a real man, yet they look for someone that fits their misguided ideal of a perfect woman. They don't know a good woman when they see one."

Devesh held off, waiting for the applause to die down.

"A good woman isn't defined by dress size, skin color, hair texture, or education level. She's defined by her heart, her devotion, her willingness to bring out the greatness in everyone around her."

The roar of approval from the studio audience took a while to die down.

"The Brothers are leaving all that good love on the table," Devesh said, then gave a five-star smile. "And I'm smart enough to pull up a chair, pick the most beautiful, ripest and intelligent fruit. And I let that love drip on me until I hunger no more."

"Well damn. Shut the front door and climb out the window," Whoopi said, causing Devesh and everyone else to chuckle.

Devesh could name one person he'd like to push out said window. Shawn Newsome, the ex Reign had put in the hospital all those years ago, had crawled out whatever slime pit he lived in. Now the good doctor was coming at her like she'd done him wrong. Well, the fact that the hospital had to give him a shot of muscle relaxant right into his groin might have something to do with it, but shouldn't he be over her by now?

"They might be right that Reign's wealth of knowledge could've been applied to a Black man to gain the same kind of success that I have achieved." Devesh put his gaze on Joy, then Paula. "But *none* of them recognized her value. *None* of them came into her life telling her how important she is; how beautiful she is; what an amazing woman she is. Not a single one.

"Black men had their chance, and they let a diamond slip through their fingers," Devesh said to Whoopi and scanned the women on the panel. Then he looked directly at the front camera and said, "There have been plenty of opportunities for a brother to slide up to her and make his wishes known. Instead of partnering up with a woman who is gorgeous, intelligent, and has a good head on her shoulders, they've been too busy chasing after the easy lays, trusting a big butt and smile." He winked, hoping that his sister Anaya was watching and caught the hint at his play on her favorite song. "But Reign is mine now. And I'm not giving her up."

"Those are fighting words," Whoopi joked.

Devesh nodded, then added, "And any man who decides he wants to test me on that—don't."

Those statements trended immediately across Twitter, Facebook, and Instagram. Memes—images created based on a powerful statement— were being retweeted, shared and distributed all over social media. An image of a plus-size beauty with the text: *Black Men are leaving all this good love on the table.* Another one with Devesh styled in the same manner as the original Dos Equis Beer spokesman which said, *"I'm smart enough to pull up a chair, pick the ripest and most intelligent fruit."* And an even coarser one that had an image of Devesh with Reign photoshopped on his lap and the text: *"I let that love drip on me until I hunger no more."*

The women were loving it.

The men were coming at Devesh with both barrels, guns blazing.

Either way, his album sales had rolled upwards to get him to double-platinum status, nearing triple if it kept going. And the people trolling his Twitter account and Facebook artist page were being taken down by women who totally understood that his relationship with Reign was about more than just the physical.

Life was good. And he would let nothing come between them.

chapter 20

Anaya watched as Kamran and Leena taught their older cousins how to play Checkers. She wondered what kind of life had Reign led that had compelled her to drive the children to be so advanced. The children knew how to play several games of chance—could identify every item in a deck of cards, all in preparation for their mother to teach them how to play Spades—a game she only recently learned to play and Pranav already knew so well. They also knew all of the chess pieces and the moves they made but did not play chess—but it was obvious what Reign intended, even though she didn't play the game herself. But Papa did, and her father was teaching them a little at a time. The twins were soaking up all of that love and attention.

She had to admit she was a little jealous that her parents now spent so much time with Devesh's children, and equally so because they were amazed at the little geniuses—who weren't even aware that they were so much further along than their cousins. She was also concerned that her own children were patterning themselves after Leena and Kamran when it should have been the other way around. Now her children were reading more, asking her questions about everything, and also wanting her to read to them every night, when her busy life didn't always allow for the type of attention they were demanding.

The twins were setting the bar so high that Anaya realized a lot of her shortcomings as a parent; she felt ... inferior. Another reason she resented Reign. The woman seemed to be able to do everything with ease—a career, children, husband, and manage his career to the point that Devesh was becoming a household name.

And now Reign was seeking out a dojo for them to continue martial arts classes. Karate? At four years old? Who does that?

These children hadn't been allowed to just be children. It's one of the reasons Anaya insisted on having them spend so much time with her own son and daughter on the weekends. But it seemed the twins had a leadership quality that mirrored their mother's in a way that not only did they learn quickly, were extremely observant, but they also ended up taking over when it came to anything where the other children were involved or at any time the others seemed indecisive. Those two were going to be something to be reckoned with when they came of age.

Her children were already mimicking Leena and Kamran when it came to school and studies; so were Bhavin's, children, and Neerav's, too. Actually, all of the parents who had children that spent time at the Maharaj house were taking notice of Reign's children. Only Tiya's children seemed to be poised to bully their new cousins. Gratefully, the twins knew how to put them on notice that they weren't having it. Several times the adults had to pull Tiya out of the children's squabbles when the twins and her children were involved. Almost ninety-nine percent of the time the twins were in the right to call out Tiya's children for some infraction or mean-spirited thing they had done. The other children would side with the twins, which angered Tiya to no end.

"Oh no," Mumma said, her voice so filled with alarm that it made Anaya shift from her thoughts of the children and to her mother at the stove.

The children were filing around the breakfast table holding their own animated conversation as they awaited lunch. Anaya's two were sitting on either side of Devesh's twins, almost like a protective barrier between them and Tiya's little bullies.

"What's wrong?" Anaya asked.

"I accidentally mixed all of the wieners in the same pot. They look so similar that I don't know which ones are for Devesh's children." She shrugged, switched off the fire and instructed the aunts to serve the other children before she began pulling out the makings for vegetable biryani. "I will have to make them something else."

"Oh just give it to them," Tiya said with a dismissive wave of her hand. "What does it matter? They won't know the difference."

"She doesn't allow them to eat pork," Mumma replied in a harsh tone frustrated by Tiya's indifference. "It must be a religious thing."

"What religion is that," Tiya asked, frowning. "She doesn't have any religion that we know of. That woman is just being particular and difficult."

Uncle Mitul glared at Leena who seemed well aware of the hatred being directed her way. "A little pork will not hurt them. It has not hurt us."

"Devesh doesn't eat it, and I don't either," Anaya countered, watching as Tiya stabbed a fork into the pot and dropped the offensive food onto a plate. "Mumma and Papa don't touch it, and that goes for the majority of the people who eat with us. We know it's not healthy. Evidently, Reign does too."

Tiya slid a plate in front of Leena and Kamran. They looked down at what had been served to them—minus the vegetables and rice that all the other children were given—but didn't make a move to eat them. Instead, they glanced at each other and Anaya saw the moment that Leena gave a slight shake of her head. Her brother nodded, and both of them pushed the plates back to the center of the table, untouched. "No, thank you," he said. "We will wait for Mumma. *She* will feed us."

"Eat," Uncle Mitul commanded, slamming his fist on the center island causing the twins to look his way. "There is nothing wrong with the food. Eat it!"

Kamran slipped out of his seat, took his sister's hand to help her down.

"No thank you," he said again and went to Aunt Kavya, who gathered the twins to her, creating a safe barrier between her husband and both children.

"You do as you're told," Uncle Mitul screamed at him, waggling a finger at them.

"Do not force them to eat that," Anaya warned, moving to stand in front of her uncle. "You know their mother wouldn't want them to."

"And who are they?" Tiya said coming to stand next to their uncle. "They aren't so special." She ignored the spatula that Aunt Kavya whacked across her hands, and gripped Kamran's arms. "Eat!"

Aunt Kavya shouted back at her husband in Hindi, but kept that spatula at the ready for Tiya.

"No thank you," Kamran said, yanking from Tiya's grasp before putting his focus on Anaya as though sending a silent message for her to intervene since Aunt Kavya and her infamous spatula wasn't getting the message across. Anaya felt ashamed that she hadn't been more forceful. But Aunt Kavya put in a few more whacks with the spatula causing Tiya to scream, "Ouch! Cut that out."

"Leave them alone," Anaya said, taking their hands in hers, allowing Aunt Kavya full access to handle Tiya. "We will not force them to eat something that is not for them."

Kamran's hand tightened on hers. She glanced down at him as he whispered a meek, "Thank you, Auntie Anaya. Thank you, Mumma. Thank you, Aunt Kavya." Her heart skipped a beat when he said her name. And she felt so foolish for her jealous feelings about them. They were children, and it wasn't their fault that their mother was forcing them into being something children should not be. Even in their manners, they were perfect and taught the rest of the children, hers included, to be more exemplary in their communications with the adults. Yet another reason Anaya realized all the things she hadn't done.

The chime of the front door snapped everyone to attention. The sounds of happier conversations echoed all the way into the kitchen and breakfast nook. Devesh and Reign wound their way toward the place where everyone had congregated and a coil of anxiousness released in the pit of Anaya's stomach. This was not going to be a good thing. The children were smart enough to realize that what had happened was not something their mother would approve. And Anaya didn't think it right for her to say they shouldn't tell Reign anything just to keep the peace.

They snatched from Anaya's grip and ran to Reign and Devesh, holding onto them tightly enough to cause a shiver of alarm to light in Reign's eyes. She swept a gaze across the group of women who were suddenly taking an interest in preparing other parts of the meal; and the men trying to appear indifferent to the sudden tension in the room by putting their focus on the television screen. Aunt Kavya's grip on the spatula turned her hands red. She whacked it across Tiya's behind, something that she'd never done to the Maharaj children when they were growing up. She also didn't spank any of the children in her care now—only Tiya.

"I'm grown woman," Tiya screeched.

"Then stop acting like a child," Aunt Kavya said in Hindi.

"What happened?" Reign asked Leena.

"Tell them, Mama," Kamran said, gesturing to the people who were posted up in the kitchen. "Tell them that we don't eat pork."

"I did," she said, eyebrows drawing in, showing her confusion. "I left food for you."

Leena pointed toward their uneaten food. Reign lowered Kamran to the carpet, and he guided her to the table. Her eagle-eyed gaze zoomed in on the contents of their uneaten meal, then squinted.

Devesh was by her side. "Reign, what's the problem?"

"They tried to feed my children something they've never eaten." She glowered at the women who were now focused on her. "Something I expressly said they didn't eat."

"It is my fault," Mumma said, taking all of the blame. "I mixed up the wieners in the pan and could not tell which ones were which."

"Mumma was going to make us Briyani. Aunt Tiya gave us that. Uncle Mitul wanted us to eat that." Leena gestured to the plate. "Mumma didn't do anything wrong."

"Don't be mad at Mumma, "Kamran said gazing up at his mother. "Aunt Anaya helped us." Kamran flickered a look at Anaya whose heart melted and guilt set in. "Aunt Kavya, too.

"Aunt Kavya spanked Aunt Tiya," Leena said. "Gave her a pow-pow on her butt."

The older woman waved the spatula and narrowed a gaze on Tiya who quickly stepped back before another spanking ensued.

Mumma placed a hand over her heart, realizing, like Anaya had, that Devesh's children were a lot smarter than they gave them credit for. They were protecting her, Aunt Kavya, and Anaya from their mother's wrath. Those two had summed up the situation and made sure that the blame stayed exactly where it was supposed to be. Everyone else who had stayed out of the fray was implicated because of their inaction. Yes, the twins were clever. Too clever by far.

"Devesh, I swear on all *you* consider Holy," Reign said, and it was obvious from the darkness in her tone that she was barely holding on to her temper. "That if they harm my children in any way, I am not going to be responsible for my actions." She looked down at her children. "Kamran and Leena are not allowed to eat at your parent's house unless one of us is present."

"Mumma, Aunt Kavya, and Anaya had everything under control," Devesh defended. "Don't be so overprotective."

"Overprotective," she snapped, hands balling into tight fists. "Then why have the other children finished their meal? And those things are still sitting on my children's plates?" She pointed toward the counter. "Don't ever question me about this again." She glared up at him, arms folded across her bosom. "Overprotective my—"

"Mama."

Reign's focus instantly went to Leena who grimaced and shook her head. She paused for a few seconds and then smiled at her child, who seemed to know that cussing was not something her mother was supposed to do.

"They do not eat *anywhere* unless we are present. Mumma, your aunt, and Anaya shouldn't have to run interference with the rest of your family," Reign said to Devesh. "If you have a problem with that, then I can keep them at the condo full time. It's all the same to me."

Devesh did not object because she was right. Seems like his mother, aunt, and sister was no match for his uncle, Tiya, and everyone else.

"Mumma, Anaya, and Aunt Kavya. Thank you," Reign said before snatching the keys from Devesh's pocket and taking the children toward the door. "I'll pick them up something from Panera."

"I am so sorry," Mumma said, gesturing to the items on the counter. "Please allow me to make them a meal."

Devesh let out a breath and Anaya was aware that he was so hoping that Reign wasn't so angry that she couldn't see an olive branch when it was offered.

"It won't be too much trouble?" Reign asked, glancing over her shoulder at Mumma.

"No trouble at all."

Reign stared at Devesh who simply stared back, but his eyes were saying so much. She then put her focus on Mumma as she said, "Thank you." Then she shifted her gaze to Tiya. "You know, this is the third time with you and my children. They say the third time is the charm, but I'm warning you that the fourth time will bring you harm." With that being said, she turned to Uncle Mitul and said in a low throaty voice, "Keep your distance from my children. You don't have any business trying to touch them or direct them. They have people who *actually* care about them. They will handle that business, not you."

Uncle Mitul's jaw tightened, but he didn't respond; though it was obvious he did not appreciate being spoken to in a such manner.

Reign ushered the twins to the table, removed the plate and placed it on the counter.

"Tiya and Uncle Mitul, I don't know what your problem is," Devesh said, cornering the counter until they were only a breath apart. "But you keep messing with my children and my wife, and you're going to find yourself on the wrong end of a problem."

Tiya's head whipped to Reign, who tilted her head and narrowed her gaze as if to say, *"You'd better listen to your brother."*

Unfortunately, Tiya had always been hard-headed, stubborn, and mean-spirited. No one could understand where that came from, but they'd put up with it all their lives.

Reign would not be inclined to do the same. That in itself was going to be a major problem.

chapter 21

Devesh dropped down on the parlor sofa, trying to get his bearings before going into the master suite to speak with his wife, who had set foot in the Maharaj place for the first time in two weeks. He closed his eyes for what seemed like a moment. Must've been far longer because when he opened them, Reign was standing over him, one eyebrow winged upward, trying to hold in a smile.

Reign had settled into married life, living with a man for the first time in her solitary life. She was handling things well, even though the only fly in the milk was some family members still seemed to be shell-shocked by his choice of wife. They were slowly building trust again after that last episode. He was growing weary of his family's interactions with Reign and his children.

"I didn't hear you come in," she said. "I just … felt that you were here."

"Awwww, grasshopper," he teased in an Asian accent. "Seems like we've just taken this relationship to the telepathic level. I must be doing something right."

"You are so silly."

Devesh laughed, got to his feet and kissed her on the lips.

Following Reign into the kitchen, he peered into the first pot on the eight-eye stove. "What's for dinner?

"Your mother taught me how to make chicken makhani, vegetable biryani, dahl makhani, naan, saag, and rasmulai. Your father's making chicken in the tandoori oven outside."

"That's awesome," he beamed, embracing her. "Thank you, Mumma."

"You are happy," Mumma said to him, accepting a kiss on the cheek. "Happier than I have ever seen you. That is all that matters, my son." She glanced slyly at Reign and said, "If you admit it to yourself, you are happy too."

Reign gasped.

"Worried, but happy," she added, patting Reign's hand gently.

"You can see all of that?" Reign's expression was so serious that Devesh wondered why his mother's words or their implications made Reign so sad.

"I am a mother," Mumma replied with a shy smile. "I see many things people do not realize."

Papa sauntered into the kitchen carrying a large tray of "red" chicken with steaming hot onions and lemon as garnish—all prepared in a special clay oven. Pranav followed him, holding several bottles of wine that would satisfy the tastes of the family and friends who would arrive in a short while. They placed their items on the wooden gathering table nearest the north end of the dining room.

Papa grinned, surveying the spread of food on the center island and on the gathering table. "This should be enough. Everyone is coming over to discuss buying a boutique hotel."

Out of the corner of his eye, Devesh noticed Reign's body tense up. He sent up a small prayer of peace. Tiya, Bhavin, and Uncle Mitul had been especially difficult and aggressive at leading the charge to keep some family members in direct opposition to Devesh, Reign, and any other family members who supported them.

"I'll take the children home for dinner," Reign said, quickly abandoning her place at the stove.

"You will do no such thing," Papa expressed, and his tone was resolute, causing her to freeze midway to the door. "Not while we are having a *family* meeting."

Reign's shoulders slumped in defeat. "I understand."

"It does not matter how you came to be the wife of my son." Papa crossed the distance between them and placed his hand over Reign's, halting her efforts. "The fact is that you *are* his wife and now a member of my family."

She took a swift glance at Devesh, who nodded and was warmed by the fact that his father and mother were trying to set the tone for the family to follow. Anaya, Pranav, and Aunt Kavya had also made strides in making Reign and their children feel welcome, but sometimes Anaya held a neutral ground if another family member was involved. The past weeks had been interesting with Reign finding ways to keep herself and the children out of sight by working at the school and then remaining at the condo, even for family dinners and other special occasions.

"Thank you," Reign said to his father, but it sounded more like a question than anything. At least her body relaxed, and she resumed making the meal.

The rest of the women were out shopping for an upcoming celebration of Tiya and Hiran's anniversary. Devesh was certain that Tiya was buying much more than necessary. As if she didn't have a million kurtas, lenghas, and saris filling every closet in the house or enough jewelry to open her own store. No one had ever seen her in the same garment twice, and only Devesh had made mention of the fact that she needed professional help for her shopping addiction.

Mumma and Reign were moving in tandem preparing for the family's arrival, and the sight of them together brought a smile to his face.

"How are things at the school?" Devesh asked Reign, sliding into a highboy at the end of the island.

"I'm actually enjoying it," she replied moving into the spot that Mumma vacated at the stove. "They're having me assist with the children who are more advanced, which means I'm working with Leena, Kamran, and a few others who might skip kindergarten or even first grade altogether."

"I still say I could keep them," Mumma said, and her tone was sad, but resigned. "You do not have to take them away every day."

Reign looked to Devesh, who kept his expression bland. This was a debate that started the moment she had moved to California, and then resumed after Reign had felt it was in the best interest of her family not to set foot in the Maharaj place at all. With the success of his music career taking off, Devesh had hoped Reign wouldn't feel the need to keep up her job search for a paralegal position and that she would somehow become more comfortable and partake of family dinners again, after this first appearance here in a while.

"I know you gave up so much to be here with my son," Mumma said, gesturing for Reign to add more salt to the makhani sauce. "And it means the world to me to spend time with my grandchildren."

"You should be enjoying this time in your life, kicking back and relaxing," Reign argued. "Not running after two rambunctious twins."

"They are not rambunctious," Mumma defended, a smile about her pink lips. "Precocious, maybe, but they are too well-mannered to be rambunctious." She turned those dark brown eyes on Reign who smiled at her acute observations of Leena and Kamran who adored their grandparents. "Since you recognize how advanced they are, maybe you can help me get this one"—she jerked a thumb toward Devesh—"to understand why I push them to learn so much, even at a tender age."

"You've taught them board and card games that are way beyond a normal four-year-old's level," Devesh chimed in, disheartened that Reign seemed to bristle anytime he brought up this issue about the children.

"They just think it's fun," she explained, pausing in her efforts to stir the sauce. "But it teaches them how to think; how to partner up. I was seven when my brother Ricky taught me to play Spades and Bid Whist. People were amazed that I could understand the game as well as I did. That I could count cards, and keep track of things. I learned to watch people. You can tell a lot about a person strictly by the way they play cards. Whether they're patient, selfish, competitive, sore loser, slow to process things, inattentive, or risk-taker."

Devesh left his place at the island, moved to the stove and stroked Reign's arm. I'm not saying stop altogether. Just ..." He held his hands in the air, slowly bringing them closer to decrease the space between them. "Cut back a little. You could start with their school curriculum."

"What's wrong with it? They're on the same learning track Jay was on." Her hand went to her hip. "I started him in a Christian school headed by a pastor and his wife. They taught on an up-slide, which meant that pre-schoolers, kindergartners, first and second graders were taught together. Third, fourth, and fifth graders were taught together, and so on. The youngest in each group learned at a higher level, and the oldest learned patience and how to teach the ones who were behind them. Jay, who was in pre-school, had been placed up with the third graders. Nothing's wrong with that."

"Honey, you also told me that by the time Jay hit first grade he was too far ahead of his peers in that public school you were forced to put him in."

Reign had lost her job and had no choice but to transfer him into a neighborhood school. At that time, Chicago public schools wouldn't let gifted children skip grades—or make a double—like they had when she was growing up. Instead, they stressed the importance of keeping each child in his or her own social group. Something that Devesh said he totally agreed with. The only concession the school administration made to keep Jay mentally challenged was to let the first grader sit in on third and fourth-grade classes part of the day. His first-grade teacher became so frustrated by the additional work involved, that she punched him and knocked him down into the seat when his escorts arrived to take him to his next class. The teacher left the school that day long before Reign arrived. Probably because she knew that Reign was going to give her the kind of beat-down that would make a long-lasting statement. The woman never returned to teach at the school again.

"All I'm saying is that pushing children so hard puts everyone under added pressure," Devesh said softly and Anaya nodded. "The twins included. I'm just trying to get you—and the children—to understand the need for balance."

"I see where you're going with this," Reign said, with a wry twist of her lips. "You're blaming me for what that teacher did to Jay."

Devesh slid behind her and wrapped his arms around her. "I would never do that."

Mumma raised a hand, as if asking permission to speak. "May I repeat my offer? I would love to keep them at least some of the time."

Reign took a deep breath and leaned back into her husband's embrace. "Maybe on one or two days a week I could leave the school early or go in later so I can bring them here. And I'll get some errands done. Maybe take in some classes or something."

Mumma's smile was a beautiful thing to behold. "I would love that, Reign. Maybe sometime soon, I can tell you more about this one right here." She nodded toward Devesh, who was now standing next to Reign, pretending to scowl his displeasure at the prospect of childhood secrets his mother might share. He stuck out his tongue and pouted. Reign and his parents laughed.

"I'm not used to sharing them," Reign confessed after a moment. "Maybe I pushed them too much, too fast, because I wanted them to be able to take care of themselves and each other." Her eyes took on that faraway look he'd come to recognize. "I know that I might not be here long enough to see them into their adult years. My son has his own life, and I didn't want to burden him with them if something happened to me. Even though he wouldn't see them that way."

"Now you don't have to worry about any of that," Devesh said, sweeping aside the morbid thoughts that tried to settle in his soul. "You're eating healthier, and you're not so stressed. You'll be here as long as God wills it."

Reign's smile was wan, not buying into his optimistic views. "Thank you for saying that."

Devesh wondered if there wasn't something going on he wasn't aware of. Some illness that was the basis for her fears. "Reign, what is this obsession you have with death? Why do you hold so tightly to not wanting to enjoy life? Help me understand."

Reign turned her focus toward the window, observing an array of flowers in full bloom. "My family. We die young," she confessed. "My mother was gone at sixty-two. Grandmother at sixty. My sister at the hands of my uncle. She was twelve. My brother from a motorcycle accident at twenty-one. My other brother went into a diabetic coma at thirty-nine and never came out. The other two got pulled into the drug trade and a rival gang took them out at the ages of sixteen and nineteen."

The pain that accompanied those words caused her to tremble. He wrapped her in his arms and held her tight.

"Of our immediate family," she continued. "besides Jay and the twins, two nephews, two nieces are still alive. And I don't have anything to do with my father or half-siblings, so I don't count them in that mix. I know my time is limited, that's why—"

"Tum marne main itne busy ho ki zindagi jeene ka ehsaas nahin hain tumko."

Reign tilted her head and studied him as he translated, "Sweetheart, you're so busy focusing on dying, that you haven't been about the business of living."

"That's not true."

Devesh pulled her into his arms. "There's so much to look forward to in *this* present moment. Your son. The twins. Me. Your friends. Your nieces and nephews. They need you to be in this present moment. Live in the now, love. Be grateful for the life God gives you—one second at a time, one minute at a time, one hour at a time, one day at a time." He pressed a kiss to her temple. "Let's be about the business of living, honey."

He allowed that to hold space in her head for a moment. Then he leaned over, tasted a spoonful of chicken makhani she held out to him, and moaned, "Oh that's good."

A real smile lifted the corners of Reign's lips this time.

chapter 22

Reign finished her call with Kerry Van Isom, the Chicago accountant who had set up trust funds for the twins and Jay. Now he was able to set up everything, all accounts for Devesh, and a marital trust for Reign and to make sure Devesh had never landed in trouble with the IRS.

She typed the last of the notes on her iPad that she needed to share with Devesh about the other financial moves he wanted to make. One was a foundation that would benefit several orphanages in India, a second would provide scholarships to American students who desired to go to Columbia College Chicago or the HBCUs Jay had attended years ago.

Reign slid her phone into her pocket, entered the family room and den where the majority of people were gathered before tonight's meal. Tiya and Hiran were set to give a presentation, then dinner would be served a little later than normal. They had Howard, a co-worker from the tech firm where Hiran worked, in the theatre fixing an issue that happened with the connection between the projection system and the server where the presentation was stored.

All eyes were on her the second she stepped in.

"What's going on?" she asked Devesh, slowing her walk, feeling that something was about to become unpleasant.

"The twins need to have their heads shaved," Devesh said to Reign. "It is a tradition in our culture." He explained that the shaving was part of Saṃskāra, a series of purification processes. Some believed birth hairs were undesirable traits from past lives and the ceremony sets the child free. "There are sixteen Saṃskāra and Chudakarana—Mundan-First Hair cutting—is one of them."

"I don't care whose tradition it is," Reign said, unfazed by all the people who were watching and hoping she'd give in. "You're not shaving my children's heads."

Reign stood stone-faced in the center of the family room, then swept a gaze across the rest of the people situated in the adjoining rooms while she pondered how she could make any part of this work. For one thing, this ceremony was supposed to take place when a child turned one. The twins were far older than that. Her biggest objection was that maybe this was part of their culture, but it was not part of hers. She'd already given in—a little—on scaling back their advanced studies, but she'd found other ways to challenge them. They were definitely staying ahead of the curve. That's something that Devesh was totally unaware of, and it was harmless, but this … was something entirely different.

"There's a story in the Bible," she began, then narrowed her look when Tiya hissed and gave her the side-eye. "Yes, I have read some sacred text from time to time. Even yours." She shifted to have a better view of Mumma, Aunt Kavya, and Papa instead of Tiya and Bhavin's sour faces. "Two harlots living in the same house gave birth to sons. One of the infants was smothered to death when his mother rolled over on him in her sleep. When she awakened the next day and realized what happened, she switched the babies so that the alive one was now in her bed. When the other mother went to nurse her son, she found that the 'infant' beside her was dead. But when she took a real good look, she realized it wasn't the son she'd given birth to. A mother knows."

Reign put her focus on Anaya. "The women took their case to King Solomon. The real mother of the live infant explained how the other woman switched the babies after accidentally smothering her own son. The other mother vigorously denied it."

Reign paced the area in front of the screen mounted behind her.

"Solomon could not determine which of the women were telling the truth. "Bring me a sword," he commanded. "Cut the living child in two and give half to one woman and half to the other."

"That's in the Bible?" Anaya asked, eyes widened with horror.

Reign nodded. "The true mother of the live child screamed, 'Please, my lord, give her the baby. Don't kill him!' However, the other woman said, 'Neither you nor I shall have him. Cut him in two.' King Solomon said, 'Give the living baby to the first woman. Do not kill him. She is his mother.'"

"So how could he tell," Pranav asked, lacing his hands with Anaya's.

"Only a mother would rather see her child stay alive," Reign answered. "Even if she wouldn't be the one to have him. She would do what was best." Reign took a deep breath, preparing to bring her point home. "There are two things that we want here." She took a seat on the edge of an open spot near Devesh. "The twins are situated partially in your culture and half in mine. Your culture practices a belief system that neither my children nor I am aware of."

"So you must be the bitter mother. Is that what you're telling us?" Tiya taunted, then added in Hindi, "Or a harlot."

Aunt Kavya's dark brown eyes flashed fire. She reached to her side for the spatula, but came up empty. Devesh got to his feet. Reign put up her hand to keep him at bay.

"Takes one to know one," Reign shot back, causing Tiya to frown as though trying to figure out the most insulting part of that statement. "But what I'm actually saying is that I like Solomon's *original* way of handling things, and I think it can work here."

"Meaning?" Devesh prompted.

"We're going to have to split the difference on this one down the middle."

The family murmured their questions and comments among themselves.

"Mumma, do you have a tape measure?" Reign asked, cutting through the throng of voices.

Her eyebrows drew in. "Yes, it is in the kitchen," she said slowly, looking at her husband as though he could explain what was going on.

"In the drawer next to the stove."

"I'll be right back."

Reign returned in the time it took to say "dinner is served," which would be happening if Tiya and Hiran hadn't insisted that the presentation go forward *before* people eat and get too comfortable to hear it.

"Devesh, I'll need you to help me with some calculations."

He whipped out his cell and prepared to enter the numbers she called out into the calculator app.

"So let's imagine that their hair grows about an inch every month. And since they're now four years old, that would be about forty-eight inches, give or take." She took out her own iPhone and checked the calendar. "Write these down," she said to Devesh, then rattled off all of the dates when Kamran had his hair trimmed, adding, "And Leena's had a couple of inches taken off twice each year."

She used the tape measure, then called the longest length of each child's head, and Devesh calculated the measurements.

Devesh took a minute to get where she was going. His laugh filled the air and caused Papa, Mama, and Anaya to join in while others shared looks of confusion.

"So, it goes without saying that the hair that they would've had on their first birthday for this tradition is no longer available."

Bhavin scoffed, but a few other family members chuckled. So did Aunt Kavya.

"But as a show of respect for the tradition," Reign said, smiling. "We'll go for a nice little trim for Leena and a much lower cut for Kamran. And I will ask them if they're alright with it."

"They're children," Tiya snapped, scowling as she flickered a disdainful look at the twins who were too engrossed in the books they held in their hands to notice.

"They are little people that God loans us for a period of time," Reign shot back, and she paced before Tiya and Bhavin. "They are not toys. The minute you teach a child that anything can be done to them without any regard for their feelings is the direct lead in that someone needs to do anything and everything to them." She scanned every single person in the room to make sure they heard her point, but put a lingering look on Mitul causing him to bristle. "They learn that *any* adult can do any old thing to them. They have to learn that they have a say in what happens to them—and why."

"The Pandit can't bless a child and say the prayers over them if they have hair," Bhavin protested, while Sana nudged him into silence.

"Then we'll have to let the Black side of the children's culture and my God do all the protecting," she countered smoothly, draping the tape measure around her neck. "Because if your prayers only work in certain conditions, that's not the kind of God I want my children to embrace." She smiled, though she was nowhere near happy. "So we're just going to have to settle for a little Catholic holy water or a good old-fashioned baptism." She whirled to face Devesh. "Are there any other traditions that we need to negotiate?"

"You could just cut their hair when she's not around," Tiya offered to Devesh. Her smile was pure evil. "Why does everything have to be about her? They are *your* children, after all."

"Are you trying to get me killed?" he shot back, seemingly alarmed that his sister did not realize who he had married.

He understood that shaving their heads against his wife's wishes would be a sure way to lose her trust; if not losing her altogether. Though Devesh probably preferred that she would allow the tradition to go through the way it always had in their family, he also realized that Reign coming up with a compromise was at least a step in the right direction.

Tiya shrugged, put a glare on Leena and said, "Just bring them here without her, and I could do it for you as a *compromise*. Problem solved."

"Not if you expect to keep your hands."

That chill of Reign's icy words resonated around the room.

"You were wrong for suggesting that," Devesh said to Tiya. "You keep playing with my wife, and it's going to be game over or lights out. Whatever best describes your trip into the afterlife."

For once, Tiya knew when keeping her mouth shut was an absolute necessity.

chapter 23

Ten minutes later, Devesh tried to stay awake as Tiya and Hiran, laid out the plan for pooling their resources—mostly Devesh's by unspoken agreement—to buy into a franchise hotel property that suddenly became available. The presentation was slick, even had a Power Point spread and Excel projections of how their money would be returned within a year.

None of it sounded right to Devesh. He wasn't putting any of his hard-earned money into the venture, but saying that outright would bring on an argument that would last for hours. And right now, he was ready for his wife's good cooking. Devesh stroked a hand across Leena's face causing her to look up from the book she was reading and smile at him. He kept his focus on her, pointing to a few interesting things in her book while tuning out the rest of the discussion where Hiran and Tiya were fielding questions thrown their way and providing surface answers to the family's concerns. He wanted an end to this façade, and since he'd already made his decision, he mentally flipped through his schedule and upcoming changes that Jay had sent over earlier that morning.

Papa's eyes slid to Reign. "You have been so quiet. Do you have something you would like to say?"

Devesh snapped to the present, definitely wanting to hear what wisdom his wife would impart.

"This is supposed to be about family," Tiya spat, leaving the front area of the theater's projection screen to address Papa from a few feet away. "She's not family."

"Be quiet," Papa snapped, his uncharacteristic tone stunning everyone.

Tiya slithered onto one of the recliners, glaring openly at Reign who moved from the seat next to Mumma and stood in the center of the theater in front of everyone.

"I think more research is needed before you put all of that cash in and end up with the same issues that the current owners have," Reign offered, gesturing to the screen. "Why isn't the place doing well? It's a boutique franchise of a *major* chain. Is the problem management or staff? Maybe the demographics have changed? Is there no longer a need for an outside place to stay? Has the area lost some of the tourist attractions or businesses? Is it taxes? Local politics?" She focused on Papa, who gave an encouraging nod. "The people who own the place didn't go into this business to fail. You need to talk with them and find out where they made mistakes and missteps. What parts of the business worked well? How did they handle times when occupancy was low? Learn what they would do differently."

She waited for a moment, giving Tiya some time to come up with answers or responses. There were none.

"There are too many variables for you all to spend that kind of money, only to inherit something that's destined to stay on a downward course." Reign looked to Mumma who smiled, then she finished by saying, "Trying to make a recovery on a place after years of neglect, mismanagement, and disrepair is much harder than you think."

"What would you know about it?" Tiya snapped, causing even Anaya to cringe at the harsh tone. "You're just some glorified secretary from the hood."

Aunt Kavya rolled her eyes heavenward, mirroring Devesh's thoughts.

She stuffed her hand in her apron, frowning when she was unable to bring out the spatula that had been missing in action for a few days.

A few murmurs followed that assertion. Anaya shifted a pointed look to Devesh and shook her head.

Devesh sighed, becoming weary of his family's distrust of Reign. They were so wrong about his wife. Why couldn't they see that? Devesh adjusted Leena on his lap so Kamran could climb on the other knee.

Reign angled, facing Tiya head on. "I have a degree in business management, with minors in both music and hospitality. And I'm a *paralegal*, not a secretary. So I definitely understand contracts. But it doesn't take any of that to see through this crap you're trying to get your family to swallow. What I'm using here is common sense. If you're buying someone else's problem, you need to know exactly what the problem is. But even a *glorified secretary from the hood* would know that. So what's *your* major malfunction, Tiya?" Then she tilted her head. "And you have a degree in—"

"Reign makes a valid point," Devesh said, moving with the children in his arms, until he stood between Reign and his sister who was about to go ballistic about that dig to her non-existent higher education—one that had been fully paid for with a pageant win. "We need to check these people out. The business too, not just the portfolio they gave you and whatever this is you threw together for us." Devesh gestured dismissively toward the projection screen. "I'd like to see …"

"Profit and loss statements, valuation reports, operating agreements, shareholder and employment agreements," Reign supplied. "Accounts receivable and payable ledgers, telling us how much money is going out as well as coming in."

"We need this investment," Hiran roared, coming to stand next to his fuming wife. Tiya fixed a glower on Devesh for siding with rationality rather than buying into a crock of bull. "We've known the Chadha family for years, yet we listen to a woman who doesn't know us or our ways. We have to be smart. This is a good opportunity to own our own hotel and hire more of our people who need jobs. We can't let slip through our fingers."

"What part of 'we need to check them out' isn't smart?" Devesh challenged. The murmurs of agreement that followed seemed to take the wind out of Tiya for a moment.

"I told him that we would help them," Tiya whispered, sweeping a look at those staring warily back at her.

"But not at a disservice to our *own* family," Devesh replied, moving so that he was directly in front of her, unfazed by the fact that she'd turned three shades darker in her anger. "That doesn't make sense, Tiya. We're talking a lot of money here. Money none of us have to waste. You brought this without doing your own research. This is all *their* information." Then he softened his tone. "You've just put some bells and whistles on it to make it look nice for people who don't know better."

Papa and Mumma's expression was a direct reflection of Anaya's— displeased.

"Consider me out of the running," Devesh said, whirling so he was aiming to take the children with him and exit to the dining room.

"Well, we can tell who wears the pants in your family," Bhavin taunted.

"It's not about pants or skirts." Devesh turned at the threshold. "Deferring to my wife's wisdom before I buy into any foolishness makes it a team effort." His gaze narrowed on his sister and he moved toward her once again as a thought hit him. The presentation was weak. Both Tiya and Hiran kept cycling back to the fact that the family "must" do this. "How much are they paying you?"

Tiya flinched, took a few steps back, but he didn't miss the flash of worry in her eyes. "What … what are you talking about?" she stammered, inching away from him.

"You've been pushing for this from the beginning," Devesh said, peering more closely at her, taking in the flush in her cheeks. "We're not all that close to the Chadhas. What's this really about?"

Tiya snatched her focus from him and glared at Reign, who simply kept any emotions she felt shielded.

Devesh was so proud of his wife. She was always reminding him to listen to what people meant and not simply what they were saying, because it wasn't always one and the same. The men in the room who had so many doubts about Reign were listening. She was more than intelligent; she was insightful. She had never made Devesh feel inferior because he wasn't well versed in how to communicate his thoughts. Reign was a perfect balance to him in so many ways.

School had not been kind to Devesh on many levels. An immigrant who barely spoke the English language, he was singled out by impatient teachers who already had their hands full with others who had no interest in learning. Devesh was bullied and beaten daily by boys who lived in the projects and the surrounding areas. Boys who didn't want Devesh near their sisters because he was so different. Taunts of "pretty boy" and "light-skinned" haunted him. He never understood why any of it mattered. Light, dark, in between—everyone was important. Everyone had beauty. Everyone had purpose.

The daily experiences caused his school work to suffer because he couldn't pay as much attention to his studies. Where he had excelled on a genius level in India, he struggled in American schools. That, too, added to a feeling that maybe he wasn't good enough. Reign could make him feel like his thoughts, dreams, and goals mattered. Words that he couldn't make come out quite right would sing when Reign put her touch to them. The fact that he wanted to work on behalf of charities that were close to his heart was admirable in her eyes. She understood him like no one else—not even his parents.

Sometimes he wondered what would've happened if he had listened to Reign years before when she tried to convince him to revamp his image. Maybe he would have been a lot further along in his career.

But then again, everything in its time. Including learning from past lessons when it came to handling family and finances.

Though their parents weren't rich by India's standards, they had been moderately wealthy at one point. Until a few bad investments with some distant and not-so-distant relatives had taken advantage of his parents' kindness and their open wallets. Anaya and Devesh stepped in to stop the practice of any and everyone coming to them with their hands out.

Unfortunately, the hit to their parents' finances had already caused them to downsize their lives. Devesh was going to do everything in his power to make sure they weren't going to be taken in by any more shady deals. Not even from his baby sister.

"I will not put any money or effort into this," Devesh said, cutting through the loud voices that were now in a heated discussion.

"You're just being selfish," Tiya snarled, waving a fist at him as the conversations circling around them trickled to a halt. "All that money you have coming in. You just want to keep it all to yourself."

"I certainly don't plan to give it away. This ain't no charity, lady," he shot back. His little girl gave a single affirming nod as though she had understood the entire conversation and Devesh had made the parting shot. "It shouldn't take my wife to tell you how foolish it was to bring this before the family without making sure we weren't putting our hard-earned money into a sinking venture. Mumma and Papa didn't own those gas stations and convenience stores just for you to drain them dry." He let that thought swim around the room before he added, "Any new requests for microloans or loans of any kind need to go through my wife from this point on. She handles my finances and has access to my bank accounts. She will set the terms and put them in writing for you to sign, so that way there's no misunderstanding." He resituated Leena and Kamran in his arms as he looked to his wife. "Reign, tell them how things are going to be."

She came to his side, taking his hand in hers and with a pointed look at the main ones who had their hands out on a regular basis. Kamran closed his book, held it to his chest, and put his focus on Reign, so did Leena. "Have a business plan when you come this way—a real one. Some of the family have outstanding loans they haven't paid Mumma or Papa. So if you haven't rolled them *their* money, don't come rolling up asking for *ours*. No more open-ended agreements where you take and take and take, and don't even realize people are giving. Those days are over."

"Big man, now that you have a woman doing all your thinking," Bhavin taunted. Jealousy was practically seeping out of the man's pores.

"I never do his thinking," Reign said between her teeth. "His brain worked well and served his best interest long before I showed up." She gave a low, throaty chuckle. "You're just pissed because I turned down your request to help with your acting career."

Devesh stiffened upon hearing those words. Why hadn't she told him?

Reign zeroed in on Devesh's hardened expression and explained, "It was a non-issue. A brief conversation I'd forgotten about until now. There's a difference between a man who has a pretty face and nice-looking body, and a man who also has charisma, a good heart, charm, intelligence and doesn't think the world owes him something because he has one out of the six." She cupped Devesh's face in her hands. "And it's why this one is doing so well. People can tell the real deal from someone who's just smiling for the cameras."

Bhavin flicked his hand in her direction, a clear sign that he didn't appreciate her telling him about himself. His brother had always thought more highly of his physical attributes. Devesh found it interesting that Reign had put him in check. And it probably stuck in Bhavin's craw that she hadn't considered his aspirations important enough to speak with Devesh to get some input.

"Having a family means making better decisions," Devesh said, scanning the solemn faces in the room. "This is not a good investment, as there are too many unknown factors and I'm certainly under the belief that Tiya and Hiran's push for this to happen is mighty suspect."

The couple of the hour fumed and remained strangely silent.

Devesh readjusted the children so that one was situated in each muscled arm again, and moved into the dining area with Reign following closely on his heels. Once the twins were seated at the smaller dining room table especially for the children, he pulled his wife into his arms and whispered, "We make a good team."

"You think so?"

"I *know* so." He couldn't wipe the smile from his face. He was so elated at the outcome of the meeting and that they were able to see through Tiya and Hiran's ruse to empty their pockets and enrich their own. "I love that we're a power-packed house. I love that you have my back."

"And your front."

"And my front," he agreed, playfully ruffling Kamran's head and putting a kiss on the tip of Leena's nose.

Reign's lashes lowered, covering any emotion he could read in her eyes, but he knew from the way her body flowed into him that she loved the compliments and she loved him, though she never said it out loud.

Reign laid her head against his chest and his heart rate increased. Soon, she would want him as much as he wanted her.

Everything in its time.

❦ ❦ ❦

"Mumma, this tastes so good," Tiya said around a mouthful of the slightly spicy spinach, mushroom, and corn dish.

"I wish I could take credit for it," Mumma responded lifting her fork in a salute. "But I did not make dinner tonight. Reign did."

All conversations came to an abrupt end. Some of the family members looked down at their plates; others shared a questioning, almost horrific glance.

No one was willing to say anything. Devesh scooped up a forkful of chicken makhani over basmati rice and moaned like it was the best thing he'd ever tasted in his lifetime. Actually, it was. This was his mother's recipe, but a few unfamiliar seasonings told him that Reign put her own touch in the meal as well.

"To eat or not to eat," Devesh said in an affected English accent, cutting through the silence that permeated the room. "That is the question. Whether it is nobler in the mind to suffer the slings and rumblings of an outrageously empty stomach."

Dinner quickly resumed. Congratulatory gestures and words were shot Reign's way. She accepted demurely while trying to keep from laughing at Devesh displaying the new techniques from his acting class. The class first put a heavy emphasis on learning to perform Shakespeare. The concept was that British actors were more concerned about being a good actor and not so much about super stardom. The next rotation would be comedy and improvisation. Devesh was loving this new process almost as much as he was enjoying Reign's home-cooked meal.

Only Tiya showed her entire ass by spitting a mouthful of food into a napkin and pushing her plate toward the center of the table. "I've lost my appetite."

Devesh snatched up his sister's plate, went into the kitchen and slid the contents into a Tupperware container. He sauntered into the dining room and presented it to Hiran, who quickly accepted it with glee.

Devesh smiled at Hiran and said, "This will come in handy when you get home since your wife's cooking leaves a lot to be desired. Except for several trips to the bathroom."

Tiya's eyes glazed over with unconcealed hatred as everyone shared a laugh.

Reign's lips lifted at the corners, and she mouthed the words, "Thank you."

chapter 24

Devesh looked over Jay's shoulder, taking in the onscreen data he had gathered on demographics and music preferences in certain cities. Jay, who was in the process of making a case for Elise, his high school sweetheart, to make that move to California with him, had proposed an idea so radical that Devesh felt no one would understand it—most of all Reign. She was more into a streamlined and solid approach to the way Devesh marketed and would perform on his upcoming tour.

The after-release marketing plans that Jay put together, and initial ideas for a small tour to promote his album had slated places like Chicago, New York, Atlanta, Detroit, Houston, and New Orleans. Devesh wanted to keep the rest of them closer to home so he wouldn't be away from Reign and the twins so much. Tonight was all about balancing Devesh's new life.

Jay had set up his office in the first-floor condo and was taking on a few clients that came as a result of his work for Devesh. He found through web trafficking and analytics that the people who made up a great part of Devesh's new fan base were middle-aged Blacks and, surprisingly, young and middle-aged East Indians. Devesh wasn't aware that so many people from his culture had a thing for R&B music.

He slid out the documents that listed the perfect places to perform. They also contained a surprise element that would connect Devesh with more seasoned artists to help him get familiar with them and their sound. Jay had hijacked Reign's playlist from her phone and computer during the last updates and dropped the songs he felt worth listening to onto Devesh's cell.

A bright green folder stashed on the other side of Jay's keyboard caught Devesh's attention. "What's this?" Devesh asked.

"I'm readjusting my life index," Jay answered, sliding out the first page so Devesh could take a gander. "So I'll know when my long-range plan will work."

"Life index?"

Jay nodded, pointing to the upper right column of figures. "Mom taught me early on about budgeting, made me keep one when I was in high school. She also taught me that everyone has a specific amount of money they'll need to live comfortably for the rest of their lives. Not rich. Not wealthy. Simply able to keep the lifestyle they have now."

"So how does that work?" Devesh asked, trying to make sense of the figures in front of him.

"My life index is pretty low," he answered, swiveling the office chair until he faced Devesh head on. "I have a car, some savings and very little in student loan debt since I went to school on grants and scholarships. The rest Mama shelled out of her pocket. I have a decent wardrobe. I'm not into material things, but I do like to travel. So as a single man, I'd need to have 6.7 million in the bank at the age I am right now in order to maintain my current lifestyle all the way until I'm sixty-five or seventy without working a single day of a 9-to-5." He extracted the sheet from Devesh's hand, gesturing to the bottom figure. "When I get married and have children, that number will go up, but I at least know what I need to be working on."

Devesh thought that over. He had only one-fourth of that number in the bank right now. If he didn't have the music thing going and the movie offers coming in, he would have to work a 9- to-5 until he was ninety—and that wasn't taking into consideration the fact that he had a family. Evidently, he needed to up his game when it came to the music part of his career. He'd make a lot more money if he added more cities to the tour, but Jay was right—balance was also important. Time with family was important. And it's one of the reasons he had Anaya put in an offer on a Shoreview home a few acres away from the Maharaj place. She had told him the minute the listing hit her desk. The condo was nice, but the children having a place to run out of the back door and straight into a yard with lots of grass and room to play, would be much better. Close to his family, but not too close. That would definitely work.

"Do you happen to know your mother's life index?"

"About 3.7 million," he answered, frowning as he seemed to give it more thought. "Maybe a little more now because that's the number she told me a few years ago and the munchkins have absorbed a lot of her cash flow. She had me start putting money in an account to fund an irrevocable trust and another insurance trust that was set up to protect my assets and always keep me with some money in my pockets. Money neither marriage nor divorce could take from me.

"Mom is smart. She's not about stocks and bonds. It's about real dollars and cents with her. Knowing what I need puts me in a different frame of mind."

"No doubt," Devesh said, pondering his own next steps.

"I screwed up a little bit in college, though. She didn't bail me out either," Jay admitted. "She said I needed to bump my head and hit that brick wall. Told me that was the best point to make mistakes because I'd have time to recover. I learned the hard way that if I had listened to her …"

"Yes, I know the feeling," Devesh said sourly, remembering all the times he'd brushed off Reign's suggestions as though she didn't understand him or the business. She understood both more than he'd given her credit for.

Devesh would not make that mistake ever again.

chapter 25

Reign stood off to the side of the United Center stage and waited, along with the stadium full of Chicago fans, for Devesh to begin. She felt that Jay and Devesh had been ambitious booking such a huge venue for the first concert Devesh would hold. Jay had asked both of them to trust him, that he knew that this plan of one concert, instead of three over a weekend, would increase attendance—and would save them a ton of money in the fact that they'd pay for one night of sound, lighting, venue use rather than three and have too much performing take a toll on Devesh too early in the game. If people knew that there was only one night to see him perform in a particular city, the demand would go up and so would attendance.

Not to mention, Jay and Percy already had some things in the works for separate music and recording deals with the background singers as a group, and the musicians as a performing jazz ensemble all their own. Multiple streams of income. That was Jay's new mantra. Then he knocked it out of the ball park by reconnecting Devesh with the companies who had used him for advertising years ago. They were the first on board to sponsor Devesh's tour, so practically none of the expenses came out of Devesh's pocket.

Devesh glanced over his shoulder at her, then smiled. And she instantly knew trouble was brewing. She studied Jay for a moment, who shrugged and put his focus back on Devesh.

He gestured for the band to stop playing the beginnings of the opening song. The music trickled to a halt.

"Can I talk to you all for a minute?" he said to the audience.

The roar of the crowd took a minute to die down. But Reign's anxiety amped up. What was he doing?

"You know, I've been accused of … what do they call it?" He snapped his fingers. "Appropriating Black culture; trying to act like I'm Black or trying to take something that's reserved for the Black folks alone."

Boos and jeers followed that statement.

"But I grew up in an all-Black neighborhood from the age of twelve, and a special woman taught me to embrace the music I grew up with in Boogie Down Bronx—"

Cheers erupted from all around.

"As well as music from my homeland of India."

A roar of approval followed that statement, and he waited for it to diminish before he said, "And she helped me combine them to make a new and unique sound. So since folks believe that I'm trying to run away with the 'Honorary Negro' title …"

Reign groaned. Jay outright laughed.

"I might as well make a good pitch to make it happen," Devesh said, smiling.

"Oh no," Reign whispered and flashed an anxious look at Jay, who had added road manager to his position of brand specialist. He had actually made some suggestions about a few family members who were well-suited to be in areas that could help Devesh. He pretended as though he was as clueless as everyone else about what was happening on stage. But she knew differently. Jay and Devesh had been meeting every day at Jay's condo for the past month, planning the tours and the direction they should take. They also had a new album in the works that would be released next year. The tours, recordings, and album releases were all planned around his filming schedule because he insisted on only taking projects in the California area.

"Some people are pissed at me because I married one of the baddest women on the planet."

The crowed cheered and applauded.

"Yes, I did," he said, sending an intense look Reign's way. "Let me tell you a little bit about my woman. She's born and bred from the South Side of Chicago."

Reign closed her eyes, trying to steady the ripples of anxiety dancing a tightrope in her mind. Devesh was so far off the reservation, he didn't have a tee pee or a horse.

"She told me that when she's feeling low, she gets in the shower and sings the type of songs that will let her get a prayer through."

"Alright now," someone yelled from the audience.

"She sings until it satisfies her soul," he said, sliding his hand along the mic stand. "So if I'm going to be accused of appropriating Black culture, I might as well do the doggone thing."

Devesh glanced at the background singers and musicians, and they knew to stand-down as he took the mic from the stand.

Reign didn't realize she was holding her breath, waiting along with the crowd to see what he would do. She took a long sip of water from the cup she held and wished it was some of the Fireball whiskey Jay and Devesh loved so much.

Devesh took a deep breath; then let loose with something so unexpected that the cup slipped from her fingers and landed on the floor with a thud.

"Father," he crooned. "I stretch my hands to thee."

"You'd better sing that," an audience member cried out.

My God. He's singing my favorite song. And he was singing it the way she sang it, in that slow building way she'd learned from the pastor when she was a teenager attending a Baptist church in Roseland.

"We 'bout to have church up in here," someone yelled from the first row.

The crowd vehemently voiced their approval, and the applause was deafening.

The song was one that the deacons would sing to start a church service and was considered a "Dr. Watts"—a deep spiritual hymn. The entire church congregation would join in, unlike the call and response of a normal Dr. Watts song. The songs would sound so sad, a sort of wailing plea for God to listen. The way Devesh belted it out, it still carried the same heaviness as a petition for God to come in the house and bring the Holy Spirit in to stay.

"No other help I know," Devesh crooned. "If thou withdraw thyself from me, oh whether shall I go?" And he sang it with such power and such pain in his voice that tears formed in Reign's eyes. They fell unchecked because she knew he was singing it for her; to let her know that he heard her and he understood. That night she was unable to save her sister's life had left a hole in her soul that nothing had seemed to fill.

She had told him that no matter what religion she'd been involved in—and there had been several—there were times when she reached back to that Missionary Baptist upbringing. When nothing else could get through, that song made her feel something deep on the inside. It said everything that needed to be said.

Reign was totally mesmerized by Devesh, listening as he transitioned into the beginnings of *Guide Me Oh Thou Great Jehovah* before moving into *I love the Lord He Heard My Cry*. She had never heard anything sound so beautiful in her entire life.

She'd sung those three songs in the shower that night when he proposed to her. Still shaken up by everything, she hadn't known which way to go or what would happen with her life. Singing a medley of these three songs was her way of turning her problems over to the Creator.

Now Devesh was singing her pain on the stage. Telling the world that what he knew about her was more than just that she was a Black woman, but that there was something deep within her that had experienced so much that she couldn't say and he understood.

The crowd responded in a way that was nothing short of amazing. Some of them sang the songs with him. Hands went up, giving praise to the Creator.

His eyes had closed. Now he was delivering the words with as much soul and power as he could summon. Reign looked out at the crowd to take in the reaction. Devesh was reaching their hearts and minds. Black, White, Latino, East Indian—it didn't matter.

When he was done, the musicians and background singers were all standing and applauding as well.

"Thank you for allowing me that moment," he said over the cheers of approval. "Are y'all ready for this?"

The answer was a resounding, "Yes."

Devesh studied his crew for a moment and sang, a cappella, the words, "You're here; I'm pleased. I really dig your company ..."

The first words of the Jill Scott classic brought the keyboards, the bass and then the percussion to life. One by one the musicians joined in accompanying him on a song that they were familiar with even though they hadn't rehearsed it with him.

By the time the first chorus kicked in, a beautiful curvaceous woman had sauntered in from the opposite side of the stage, put her mic up and joined him. The crowd recognized that familiar voice as the one who recorded the original, which put her on the map. And so did the background singers and musicians who seemed to be just as shocked as everyone else.

Devesh lowered his mic and let Jill have a run with the song before lifting the mic again and saying, "Chicago, I present to you the incomparable Jill Scott."

The audience's enthusiastic response to her appearance meant they could barely hear the vocals at first.

They finished the song together, then Devesh left the stage giving Jill the time and space to do her thing.

Reign couldn't put a voice to what she felt. Devesh looked at her, waiting for her to say something, anything to let him know that she was alright with the direction he'd taken. She embraced him, held onto him as the music flowed around them.

chapter 26

Anaya situated herself across from Mumma and Papa in the game room, watching as Pranav took a beating in billiards from her father.

"I think his marriage is a good thing," Pranav said to Papa, but more for her benefit. "Devesh is different, all of a sudden he's more … something. I can't put my finger on the reason, but this marriage is working for him."

The words Pranav had said to Anaya a few weeks earlier in the privacy of their home echoed in Anaya's mind.

"That man has a hunger for that woman like you would not believe. His heart has not been satisfied without her, and he wants her in the worst way. I love you, but for the first time, I'm beginning to not like some parts of you. You are denying him happiness when you already have your own."

"It works because he's a mama's boy," Tiya taunted, plopping a red grape into her mouth. "And he married a woman who has a few years on him. She can pick up where Mumma left off—taking care of him."

"Actually, I love both parents with equal measure," Devesh said entering from the patio, causing the few family members in the room to shift their gazes his way. "And there are things I think of doing to my beloved that I would *never* dream of doing to my Mumma."

Anaya and Mumma blushed a deep red. Papa gripped Mumma's hand to keep her silent. Tiya blinked back a retort. Bhavin rolled his eyes. Pranav actually chuckled.

"Don't be upset because I married a woman who knows how to handle her business and mine, too," Devesh said, using a bath sheet to wipe off some of the excess moisture from an early evening swim. "While you're shopping your husband into the poor house trying to keep up with Anaya."

Hiran's shoulders drooped. Something that Anaya didn't miss, neither did their parents.

"You're going to lose your husband trying to be something you're not," Devesh warned. "Anaya has a two-income household. They can afford everything they have." He draped the bath sheet about his shoulders. "So instead of worrying about whether I have *mama issues*, you need to be focusing on your own household."

"Well, there's some truth to that," Aunt Kavya said in Hindi, causing Tiya to glower at her.

"Who are you to say anything about my life? You make money off your body, just like a whore," Tiya snarled at Devesh putting her bowl of grapes to the side. "You're nothing more than a pretty face."

Bhavin's snicker set Anaya's nerves on edge. Oh yes, her big brother was still pissed at Reign for not taking him on as a client. And to add insult to injury, she'd tested the waters of this new entertainment management career of hers by taking on another East Indian male as a client. The newcomer, who was a referral from Devesh, was starting to see traction in his career following on the heels of Devesh's success.

"Actually, he's not pretty. He's handsome. Get it right, sister," Reign teased, putting a steely look on Tiya. "It's not what he does on the page, in front of the camera, or on stage that's the reason he's doing so well. The real money comes from investing, saving, and living within a reasonable limit."

"But if you really were about the almighty American dollar," Bhavin countered around a mouthful of garlic naan. "Then it wouldn't have been a problem to help me in my career. I look just like Devesh. Some say I'm even more handsome."

"It takes more than good looks and a great body," Reign explained. "He has more to offer—and that's what the industry sees. And so do I."

Bhavin slyly glanced at Devesh. "There were rumors that Devesh ..." He grinned, and there was something evil in that expression. "May have given those directors a little more than just acting."

The implication was out there and so was the bitterness in which it was delivered.

"The reason I left Bollywood is because I wouldn't do that sort of thing," Devesh challenged, but the fact that his brother would put that kind of thing out there was foul.

"The difference between you and my husband," Reign began. "Is that you'd do *whatever* it takes to climb up that ladder, whether you had to sleep with a woman ... or a man. Trust me, there's more than rumors floating around about that. And what do you have to show for it? So I think your sister's calling the wrong brother a whore."

Bhavin turned beet red.

"I hate what this is doing to our family," Anaya said, and her tone was so despondent that Pranav rushed to her side.

"You all are letting things that don't matter become a big issue," Devesh shot back. "You don't approve of my wife, but you certainly don't mind using her to your advantage. She's not having that. Neither am I."

Bhavin stormed from the room.

"What she said earlier," Hiran chimed in studying Tiya as he polished off the snack he had swiped from the kitchen. "Live within a *normal* life budget."

Tiya leveled a stony look at him, and he fell silent. "If you worked harder then—"

"I have three jobs to support you," Hiran shot back, and the bowl almost toppled from his lap. "And it's killing me."

"You think you're so clever," Tiya growled at Devesh, ignoring her husband's heart-felt admission.

"I'll take that," Devesh said cheerily, then he kissed his wife who followed him out of the game room.

❀ ❀ ❀

"Does she have a point?" Reign asked Devesh as he closed the door to the master suite behind them. "Are you with me because you've got mama issues?"

"It's nothing like that," he replied, angered that his sister had managed to plant a seed of doubt in Reign's mind. "When I saw you at the convention, my world shifted again. Being with you, listening to you talk—the feelings all came back. I realized I could not live without you being in my life. No other woman had made me feel as wonderful as you did. Like despite all of my obstacles and challenges, I could still be the best me possible."

Devesh situated her next to him on the chaise. "A lot of women came at me because of my looks."

That had been the case ever since he'd morphed from a scrawny dude to a muscular heart throb. He had to ask himself if he didn't have those two elements going for him—handsome and a bodybuilder's form— would they still want him. He would have to honestly say no. And that was sad. He wanted a woman who loved him for him.

"They'd all tell me the wicked things they wanted to do to me," Devesh said. "But you never paid me empty compliments on my looks or body. You praised any achievements, my charity work and things of that nature. That meant everything to me. You saw who I really was."

Reign laced her fingers with his.

"That night when I was laid up, I asked you to stay with me because simply your presence was enough to make me feel better. Your sitting in the chair across from the bed eased my mind. I loved talking to you, as you had insight about life that was incredible. I didn't want you to leave."

"Is that why you asked me to rest on the opposite side of the bed?"

"Exactly. And you laid so far on the edge that one inch more and you would've been on the floor." He touched his forehead to hers and they shared an easy laugh.

Sometime during that night, he had reached for and resituated her so she wasn't nearly falling off. She had turned to him, and he'd held her in his arms. They stayed that way all night, and it had felt so right. "You were smiling the next morning," he said. "I wasn't ready to let you go, but when I said we needed to talk, you said "tomorrow. We'll talk tomorrow. We have things to do today.'"

Tomorrow never came. They were always working, busy, recapping their day. He had never said what he needed to say, that he loved her, that he wanted to be with her in every way.

"With you, life felt right; it felt good, it felt … awesome. I wanted you regardless of what my family felt. But then you disappeared."

She looked away, then cast her eyes down as though maybe she was beginning to regret the years they missed out on. He gently turned her face toward him. "But you're here now. I want to do right by you and our amazing children."

They would have a two-parent household with a mother and father to look out for them. The children would see them working together. The same way his parents had done for many years. That's how marriages worked. The parents stayed together, made good choices, achieved things together. He could do that with Reign.

"Can I tell you one of the things I love about you?" he asked.

She broke eye contact with him again, seeming to resist the pull the sound of his voice had on her.

"You pay attention to the little things. For example, I've never reached up for the shampoo and come back with an empty bottle. And these." He gestured to the few clothes he still had in the closet. "Don't think I haven't noticed that you put some of my old clothes somewhere and kept the ones you said make me look good."

Reign gave him a sheepish smile and averted her gaze again. "I did that?"

Before he answered, he pulled her into his arms and kissed her gently. "You're slowly slipping in some new garments that fit my new style."

Reign didn't bother to deny it.

"I noticed how you schedule my personal appointments, coordinating them with Jay, making sure to space them so I have time to breathe and spend time with the twins. I notice everything you're doing, honey. And I appreciate you. Thank you, my love. Thank you," he said and slid her hands into his. "So if Tiya's going to believe that I chose to be with you because I've got mama issues, then I'm going to let her believe whatever she wants." He gave her a sly smile and puckered up for a kiss. Reign gave him a peck on the lips, then he added, "I'm happy, and Tiya's miserable. So is Bhavin. Let's leave them that way."

She inhaled slowly and let out a calming breath. "At the convention, when you were so attentive, I was confused," Reign confessed. "You know, sometimes men smile at a woman. For some reason, she immediately reads more into it. She'll have them married, with children, and a white picket fence, when all he meant was a simple smile."

Devesh chuckled.

"I didn't want to be that woman," she said. "Reading more into it than you meant. You embrace everybody, but it seemed like you held onto me a lot longer. It could've just been my imagination—"

"Running away with you?"

"Good one," she said about his reference to a Temptations song.

"I meant it, honey," he said. "Everything I did, I meant it. I was so happy to see you after all that time, but the feelings that I thought were long gone came back full force."

"So … did you plan on…"

"No. I … No. I planned to come at you the right way, after I told my people what was what. Blessing or no blessing, I was coming for you."

Reign locked gazes with him.

"That night was phenomenal, Reign."

"Truthfully?"

He nodded. "If I had known that making love to you would cure what ailed me, I would've put in an order for that before I landed in Atlanta. No Biofreeze. No anti-inflammatories. No Aleve or Tylenol. Just some good old-fashioned loving. That right there should be on the market."

Reign laughed, smacking him on his rear end. "You are so silly."

chapter 27

"Mama, is it okay if Papa washes me?"

Devesh trailed behind his quick-footed daughter, soap in one hand, soft sponge in the other and a scowl that voiced his displeasure more than words ever could.

Leena's bath towel was barely wrapped around her, and it was so large she was having a time of trying to keep it around her body. Amazing how she'd managed to do so after covering so much square footage of the Maharaj house. The twins knew how to bathe themselves, but they'd been in the pool and needed to get the chlorine out of their hair. Jay was coming to get the munchkins in an hour to take them back to his condo to watch the original Wizard of Oz and The Wiz, so he could show them why he called them *munchkins*. Devesh had taken up the task since Reign was helping Mumma with planning Aunt Kavya's birthday celebration.

"Yes, sweetheart," Reign answered slowly, taking in the glint of anger that flashed in Devesh's eyes. "It's alright."

Kamran peered around the edge of the threshold and Reign waved him back, figuring that he hadn't shown his full body because he, unlike his sister, had covered the entire walk to the den in his birthday suit.

Curious glances shot their way. Once again, she hated the close proximity of his family and the fact that privacy was only relative in the area that Devesh still claimed whenever they were visiting. The closing on their new home couldn't come fast enough. He finally had to let Reign in on the secret because packing up the condo was going to be a lot more involved than their move from the Maharaj place. If things had gone as planned, they would have already been in the new place.

Devesh lowered until he was eye level with Leena. "Go on back to the bathroom and brush your teeth. I'll be right back to help with your hair, baby girl."

"Okay," she said and dashed off.

He waited until Kamran and Leena had cleared the area before he spun and faced Reign full-on. "You're projecting your fears onto our daughter?"

"It's about safety," she defended, trying to keep her voice level. "She knows her body belongs to her, and that no one should *touch* that part of her. That's not me being fearful or making her fearful. That's smart."

"Just because that low place you come from isn't safe," Tiya said, interjecting her unwanted thoughts and presence into the conversation. "Doesn't mean that it's not safe here."

"Oh, you want to go there?" Reign taunted, placing her iPad on the end table as she stood. "Alright, then let's talk about the fact that *none* of the girl children in your family want to go anywhere near one uncle in particular. Yet, the adults force them to."

"Reign," Devesh warned as his parents came to their feet, putting an intense focus on his wife.

"Y'all are so involved in eating, dancing, drinking, and having a grand old time that you forget to keep an eye out for your children, grandchildren, nieces, and nephews. There are things happening right under your noses." She scanned the faces of everyone. "And you have the nerve to question me?"

She whipped around to face Devesh, whose expression was

thunderous. "I was in the Nation of Islam for five years. When I left, three things remained with me. A Nation can rise no higher than its woman. Pork is something I should never consume. And a girl child over five years of age should not sit on the lap of any man. Not even their own fathers."

Reign slowly pivoted until she put her eyes on Mumma. "Now, I didn't give a lot of thought to that last one because I had a son at the time. But given what happened to my sister, I began noticing when people say give Uncle So-and-so a hug or a kiss, and that child doesn't want to." She slid a glance at the women who wore expressions that ranged from shocked to perplexed. "The grown-ups either didn't see—or worse, didn't care that the child is anxious or reluctant about being near someone. But we adults *can't* overlook something like that. A child's instinct can be more accurate than ours, and if you give them the idea that their bodies can be commanded by any adult, that's just the thing that teaches the child that they don't have the power to say 'No.'"

She moved forward until she was only a few inches from Tiya. "And I let my children know that they can talk to me about *anything*." She studied some of the men who were spread out near the entrances to the living room and the den. "That no one can threaten to harm them, me, or their father just to keep them quiet about something hurtful that's being done to them. Children are counting on the adults to keep them safe. So don't question how I choose to make that happen."

"We don't have anyone here that does that," Tiya said, smirking at Reign. "This family is safe."

Reign laughed, and the sound of it was bitter to her own ears. "Let's go there, then. Notice how one relative in particular only wants the *girl children* to sit on his lap? Never the boys, though." She moved until she was facing Anaya as she said, "Or how your daughter cries and squirms to get away every time you force her to touch him?" Reign shrugged and threw up her hands in a show of nonchalance. "But hey," she crooned. "That's not *my* business, though. You're so busy trying to be all up in how I'm raising my children that you're slipping on the fact that something's not quite right with yours."

The men seemed especially tense as Papa looked their way and frowned, his eyes darting to each one, trying to ascertain who Reign meant.

"So you get all up in your feelings because my daughter is aware of her body, her father is new to her, and she asks if he is allowed to see or touch her naked body. And you also have issues when Leena doesn't want to slide up onto that uncle's lap, and he tries to scare her into obeying." She let that hang tight for a minute as people mentally flipped scenarios, trying to figure out who she meant.

She tilted her head. "Notice that the only adults in this house that my children ever go to is their father, Papa, Mumma, Aunt Kavya, Anaya, and Pranav. No. One. Else." Reign quirked a questioning brow. "They avoid Tiya as much as possible, more than anyone else in this house."

Tiya cocked her head. "That's because you've taught them to be as stubborn, standoffish, and close-minded as you are."

"I didn't have to say a word. Children want love, and they are well aware who's giving it and who doesn't have an ounce of it in their souls. They can feel the hatred or indifference coming from the rest of you. You view them as something less than children. They are not as important as your full-bred Indian children."

Tiya blew out a cynical breath and rolled her eyes.

"So forgive me if I err on the side of keeping my children safe," she snarled. "Rather than have them spend a lifetime in therapy trying to deal with the pain that could've been avoided if adults had been doing their job."

Silence followed. The kind where folks stewed in their own thoughts.

"Oh, and maybe my children are doing your job as well," she said with a pointed look at a red-faced Tiya. "Why do you think my daughter always comes to *your* daughter's aid, asking her to play with her when you're forcing her to do as that uncle says? You thought Leena was being bossy, but she was subtly forcing him to relinquish his hold on your daughter. And it happens more times than you realize." She gave everyone a patient smile. "My four-year-old has better sense than some adults around this camp."

When no one responded, she continued with, "I may not have been your ideal choice for Devesh's mate, but I'm definitely God's best choice to be the mother of his children." Reign scanned the range of solemn faces focused on her. "In the back of your minds, y'all know that something's off with that uncle I'm talking about. You can keep ignoring it, but he will never have an opportunity to hurt my children. No one in this house or on this earth will do to them what he's been allowed to do to your little girls."

Anaya froze, stared down at her child, then at Uncle Mitul who met her startled gaze head-on, almost daring her to say something. Realization dawned, and she snatched her daughter from his lap and ran from the room.

"Uncle Mitul, aren't you going to defend yourself against what she's saying?" Devesh asked, putting a glare on the man with hawk-like features and beady eyes.

"Why should I?" he shot back with a shrug. "The accusations do not hold. I have not done anything wrong. Why should we listen to this kalankani?

Devesh crossed the distance in six smooth strides. "She. Is. My. Wife!"

Uncle Mitul was off the sofa. Bhavin stepped in and quickly slid between Devesh and his uncle, holding Devesh back after that derogatory word left the older man's lips. A word that meant a woman who has a blackened face because she has committed a sin or slept with or married a man outside of their culture.

"Tune your lips to call my wife out of her name again," Devesh growled, craning his neck around Bhavin's body. "And I will show you how much respect I don't have for you." Devesh gripped Bhavin's arms and said, "If I'm going to do some damage, you won't be able to stop me."

Bhavin raised his hand in mock surrender.

Mitul laughed, his round belly shaking with the effort. "Get a little taste of some black magic and all of a sudden you are turning against family."

"I'm not turning against anyone," Devesh defended, facing the man who puffed up, trying and failing to match Devesh's towering height since he was a whole foot-and-a-half shorter. "Sometimes outsiders can see things the family is too close to notice. She might be wrong, but guess what I'm not going to do? Wait and find out. Not on my watch."

"You are going to take the word of that … that—" Uncle Mitul caught himself before he used that word again and suffered the consequences. Devesh was not in a playing mood. "You have chosen her over your family. She has no proof of anything," he cried, jamming his hands in his pockets. "None of the children have said any such thing."

"She's not lying," Anaya called out from the entrance to the den. She must have left Keva in another part of the house.

A chilling silence descended on all of the rooms.

"She's not lying," Anaya repeated, moving further into the family room until she was in front of her parents. "You always let him babysit us while you were traveling to India. He insisted that Aunt Kavya go with you and he'd stay behind." Anaya put her focus on Uncle Mitul. "No one questioned why."

"She's the one," Mitul roared, pointing an accusing finger at Reign. "She says these bad things and all of a sudden people are believing them. She is crazy."

Papa's hands clenched into fists, his trembling lips a sure sign he was making every effort to remain calm. Mumma put a grip on his hand, struggling to hold him in place.

"He said I was the pretty one," Anaya whispered, forcing Mitul into silence. "I was special. No one was more special than me." She ran into Devesh's open arms and absorbed his comfort before focusing on Tiya, who was rigid with shock. "But Tiya was *special*, too. So were his daughters Ritu, Savina, and cousin Monika. That's probably why Rita and Savina left home the moment they turned eighteen. We haven't seen them since." Anaya's focus landed on her mother, who had covered her face and cried. "I was too afraid to say anything because you all loved him so much. Who would believe me? He said no one would believe me."

Yet, your silence allowed that man to continue doing this to others—even your own child. Devesh kept that thought to himself, though the moment he locked gazes with Reign, he was certain that was going through her mind as well.

Papa slowly circled until he was a few feet from Uncle Mitul. His expression was so pained, it took everything within Reign not to cry.

"I pushed it to the back of my mind," she whispered, and wrapped her arms around her midriff.

"What he did made it hard for me to love my wonderful husband," she said, lips trembling as the words flowed from her lips. Pranav couldn't know how much I hurt. Not just my body, but everywhere. Being "special" was not supposed to hurt."

Pranav finally got over the shock that came with that hurtful admission. He rushed to his wife's side, taking her from Devesh's hold.

"You are not even her *real* husband," Mitul taunted Devesh, beckoning for Aunt Kavya to come toward him. She remained squarely in place. "Could not even demand a *real* marriage. What kind of man allows that? And you are listening to her lies. I have never touched Anaya—ever."

"Anaya is telling the truth," Meenu said and slumped down on the nearest chair as though weighted by that admission.

Mitul abandoned any other attempt to get to his wife and tried to make his way to the front door by himself. Devesh slid to the side so he and his father fully blocked the man's path.

Soon stories spilled out from Anaya and Meenu on how they had been violated in the worst way. They all felt that it was their fault because he'd given them one reason or another to believe that lie. He said it would make them good little Indian girls; cure them of their "American ways". Only he could make them good. Only he could make them special. For some reason, it took harming them, destroying their innocence to make them that way. It also took threatening them, shaming them to secure their silence. Their secrecy had allowed him to run his ugly game on nearly every female in the family long before they had their first menses. Tiya had not admitted anything, but her shell-shocked expression spoke a truth her tongue would not utter.

Devesh's expression was murderous and a direct match for Papa and Pranav. His tone was barely civil when he said, "Uncle Mitul—"

"Come, Kavya," Mitul commanded his wife who seemed to shrink in a matter of moments. "They need to cool off and figure out that these girls are lying about me. Let us go for a walk. Now!"

Mumma quickly translated a summation so Aunt Kavya would understand what had transpired.

Aunt Kavya's face flushed with embarrassment. Her husband's shame was now her own. She adjusted her weight on the sofa and moved to stand next to Mumma, tears streaming down her face; the same as nearly every woman in the four connecting rooms. Her chest heaved and then with a speed and strength no one could have ever believed possible, Aunt Kavya streaked past Papa, lunged for her husband, hands encircled his neck. She tightened her hold as she shrieked a barrage of curses in Hindi.

"Help me," Uncle Mitul screamed, lashing out, first trying to extract her hand, then to block the strikes coming at him in rapid succession. Aunt Kavya had a mean right hook and wasn't afraid to use it.

Several men moved forward.

"Her daughters ..." Reign said, causing the men closest to Aunt Kavya to stay in place.

Pranav and Devesh stepped back, giving Aunt Kavya free range to pummel her husband with blow after blow.

Bhavin finally stepped in to put an end to the skirmish. Only then did Pranav and Devesh extract her deadly grip from Uncle Mitul's neck.

He slumped to the ground, coughing and trying to breathe.

"Uncle Mitul," Devesh began and then waited for the man to wipe the blood from his face with the edges of his plaid shirt. "Someone will pack your things, but you'll need to leave here tonight."

"This is my home," he cried, trembling with equal amounts of outrage and fear. "Where am I supposed to go?"

"Back to India," Uncle Samar said, folding his arms across his broad chest and a few of the men nodded and voiced consent. All except Papa, Devesh, and Pranav who pulled out his cell to make a call.

Reign laughed, and it caused all the attention to snap to her. "So you're going to pack him back to India, where he'll be free to molest more children?" she scoffed, leaning on Devesh for support. "That's one thing my culture, yours, and the Catholic Church have in common. Playing musical chairs with the pedophiles."

Papa's eyes closed, trying to calm that rage that was evident in his expression. When he opened them, he focused on Reign.

"Rape and molestation are the most common crimes against women and children," Reign said with a pointed look at Devesh. "Here and in India." Reign narrowed a studying gaze on Tiya, who was too frozen to do anything but listen. Her husband hadn't bothered to give her the kind of comfort that the others were doing for their wives at the moment. "So don't ever talk to me about Indian culture being better than anyone else's. You all don't protect your women and children any better than anyone else does. And men like him get away with it because you, like other cultures, don't hold women and children in high enough esteem to punish predators like him." She shrugged yet again, spread out her hands in supplication. "But hey, that's not my business, right?"

"No, that is not how we will handle this," Papa said, finally finding his voice.

Devesh trembled with unspoken rage. He struggled to keep a steady gaze on Reign. She realized that she shouldn't say anything else. Unless she helped her husband find a sense of calm, she was going to lose him to the penal system. She did have his bail money, but that was beside the point. The victims in all this had said everything that needed to be said.

"As long as he's not here, India will work fine," Samar said, his face moist with a thin sheen of perspiration. Several of the men agreed.

"You think he's going to stop?" Devesh roared, snapping everyone else to attention. "How old is Anaya? How old is Ritu? Savina? Tiya?" He scanned the expressions of family members who were suddenly transported inside a nightmare they didn't know existed. "He hasn't stopped in all this time because he hasn't had to. We keep providing him new children and opportunities."

Only the men were making the decision in this, when it was the women and their children being violated.

"Her father guards her in her childhood; her husband guards her in her youth; and her sons guard her in her old age. A woman is not fit to act on her own," Reign said, repeating an ancient Indian Dharmasastras as she looked first to Anaya, then to Mumma, Sana, and even Tiya. "You can love and respect the men of this family, but you can't allow them to let him get away with what he's done to you."

She went into Devesh's waiting arms, and he whispered into her ear, "I apologize. I took it personally that Leena asked you if I could bathe her, and I should not have. If we had been taught that way, my sister wouldn't have had to endure the things she did." He tucked a few strands of hair behind his ear. "Why wouldn't she tell me? All that time, he'd been hurting her, hurting them, and no one knew?"

"Because the adults love him and never suspected he'd stoop so low."

"I never liked him," Devesh growled. "He's always been a bully—not just to the children. Mama insisted that her sister come to California. We thought Uncle Mitul would remain in New York, since he loved it so much and had several business dealings there. I was disheartened when he arrived two months later. Should've picked up on the fact that he was a pervert long before now."

Leena appeared in the doorway fully dressed with Kamran directly behind her. "Papa?"

Reign put a grip on Devesh's arm to get him to come with her. She quickly placed Leena in his arms. Only then did he let out a long, slow breath and place a kiss on Leena's temple.

"Papa, we took a shower," Leena whispered so only her parents would hear. "Jay said he would wash our hair when we get to his place."

"That's fine," Devesh said. "And I'm sorry that I didn't get back up there in time."

"Grown up stuff?"

"Yes, sweetheart," he replied, tweaking her nose

Reign picked up Kamran who tightened his arms around her neck and laid his head on her shoulder. In the center of the family room, Mumma held onto Anaya, whose sobs mingled with several other women who were now locked in the prisons of personal secrets that had been revealed.

Devesh transferred Leena to Pranav, then held open his arms. Tiya ran to him, nearly knocking him over as she held on, shedding her own tears. Papa eventually released Anaya and came to take Tiya from Devesh's hold and continued consoling her for a moment. Mumma soon realized that Tiya's tears meant that even though she did not admit it out loud, there were things that happened she was still too ashamed to admit.

Reign scanned the range of expressions of the men in the room, then to the grandmothers, mothers, sisters, and aunts. "Whether Mitul goes or you decide to let him stay," she said. "Just make sure it's understood that if he ever comes near my children, I. Will. Kill Him."

"She won't get the chance," Devesh said, extracting the cell from his pocket. "He'll stay here for as long as it takes for the police to get here and sort things out."

Pranav clapped a hand over Devesh's shoulder plucking the phone from his hands. "They're already on the way."

❁ ❁ ❁

Reign watched Aunt Kavya for a moment, her pained expression and eyes darting everywhere were sure signs that she was filtering through her memories, trying to figure out what she'd missed. Thoughts were probably leaning toward: *How could such a thing happen without my knowledge?* Most of the family was going to fault her, even though she very well could have been in the dark about all of it. She had just witnessed her life imploding in front of everyone she loved, but the looks a few of them were sending her way said they had already considered her guilty.

From what Reign had heard tonight—Uncle Mitul's inability to travel with everyone else because of some unspecified "illness," also letting his passport expire on purpose; and the clincher—that Aunt Kavya was not a good wife so he didn't want to be around her much. All of this meant Aunt Kavya was as much a victim as the girls he'd molested.

"Aunt Kavya, please get your things and come with us," Reign said.

Devesh was in total agreement. They had more than enough room at the condo.

"She needs to be around family right now," Tiya challenged, straightening her shoulders in a defiant move that made some of the conversations trickle to a halt.

"She needs to be around people who will support her," Reign countered, sweeping a gaze to some of the family members behind her. "Several of them believe that she knew something. They're not taking into account how slick pedophiles can be. They are crafty liars. He did these things when she was out of the house or traveling with your mother. He groomed those girls right in front of *every last one of you*— not just in front of Aunt Kavya. And he's still doing it with the current generation of children. All except mine."

Reign placed a hand on Devesh's chest as she looked up at him. "Aunt Kavya's been lying next to a man who's brought shame to the family and hurt her daughters in unspeakable ways. She needs a fresh start." She searched his eyes for a moment. "Ask her what she wants to do. Give her a way to make money on her own so she doesn't feel like a charity case. But more importantly, find her daughters and bring them back to her. She needs to know that they're alright and they need to know that everyone will believe them." Reign's hands trailed upward to his face. "Devesh, you've been all about charity for others. Now, charity needs to begin right here at home."

chapter 28

Family and friends dinners were suspended for two weeks to give the immediate family a chance to get a handle on what happened that night and to give statements to the police. The experience was hardest on the children who had to be consoled by their unsuspecting parents, and later counseling with a therapist who specialized in sexual abuse.

Aunt Kavya moved in with Devesh and Reign. And in a few days time, with Jay's help, they had found Ritu and Savina. Jay set up a video conference for the women to speak. His cousins promised to consider coming to visit for the next East Indian holiday. Aunt Kayva was still weeping with joy over seeing and speaking with her long-lost daughters.

Today's dinner celebration was centered around Raksha Bandhan—or Rakhi. This evening when Jay arrived to the house after taking his siblings out for a day at the beach, Anaya and Devesh gave them the material to tie a thread—making a talisman or amulet to place on their wrists as a form of protection. The protection is offered principally by sisters to brothers and the day is observed to appreciate the bond they share. Devesh had given one to Anaya and Tiya. Now Jay and Kamran had made ones and gave them to Leena. She beamed at Anaya and held up her wrists, matching her amulet to the one on her Aunt's wrist. Anya kissed the top of Leena's head and smiled. "Yes, I think yours is prettier."

Reign watched all of them leave the den where others were making their own bracelets for their siblings. Then she placed the plates around the dining table at Maharaj place, preparing for the family dinner that was taking place for the first time since that night Uncle Mitul was taken into custody. Jay had finally accepted an offer from Devesh to have dinner with the family, and the men quickly shuttled him into the game room for Spades.

Pranav wandered in from the kitchen, then watched Reign for a brief moment before picking up the last of the plates on the buffet and sliding them into the empty spaces.

"Your son is killing it in there," he said causing Reign to smile.

"Were you behaving yourself in there?" She nodded toward the game room where the sounds of laughter filtered in from time to time, including Jay's, who seemed to be having one heck of a good time with the men of Devesh's family.

"I was trying real hard not to. Still got my butt kicked, but I'm going to get a little payback later."

Reign chuckled. "Yes, you are definitely Devesh's friend."

He paused in the middle of repositioning the floral centerpiece. "And as his friend and yours, too, I'd like to say something."

She paused and looked over to him.

"Don't let the family get to you."

Reign opened her mouth and was about to say that they hadn't, but couldn't tell that lie. "I hear you, but it's a little hard. Thankfully, this is only for eight years."

Pranav's instant scowl was an unexpected thing.

"What?" she asked, slowly flickering a look over his scrunched up face.

He shrugged and continued setting out the dinner plates. "If that's what you want."

"I think that's what the family would prefer."

"It's not about them," he said, and his hard tone pulled her up short. "Devesh is in this marriage with *you* – not *them*."

"They mean a lot to him."

"*You* mean a lot to him," he countered gripping the edge of the table, abandoning all efforts to help her finish. "Don't let anyone tell you otherwise."

Reign didn't have a response to that, but if his best friend was saying this, there had to be some truth to it.

"I'm glad you're here," he said, sliding into the seat at the head of the table. "I consider Devesh my brother, and I want for my brother the very thing I have for myself. Contentment and happiness."

She slid a plate and fixed the silverware in front of him.

"Reign?"

"Yes."

"Give him a chance to show you what you all are made of," Pranav said, holding both of her hands in his to halt her movements. "Don't miss out on something that's good for you too."

"I'll keep that in mind," she said, extracting her hands and returning to the task.

Anaya glided in from the kitchen carrying a silver tray of naan. She winked at her husband, who gave her a lengthy onceover that spoke to the fact that he wanted to do some unmentionable things to her later on.

"Get a room," Reign teased, and they both laughed.

Devesh came sauntering in off the solarium, sliding into a shirt to cover his massive chest and six-pack abs.

Leena ran from the solarium right after him, still dripping a little water from the pool even with the towel she had around her body. She barreled straight to her father who picked her up, planted a loud raspberry on her cheek that made her giggle.

"Tum mujhe bahut Khushi deti ho beti," he said, smothering her cheek with kisses

"You bring me joy, too, Papa," Leena quipped as a reply.

Devesh frowned, tilted his head, peering closely at her face as he asked, "Do you speak Hindi?"

Leena froze. Shot an alarmed look toward Reign, her green eyes wide with fright. "Mama?"

"Reign," Devesh said through his teeth, placing his steely focus squarely on his wife. "Do the twins speak Hindi?"

She didn't say anything for a long moment as Pranav, Anaya, and Devesh awaited the answer. Then her shoulders slumped in defeat. "Woh hindi bolte hain aur main bhi."

Yes, they speak Hindi and so do I.

Devesh winced as though she had struck him. Pranav's jaw nearly hit the table.

"Don't tell anyone," she pleaded in a breathy whisper, reaching for him but he evaded her touch.

"Why?" he roared, hardly able to contain his true thoughts. "It's something to be proud of, not hide like it's a dirty little secret."

Aunt Kavya rushed into the room, quickly surveying everyone to figure out what was wrong, and quickly scanned for Tiya. Anaya reached for Leena, but the little girl shook her head and pulled back. A movement he had seen too often as of late.

"People are able to speak their minds right now," Reign said in a quiet tone.

"What difference does that make," he snapped, as Leena allowed Aunt Kavya to take her from his arms causing Anaya to grimace at the slight. What had happened between Anaya and Leena?

"Knowing who's for us and against us keeps us safe," she said gesturing for the children to go into the solarium.

Devesh weighed those words for a moment. "I don't like this, Reign. Maybe people will be more mindful of what they say."

The strangest movement transformed Anaya's expression from blank to alarmed, and it caused both Devesh and Pranav to study her for a moment.

"What?" Devesh asked his sister.

"Some of them have said some pretty horrible things about … her." She placed a wary look on Reign.

"Within your hearing?" Devesh challenged.

Anaya snailed a nod.

"And you said nothing," Pranav interjected, and his tone dripped with contempt.

She didn't bother to reply.

So much for getting a little pickle tickle tonight.

Now Reign understood why the children tended to avoid even Anaya these days. They were well aware she, even after all this time, still did not care for their mother. They were well versed in showing their displeasure. Not allowing her into their world—was one. No fake friends. No fake family, either.

"Like I said," Reign continued, her face a mask of indifference. "It's nice to know who our enemies are."

Devesh gave a parting contemptuous look at Anaya and aimed for the kitchen, but paused when Bhavin's voice carried from the game room.

"Turn that off," Bhavin said, his voice dripping with disdain. "All that Black Lives Matter crap. If Black people spent more time being productive than criminals, then there wouldn't be the need for all that foolishness. They're just lazy and don't want to do anything with their lives."

A hushed silence fell over all four corners as some of the family seemed angry, but looked at Reign and Jay to gauge their reaction. Even the children's board game in the solarium slowly came to a trickling halt. Reign's chest heaved. She stepped forward, but Devesh, who had his eye on Jay, held her back.

Leena and Kamran burst out of the solarium, ran past the kitchen, to the dining room and rushed to Jay's side. They took one of his hands in theirs, as though to ground him. Lengthy or sudden silences in the Maharaj house tended to be because of Tiya, Bhavin, or Reign—two troublemakers and one rebel. Evidently, Jay was about to be on that same trajectory.

"And East Indian men would be better off if they didn't rape and mutilate their women," Jay tossed out.

Shocked gasps and roars of discontent swept through all of the rooms as Jay locked a steady focus on Bhavin.

Devesh leaned against the gathering table, shifting uncomfortably as he remained silent, waiting for Jay to bring the point home. He was certain that those weren't Jay's true sentiments.

"All East Indians aren't rapists," Bhavin said between his teeth.

"And all Blacks aren't criminals."

The silence behind that truth lingered for a hot minute. Bhavin scanned the people nearest him and found that most of their expressions had transformed from anger to totally blank. Point taken.

"You don't get to throw that kind of verbal Molotov cocktail out there and not expect for me to rise up," Jay said taking a few steps toward Bhavin who was more than a little taken aback that he was being challenged this way. "You've got the wrong Black man."

"So all this marching and protesting is about what?" Bhavin said, gesturing in a wide circle. "If y'all are so unhappy here, why don't you go back to Africa."

Devesh let loose with a curse under his breath. This time Reign's hand snaked out to keep him from interfering. He exhaled, steadying his focus on the two men in the center of the room.

"Jay—" Reign began.

Her son held up his hand to stave off anything she could say. "No, no, no. I'm not going to let that slide either. Go back to Africa?" he asked, and his voice was hard and intense. "Seriously? And where did y'all come from?" He tilted his head as though studying Bhavin for a major malfunction. "You get to enjoy being here, working here on American soil? Living here, why? Because *we* built the foundation of this country and its economy. *We* built this city, and I'm not talking about on Rock 'n' roll, either. It was our blood, sweat, and tears. Because the people who took this place from the First Nation, didn't want to do any of the heavy lifting. So they enslaved the ones who were already here and brought millions over in ships under deplorable conditions." Jay inhaled and let out a long, slow breath. "This place was built on the sorrow of Black women who were—" Jay looked down at his siblings and said, "Leena and Kamran, why don't you and the other children go back into the solarium and play for a little while."

Kamran frowned and looked up at his brother defiantly and said, "We know this stuff already."

"Yes," Jay agreed, nodding toward the children at the entrance point between the kitchen and the dining room. "But they don't."

"They should," he countered, and his little lips set in a thin line—a perfect imitation of his father.

"You're right, but not now," Jay put his eyes back on Bhavin. "Seems like I need to take their parents to school first."

"You called us by our names," Kamran said, still keeping a hold on Jay's hands. "We're not munchkins anymore?"

"You'll always be munchkins, because I'm the oldest," he countered, struggling to hold back a smile. "I'm fine. Really. Now scoot."

Leena grinned before Kamran gave his brother's hand a final squeeze then led her away. The twins corralled their cousins, ushering them back into the solarium.

Some of the tension in the room eased during that exchange before Jay continued, "This place was built on the tears of Black women and little girls who were raped by slave masters, mutilated, killed, their children were taken and sold like cattle. This place was built on the anger and frustrations of Black men who were violated, beaten, had their families separated never to be seen or heard from again. And they were helpless to do anything to help their women, daughters, sisters, mothers while anything and everything was done to them simply because they had no power.

"This place you want us to leave, was built on the backs of people who were property from the time they were born to the point when slavery sent them to a much too early grave." Jay paused, scanned the horrified, anxious, and saddened expressions. "Almost, but not quite, the same as it was in India, right? But how long did y'all put up with that? How long did the British violate your women? How long did they force your people to build their railroads? How long did they kill off thousands, maybe millions of those who fought back?"

Devesh slipped his hand inside Reign's, and she laid her head on his shoulder as they continued to listen.

"See, the difference is," Jay said turning slowly in a circle to look at everyone. "Y'all had the home court advantage. You ran them up out of there, took India back, retained your culture and your land, became a powerful nation again. How many of your ancestors died for that?" Jay lined his body so he was mere inches from Bhavin. "How many of mine died on—This. Soil. Right. Here." He punctuated each word with a finger pointing to the ground. "Enduring things that were much worse than what was done to *your* ancestors." He laughed, but the sound was hollow. "What part of America does not belong to us, too? And you want us to do *what?!*"

Leena tipped in and said, "Is it safe now? Are y'all done with grown-up stuff?"

"Give us a minute," Jay replied, and she ducked away while he locked in on Bhavin once again. He looked at his mother. "Do you feel comfortable sharing your encounter with the police?"

She gave a pensive look in Devesh's direction before starting. "About three months before I moved here, I was pulled over by the police."

Devesh's shoulders tensed and she held up her hand to signal that he should be calm.

"I wasn't speeding or anything," she said. "They believed I was holding my phone and talking while driving. It was dark. They couldn't see into the car to know that I had a blue-tooth connection with a hands-free feature." Reign scanned the family. "For the first time in my life, I felt afraid of the very people who are supposed to serve and protect. Sandra Bland had been killed because a White police officer got pissed at her questioning his motives. She was killed because he felt she'd been arrogant. A simple traffic stop cost her life. Cost Eric Garner his life. Cost Philando Castile his life. And so many others. And people who don't understand the dynamics, justify those lives being taken by saying, 'Well, she should have just put the cigarette out. Well, he shouldn't have done x,y,z. How depraved have we become that we cannot see that injustice is being doled out toward one group more than any other?"

"Don't come for me unless I send for you," Jay warned. "Because I'm going to be ready for you every single time. I am *not* my mother. And truthfully, she can read y'all a whole lot better than I ever could. Y'all better be glad she loves this man right here," he said gesturing toward Devesh.

"Jay, you don't—"

"Mama, quit playing," he said, turning to face her. "You love him. And you need to be a grown up and own up."

Reign flinched under the intensity of those words. Pranav nodded and looked as though he wanted to give Jay a high five.

Devesh's eyes glazed over and he quickly averted his eyes, saying, "There's something in my eye. Must be these allergies or something."

"Or something," Jay said, chuckling. "You don't have allergies."

Devesh held out his fist and gave Jay a pound. "True."

Papa removed his hand from Mumma's waist and stepped forward to speak to Jay. "How do you know so much about our history?"

Jay looked Papa square in the eye. "I felt that if I was going to be part of this family, I needed to learn something *about* this family. I would hope y'all did the same for us. How else can we have a peaceful and respectful understanding built on knowledge and not assumptions? Built on truth and love. If you want our respect, earn it in the same way we hope to earn yours." Jay's gaze went to the entrance. "Kamran is that your tummy growling so loud?"

"Yep. It sure is," Leena answered for her brother who was nodding. "Y'all can do this grown-up thing some other time, but we'd like to eat now, thank you."

Kamran gave a single nod. *And that's that.* The rest of the kiddie crew was in total agreement.

"Alright, Leena," Jay conceded. "I'll climb down off my soap box now."

"Good, 'cause I was gonna throw you a washcloth and some water."

Jay moved toward Leena. She took off running and giggling as everyone laughed at her feisty response to her big brother.

The family and guests began to disperse into different areas, but not before coming to say something encouraging to Jay, beginning an exchange of understanding that was sure to have a lasting impact.

Aunt Kavya pointed the spatula at Bhavin and gave him the evil eye.

Bhavin quickly held up his hands in complete surrender. She leaned in, kissed his cheek, then playfully swatted his rear end on her way to the kitchen to help with dinner service.

"I apologize," Bhavin said to Jay.

All conversations trickled to a halt—again. Even Mumma's head snapped to Bhavin, eyes as wide as saucers. "Did … did he … he just apologize?" she asked in a breathy whisper.

Papa simply nodded as his jaw went slack.

"I meant no disrespect," Bhavin continued.

"Yes, you did," Jay countered smoothly, but added a smile to take away the sting. "But now that you have a little understanding, things could change. You know my mother and my sister and brother. We are nothing like you said. And there are more like us, than the media likes to portray. There's good and bad in every ethnic background. I chose to believe the best in everyone I meet, until they show me something different."

"You're right," Bhavin said smiling as he extended a hand to Jay. "I'm learning."

Anaya gripped Pranav's chest to steady herself, when Jay shook Bhavin's hand and then embraced him before he said, "And don't be mad because we ran a Boston on you and won the game."

Everyone broke out into laughter, chuckles, and guffaws.

Papa and Mumma went to Jay and embraced him warmly and said, "Welcome to the family, son."

A short while later, all of the family filed in from the patio, solarium, game room, theatre and into the dining room where tonight's spread of food was situated.

Bhavin was the one to put his gaze on Pranav first and then to Reign, peering at them as though he had missed out on something. Then he looked down at the desserts and frowned before putting his focus on Mumma. "Where's the rasumulai?"

"Devesh asked me to only serve rice khir instead," she replied unbothered by the curious glances shot her way.

Everyone's attention shifted to Devesh. Those seated around the main table began serving up their meal.

Anaya gestured to the serving bowl of rice khir, then looked at her brother and asked, "What gives?"

He shrugged and said, "Well it's white."

"But it's not the same," she shot back.

"It's creamy," he countered, peering over the rim of the bowl to check the contents.

"And it's different," Sana said.

Mumma leaned into Papa, who gave her a kiss on the cheek before the both of them settled into the head seats on opposite ends of the main table, watching their youngest son.

"And it has most of the same ingredients," Devesh said, stirring the dessert a little.

"Rice khir is not the same as rasmulai," Bhavin offered.

"Right," Devesh said simply. "Now you understand."

Anaya shared a speaking glance with her parents, then her husband before scanning all of the confused expressions at the table. "I don't get it."

"You all are trying to make me have *rice khir* when what I want is *rasmulai*."

Dinner came to a screeching halt. He let those words bounce off the walls for a minute.

"We're going to have this discussion *one last time*," Devesh said, and there was a warning in his tone. "The moral of the story is, you have a problem with my woman, then you have a problem with me. And what that means is that I'm tired of the side discussions and the disrespect aimed at my wife and children. There are *no more* warnings about this. I will not have my woman subjected to it any longer, and that means I'm about to clean house and some of you all will not be welcome here."

The only sound in the house was a Buick commercial playing on the television filtering in from the game room.

"You have an issue, let it stay *your* issue," Devesh warned with a stern look at the people spread across the different rooms. "That means leave it at home or stay home with it. This place benefits all of you. Not simply for these awesome meals, but that your children stay here during the day or after school and receive excellent care. They learn Hindi and

Indian culture. That's a bonus. But it's also a privilege. I will shut it all down and take my wife and children, Mumma, Papa, Aunt Kavya, Pranav, and Jay on the road with me and leave the rest of you to figure it all out on your own."

Mumma and Papa perked up at hearing that suggestion. Mumma leaned over to whisper something in Aunt Kavya's ear. The older woman grinned and gave a thumbs up that almost made Reign laugh out loud.

"You're sounding mighty Black, my brother," Jay said low enough so he could hear.

"Gets the point across?"

"Indeed."

Devesh held back his smile and continued speaking to everyone else. "Reign is beautiful. She is *everything* I desire in a woman. All the right ingredients *for me*. You all want me to put my desires aside so you can serve me up something that is not to my taste."

He gently pushed the huge serving bowl of rice khir toward the center of the dining room table before accepting the smaller bowl that Mumma held out to him.

"Rasmulai," he asked, though he was certain that everyone was already aware of the contents.

"Of course, my son," she said, with a loving smile.

Devesh snatched up the closest spoon, then teased everyone by moaning as the creamy dessert slid down his throat. He placed the spoon on a napkin, then scanned the faces of his family.

Anaya's tongue snaked out to wet her lips. Tiya's infamous sour face was in place again. Bhavin looked as if he was ready to snatch the bowl from Devesh's hand.

Devesh lifted the goods and said, "Enjoy your dinner. Oh, and dessert."

Then he nodded toward Jay and Pranav, gesturing for them to grab up a few spoons to share in the bounty and follow him. Then hooked his free arm under Reign's, and whistled all the way to the living room leaving an angry family behind.

Laughter from Mumma, Papa, and Aunt Kavya trailed after them.

❦ ❦ ❦

"I never realized that people we consider the beautiful ones have a whole set of issues that don't come into play for everyone else," Reign mused from the lounger out by their condo's pool. She said the calm of the waters soothed her soul.

Devesh studied Reign's face, and saw that she was serious. These sentiments must stem from the discussion that took place at the dinner table tonight. Bhavin still took exception to Devesh and Reign not helping him with his aspirations. He was extremely vocal about it tonight when a commercial came on and Reign's new client was front and center.

"How do you mean?" Devesh asked.

"I didn't understand that people sometimes become so obsessed with their looks and their bodies that they spend all their time chasing beauty." She showed him the image of a social media queen who'd become famous because of a sex tape with a young singer. "Face lifts, drugs, injections, overkill when it comes to diets and workout regimens. Whatever will keep them looking young and pretty."

Devesh wasn't sure how to take that. He was careful about what he ate—no pork or beef, organic chicken, and fish, lots of fresh vegetables and grains—worked out every day, ran a few miles every evening. Was she saying that *he* was vain?

"It's the same with prosperity. People want it so much because they don't understand it," she said, and he ascertained from the abrupt switch in topic, that this was the real reason for the conversation. Something to do with Tiya, or maybe the issue they were currently experiencing. Money was rolling in faster than they could decide what to do with it.

"It's like when people think that hitting the lottery will solve all of their problems." She let her gaze pass over the smiling faces in the magazine—Devesh and Krish, Reign's new client, in an advertising spread for Marc Jacobs. "Then they win all that money and have even more problems." She swiped a hand across her iPad. The characters from House of Cards faded to black. "Remember that guy who was killed because he won a hundred thousand dollars? It cost him his life. Or that woman who spent a good majority of her winnings on a boyfriend who kept landing in jail?" She turned another page. "She wasn't ready for all that prosperity. Most of it is being whisked away by the government. They're holding her money hostage because a man she's too afraid to let go, keeps getting in trouble and they know she's going to bail him out."

Devesh's forehead furrowed with thought.

"Then the problems didn't end there. A church sued her because she told them she'd give them some of it and they wanted their cut." Reign shook her head. "There are folks who had to go into hiding because of family members always having their hands out."

Devesh was all too familiar with that scene. Only Anaya, Pranav, his parents, and now Reign knew that he actually bought the house on Shoreview Drive. They continued to let everyone believe that their parents were the ones who had all the money.

"That's why I've only told three people what kind of cash I have. I didn't want to lose people because of it. My parents sacrificed a lot for me to be able to do what I love. That was no small thing. I owed them, but they insisted that the house should be in my name, so there was no misunderstanding with my brother and sister if ... if something happened."

"And then you break your trust for your children," she said, and her tone was sad.

"That wasn't a sacrifice, honey," he confessed, sinking further into the padded lounger next to her. "That's what a husband does for his wife; it's what a father does for his children. I couldn't very well ask you to leave everything to be with me without putting some type of security on the table. You gave up a lot, simply because you wanted to do what was best for our children. I will never take that lightly."

Devesh extracted the magazine from her hands, flipped it until he came to an advertisement for an island vacation with a couple grinning while on their walk along a tropical beach. "Money has never been all that important to me. Simple things mean so much." He flipped the pages to the article written about him and the wildly positive reception to his success within the East Indian community. "When I was traveling to Africa, Sri Lanka, Dubai and all over Europe, people took me in, fed me, treated me like family," he said, giving her a wry smile. "That's why I was able to meet so many wonderful people and see things, visit the temples and learn what connected and separated people of different cultures. I didn't have any reason to be afraid; I knew that God had me." Devesh took her hand in his. "There's only been one time when I felt any kind of anxiety. When I first told my parents about you, what I saw in their eyes—the disapproval—that was something I couldn't bear." Devesh waited a moment to see how she absorbed that piece of information. "So I didn't pursue what I felt about you seven years ago. How could I go against my family? I wanted children; you had already said you didn't want any more and I understood. When we talked, there was so much you told me, not knowing that I was keeping all of that information in mind."

He watched as her eyes clouded over with some emotion he couldn't name. Devesh let himself relax slowly, allowing his feelings to come forth in a way that he could share with his wife.

"But that week in Atlanta—especially that night—sealed it for me." He slid his hands over hers. "No matter what the differences were, no matter how my family felt, you were going to be mine. And I told them that when I came home. I told Anaya and Pranav how much you helped me, and how much I loved you," he said, and his voice took on a breathy sound as the emotions he felt back then resurfaced, especially the feelings associated with the loss of her in his life. "Then you disappeared from social media. My emails bounced back. Phone calls went straight to voicemail, which you didn't return. I didn't know what to think. My heart hurt. It was actually a physical hurt—a pain like I never knew."

"Oh, sweetheart, I—"

"No, I understand, honey," he whispered. "I thought I knew what love was. I thought I was ready to be with a woman like you. I really did."

He tightened his hold around her more delicate fingers. "But I would've messed things up. I wasn't mature enough to be in a relationship that people were not ready to accept I wasn't in the place that I am now, and that would've been the wrong dynamic for a relationship. I know that now." Their eyes met. "You saw me in a different light."

Before she could take her next breath, he went in for a kiss that was milder than ones he'd given her before. When he pulled his mouth away, she moaned her protest. He was elated.

"If we didn't have that night together five years ago, I would not know that this is making love." He draped a kiss across the smooth skin of her exposed shoulder, causing another tremor of pleasure to shiver through her body. "Or this…" His lips lowered to the swell of her breasts, and she shivered with undisguised heat. "You're so in tune with your sensuality. I learned from you that making love starts in the mind and then travels everywhere else."

Reign shook her head as though trying to clear her thoughts. "Devesh, we're supposed to be having an adult conversation here," she whispered, her arousal evident in her voice and in the heated look in her eyes.

"Yes," he whispered. "I think there is no adult conversation more important than what I want to do to you right now. The children are with Jay and—"

"You said you would give me time," she said, extracting from his embrace.

Devesh froze. The disappointment in his eyes was nearly heartbreaking.

chapter 29

Devesh's lips paused a few inches from hers before pulling away; his erection was straining against his pants. He leaned in to kiss those sensually curved lips he had always found so inviting. He teased them, tasted them, allowing the warmth from her to extend to him.

She responded, opened to him.

Devesh took that to be significant and cupped her hips, pulling her in so they were as close as two people could be.

When he finally looked into her eyes, he said, "Mine. All mine. In every way."

Reign slowly nodded, but the look she gave him was a blend of slightly fearful and anxious as though she still wasn't sure this was the route that they should take.

How could she feel that way after all this time? He knew she loved him. He could feel it.

"What keeps you from loving me?" he asked.

She quickly looked away.

Devesh guided her face back toward him so their gazes would be connected again. "Talk to me," he whispered. "Why are you so afraid of this?"

Reign shook her head.

"Let me know your thoughts, honey," he whispered, in a husky tone. "I don't want to make a misstep here."

Reign swallowed and seemed to lose her ability to speak.

"I know that this marriage was not your choice," he said. "I know you valued your freedom, being single. You once told me that you were prepared to spend the rest of your life alone. But what if God had something different in mind? What if *this* is the way you're supposed to spend your life? With me. My family believes in arranged marriages, but I think God arranged our marriage."

She fumbled with her hands, clearly uneasy with this turn of the conversation.

"This does not have to be something that frightens you; something that makes you afraid to love me. There's nothing wrong with loving me."

"My son is your age," she said.

This again? Seriously? "And? What difference does that make?" he asked, his tone a little harder than intended. "You might not love me the same way that I love you, but that's going to be alright, too. We will give it time." He stroked a hand across the small curve of her back. "I've wanted you a long time, Reign. I've wanted *this* for so long."

She pulled herself up to meet his eyes.

"I love you, honey," he confessed, fingertips gliding over the graceful lines of her neck. "I've loved you from the first day we met. When you bypassed all those other cover models and said, 'My God, I've got to get a picture with *this* guy,' and everybody at the banquet table followed you."

Reign smiled, glancing down at her pink toes.

"Then the next day you came up to me to talk about foods and movies you love, we connected so well." Devesh lifted her chin so that their eyes locked. "That was my first time at that convention. I was kind of a stranger there, and the other models and some of the executives were giving me a hard time. Especially when they heard my accent and didn't think I was American. It felt a little lonely. Then you came, and we had those conversations, and I was laughing and enjoying myself. When everyone else saw us having such a good time, that's when company representatives started coming to check me out, wanting me to be part of their advertising campaigns."

She crooked her mouth into something that was part smile and part something else.

"We don't have to make love tonight," he said, and he was certain that this was the path to take. "When you want me, when you're ready, you reach for me. Then I'll know it's your decision."

Moments ticked by. This time it was Reign who kissed him passionately, then wrapped her arms around his neck, guiding him to her. They were now so close that he could feel her heart beating out of control.

"Are you sure?"

"Yes."

Devesh scooped Reign off her feet and carried her past the gazebo, and the game area into the building, slid in the elevator to their condo, and maneuvered to their bedroom she had furnished in warm colors of reds and creams with charcoal accents.

"You're not settling for second best?" he asked gently laying her on the bed, and there was more in that question than he was willing to put to voice.

She shook her head, realizing he meant the man she'd given up.

"Because I want you to know that you've always been my first choice."

Devesh placed a kiss on her temple. "I'm so glad God saw fit to bring you back to me." He peeled the form-fitting dress from her shoulders and arms, unveiling, undressing, kissing along the smooth expanse of skin, teasing, letting his tongue do the talking for him. He draped his lips across the stretch marks, recognizing the ones that were there a few years ago.

She quickly drew the bed sheet about her body. "I can't have you look at me straight-on," she admitted. "In the past, men wanted me for my personality, but when I took my clothes off, they somehow expected everything to straighten up and fly right."

"Then that's their issue if they don't understand the basic laws of gravity. What comes up, is coming down at some point—they should know that simply from what happens after getting an erection." He cupped her left breast in his hands, lowering to kiss it.

Reign gasped, and there was something in her eyes that she wasn't able to shield before averting her gaze.

"Let's be honest," he said. "We're not talking about *them*. It's *him*. He's still affecting you after all this time?" Devesh whispered, unable to believe this barrier still existed. "You can't let him be this important to you. What I say—what *your husband* says—overrules some donkey who didn't see your value in the first place." He peered at her a moment. "How long ago were you with him?"

"Jay was maybe six, seven," she said, frowning.

"And how old is Jay now?"

"Thirty-one."

Devesh leveled an intense focus on her. "So that man has been holding your self-esteem hostage all this time?"

Reign grimaced but didn't come up with a reply.

"Will you allow me to set you free, my love?" Then he touched his lips to the few stretch marks that had to come from carrying his children. The battle scars that added to her beauty, that told the story of her life. He moved lower, kissing the place on her knees where she had run from a schoolmate and tripped over a concrete barrier, creating a wound that took a year to heal. Then he pressed his lips to the healed mark where the phone charger had accidentally disconnected from her cell. The open end had seared her skin while she slept.

Devesh kissed the fullness of breasts that had nourished his children and were now so sensitive that a slight bit of cool air would make them aroused. He draped his hands along the width of her hips, which provided a welcome pleasure. He kept his focus on her eyes, watching the emerald orbs as the desire lit a pathway to arousal. Her breathing became labored as though she was struggling for each breath. Then he prepared to join them—body and soul—knowing that this final threshold in their relationship would only serve to bring them even closer.

"I'll be right back," Devesh said, sliding from the bed.

"Alright," she sighed.

"I have to find a condom."

She sat up, frowned at him. "Do you have something I need to know about?" she asked, stopping him in his tracks. "I mean, it's a little late to ask but ..."

He didn't turn to her when he answered, "No, but I thought you wouldn't be too happy if you got pregnant again."

She laughed, hard. "No worries about that. After the twins were born, I told Dr. Taylor I'd tie those tubes myself if she didn't do it."

Devesh lowered his head and joined in her laughter. He turned, and still completely mesmerized, he slowly undressed. Then he drank in the lusciousness of her curves; raking a slow gaze from the tips of her pedicured toes to those lovely thighs, hips that were made for him to hold onto, and small curve of her belly that held a few small signs of how she had given three people the opportunity to come into this world. Her breasts—so full and ripe, brought an excitement all their own. Her beautiful lips were slightly parted in wanton expectation of the exquisite torture he would put her through.

Completely in all of his naked glory, Devesh crossed the distance between them, took her hand and brought it to his lips. He guided her into his arms and captured the gasp that tried to escape from her mouth.

She closed her eyes when a heated response shook her body the moment Devesh took a nipple into his mouth, curled his tongue around it, and began teasing her to the point that she couldn't take in a solid breath if she wanted to.

❧ ❧ ❧

Those well-defined muscles felt hard and firm beneath her trembling fingers, and he guided her forward, pressing her even more tightly against him. His scent, warm and heady, forced her to inhale him, take him in and let it explode in the corners of her mind.

And then splaying his fingers across her buttocks, he opened her up, leaned forward and sank his mouth into her. He teased here, nibbled there, and when she cried out his name he put so much intensity into that never-ending kiss that she nearly lost her hold on reality and him. She moaned in response to the shivers of pleasure that whipped through her like a tornado in search of vulnerable land.

"My woman," he said in a deep and throaty voice. "Every inch, every curve, every dip, breasts I can barely hold in my hands, thick thighs that are meant to be wrapped around me—all of it belongs to me."

She watched as he studied her features and figured he was wondering how to give her what she needed most. She didn't realize until this moment that she already had it.

Unconditional love.

❀ ❀ ❀

Devesh exhaled deeply as he moved toward her, fully aware that he still had his work cut out for him. More than simple insecurities had a hold of her. The pain that she had harbored ran deep, and it had provided more resistance than she probably knew. But that was alright. For a time, he had loved enough for both of them. Tonight she would realize she could open to him, and his love.

He parted her thighs and eased into that part of her world that had been denied him for what seemed an eternity. He moved with her, entering that classic dance of love which is something they both wanted and needed. Devesh held on to her, dragging in a deep breath when those moist walls clamped him tightly, squeezing and demanding a release that he had prayed for so long.

Five years, and this was his jubilee. To be inside her this way, to be fully aware, connected in all the ways that a man should be when he loved a woman this deeply, was heaven unto itself. She trembled in his arms, gripping him, using his body as a stronghold keeping her tethered to reality. He was inside her again, crushing her to him, unwilling to let her go now or ever.

"I love you, Nareigna Lisa," he whispered in a breathy moan.

"I love you more, Devesh Ahn—"

Devesh was inside her once again, his mouth swallowing the sound of his name, taking her within, relishing the taste of her, the feel of her soft skin, the sound of her moans trapped and unable to make their presence truly known.

"Main tumse pyaar, karta hun, mera suraj, meri duniya, meri Hukumat," he whispered.

I love you. My sun. My world. My universe. My Reign.

The orgasm that ripped through her triggered his own. He barely managed to hold it at bay for a few moments longer, watching as her eyelids shuttered to close over emerald orbs that were gleaming with passion.

The moment she went still from the throes of that subsiding orgasm— He. Came. Undone.

chapter 30

"Mumma, this is for you."

Anaya smiled at Leena, who left her side carrying a glass of fresh mango juice that she'd helped press with Anaya overseeing the process.

The children were adjusting to life with the Maharaj family extremely well. Reign and Jay had won over even more of the adults because they couldn't deny the positive impact her twins were having on their children.

Anaya had marveled at how the cousins were shifting their focus from video games to the board games that the twins favored. Reign pointed out that while videos games were great for developing eye-hand coordination and reflexes, the children were thrilled about the confidence they found as they tapped into skills they'd never been encouraged to use before. They were learning, thinking, reasoning, strategizing, and partnering up to win. She knew from experience that when children are taught to observe, think, and communicate, they can learn anything—do anything. She simply offered to share the things that had worked in her experience.

Reign had brought out a system called Sing, Spell, Read & Write that she'd used with her oldest son and then the twins, and it, along with how she approached getting them to see the outside world, was one of the reasons they were so advanced. Even some of the adults who wanted to learn better English were using it. Anaya was happy that some true bonding was taking place and she was certain that Devesh was pleased that Reign was trying to be more open with the family.

Anaya took a glance across the room to see how far her little niece had made it in her trek to deliver the glass of mango juice to Mumma who was sitting in the solarium.

When she passed the gathering table that was closest to the solarium entrance, Tiya's little hellion son stuck out his foot, causing Leena to lose her balance. Instinct made Anaya reach out to catch her niece, but she was much too far away. The cup went sailing forward, splattering its contents all over Tiya's brand new dress.

Tiya's shocked gasp did not last more than three seconds.

Neither did her reaction.

Her hand went back, made a wide arc, then swung wildly forward. That hand cracked against Leena's face with a loud gunshot sound that sent her sprawling. Leena defensively curled into herself and let her body go limp. The far right wall of the kitchen broke her airborne trip.

Leena's scream is what forced Mumma and Anaya into action. It also brought Reign sprinting from the master suite all the way into the kitchen.

She scooped Leena up into her arms, comforting the little girl as she fell into hiccupping sobs. Tiya mindlessly rubbed a towel over the lower half of her dress.

Some of the women looked on, unable to decide how to help. Aunt Kavya picked up a spatula and whacked Tiya upside the head three times, causing her to yell, "Ouch. Cut that out."

Reign's green eyes zeroed in on the floor.

The orange splatter.

Gaze slid to the mess on Tiya's dress.

Her focus swept across all the anxious people waiting to see any reaction.

Anaya's heart broke when Reign examined her child, who had clamped her lips to stop wailing but whose silent tears flowed endlessly.

Reign trembled with a rage so profound that Anaya wasn't sure she could keep her hold on Leena for much longer.

Leena pointed at Tiya. "Mama. She hurt me." She looked up at her mother, saying, "I did not hurt her back, Mama. I did not ..."

Marital arts. Karate. That child could have taken Tiya on herself if she chose to.

"I know, baby. I know." When Reign put eyes on the wall, Anaya saw her sister-in-law's face cloud over as the realization dawned that the dent was caused by the impact of her daughter's body. Leena had been on a trajectory so fierce that it wasn't minor damage, either.

"Leena, stay with Anaya for a minute, alright?"

Her little chest heaved and settled twice before saying, "Yes, Mama."

Reign placed a kiss on her daughter's temple.

Kamran inched into the room, having left his cousins out on the patio who were well into a game of Cricket. He took in everything at once, and asked, "Mama, is Leena okay?"

"She will be."

Anaya rushed forward to take Leena from Reign's arms. Kamran marched purposefully into the room, stopping when he made it to his sister's side. Their cousins looked on, faces solemn as they took in the scene and realized that one of the adults had done something wrong.

All anger seemed to seep out of Reign's pores. She now seemed to be filled with a calm that was more frightening than her rage could ever be. Tiya had no better sense not to be afraid of this profound change in a woman they were just getting to know.

Reign was on Tiya in a flash, bypassing everyone in the crowded kitchen by taking a giant leap across the center island. She slid across the countertop of the granite island, forcing the meal prep items out of her path and clattering to the floor as she snatched up a butcher's knife along the way. She landed directly on the other side, a few feet from her intended target. Reign yanked up a handful of Tiya's hair, snatching off the band that held the thick black strands before twisting it tightly around her fist. The hair that flowed all the way past Tiya's ankles were now a way for Reign to hold her hostage.

As the women tried—unsuccessfully—to separate them, Reign dragged Tiya by the hair to the stove. A pot of Basmati rice was on full boil. She carefully inched it partway off the burner, exposing the bright orange and flickering blue flame. The shrieks of horror and panic that filled the air brought the men running from the outside patio, the theater, and the den. They were just in time to see Reign lower Tiya's face until it was several inches above the fire.

"Honey," Devesh yelled, trying to get around Aunt Kavya who blocked his way, shaking her head so he would stay put.

Reign glanced over at him, face devoid of any expression.

Aunt Kavya whispered a few words to him in Hindi. He finally gave in with a defeated set of his shoulders, fully realizing that there was no reaching his wife at the moment.

Reign's body pressed against Tiya's to keep the struggling woman in place. In one slice starting from the base of her neck until the knife touched open air, the bulk of Tiya's silky hair slipped to the marble tiles.

"Reign," Mumma screamed, pressing her hands to her mouth. "Please do not kill my daughter."

Aunt Kavya scoffed at the sentiment, giving Reign an encouraging nod to finish whatever she'd started.

Tiya squirmed, trying to loosen Reign's tight hold on her.

"You move, and I will push your face into this fire," Reign said through her teeth.

"Please think of your child. She shouldn't see any of this," Bhavin cried, inching closer to the stove, but still staying a few feet away or he might cause Reign to make a deadly move.

"I *am* thinking of my child," she said, lowering Tiya's face so that the fire nearly touched the skin. Shrieks of horror and shocked gasps filled the air as a slightly red area surfaced where Tiya's skin was closest to the heat. "She needs to see this and so does everyone else."

"Please don't," Tiya screamed, clawing at Reign's hand.

"Please don't what?" Reign shot back, looking up from her handiwork. "I warned you about putting your hands on my child. You didn't listen. Nothing she did to you warranted you striking her so hard that she put a dent in the wall."

Devesh's focus snapped to the far end of the kitchen. He flinched when he saw the damage, and his thunderous expression meant he was ready to vindicate his daughter himself.

"You'd better be glad I'm in a generous mood," Reign said through her teeth. "I cut up a chicken real well. A human should be no trouble at all."

Devesh gently extracted Leena from Anaya's arms, and said, "We need to get her to the hospital."

Reign chopped off every inch of Tiya's hair, leaving bald patches and splotchy terrain that was horrid to behold. "If my child needs a hospital visit, so will you."

"Reign," Devesh warned, but she totally ignored him.

"Who would think a woman as loving and compassionate as your mother would raise such a mean-spirited child," Reign said. "They've given into your tantrums and ugly ways, and now you think it's acceptable." She looked at the other women. "And you're just as bad, pleading for mercy on her behalf and nobody except Aunt Kayva got on her about what she did to my daughter." She locked a gaze with Anaya and then Mumma. "Don't expect me to have any mercy for this witch. I'm all out."

No response.

"Apologize," she demanded of Tiya, shaking her body so it came even closer to the flame. "Apologize!"

Tiya sobbed into her hands, but didn't comply. Aunt Kavya moved forward, whacked her on the bottom a few more times and spoke harshly in Hindi.

"I'm sorry," Tiya screamed between strikes. "I'm so sorry."

Reign moved away from the stove, allowing Tiya to slide to the floor, sobbing uncontrollably as she joined what used to be her pride and joy. "Try me again, hear?" Reign warned. "And I give you my word that you'll meet your maker faster than He intended."

She stabbed the knife into the wooden butcher block, took Kamran's hand and ran to catch up with Devesh.

"She's a beast," Tiya cried, holding a hand to the damaged areas of her face.

Bhavin, Sana, and Neerav all made a move to converge on Tiya.

Aunt Kayva held up a hand to make sure everyone stayed in place, sending a message that no one was to help Tiya behind what she had done.

"You drove her to this," Anaya said, first to her sister, then to everyone else. "All of you. How long did you think she'd take it and not fight back?" Anaya stepped over to her sister who was holding a trembling hand to her injured face. "You deserved what she did. You should have never hit my niece like that. You'd better be glad she didn't slice your neck."

chapter 31

Reign and Devesh were outside of Leena's hospital room to hear what the doctor had to say about her condition. The blend of bright blue, taupe and beige walls failed in its effort to make the place more cheerful.

"Ms. Maharaj, as a courtesy, I want you to know that I had to call Child Protective Services."

"Why?" Reign asked the doe-eyed woman who didn't seem old enough to actually be a doctor. "I didn't hit her. Neither did her father. Her aunt did this, and my husband called the police who met us here. We made a report already."

"It's mandated when a child has these types of bruises," she said, sadly.

"Are they going to take my child because of this?"

"It's out of my hands. She has to remain here until someone from CPS arrives," she said, looking over the chart. "I put in the referral after the tests came back. They'll send an in-person response staff member out to obtain the facts to determine what kind of abuse your child has suffered."

"I understand," Reign said in a resigned whisper. "Thank you, Doctor."

"We'll need to keep her overnight. Your child is lucky that it wasn't worse," Dr. Wade explained. "I don't know how she braced herself for that hit, but it saved her from having a broken arm, ribs—so much more."

"They teach that in karate class," Reign explained with a pointed look at Devesh. "How to fall properly, how to absorb a blow. She had tucked her body inward so ...." Reign swallowed around the lump in her throat. "So the impact ..." She inhaled slowly. "So ... so it wasn't so great."

Devesh attempted to bring Reign closer to him. She refused his efforts.

The doctor gave Reign's shoulder an encouraging pat. "I'll be back to check on her a little later."

Reign squeezed the bridge of her nose, then let her head rest against the cold stone pillow that was the hospital wall. "They could take our children away."

"Is Auntie Tiya okay?" Leena asked, her voice echoing from the hospital bed as Kamran left her side to peer out at them and hear the answer.

Their daughter would still be concerned about a woman who didn't care one fig for her.

"She'll be fine," Devesh replied, glaring at Reign, who didn't have an ounce of remorse for what she'd done. Kamran nodded and went back to his sister.

Inwardly, he applauded his wife's efforts, but the fact that she took it to such extremes was cause for alarm. She could've easily killed his sister. One slip of her hand and Tiya would have been six feet under, pushing up daisies.

With all the crazy, mean things Tiya had done over the years, he wanted to ring her neck himself. But he never came close to taking her out like Reign had tonight.

"Reign—"

"I don't want to hear it," she snapped.

"Honey, we need to talk about what happened."

"She struck our child," Reign growled, stabbing a finger in his chest with each word. "Hit her so hard she put a dent in the freaking wall.

There's nothing to talk about. You're forcing something to work that's *never* going to happen." She put her back on the wall again, eyeing the half-eaten tray of food on a nearby cart. "When my child was on the floor screaming, only your mother, Anaya, and Aunt Kavya even tried to come to her aid." She grimaced as she looked up at him. "But none of those women had any problem standing up for a grown woman who had battered a child."

"They were in shock," Devesh defended.

"Really?" she shot back. "They weren't when I put a hurting on Tiya's behind. There wasn't any slow dragging or being"—she crooked her fingers as quotes—"In shock then. So they can kick pebbles because rocks are too strong for them."

Devesh realized getting Reign to see that her reaction may have been over-the-top was a lost cause. Slicing her hair off? Well, that one he could shrug off. But putting his sister near the fire and nearly burning her face off—yes, that was cause for concern.

"Your mother and father, they love you, they love our children, but they are blind to your sister, and they're also blind to anyone else in the family who doesn't care for Leena and Kamran." Reign folded her arms across her chest. "Tiya has never hidden the fact that she hates them. Leena spilling that juice on her only gave her an opportunity to do something she'd wanted to do all along. She's insanely jealous of you and your children. Hitting our child that hard was deliberate. She didn't swat her on the bottom. She didn't pinch her arm. She didn't have any control whatsoever. And when it comes to someone harming my children, neither do I." She pulled herself upright. "Now if you don't mind, I'd like to focus on my children before Child Protective Services whisks them off to some unknown place and puts them in foster care, compliments of y*our sister*."

"Reign—"

"Now isn't the time," she whispered, shaking her head. "I have a lot of regrets right now, and every one of them is tripping over the other for first place." Reign locked a steady glare on him. "But know this, there is no way in West Hell or East Jesus that I'm setting foot in that house again with my children. Next time, I won't even come close to just doing bodily harm. I would succeed to the measure you all aren't prepared to handle. If protecting our children is not your priority, it damn sure will be mine."

She swept past him to go into the room where Leena was situated on the bed. Kamran was right by his twin's side, holding her hand.

"Honey, you and they are my—"

"Mr. and Ms. Maharaj?"

"Yes," Reign answered, turning toward a woman wearing a white blouse, gray pinstripe pants, and a severe bun pulled to the back of her head.

"I'm Priscilla Jackson with Child Protective Services. The police gave me a copy of the report. It seems a Tiya Singh hurt your child?"

"Yes. My daughter's care was my first concern," Reign responded. "Making sure the woman who hurt her was brought to justice was my second."

"I understand," she said in a patient tone. "This is the first time something like this has happened?"

"Yes ma'am."

Ms. Jackson nodded, scribbled something on a yellow notepad. "I did some checking in Chicago, and there doesn't seem to be any cases of neglect or abuse there."

"That's because I've never neglected or abused them," Reign said sourly. "Not even this time."

Ms. Jackson gave her a patient look. "I understand your frustration, ma'am, but your child was injured by something other than accidental means and was brought in with severe bruises to her body. We have to investigate before we can release your children back into your custody."

"And we told you exactly who did it," Reign countered, her tone barely civil.

Devesh sighed. "Reign, please don't make this difficult."

"Your sister already has," she snapped and finally laid eyes on him. "And why isn't someone from the family here to back up our story? God only knows the lies Tiya told the police."

Devesh pulled up a text on his screen and showed it to her. "Mumma,

Papa, Anaya, Aunt Kavya, and Pranav are here in the ER waiting room. The police are verifying things with them so I can get a temporary restraining order. They won't let them upstairs just yet," he said. "A few others are on the way."

"I'd like to hear what happened in your words, please," Ms. Jackson said, jotting all of the new information down. "And I'll have you to know that Ms. Singh has filed a report of assault against you."

"Of all the nerve," Reign spat.

"My wife didn't assault my sister … she …" Devesh grimaced, not knowing how to sum up today's experience. "merely showed her why she should never lay a hand on Leena again."

"What happened with your daughter today?" Ms. Jackson said, studying Reign's tight face for a long moment.

Reign recounted the story, and though Ms. Jackson tried to keep her expression neutral at the point that Reign told of cutting Tiya's hair, the woman's eyebrow shot up and her pen stopped scribbling across the page. "Say that again."

"I cut off all of her hair," Reign repeated. "I thought it was a small sacrifice for what she did to my daughter. Since I couldn't break my foot off in her—"

"Reign," Devesh said, trying to put his wife in check before she said something damaging. He was having enough of a hard time keeping his own anger at bay. Hearing how they ended up here in the hospital from something so minor lent to the fact that Reign was right. There was some deep-seated hatred from Tiya and still some indifference from the rest of his family that he needed to be concerned about. When they left the hospital, he was keeping his promise to clean house. A lot fewer family members, friends, and co-workers having full-time access should put everyone on notice that Reign or his children were not to be trifled with.

Devesh snapped from his thoughts in time to see a slight smile lift the corners of Ms. Jackson's lips as she looked at Reign, giving her an approving nod and a sly smile.

chapter 32

Devesh was relieved when things had calmed down after the incident with Tiya. Ms. Jackson had allowed Leena and Kamran to come home with Reign and Devesh under the instruction that Tiya could not be within one-hundred feet of Leena. This new development meant that Tiya and her family had to move from the Maharaj house immediately.

This was unfortunate and untimely in a number of ways. The closing on thee new home that Devesh had picked out was taking a lot longer than expected as the buyers had somehow found out that Devesh was loaded and also that the reason he wanted the place to be in close proximity to his parents.

A simpler solution would have been for Devesh's family to move into the Maharaj house temporarily and put Tiya and her family in the penthouse. No way was Reign comfortable with giving up their penthouse for Tiya—period.

Problem solved by moving Jay and his girlfriend, Elise, into the Penthouse, then shifting Tiya and her family into Jay's much smaller first-floor condo.

Even that exception didn't prove to be enough for Tiya who complained—loudly—that she should have the larger space since they were a family of four, and Jay only had himself and his girlfriend to consider. Reign flickered a gaze over Tiya's bandaged face and said, "We could put you out on the street. Remember, you're not our child, we don't have to do a damn thing to make life easier for you."

The twins were elated. Now they were now able to spend more time with their favorite family members.

Now Reign and Devesh were living once again in the master suite of the Maharaj home until the closing took place.

Two weeks later, the initial charges against Reign were dropped, but the judge had given her a stern warning.

They were still waiting to hear from Ritu and Savina on whether they would visit Aunt Kavya for the first time in fifteen years. Devesh could only hope that with Tiya out of the picture everything would go smoothly.

❀ ❀ ❀

Devesh was seated on a panel with Sheryl Underwood, Sara Gilbert, and Sharon Osbourne of *The Talk*, shifting his focus to Toni Gaytan, an actress who had been aiming for her own talk show, and was sitting in for Julie Chen., "And to make things more interesting," Toni said with a pearly white smile. "We have a special guest. Someone who can provide an opposing view on interracial relationships."

Sheryl Underwood shook her head. "No, that's not what this show is about."

"Don't do it," Sharon warned, visibly uncomfortable before even hearing what Toni had to say.

"Things are going to get pretty hot." Toni smiled directly at the lead camera and said. "We understand that Devesh Maharaj has avoided this at every turn, but it's something everyone has wanted to see for a long time. A dust-up between two men who have one woman at the center of their worlds."

Devesh flickered his dark brown orbs to the front row and saw every ounce of color drain from Reign's face. Jay's hand snaked out to grip her arm, holding her steady, but from his heated glare, he was having a tough time getting his own emotions under control.

"Everyone, please give a warm welcome to Dr. Shawn Newsome."

There was a splattering of applause as some of the audience members looked to each other, trying to figure out what this new development was all about. A man with mahogany skin, a shiny bald head, and a slight build draped in a two-piece suit and Stacy Adams, sauntered down the path until he was in the empty seat that was brought out for him.

"Well, Devesh, this man has been coming at you publicly for a minute. What do you have to say to him?"

Devesh settled back in the chair, gave Toni a smile that didn't quite reach his eyes. "First, I want the producers out here. *Now.*"

"We … we can't. We can't do that," Sarah Gilbert stammered.

"They come, or I walk," he snapped.

Shawn moved forward but Devesh gave him a look that stopped him in his tracks. "I wouldn't if I were you," Devesh warned. "You've already done too much."

"We'll just take a little commercial break," the blonde whispered in a conspiratorial tone, her smile faltering. "The show doesn't pay for itself."

"Oh no, we're not cutting to commercial," Devesh warned, firing a stony look at her. "You all did this under the cover of darkness. You need to make it right in daylight."

A woman with owl-rimmed glasses stepped out, joined by a round-bellied man with a cap over the wisps of hair head.

"Apologize," Devesh said through his teeth. "You are well aware that there is a major issue between this man and my wife. This man's been stalking her on Facebook and all other social media. He's been badgering their old classmates, trying to get them to give him her number." Devesh stood. "Then you blindside me by having him here? I would not have had my wife anywhere within one-hundred feet of him. I don't appreciate this."

"We are truly sorry about this," the spiky-haired woman said, chancing a glance at the shorter man next to her.

"He waived his appearance fee to be here," the balding one said. "I apologize."

"We couldn't turn that down," Toni said, seemingly unconcerned at the position that Devesh had taken.

"So it's all about ratings and money for you," Devesh snapped at Toni. "But for my wife, it's about the restraining order she has against him."

The audience gasped, and the producers scurried off the set but not before sending a pointed glare at Toni. Devesh left his position on the stage and went to Reign in the audience. "Are you alright, honey?" He looked to Jay, whose expression was deadly and firmly set on Shawn. "Why don't you take her out of the studio."

"I'll stay," she said, placing a hand on his chest. "I have to make sure you don't do something that requires me to come up with bail money."

Devesh pressed a kiss to her lips, causing the audience to voice their approval with "ooohs" and "ahhhhs".

Shawn grinned at Devesh when he reclaimed his seat on the panel but then put his focus on Reign who kept her attention on her husband. Jay, though, was studying Shawn as though he was ready to tear him apart.

Toni looked at the camera and said, "We welcome Dr. Shawn Newsome to the show. He has a doctorate in African-American Studies, and a masters in sociology. He's here to speak today on the controversial interracial relationship divide."

Shawn launched into his normal diatribe about Black women stepping outside of their race to date men of other ethnic backgrounds. "The only reason a White man would be interested in a Black woman is to fulfill some fetish. White men view Black women as either a "mammie" or primal and hypersexual. In order for a Black woman to truly be valued and appreciated, it takes a Black man, not some little White boy with sexual issues."

The audience murmured their discontent with that volatile explanation.

All of the hosts—except one—looked mighty uncomfortable. They cut to commercial break and when they did, Devesh exhaled and looked in Jay's direction, mouthing the words that he should take Reign out.

Reign saw the exchange and shook her head. Instead, she gave him an encouraging smile to let him know she was fine.

"And we're back with superstar Devesh Maharaj and Dr. Shawn Newsome speaking on interracial relationships," Toni announced. "Before the break, we heard Dr. Newsome's take on things. Now Mr. Maharaj will speak his peace."

"First of all, I'm not White, I'm East Indian," he explained. "And to be honest, there are not enough good Black men for all those wonderful, amazing, talented, and gorgeous Black women out there. Someone has to cross on over to ..." He lifted his eyebrows twice. "The *Eastside*."

Reign rolled her eyes heavenward as the audience laughed at his pun.

"It's not a slight; it's not on purpose," Devesh continued. "It's the law of average. Nature hates empty spaces. And those empty spaces in a Black woman's heart are going to be filled with something or someone." He put his eyes on Reign. "And let's hope that it'll be a grown ass man and not some whiny little boy who's still trying to figure his life out—no matter how many letters he has behind his name."

The audience heartily applauded their approval.

"I don't know what your problem is, Mr. Maharaj," Shawn said when the audience enthusiastic voices dimmed. "But since you want to take me to task over those letters. I am the type of man that Black women should be with. Black women are always talking about Black men making it and not being with Black Women, but when there are good men, like me, they're still flocking to White men ... or men like you."

"With all of those degrees," Devesh countered. "I'm sure you're very much aware of the numbers. Black women outnumber Black men nearly three to one. More if you count the ones who are not available to them—married, in jail, gay, or those who don't want to commit to marriage."

The audience clapped, the more enthusiastic applause coming from Black women.

"They'll go to their graves while waiting for the Black man who God's supposed to mysteriously recycle so she can have her turn," Devesh said. "He took two fish and five loaves of bread, and it became enough to feed a multitude. But I never heard of Him using His power of multiplication to create extra brothers when there are already so many other desirable seeds. Those seeds on the ground might at least bloom into a relationship that is more than a placeholder until a good Black man mysteriously comes along. And it might be the best thing that's ever happened for both of them."

This time the audience whooped, hollered, and laughed and Sharon placed an encouraging hand on his shoulder. Sheryl nodded and had an ear-splitting smile.

Shawn's face darkened with anger. "So now *you* speak for Black women?"

"I don't have to speak for Black women because I only have to focus on *one* woman." He took a sip from the coffee mug and returned it on the coaster. "A woman I love, a woman whose spirit I'm not going to crush just to satisfy my ego. You have a wife—she's *your* business. I have my wife—she's *my* business. I'm not all up in your finances. I'm not all up in your bedroom." From the corner of his eye, Devesh saw Sheryl and Sara nodding and putting the evil eye on Shawn. "Your ego took pleasure in hurting Reign. I take pleasure in helping my woman to heal."

"My woman?" Shawn examined Reign before looking back to Devesh. "Sounds like some cave man white boy mess."

"Too many men have used the word *wife* in a way that implies property. Saying *my woman* is primal, instinctual." Devesh's smile disappeared as his eyes narrowed to slits when they focused on Shawn. "It means I will nail someone's balls to the wall if they come at her the wrong way."

"Are you threatening me? On live television?" Shawn said, shoulders stiffening.

"Not threatening anyone. I'm going to need you to keep *my woman's* name out of your mouth." Devesh leaned in, causing Shawn to slide back. "See, you're not upset about the most important part of the equation. You're upset about *the money*. If I wasn't rolling in it right now, you wouldn't blink about who I chose as my mate." Devesh wagged a finger in Shawn's direction. "So my brother, you're going to have to stay mad—I mean the next seventy years worth of mad, because I'm going to be loving my woman until there's no more love to be had."

Amid the roaring applause, Jay hopped from his seat next to Reign, tipped out on the stage like he was a teenager sneaking into the house after curfew, extended his fist to Devesh for a pound.

Devesh tapped his fist to Jay's right before Jay slow-walked past Shawn giving him the evil eye, then tipped back out and took his seat amidst laughter from the audience.

"She didn't want you," Devesh said to Shawn. "How could she after you hurt her like that?"

"I was tipsy."

"A drunk body speaks a sober mind. You were thinking it. You just weren't prepared for her to put your ass in the hospital behind what you said."

Toni piped up. "What did he say?"

Devesh ignored her and said to Shawn, "Instead of being happy that she's moved on in her life, you're all on the airwaves about what we're doing wrong." Devesh flipped a stony look at Shawn. "It's obvious you're still in love with her because you seem to be campaigning for her to take you back, because I don't see you dragging any other interracial couple through the ringer this way. You have a wife, that's the only Black woman you should concern yourself with. Why don't you make sure you've handled *that* business and leave mine alone."

Toni asked again, "Tell everyone what he said to her."

"Oh no, I'm not breaking my wife's confidence," Devesh said to her. "And you all pulling a stunt like this, should not be rewarded with any inside information."

Toni shifted her focus to Shawn, who lifted his chin in defiance and said, "I mentioned that she could lose a little weight."

"That's nowhere near what you said," Devesh snapped. "You know it wasn't anything so tame. If I had said something so foul to any woman, I'd find a way not to own up to it, too."

Shawn found a sudden interest in his shoes.

Devesh unclipped his mic, stormed off the stage, extended his hand to Reign who stood and placed her hand in his.

Jay was right behind them on the way off the set. He turned to the cheering audience and the panel, gave a head nod and the "Peace, we're out" sign.

chapter 33

The Maharaj women arrived at Reign and Devesh's new home before dawn intending to pull Devesh and Kamran from their beds and out of the house. They were to prepare breakfast as a start to their observation of Karva Chauth (करवा चौथ), a one-day festival where married women fast from sunrise to moonrise for the safety and longevity of their husbands.

The closing took place a few days before. Reign was excited to have their first guests, besides Jay and Elise, to walk into the home that was slightly smaller than the Maharaj place. This home was eight thousand square feet and situated in the oceanfront community of Pelican Point. Guests had to enter a front gate that provided some protection from fans and Paparazzi who were quickly taking an interest in seeing a bit more of Devesh than he would like. Exquisite stonework covered the exterior, artisan lanterns brightened the perimeter, and walnut, stone and ebony floors glowed from the interior. Gardens and covered porticos led to the glass mosaic-lined pool that was perfect for Devesh's early morning swims.

A magnificent paneled office anchored one wing of the main level, with a stunning dining room and formal living room at the other. The master retreat had two fireplaces and sitting rooms. Six bedroom suites, multiple media rooms, a gym, elevator, and a masterfully designed kitchen topped off the elegance of the place. Thanks to Anaya's diligence and their patience at waiting out the buyers who became a little greedy and pulled back when they thought they could get more money for the place. When Anaya told the Seller's agent that Devesh was going to walk away from the deal and put stakes on another property, the owners caved.

Devesh had offered Jay a suite in the new house and he first declined saying, "The next move I make is buying this condo. I've already started that process with Anaya. Your one year rent-free deal is up in a few months."

He could totally respect those sentiments, but Devesh knew Reign really wanted to have all of her children in one place—at least for a while. So he sweetened the deal saying, "How about you buy the condo, lease it out and rake in some cash for your life index, and still have yet another year with no living expenses. Then you an Elise can save up to get a house close to us."

"Sounds awesome, but no." He eyed Devesh for a moment. "Didn't y'all just leave a spot that had like a kabillion folks living there?"

True, but two was a far cry from a kabillion. "How about two?"

Jay hesitated, and Devesh could tell he was mentally calculating things against his life index number, so Devesh said, "Three, and you get to have your own studio space to write off on taxes?"

"Sold," Jay said, obliging a fist bump. "But I need to talk it over with Elise. And let's revisit this idea in a few weeks. You might like the privacy that comes with having the house all to yourselves."

"As huge as the place is, I won't see y'all for at least two weeks."

"True that," Jay replied, laughing.

Now a few days after that conversation, Kamran stumbled his sleepy form into the kitchen where all the women had settled. Leena was stationed at the juicer, her favorite thing to do with Anaya.

Karva Chauth is a special time for women to commune and learn more about each other and exchange gifts. Even unmarried women sometimes joined in, fasting for their fiancés or desired husbands. In the hopes of bringing unity between Reign and the Maharaj women and their friends, Mumma suggested that the first meal on this year's celebration should happen for Reign, to bless her new home.

Kamran frowned and said, "Why is Leena allowed to stay and I have to leave?"

Devesh lowered to Kamran's eye level. "Because this is a woman's festival."

"And they're going to have food?" he said, yawning, eyeing all of the breakfast items.

"A little this morning, but not any real food until later tonight," Devesh explained. "There's going to be a major spread at moonrise at Mumma and Papa's place, but only some for Leena and her other girl cousins for the rest of the day."

"Well, in that case," he said, shaking his head and sending a sorrowful look toward his sister. "Let's hit the road."

The women all laughed at him. Aunt Kavya planted a kiss on the top of his head.

Kamran embraced his sister, mother and the women and ran to Devesh.

"We can go hang out with Jay or go to Papa's."

"Why don't we get Papa and take him with us to Jay's?" Kamran offered. "Jay just got some old school video games. Papa loves Pac Man. Me too."

Reign exhaled, accepting that there were some things that she was not going to control. Video games was one of them. She reached in, taking the purple garment that Anaya held out to her, but put her focus on Kamran, simply saying, "Have a good time."

"Thank you, Mama."

The fasting women collectively sat in a circle and sang while performing the feris, the passing of their thalis around the circle. Reign ended with her own prayer of the 23rd Psalms, followed by the 112th Psalm, which Anaya translated into Hindi and the women all found to be beautiful and fitting. Only a few people knew Reign spoke Hindi.

When she was done, Reign was silent for as long as she could manage, but had to ask, "Why do we observe this holiday? How did it begin?"

Anaya settled onto a large purple cushion and said, "Some believe that since the men were off to war with the British and left their wives and children, the wives would get together to pray for them to come back safely."

"Others believe that the festival happened around wheat-sowing time, the beginning of the Rabi crop cycle," Mumma explained, holding Leena close. "Big earthen pots, in which wheat is stored, are sometimes called Karvas, so the fast might have been a prayer for a good harvest."

Aunt Kavya took hold of Reign's hand as Anaya translated her words. "There is another story about the origin of this festival. Girls barely in their teens would get married, go and live with their in-laws in very remote villages. Everyone would be a stranger to the new bride. If there were problems with the husband or in-laws, she would have no one to support her. Telephones, buses, and trains were not heard of in those days. People had to walk almost a whole day to go from one place to other, so her own parents and relatives would be too far away to help if she needed them."

Reign leaned forward and rested her chin in the palm of her free hand, taking in the exotic flow of Aunt Kavya's words before looking to Anaya for the translation.

"A custom started at the time of marriage," Mumma added, pulling Reign's attention from Aunt Kavya. "The bride would make friends with another woman in her new village. They would be recognized as kangan-saheli, which is something like god-friends, or dharam-behn, or god-sisters. These were lifelong bonds. The new sister-friends would keep each other's confidence. The family would recognize the sister-friend as a revered member of the family who stood in the stead of the bride's real family. Karva Chauth started as a festival to celebrate this special bond of friendship between the brides and their god-friends."

"So, is Aunt Kavya my kangan-saheli?" Reign asked, causing the women to burst into giggles and laughter. "What's so funny?" she asked, looking from one woman to another. "She's the first woman who accepted me when I came." She frowned, looking around at the women.

"The bride's new friend would usually be of the same age, maybe a little older," Anaya answered, seemingly put off by the fact that Reign would align herself with an elder instead of someone who was closer to her own age.

Reign stroked a finger on the weathered hand that had not released hers since the beginning of the last prayers.

"I would be honored if you would consider me your kangan-saheli," Anaya offered. "I might not have been an advocate for your relationship with my brother in the beginning, but I was wrong for letting my own issues cloud my judgment. You have been the best thing to happen to my brother. His happiness and yours are all that matters."

The two women embraced and the smiles from the rest of the women brought warmth to Reign's heart.

"In earlier times," Aunt Kavya began, in her halting English, causing several women to smile. "The sister-friend was not someone related to the groom's family. The bride couldn't very well complain about the groom or his family to someone who knew them so well." She held one hand out to Anaya and said, "We could change that part of the tradition, don't you think?"

Anaya kissed her aunt's cheek, then scooted close to Reign. Her voice caught in her throat and her eyes filled with tears. Reign was impressed with Aunt Kavya's progress with English. She'd absorbed enough of it over the years, but had been hesitant to use it because her husband had preferred her to remain silent.

Mumma left her place next to Sana and Priyanshi. She moved onto one of the cushions nearest Aunt Kavya as she launched into another version of the origins of Karva Chauth.

"A beautiful queen called Veervati was the only sister of seven loving brothers. Her first Karva Chauth as a married woman was at her parents' house. She began the fast after sunrise but by evening, was desperately waiting for the moonrise because she suffered severe thirst and hunger.

"The seven brothers couldn't bear to see their sister in such distress, so they created a mirror in a tree which made it look as though the moon had risen. The sister was deceived into breaking her fast before the appointed time. The moment she took that first bite, someone came to tell her that her husband, the king, was dead."

Some of the women looked shaken, as though they didn't want to imagine life without their own husbands. A few of the others were looking like they wouldn't mind switching places with Veervati. Interesting.

Aunt Kavya continued the story with, "Veervati was heartbroken, and wept through the night. A Goddess appeared and revealed to Veervati what her brothers had done. She told the queen to repeat the Karva Chauth fast with complete devotion. When Veervati did as she was told, the Goddess was forced to restore her husband to life."

Nalini, one of Pranav's coworkers, chimed in with the version that she'd been taught. "When Lord Yama—the god of death—came to take the soul of a man named Satyavan, his wife, Savitri, begged Lord Yama to grant him life. When he refused, she stopped eating and drinking, and followed Yama as she carried away her dead husband.

"Yama said that she could ask for any other favor *except* for the life of her husband. Savitri asked that she be blessed with children. Yama agreed, without realizing one thing. Being a *Pati-Vrat*—devoted wife— Savitri would *never* let any other man be the father of her children. Yama was left with no other choice but to restore Savitri's husband to life to fulfill that wish. They lived a long and happy life with their children."

Reign chuckled and said, "I *like* that version."

"Of course," Mumma responded, grinning. "That sounds exactly like something you would do."

The women laughed and Reign joined them.

The stories of their personal journeys continued all day as the women fasted, along with other legends and myths surrounding the event.

Later in the day, the sound of the front door opening forced Reign from her place in the circle. They weren't expecting anyone else today. She wondered why Devesh or Jay would return to the house, knowing the importance this bonding time for the women.

Two beautiful women, draped in elegant saris were standing in the foyer with suitcases perched on the floor next to them. They looked at Reign, then back to Devesh and raised a questioning eyebrow as Devesh swept past them saying, "I'll be right back."

"Welcome to my home," Reign said, eyeing the women closely and seeing a familiar resemblance.

"Thank you for having us," the taller of the two women said. "We—"

"Ritu. Savina," Aunt Kavya's wavering voice echoed off every corner of the foyer, living room and parlor.

Her hands went to her mouth as her steps halted along the path to where her daughters stood. Devesh hooked his arms under hers, moving the older woman forward.

Ritu and Savina left Reign's side and ran to their mother, both of them embracing her warmly.

"Oooooh, my babies," Aunt Kavya crooned, swaying with them in her arms. "My babies."

Reign tried to look away to give them a moment of privacy, but the beauty of the reunion was something she did not want to miss. This had been a long time coming.

"I am so sorry," Aunt Kavya said, still holding them in her arms.

Ritu pulled away to stare down at her mother. "Mama, you're speaking—."

"Yes, I speak English now," Aunt Kavya said proudly with a lift of her chin and her daughters both smiled. "Not good, but better every day." She stroked a hand through Ritu's cap of curls. "I am so sorry for what happened, that I wasn't a better mother. I should have known, by the way he treated me, that he would also treat you so horribly." She pressed a kiss to Savina's temple, then Ritu's forehead. "If I had known, I would have—"

"Killed him," Ritu supplied. "We know. That's why we couldn't say anything. I thought we needed our mother more than we needed to tell what he had done."

"Oh, my darlings," Aunt Kavya said. "What a burden you had to bear. We would have found a way to be together. He had no right to hurt you that way and still draw a breath." She pulled both of them to her again.

"I failed you. Failed to protect you."

"No!" Savina said, as Ritu shook her head. "It is his shame, not yours. We do not blame you. He is who he has always been, but we will not put the blame on you in any way."

"Devesh talked with us," Ritu admitted. "He explained a lot of things and we understand more now than we did back then. We should never have left you behind."

"You are here now." Aunt Kavya patted her hand gently. "Nothing will come between us again. I love you so, so much. There is no better gift than having you back in my life. Thank you for coming home. It is safe for you to come home for good, if you want. I will make a place for you. I have work now—I make garments for the women—design them, and I have my own money now."

Reign's heart swelled with pride. Aunt Kavya had been delighted when Devesh asked her heart's desire. Her small business started with making clothing for members of their immediate circle and friends—designs that blended both Indian and American styles. Now she had so much work coming in that Devesh was scouting out a place for Aunt Kavya and two of the aunts who helped in the work, to have a small store not too far away from the Maharaj place.

"You will remain here in our home," Reign said with a nod from Devesh.

"No," Aunt Kavya replied. "You are husband and wife, a family just becoming. You need time alone before so many people come. Later, then maybe you can have us."

"I'll make room in the Maharaj home," Devesh offered. "Reconfigure my old suite to accommodate the three of you. If you would like."

"That would be more than fine," she replied with a teary-eyed smile. "Thank you. Thank you both for this gift." She went to embrace Devesh and Reign, then said to her daughters, "We are in the middle of Karva Chauth, but we can go somewhere to have a meal. I am only participating to help Reign to understand the tradition. I am not fasting for my husband. Soon to not be my husband."

"No," Ritu said, and Savina took Aunt Kavya's hand. "We would like to join you, even though we are not married. We have all the time in the world to be together, but this is a special moment we should share."

When Ritu, Savina, and Aunt Kavya entered the family room, the women left their cushions and swarmed the daughters, smothering them with embraces and kisses, welcoming Ritu and Savina home and sharing in Aunt Kavya's joy.

Reign went to Mumma when the women took a break from the circle and said, "It's no secret how Tiya and I feel about each other, but for your sake, I'm sorry that she couldn't be here."

"It is alright," Mumma said. "Tiya lost her place among the women here when she hurt you, your child, and my son. That is not unity. She continued to try and separate the women from you, my son's beloved, that is not unity. She is not a good example of what Indian women represent—compassion, understanding, and support." Mumma embraced Reign, then pulled away. "Devesh loves you. I have not witnessed that kind of love with anyone. Not even in my own marriage, which was arranged by my parents." Mumma smiled, and it seemed to light up the entire room. "I did come to love Suresh after time because he is a wonderful man, but the kind of love that you share with my son, it is beautiful to see." She clasped Reign's hands. "Many women are not so fortunate."

chapter 34

During the moonrise meal to break the women's fast, the men served their first drink, followed by the first taste of a meal since before sunrise.

Tiya sidled up to Devesh who was in the middle of a conversation with Bhavin in the game room, and said, "Now that you no longer live here, my husband and I would like to move into your old suite."

"No," Devesh said, and continued the conversation about his recent trip to New York.

"But it's not like you're going to be using it," she protested, still ignoring the fact that he was already in a discussion with someone else.

Devesh sighed, put up a finger and said to Bhavin, "Can you give us a minute?" Then he put his eyes to Tiya and repeated, "*No*. I have plans for the space. And do remember that the only reason you're able to visit right now is because my children are with Jay. Who, by the way, is missing the first part of this important family event because of you. He'll be here in ten minutes with the children. The answer, since your ears must've been filled with wax the first time I said it, is no."

"You're so selfish," she spat and raised her voice to a level that caused nearby conversations to fall off. "You don't even need it. Don't you mate enough with that she-bear at your own pad?"

Devesh tossed back a shot of FireBall whiskey and put the empty glass on the table behind him. "I don't know about any she-bears, but my queen is standing right behind you. Why don't you ask her how often we mate? You could probably learn a thing or two. Especially since your cooking would be turned down by a starving man. You might as well perfect something else."

Tiya's complexion went from olive to pure white.

"I'm going to say this, and then I'm going to let it alone," Reign spoke in a voice that commanded everyone's attention as she came to Devesh's side. "I'm not going to be called too many more names and let it ride."

Somehow Tiya's bravado surfaced at the wrong moment. "And what are you going to do about it?"

Reign tilted her head as though studying her for the first time. "Hmmm. Nice haircut." She winked and let the threat hang in the air for a moment before adding, "Next time, I'll take a little more off the top. What do you think?"

Tiya shuddered and rushed out of the room.

"I have a question," Reign said, causing the rest of the people, who had pretended not to listen in, to look her way. She stepped further into a central spot that gave a view of everyone in the four corners. "So what's the name of the holiday where the men fast for the women?"

The rest of the conversations from the living room, den, parlor, and the family room all fell into complete silence.

"There is no such thing," Bhavin said, and had the nerve to sound incensed that she would suggest such a thing.

Devesh's lips quirked as though he was already prepared for where this line of questioning would go.

"What do you mean, *there isn't one?*"

"This has been a tradition for hundreds of years," he answered, garnering nods and verbal agreements from most of the men. "Only for women."

Reign lowered her gaze to the carpet, but the wheels were turning in her mind. "So let me get this straight. The *women* have a particular holiday where we fast for our husband's longevity and good health. But there isn't one where men fast for *our* excellent health and long life? Where is the fairness in that?"

Anaya nodded. Mumma blinked twice. Aunt Kavya grinned. Most of the other women wore perplexed expressions and talked amongst themselves.

"We don't have to do that," Bhavin said. "The women should *want* to do this. We are the ones to take care of them, not the other way around."

"Is that right?" Reign favored Bhavin with a look that was every bit of alarming. "We will see."

Bhavin's wife raised a questioning brow at Reign and gave her a small smile.

"Honey," Devesh began, realizing that covering his ass was of paramount importance. "I'm sure I'll support whatever you're about to do, but don't leave me hanging."

She nodded, then asked everyone. "All in favor of the men showing the women that they also wish their wives long life and excellent health, raise your hands."

Every woman's hands instantly went up—high. Only Devesh, Pranav, and Papa's hands were up on the men's side.

"Women, I see we have some work to do," Reign explained, and all of the females put their focus on her. "Can any of you take off work anytime soon?"

The next day, Reign secretly coordinated with the women's schedules and orchestrated a trip to the Atlantis Resorts on Paradise Island, Bahamas. All of the women, Anaya and Reign's children, and the three men who showed support were set to go. And for an entire week, the rest of the men were left to their own devices—cooking, cleaning, and taking care of the children—for an entire week, with no word where the women were going or when they would return. The women were instructed that to get the message across, they would have no contact with their husbands whatsoever as they enjoyed everything the resort and island had to offer.

Suffice it to say that the men were relieved when the women came home. A new holiday was created for the Maharaj men and their male guests to observe a day of fasting for their mates.

Even Papa couldn't stop laughing about that one.

chapter 35

The adult members of the Maharaj clan centered around the wide screen television in the den, horrified at the accusations Tiya had leveled against Devesh and Reign on TMZ. Leena, Kamran and Anaya's children were with Aunt Kavya at Reign and Devesh's new home they had named Universe. Aunt Kavya's daughters—Ritu and Savina—were settling into the Maharaj house for a month-long period to reconnect with their mother, and then the rest of the family.

Tiya and Hiran stood off to the side, a sly grin playing about Tiya's lips as she watched the family's reactions to the show that had been taped earlier that day.

"He was drunk and didn't even remember that he'd slept with her that night," Tiya said, reaching a hand up to flip her hair, then putting it down when she remembered it wasn't there any longer. "That's why he didn't know about Leena or Kamran. Then she married him. What kind of foolish woman marries the man who raped her?"

Devesh closed his eyes against that Punjabi heat that threatened to overtake every smidgen of common sense.

"I hope the money was worth it," Reign said as Anaya switched off the telecast and put a heated glare on Tiya. Everyone's focus was on Tiya. It was obvious from the range of expressions that they did not approve.

"You think you're so above us," Tiya scoffed as she maneuvered past the first rows of recliners until she was a few feet away from Reign. "You think because you put your hook out and reeled in the most handsome man that India's ever seen, that your shriveled up self is a prize. You are nothing," she spat. "So I did whatever it took to let the truth come out. No need for you to stick around and make our lives any more miserable than they already are." Tiya smiled, and it did not quite reach her dark brown eyes. "If you and your little bastards are gone, then there's no need for me to be in that little matchbox of a condo."

Reign moved her hands, and Tiya flinched. It almost caused Reign to smile. Almost. Thankfully, she quickly controlled her need to slap the cow-walking crap out of Tiya. "And you did this regardless of the fact that my children will be affected by it? That they would hear this from people who are crueler than you could ever be. That your lies will follow them the rest of their lives." Reign's hands balled into fists. For a moment Tiya was truly closer to getting stomped than that day she lost her hair. "You would do this, knowing how much it would hurt the man who helped so many out of tough spots. I hope the money was worth it, I truly do. Because he might forgive you one day, but I never will."

Mumma raised up out of the chair and faced her daughter. "Take your husband and go."

Tiya's eyes widened to the size of saucers. "Mumma, you can't mean that."

"Leave my house and never return." Her voice was soft, but there was no mistaking the anger that laced her command. "You have brought great shame to this family. Reign is right. It is more than just her that will be hurt. It will be their children and our family that suffer."

Papa moved to stand by Mumma's side. "Your thirst for revenge has no boundaries. If you do this to a man who has helped you on so many occasions, what will you do to any of us?"

"We cannot trust you or abide you any longer," Mumma whispered with tears streaming down her face.

"Your precious son," Tiya roared, gripping the edge of the recliner so hard her knuckles turned white. "The son who has lived off of you like a parasite and would still be living here like some little boy who never grew up if his little brats and she—uh, wife"—she quickly corrected and put more space between herself and Reign—"hadn't shown up."

Mumma rounded the front row of the recliners, shaking a fist in Tiya's face. "We don't take care of him. He takes care of us. This—is—*his*—house!"

Gasps, murmurs and shocked sighs followed that admission.

Devesh grimaced at having that piece of information confirmed and floating around. He moved forward to put a restraining hand on his mother's arm. She exhaled and placed her hand over his.

"Every dime he could send us from India and abroad, he did. It paid for *this* house, for us to travel. *He* did that and never wanted anyone to know," she confessed, hammering that point home. "He was trying to keep from having a long line of relatives asking him to solve their financial problems because they were too lazy to figure their lives out on their own." She flickered a disdainful scan over her Tiya's body. "I will not call names."

Anaya stroked a reassuring rub along the length of Mumma's other arm.

"When I had my knee surgery Devesh was here taking good care of me along with Suresh. He did that, so I would not have to ask any of you to disrupt your busy lives to nurse me back to health."

"He did it," Papa interjected, taking Mumma's hand. "Because he did not want to see his Mumma get her feelings hurt when she realized that the people she had made so many sacrifices for, were not willing to give of themselves the one time she needed them." He glared openly at his daughter. "You, who do not have a busy life at all since you have not worked a day in your life, was the first one to say that you were not able to come to be with your mother. And that was before we even thought to ask."

Tiya stiffened, and her lips parted to offer some reply, but didn't manage to get anything out before Mumma pointed toward the door and said once again, "Get out of my house."

chapter 36

Enough men to make quick work of the task at hand were gathered around three moving trucks outside of the building that housed the first-floor condo that Tiya and Hiran lived in. Reign had also called a locksmith the moment she left the twins' school, who was now in the process of changing the front and rear door locks and putting in a keyfob system for all the remaining residents.

Tiya pulled up in a brand new BMW, scrambled out of the car without bothering to close the door behind her. Her children stayed put in the rear seats, totally engrossed in whatever was on their iPads.

"What are you doing?" she yelled, running to within a few feet of Reign. Always that few feet between them. She might be stupid, but she wasn't altogether dumb.

"I can't smack the entire Bollywood crap out of you," Reign said, without putting eyes on the woman. "But since your little episode landed you a nice little chunk of change, you won't have a problem living *elsewhere*." She scanned the area and found that the neighbors were filing out of their houses and other nearby buildings to check out the scene. "Because after what you pulled, you can't live here."

"You can't do this," Tiya screamed.

Reign waved the two documents that gave her the authority to do exactly what she planned. "I can and I will." She shifted to face the house again. "You have two choices. You can go in and take what you can carry then come get all of your stuff off the street. Or the movers can put everything on the truck, and it'll go into storage." She placed a document with the terms in front of Tiya. "You'll need to sign this first, though. And if it's not done within the next five minutes, my people are going to do exactly what I paid them to do."

A brand new Mercedes convertible came barreling into the empty space behind Tiya's car, "What is going on here?" Hiran demanded, scrambling out from behind the driver's seat. He pulled a phone from his ear. "Who are all these people?"

"They're here to evict us," Tiya said.

The children finally left the car, realizing that something major was going on.

Hiran swung a look toward Reign then to the burly men camped out on the front lawn. "That can't happen."

"Devesh owns this place," Reign said, grinning. "And I'm here to evict you—unless you have an *executed* lease. You know, the one you refused to sign because you were haggling over getting a lower price. When you were also trying to get my son out of his condo so you could have it because *you* deserve to have a better living space. Not to mention the space you were living in has three bedrooms to accommodate you." She tilted her head, taking in their panicked expression. "Do you even have the money you owe him? No? Didn't think so. No lease? You are guests, not tenants, and you are no longer welcome here."

Tiya snatched the sheet, scribbled her name and thrust it into Reign's chest.

Reign nodded toward Hiran. "You need to sign it, too."

"I want to talk to Devesh first," Hiran growled.

"You do that," Reign shot back and signaled for the movers to get to work. "Put everything on the street, fellas."

"Noooooo," Tiya screamed, pushing against her husband's chest. "Sign that thing."

Reign raised her hand to stall the men's movements. They halted—in unison, just like a synchronized swimming team.

Hiran placed his signature on the space provided right next to his wife's then held the sheet out for Reign. Before she could grip the end, he released his hold and let it float to the ground.

Reign left the document where it fell, refusing to pick it up from the ground. Instead, she turned to George, the bald man in charge of the teams, and said, "On the front lawn works for me."

"You can't do that." Tiya quickly scooped the pages off the grass and tried to fall in step as Reign walked away.

"You keep saying that and I keep proving you wrong." She opened the driver side door of her Buick Enclave and said, "I was going to pay for them to move it to storage. But you all still don't seem to get the fact that you're on the low end of this equation. If you want your stuff on the trucks, *you* pay for it. I'm not spending a dime to help you after what you did."

Hiran whipped out his wallet and produced a credit card.

George signaled a look at Reign, who shook her head. He put his eyes on the card and down at Hiran "Sorry, we'll need to have cash at this point."

Hiran glared at Reign, and said to his wife, "I'll be back. I need to hit a cash station."

When he drove off, Reign leaned on the passenger door closest to where Tiya stood. "Think I can't put my hands on you for your willful disregard for me and mine? Oh yes, you brought it to my house, and now I'm bringing it to yours."

Reign stroked a hand through Tiya's short-cropped hair. "If you ever come against my family and me again, this right here"—she gestured to the men going inside to start the process—"is the tip of what I'm willing to do."

Tiya was trembling with an anger that she didn't dare let run wild, or else she would receive another valuable lesson right on the front lawn.

"I'm more than willing to live down to your low expectations of me."

"So my brother did this?" Tiya asked.

Reign smiled, started the truck and left Tiya standing in the front yard while strangers dismantled her life.

chapter 37

"Nareigna Lisa Maharaj."

Reign swiveled her office chair to face Devesh, only slightly alarmed by his tone. She was grateful that the twins were with his parents tonight. She had a feeling that this storm might take a while to blow over. "My whole name, huh? Means I'm in real trouble, yes?"

"You evicted my sister without discussing it with me first," he said, as a vein throbbed at his temple. "Probably because you knew I wouldn't have been alright with the viciousness of it."

"That whole *everything in its time* thing was not working for me," she shot back. "Truth be told, I would have preferred putting my entire foot up her—"

"Come on, Reign," he warned. "Behave."

"But that wasn't an option," she finished, getting to her feet. "So I did the next best thing. No way does that heifer get to live on our dime after doing something so foul."

"Now, Reign."

"Don't you 'now Reign' me." She put a hand on her hip and studied his face. "I had to take the children out of school, Devesh. Their friends say their parents call you a *rapist*. Imagine having to explain that word to Leena and Kamran when I took them into school this morning," she said sourly. "They don't want you anywhere near their children. And they don't want our children playing with theirs because in their eyes, there's a thin line between rapists and pedophile. The director of the center disagreed with the parent's stance and asked me to stay. But the outcry from women everywhere has been devastating. This is not going away anytime soon."

"And putting Tiya and her family out on the street is going to make it go away?"

"Oh no," she said with a mild shrug. "I was being real petty on that one, since putting my fist in her face would've meant going to jail and paying her more money." She grasped his hand. "She hurt you. She hurt our children. I couldn't let that ride."

"You're acting real twenties right now," he shot back, scowling as he took a seat.

"No love, I'm being straight up hood," she admitted without an apologetic bone in her body. "My kind of twenties would mean stomping her correctly. And I would've made it worth the jail time, too."

Devesh flinched.

"If I'm going to be sitting in the pokey," she confessed, chest heaving with indignation. "I want to be smiling the entire time. She will not come for me and mine thinking that there won't be a piper to pay."

"Pokey?"

She looked upward as though accessing her memory banks. "Another word for jail."

"Should I ask why?"

Reign released her anger long enough to chuckle. "I don't believe it's for the reason you think. And it would be the pokey for you"—she pointed a finger at his chest—"and certainly not for me."

Devesh smiled a little but was obviously still processing her earlier statement as he pulled her into his arms. "Honey, I need you to be the adult in this relationship."

Reign outright laughed at that one. "So what does that make you?"

"Alright, let me rephrase the statement," he said, releasing her so he could guide them to a different area. "I need you to be the grown ass woman that I fell in love with. You can't be going around kicking butt left and right. How would that look?"

"It'll look like I'm a grown ass woman who doesn't stand for anyone's bull."

Devesh's shoulders slumped. "Don't have me put you over my knee and—"

She perked up. "My God, you're into that, too?"

"Reign, I'm trying to have a serious conversation here," he said failing to hold back an ear-to-ear grin.

"I hear you chirping, Big Bird." She took a moment to think about what he said and sighed. "And I'm sorry that—" She shook her head and waved him off. "I can't even tell that lie."

Devesh exhaled slowly, weighing his next words carefully. "I'm going to say this, love. God doesn't need you to help Him along with that karma thing, alright, honey?"

"Alright," she replied, completely deflated.

"That doesn't mean you can't—how do you say it? Get in that tail. But only if it's necessary. Even Jesus turned over the tables in the temple, right?"

She gave a victory fist pump. "That's what I'm talking about."

"But I'm going to need you to make sure you don't do something that will require me to come up with bail money."

Reign lowered her hands and pouted at hearing her own words thrown back at her. "Do I have to?"

"Yes, my love. You're no good to me if you're behind bars."

Devesh took her in his arms again, placing a kiss on her temple. "I understand why you did this, but we can't start giving an eye for an eye, or it'll never end. Good never follows bad when we know better." He stroked a finger across her cheek. "And we've been so blessed. Things that I've wanted for so long are finally happening for me, and for your son who's getting more business than he can handle. He's had to hire assistants. Even Anaya is thinking of accepting Jay's offer of a position that will allow her to help with my upcoming world tour. He says having people I can trust in key positions will benefit everyone in the long run. We have to be above board on how we do things."

"Tiya shouldn't hurt you that way," she whispered. "All because she wanted money to fund her shopping addiction? They weren't even using it to pay their bills. Please."

Devesh waited a moment and took a deep breath. "Yes, I'm hurt by what she did, but I'm not going to let it change how I do things." He leaned forward, laid his forehead against hers. "She's hurting, honey. All the jealousy, all the pain, we know where it comes from."

"But that doesn't give her the right to screw with everyone else just because she's had bad things happen to her," she whispered. "Hell, they happened to Anaya. They happened to me. You don't see us going around bending people over without oiling them up."

"I didn't need that kind of visual, honey."

"Sorry, but it's the truth," she countered. "She's mean because you all have allowed her to get away with bullying everyone for so long that she thinks it's normal. I was just her latest victim. Well, she *thought* I was a victim."

Devesh stroked a hand across her bare arms. "I understand how you feel, Reign, but God has been merciful and kind. We have to know that these blessings won't come to us without a challenge. That's how life is, but what will make the challenges less chaotic is facing them together. Understand me?"

She gave him a weak, "Yes."

"So no more going gangster on folks."

The defeated set of her shoulders told him she couldn't make that promise. "We have to move her back in?"

"Oh hell no," he confirmed, waving that off. "I'm riding with you on this one."

She roared with laughter, and when it died down, she said, "Your family's mad at me again."

"No, honey. They're upset at the lengths that Tiya would go to discredit me. I'm more amazed that my mother stood her ground and wouldn't let Tiya move back into her house. She told her that the children could stay, but not my sister or Hiran. I didn't think Mumma had it in her."

Reign grinned and sang, "Mumma don't take no mess."

Devesh frowned, trying to figure out the reference.

"James Brown," she supplied.

"Ah! Godfather of Soul."

Reign checked her cell. "*TMZ* called." She scrolled up the screen. "*The View, The Talk* all of them want an exclusive."

Devesh shook his head. "I'm not into any of them. They've been raking me over the coals without trying to check out the story first. Ellen? Iyanla?"

"Even she knows she can't fix this family."

Devesh struggled not to laugh. "As long as Mumma and Papa, Anaya, Aunt Kavya, and Pranav are alright, then we'll be cool." He sighed and it seemed like the weight of the world was hanging on that sound. "I never wanted this. For money to tear my family apart. I thought we were stronger than this. I believed we could survive anything. We even made it through Uncle Mitul's actions. Though, he might not survive the prison time they're going to give him."

"Do you regret that we—"

"No," he said, and his tone was adamant. "Never that. I am at peace. I haven't felt this in a long time. Peace is within us. We're not going to let Tiya, Bhavin, Hiran, or anyone steal that away."

The cell rang. She peered at the screen. "One of the producers from Oprah. They left a voicemail earlier."

Devesh thought about that for a minute and said, "Take it, if you feel we must."

"Your silence keeps everyone wondering if what Tiya's saying is true."

"No, we can't … how do you say it … let that ride." He held his fist out for a pound, and she obliged. "But next time …" he warned.

"Yes, yes. I hear you," she playfully whined, switching over to take the call. "Take the high road."

chapter 38

Reign helped to prepare the Maharaj home and her own place for Diwali, one of the most popular festivals which spiritually signified the victory of light over darkness, good over evil, knowledge over ignorance, and hope over despair. With Tiya and Uncle Mitul, that had been the most recent instance of that kind of challenge.

Diwali is a five-day festival that typically falls toward the end of October, or the first half of November and comes right after Navratri, the nine-day festival that is observed in honor of the divine feminine—Devi. The main night centers on the new moon—the darkest night of autumn. Candles and lanterns called diyas, make Diwali the festival of lights. The sights, sounds, and feasts of Diwali ritually bring family and friends together every year.

Everyone in the family had been cleaning, clearing out unwanted items from their home, renovating, and decorating their homes and offices. Devesh had shown Reign a video of last year's celebration in India where millions of lights were shining on housetops, doors, windows, temples and other buildings.

Reign had suggested that he ask the neighbors if they would like to participate so they could learn about the festival—also so they wouldn't mind that the festivities were going to be loud when the fireworks were lit. Surprisingly, most of the families in the area accepted the invitation. For the first time, the Maharaj family applied for a permit to erect formal white tents on their property, and rented chairs and tables to accommodate the outpouring of guests they expected.

Tonight, for the main celebration, people dressed in new clothes or their best outfits. While the Maharaj family participated in family puja—prayers—to Lakshmi, the goddess of fertility and prosperity, other families said prayers that were reflective of their own cultures and religions.

At Reign's suggestion, the outdoor food spread accommodated all levels of tastes. Spicy foods were on one side of the tent, and mild foods were on the other.

"Sort of like a Heaven and Hell party," Reign explained to Mumma. "When I was growing up, our church had a fundraiser where R&B music and hot foods like chili, tacos, spaghetti and devil's food cake for dessert were in one place, while gospel music and cold foods—like salads, sandwiches, and angel food cake were on the opposite side of the room. Those were so much fun."

"I think I know what side appealed to you more," Mumma teased.

"The angelic side, of course," Reign replied, batting her eyelashes innocently causing Mumma to laugh.

A lavish salad and fruit bar was laid out for those who might not find Indian cuisine to their liking. All were encouraged to at least have a taste, and some found they enjoyed it, though they had been afraid to try it before.

"Wow," their neighbor Angela Levin said to Devesh. "This is amazing. Thank you for inviting us. Are you guys going to do this every year?"

Papa hesitated, then nodded as he nudged Devesh who said, "Looks like we will if it's something everyone would be interested in being a part of."

Jackie, a robust woman who was filling her mouth with some Tandoori chicken, said, "If the food is always this good, then I'll be here."

Reign smiled and asked Angela, "You're Jewish, right?"

"What gave it away?"

Reign gestured to the emblem around the woman's neck.

"Yes, I am," she said, fingering her necklace. "A traditional one."

"It would be nice," Reign said where Mumma, Papa, and Anaya, could hear, "If we could celebrate a Passover and learn something about Jewish customs."

"That would be awesome," Angela said, and her barrel-chested husband agreed.

"The more people learn about the religions and cultures outside of their own, the more tolerant and understanding we all will be," Reign said. "Some of us barely know each other around here. I'd like to change that."

"Sounds good," said Lu McCoy who moseyed up arm in arm with her husband, Darek.

"I know there are some important things involved with Passover," Reign said, peering over their shoulders watching as Jay pretended to chase after his siblings who were quickly outdistancing him and laughing so hard they couldn't keep their balance. "Like clearing out non-Kosher items from the home, but we could host it outdoors for the whole block, like we're doing today. And we'd make sure everything conforms to Kosher standards."

"You know of our ways?" Angela asked, smiling.

"Being a Black woman in America means I don't know what my true religion might have been before my forefathers were brought here. I took the time to learn a little of everything—the spiritual chit'lin circuit. Being immersed in the entire Indian *culture* experience is new for me. Indian movies, food, music and … men, are not."

"Thank God." Devesh comically raised an eyebrow and gave a wide smile that caused everyone to laugh.

The night ended with the Maharajs giving presents to all of their neighbors.

Mumma and Papa thanked Reign for helping others who lived close by learn more about Indian culture, and Papa asked, "Is there something you would like to do to share your culture with us?"

Jay's head whipped up. He scooted over with his favorite munchkins in tow. "As a matter of fact …" he edged, with a pointed look at his mother.

"We can plan something around Kwaanza," Reign said, smiling when Jay nudged her in the side with his elbow. "Which is a seven-day experience in December."

"Maybe a little more open discussion for people to ask questions they've always wanted to ask with no judgment. It'll foster a better understanding all around."

Mumma piped in, "And maybe some of Reign's good food and some dancing too?"

"Of course," Reign said.

Papa beamed, saying, "We would love it."

chapter 35

Thanksgiving dinner was a wicked spread of soul food that nearly had everyone in a coma. Yes, Reign and Jay threw down, and those soul food delicacies were that good. Before dinner was served, Jay had to step out to the airport to scoop up Elise who had leased out her condo in Chicago and took a job with an architectural firm in California. Devesh made sure to slide a plate for him in the microwave since some of the family was scouring for second and third plates and wouldn't leave a crumb if they had their way. Reign was guarding it closely, even borrowed Aunt Kavya's spatula and playfully tapped a few hands of those who were teasing her by pretending to snatch up the goods.

Devesh practically skipped from the dining room with the dessert he'd managed to snag at the same time he fixed Jay's plate. Pranav and Kamran rounded the corner alongside him on their way to join the others who were watching an action flick in the theatre.

He was nearly knocked off his feet as a group of men burst through the theater's doors running as if the very devil was on their heels. Some laid eyes on Devesh and froze, eyes widening with fright and shock. That alone sent a shiver of alarm up his spine.

Devesh made it to the theatre in time to see Bhavin laying a fist to Hiran's gut. Howard, one of Hiran's co-workers, made a mad dash back into the theater. Devesh tried to peer in to see what could have caused such a ruckus. Unfortunately, a few other men had bunched together to keep whatever was going on behind them hidden.

"What happened?" Devesh demanded. He thrust the saucer of sweet potato pie into Pranav's hands and rushed forward. Pranav foisted the dessert on Kamran and was right behind him.

"Devesh don't go in there," Cousin Neerav warned, holding his hands out to keep Devesh from moving forward as Howard was frantically fiddling with the projection system.

Devesh ignored that warning and pushed through the barrier of men and went straight into the theater just as an image flickered off the screen. He whirled to face Hiran and Howard. "What is it that you don't want me to see?"

Kamran ducked under Hiran's arm and sprinted into the theater. Hiran scrambled behind him, but he was too late. Kamran snatched up the remote before Hiran could get to it, then faked to the left to avoid being captured by Howard. He zipped past Bhavin, jumped up on one of the theater's recliners and used the rest of them as a path to his father.

"No," Hiran yelled, tripping over his own feet and sprawling onto one of the recliners.

Kamran rushed to Devesh, with Howard on his heels, close enough to almost get their hands on him. Instead of finishing the journey on foot, Kamran tossed the remote to Devesh, who caught it in midair, curled his hand around it and waited for a moment to see what the two men bearing down on him would do.

Howard and Hiran pulled up short as Bhavin grabbed them both by the shoulder to hold them in place. Whatever was on that screen was something the men didn't want him to see, so he knew it was something his son shouldn't put his eyes on either. Devesh pulled Kamran to his side and said, "Thank you, son. Now go to your mother."

"Yes, Papa," he replied and made off for the dining room.

Devesh rushed further into the theater. Most of the men stayed in the hallway—a safe distance away. Someone closed the door behind them. *Oh, this must be really bad.* He lifted the remote, pushing the button to resume whatever had caused the commotion.

Bhavin braced himself against the patio door. "Devesh, I'm trying to save you some anguish, brother. You shouldn't see that video. Trust me." Hiran and Howard tried to tip out of the room and into the hallway, and he said. "And you should've let me take Hiran's head off."

Devesh inched back, so no one could leave out of the front way. "No, you two stay right here."

The image that came to life nearly took the wind and the life out of Devesh. He closed his eyes bracing against the rage that threatened to take over completely.

Reign.

On her knees.

In front of Devesh.

Pleasuring him to the point of orgasm.

Supposedly in the privacy of their master suite in the Maharaj home.

Devesh centered his soul, trying not to let the anger have its say.

He failed.

Devesh slid an angry gaze at Howard, the red-haired freckled man cowering behind Hiran. No wonder the men in the family had run out of the theater as if their pants were on fire. No wonder Bhavin was trying to put Hiran in the hospital. They weren't stupid.

Howard's blue-eyed focus went to the nearest exit, gauging if he could bypass Bhavin and make it to safety.

Devesh made sure he didn't.

In seven strides that ate up the carpet, he grabbed the man by the scruff of his neck and dragged him toward the series of glass doors leading out to the patio and pool. Bhavin lifted the remote and switched off the recording. And not a moment too soon.

"Devesh?" Reign screamed from a place far behind him. Too far for her to have witnessed what had been displayed on the screen. The men were trying to back her out of the theater.

"Take the children home."

"Please tell me what's going on," she said over Bhavin's shower.

Devesh shot a look at her, and she shrank back, quickly directing the children to come to her. The women had gathered around her, concern etched in their expressions. Aunt Kavya gave Hiran the evil eye. The man had barely been allowed back in the house. Bhavin had vouched for him saying that it was only Tiya that had the two restraining orders and their children needed to be around family. Now this.

"Devesh, I'm going to need you to be the adult in this relationship."

"I don't want to hear that bullshit right now," he growled at Reign, signaling for Bhavin to open the patio doors. "I am so beyond trying to be rational." He gripped Howard's arms, lifted, and ejected him from the theater, causing the man to go airborne, then land face first on the stone patio. Seconds later, Devesh was on top of him turning him over, landing a few punches to his gut, then to his face.

Howard screamed like a girl.

"Who made it??" Devesh roared with each punch.

"I don't know," came the man's muffled response, as he tried to block another series of blows. "That's not the movie that was supposed to be in the package. It said Long Kiss Goodnight."

Long Kiss Goodnight. The action film Hiran brought over for them to watch. But he had to call Howard in to get the projection system working correctly.

"So how did *this* DVD get into the house," Devesh demanded. "And have that label on it?"

"Devesh, stop this," Hiran warned, trying to separate him from Howard. "You're going to kill him. It's probably one of your little private sex tapes."

"Reign would *never* do that. Neither would I," Devesh responded. "Where did it come from?" Devesh roared, straightening to face his brother-in-law, who was shaking so hard his teeth were chattering. "You were the one to wire this house. How did he get access to record us like that?"

"I had Howard do the wiring," Hiran whined, with a frightened glance at his co-worker. "I was busy, and he was really, really cheap."

Devesh tightened his grip on Hiran's shirt. "After we paid you, you let a *stranger* into *our* home because you were too lazy to do it yourself?"

And he hadn't even considered why the prices were really, really cheap?

Devesh jammed his hand into Howard's pocket, fishing for the man's wallet and keys. "We're going to take a little trip."

"I swear there are no others," Howard screeched, trying to wipe the blood from his face with the back of a trembling hand.

Devesh dropped Howard and ran toward Hiran, whose reflexes were a lot slower than was sensible. Devesh lifted him from the ground, traveled a few yards, and dropped him headfirst into the deep end of the pool. Which would have been fine, except everyone knew Hiran couldn't swim.

As some of the family men waited a few minutes before making a half-hearted attempt to fish Hiran out of the water, Howard snailed his body across the stones, trying to put some space between him and Devesh.

Not enough.

Devesh snatched up someone's unused beach towel from a lawn chair. He forcefully escorted Howard to the front of the house, ignoring the protests from his family along the way. He pushed the activation button on Howard's keyfob to figure out which vehicle belonged to that snake. The headlights on a blue Mercedes flashed on.

Anaya sprinted past the patio, rounded the gardens, and picked up speed as she streaked across the front lawn, struggling to catch up with them. Devesh slammed Howard into the passenger seat before tossing the towel over him and saying, "Clean your face." Then Devesh adjusted the driver's seat as far back as it would go and slid behind the wheel.

"I'm going with you," Anaya said, jumping into the back seat.

"No, you're not."

"You can't kill him, Devesh."

"Oh, I have something much worse in mind," he said, glaring at Howard, who shrank down in the passenger seat.

"Reign made me promise that she would still have a husband in the morning. Said she didn't want you in ..." Anaya tilted her head, looking at her brother as he eyed her in the rearview mirror. "What's a pokey?"

"Let's hope you never find out."

chapter 40

Devesh kept a tight grip on Howard's upper arm, following closely on his heels before they waited, peering through the glass doors of an upscale building overlooking downtown Los Angeles. One of the guards finally went on break and the other settled in and became engrossed in whatever was on one of his monitors. They slid in the back way, took the elevator to the eighth floor, then wound their way through a maze of hallways leading to a corner apartment.

The three of them entered a place with sparse furnishings, a small dining table along with a glass desk and two chairs, some artwork, tech books, and a single television.

"For a tech guy," Devesh mused, scanning the immediate areas again. "This place is a little light on hardware."

Devesh and Anaya secured his hands and feet with neck ties and belts they snatched from the drawer in the bedroom. Then they scoured each of the rooms more thoroughly, trying to locate where the man would keep things that would be damaging to someone else. All they found when they slid open the door to the closet in his tiny bedroom were clothes more suited for a corporate hack than a lazy bum of a tech guru.

"Where are they?" Devesh demanded, nearly winded from turning the place over for a half hour and unable to find anything that pointed them in the direction of where the real dirty work was done.

"I don't know what you're talking about," Howard chirped, inching back, before struggling to use his shirt to clear away the blood that pooled at the corners of his mouth.

Devesh quirked an eyebrow, flickered a glance toward the kitchen, putting a particular focus on the butcher block of knives.

"I hear that taking off fingernails from the nail bed can be quite painful."

"My other place," Howard offered up without another second of protest.

"How far is it from here?" Devesh asked.

Howard parted his lips to speak, but when his eyes shifted to the left to avoid looking at Devesh head on, that was a sign. Devesh put his hands around the man's neck and said, "And don't lie to me. I cut up a chicken real well, and a human should be no trouble at all."

"'That sounded better when Reign said it," Anaya whispered.

"Maybe we should get her over here," Devesh suggested. "She almost killed Tiya with that knife and if she sees this video—"

"Through the closet," Howard quickly said, swallowing hard.

Devesh and Anaya shared a speaking glance between them. "Show us."

Howard lifted his hands. "Untie me first."

"Not a chance," Devesh responded at the same time Anaya said, "No."

Howard hobbled toward the closet, pushed an obscure button on the underside of the door, then keyed in a set of numbers. A secret panel whooshed open. Without waiting for Devesh, Anaya stepped through. The lights automatically came on. Devesh dragged Howard and entered an expansive world of tech-savvy genius. Ten monitors were positioned over several glass desks. Computer towers stationed on a series of shelves were flashing with red, green, and white lights. CDs, flash drives, and packaged products were all lined up on the shelves in neat rows. The front cover on one of the packages sitting on the main computer had an image of Reign smiling up at Devesh.

Devesh's heart plummeted. She would be devastated if something like this got out. Devesh flickered a gaze to a set of CD labels. All of them printed with the title *The Long Kiss Goodnight.* Evidently, Howard was also in the business of pirating music CDs, movies, and porn. Another reason to smack Hiran upside the head the next time he laid eyes on him. They had given him funds to procure the real deal. Somehow one of the labels had gotten mixed up in the process.

He couldn't trust the man to tell the truth, but still had to ask, "Who did you sell these to?"

"No one, yet. Vivid Entertainment turned me down," he confessed, and he seemed more upset about that than the fact that he had violated them or that Devesh wanted to put him six feet under.

"Those are the same people who did the Kim and Ray J tape?" Anaya asked, dark brown eyes narrowing on him.

Howard nodded. "They don't take videos anymore unless the people in them show identification and sign release forms," he admitted sadly. "*Now* they're concerned about the legalities of things." Then the freckled man perked up. "But if you give your consent, we can make *millions*," he said, eyes glazed with greed. "All you have to do is sign. You both are hot right now. They were talking five, maybe six million."

"A lot of good that's going to do you where you're going," Anaya said, then pulled out her cell. "I'm calling the police."

"Pull every one of the masters right now," Devesh demanded, holding up a hand to Anaya so she wouldn't complete the call. "You give those to me, and we'll go."

"But we can't let him get away with this," Anaya protested, her face a mask of pure fury.

"Anaya, all I care about is making sure Reign is safe," he replied in a determined tone.

Seeing that Devesh was on his side, Howard quickly plopped down at the desk and pecked in a password. Movie icons spread out from one end of the screen to the other.

Over the man's head, Devesh favored Anaya with a long look, sending a silent message to trust that he knew what he was doing.

Her shoulders relaxed. "So why can't I call the police?"

"We can't trust them," Devesh explained. "Some are corrupt. They'll be looking at her, and one of them might find it's in *their* best interest to make a copy to keep for themselves or maybe even sell." He put his focus on watching Howard delete their files from the computer and the cloud storage.

"Just think about it," he said to Anaya. "They'll drag her into court, and then the jury will see it. Those tapes could go anywhere, fall into the wrong hands; too many hands. She would be devastated."

"How do we know we've got all the files," Anaya asked. "That everything's erased? You're good, Devesh, but not *that* good."

"Jay," Devesh answered after thinking about a moment. Then he whipped out his cell and dialing the number. "How far are you from the airport?"

"Actually, we're almost at the Maharaj house. Hopefully, there's some of that good food left."

Devesh exhaled, hating to disappoint Jay because the guy really loved a good meal—and one that he had helped to cook. But he couldn't allow Jay to go to the house. Someone would say something about what happened tonight and Jay would lose his natural mind. "I need you to drop Elise at the condo and make a detour to where I am."

"What's up?"

"I'm going to give you an address," Devesh replied, flickering a angry look at Howard who was slumped down in the office chair, whimpering like a newborn baby.

"Text it to me," Jay said. "I'm driving right now."

"I don't want this in a text," he responded cautiously as Anaya nodded, also realizing that they didn't want an electronic trail. "Have Elise write it down."

"What are you about to get me into?" Jay asked, and his tone was cautious.

"I need you, Jay," Devesh said. "I wouldn't ask if it wasn't important.

I'll tell you when you get here."

Devesh gave the address and disconnected the call. "We have to get rid of anything that has Reign on it. If Jay lands in the pokey, Reign will kill me." He gestured to the secret door. "Grab the fire extinguisher and that metal trash can from the kitchen."

Anaya rushed to comply.

Howard's wide-eye panic was warranted. Devesh stood on a chair and removed the batteries from the smoke detectors throughout the place.

She came back, fumbled with the pin a few seconds, pulled it, and aimed in the direction so that whatever blast would come would go directly into Howard's face. She was poised for whatever action Devesh needed.

Devesh snatched open the packages that had him and Reign on the cover, and put a match to the DVDs before dropping them into a waste can. "Make sure its contained right in there. We'll drop in more of them once those are destroyed."

"I'll go out to meet Jay when he gets here," Anaya offered.

"No, I'll do that."

"You can't leave me with him," Anaya warned nodding toward Howard, then the blade she had brought in from the kitchen. "He might not be alive when you get back. Reign's not the only one who knows how to cut someone too short to shit."

❀ ❀ ❀

Twenty minutes later, Jay slid the mouse from Howard's hand and clicked on another set of folders—ones that Howard kept avoiding.

Anaya stiffened as snippets from recordings of women who had been drugged, then raped by Howard and some of his friends played on the screen.

"My God," Anaya whispered, hand fluttering to her chest.

"How many are there?" Jay demanded.

"I … I don't know," Howard stuttered, clasping his hands so he wouldn't interfere with Jay's efforts.

"What do you mean you don't know?" Devesh roared, yanking the man's ear so he was forced to look at the shelving system. "You have everything organized, cataloged, taped, and measured. Don't tell us *you don't know*."

"I stopped counting a long time ago," Howard whined, holding up his hands to protect himself.

Devesh slammed him further into the chair. "Pull their names and addresses."

"I don't—"

"Don't lie to me."

"Just calm down," Howard said, trying to ward off any further blows. "Okay. I'll get them for you."

Howard wobbled over to the silver file cabinet, rifled through the contents, then slid a folder to Devesh.

"We're going to stay here until you write a letter of apology to each and every one of them," Jay said, and his tone was deadly.

"But that'll be like I'm confessing," Howard cried, as he flickered a look to the three people surrounding him.

Devesh flipped through the rest of the masters to find out what else the man had done. He froze when another familiar name came into view.

Before Devesh could drop those into the metal container, Anaya leaned over, glanced at the cover image and exhaled.

This time she was the one to lay a fist to the man's face, tumbling him to the floor.

"He had our whole house wired," she screamed as Devesh pulled her away. "He probably has something on everyone."

Devesh gripped the chair and swiveled it so Howard was facing them. There was some truth in what Anaya said. "I want all of them."

"Okay, okay." He gestured toward the bottom shelf, and Anaya swiped the first ones within reach. Bhavin, Priyanshi. More of Reign. And even—

"Oh my God, Mumma and Papa," Anaya yelled, smacking the top of Howard's head, causing him to duck down.

Devesh put a vice grip on her arm to keep her from hitting him again, though he actually wanted to do so himself.

"None of Tiya," Devesh said at the same time as Jay who narrowed his gaze on Howard, asking, "How is that possible?"

Howard first looked to Devesh and then Jay. "She's the one who wanted the recordings," he confessed. "She paid me to make them, let me back into the house late at night to adjust the cameras and put in new ones. She just wanted ones of you and Reign. She didn't know about the others."

Devesh was so livid he couldn't put a voice to how he felt.

"We'll only put fire to the ones of our family and leave the rest for the police to find."

"But you said—"

Devesh glared Howard into silence. "I lied."

"He could go to jail for those others," Anaya offered, placing a hand on Jay's shoulder.

"You're right," Jay responded, clicking the keys to bypass firewalls, find hidden falls, making sure everything related to the Maharaj family was erased off the hard drive. "These women are someone's sister, or daughter, and by now maybe someone's wife. He did this to them without their knowledge."

Devesh gestured to the screen, then glowered angrily at Howard. "They should have a choice in whether they want to be subjected to police scrutiny and the court system. Some of them know you did something, but couldn't prove it. Now ..."

While Howard ranted and raved, pleaded and begged, they wiped the recordings he'd made of the women in their family and their mates. Devesh was barely holding it together with each one they uncovered. Jay watched closely as the man extracted every file from his digital library, the cloud, a backup server, and a file-sharing network. There was also a backdoor website that Devesh couldn't navigate earlier. And he had tried several times.

"Put in the password," Jay commanded.

"I can't do that," Howard cried, and he was trembling with fear. More fear than he'd shown all night if that was possible. "They'll kill me if I do."

Jay turned to look at Howard. "I'll kill you if you don't."

Howard held out his hand for his keys. Devesh reached into his pockets, then slapped them in his palm. Howard placed the keyfob near the right computer tower. Jay slid the mouse and clicked on a secret folder, and a series of earth-shattering images sprang to life across several screens.

At the point when Devesh didn't think things could get any worse ...

They did.

chapter 41

Devesh, Jay, Howard, and Anaya left Howard's place an hour later and slid by two late night convenience stores to buy enough stamps to mail off those letters and DVDs, and pick up three pairs of rubber gloves as well as a burner phone to report the crime. Both Devesh and Anaya had to ignore the constant calls and texts from their significant others, but Jay finally suggested, "At least say something. They're probably worrying themselves sick about what's going on." They complied and simply sent an "everything's alright, just tying up some loose ends" kind of text. The calls and texts from Reign and Pranav finally died down.

Then the group slid to the main post office in Los Angeles for Howard to drop more than seventy packages addressed to his victims in the late night slot, before taking him back to his apartment. They covered their bases by wiping down everything in the apartment that would have their fingerprints. Anaya put the extinguisher and other items back in place, but the metal trashcan was taken to Jay's car.

"We've been watching way too much television," Jay mused, as they moved out of Howard's hearing to discuss the details of things they should do to cover their behinds.

"If that were true," Anaya countered. Her voice was pure ice. "We'd be hiding a body right now."

"That's not funny," Devesh said, locking gazes with his sister whose demeanor was colder than he had ever witnessed.

"I don't think it was meant to be," Jay replied. "We're all on the security tapes. If something happens, we might be in the hot seat right along with him."

"Can you do something about that?" Anaya asked, and her expression was slightly alarmed. "We were doing something right. We shouldn't be penalized for that."

"Officer friendly won't see it that way," Jay answered. "If dude was so key on keeping this operation on point, he'd have some way of seeing who's coming and going and a way to manipulate things."

Devesh went to Howard, who was so unbothered by this that he'd lost his sense of fright and had fallen asleep. He shook the man hard enough to snatch him from his nap. "Do you have a feed into the building's security cameras?"

Howard blinked, cowered in the chair and then shook his head as though to clear his thoughts. "Yeah."

"Show me," Jay demanded, wheeling Howard's chair to the desk.

Howard leaned forward, stretching his tied hands toward the keyboard.

"No, just navigate me to it," Jay said, settling into the chair. "I'll do the rest."

"He can do it faster," Anaya offered with a pointed look at Jay.

"He could also hit a few keystrokes that we aren't aware of and wipe his entire computer. Then all of those children will stay lost."

Minutes later, Jay had processed the video that had been taken when they first arrived. The sun was rising when he finally figured out how to splice the images where it removed the clips that showed when the threesome had come into the building and when they left. Those guards needed to be fired. They were so busy between sleeping and watching a porn vid—Jay recognized as Howard's work—that they never caught on to the perfectly-timed blips on the screen when Jay looped in earlier footage.

They decided against using the burner phone, and with the threat of losing an entire finger, Howard made the anonymous call to local law enforcement right from his cell and house phone, then another to the FBI directly. To speed things along, Jay had Howard send a few of the most explicit and damaging of the pictures to the tip line for the police department.

Anaya and Devesh followed Jay's lead and unplugged all the wiring and connections between the computers so that Howard would have a hard time wiping out any evidence in the time it took for the police to arrive. Jay queued up the security video so that it stayed in one final thirty-minute loop before he and Anaya left the apartment and waited in the car which they drove to the back entrance. They signaled to Devesh with a text when the first of the patrol cars arrived.

Devesh left some of the more incriminating evidence spread throughout both places, jammed a nail in the secret door so it wouldn't close, then beat a hasty retreat down the back stairwell. The three of them took off in Jay's car, dropping the metal trashcan off in a dumpster near the meat market a little distance away from Howard's place.

The entire episode had taken nearly all night, and when they were done, Devesh told Jay, "Remind me not to ever get on your bad side."

"You married my bad side," Jay replied.

🪷 🪷 🪷

Devesh hadn't made it into the foyer of his home when a call from Anaya came through.

"They just rushed Mumma to the hospital," she said, then filled him in on what little she knew.

"I'm on my way," he said and disconnected.

"What's wrong?" Reign asked, placing the last of his clothes in a garment bag. They were supposed to leave for Chicago tomorrow for the closing on Reign's house that her nephews purchased. Looks like there was a good chance they wouldn't make it.

"All this drama has taken effect on Mumma. Seems that she had a heart attack or something." He exhaled slowly, trying to tamp down on his fear as the realization that he could lose such a precious woman because of his baby sister's actions hit him full force. "I could give Tiya the spanking my parents should've given her a long time ago."

"I'll stay here," Reign said, watching him frantically gather up his things and make his way toward the front door. "Call the minute you know something."

Devesh froze with his hand on the knob. "You know, I miss them so much when they're traveling," he whispered. "I don't think I could ever … if they …."

She went to him, wrapped her arms around his waist. "Don't think about any of that right now."

"Go on and get Aunt Kavya and the kids." He took her hand. "You all are coming with me. "

❀ ❀ ❀

The Maharaj family were gathered in the waiting area down the hall from Mumma's room in the intensive care wing. All of the children spilled out into the brightly lit hallway, with the parents hanging nearby.

"This is your fault," Tiya screeched, causing everyone—even other families—to focus in their direction. "You brought this woman into our lives, and it's been chaos ever since."

"Wasn't chaos until you took it there," Devesh snapped, and Anaya quickly came to his side. "Wasn't chaos when I wrote you that check. Wasn't chaos when we saved your ass. Well, Reign's presence in my life correlates to all of that new money in my bank account when you're asking me to … 'help a sister out'". He scanned the solemn expressions from the rest of the people in the waiting room. "Any one of you have something to say about Reign being here, make sure you have an open wallet to go along with your big mouth."

The nurse with a mocha complexion nodded her approval, but gestured for Devesh to use his "inside voice."

"And since my children are here," Devesh said in a lower tone, leaning in so there was only a few inches of spaces between them. "This is where you take a hike."

Tiya huffed, ran to the elevator and Hiran was right behind her.

Leena and Kamran rushed down the hallway to be with their cousins. Reign moved to Anaya, whose tear-filled eyes mirrored those of several others nearby. "What are they saying?

"They're still doing tests," she said, and Pranav placed his arm about her shoulders, but his expression was grave.

"What happened, Papa?" Devesh asked.

"She was in the living room. Tiya was pleading with us to let them move back in. They have been living in a motel. We said no. Then she demanded that we give in to her wishes." Papa ran a hand through his salt and pepper hair. "She said we owed her because we were to blame for what Mitul did to her. She said it's entirely our fault. I thought we were going to have to call the police. She was so... difficult."

"She's always been difficult; you just spoiled her a little too much," Devesh said, taking in the people who were watching their exchange, but keeping their distance. "Now she has to be a grown-up, and she doesn't like it."

"True," Papa said, grimacing. "But we spoiled you, too, my son."

"Not quite as much," Devesh said, clasping a hand on his father's shoulder. "But I still turned out alright."

Leena and Kamran came back to be near Papa who held them to his side, despite the worry in his dark brown eyes.

"That you did, son," Papa said, finally giving up a smile. "That you did."

"And I'm glad you didn't let Tiya guilt you into anything. She's not right about that. Mitul is to blame."

Leena left Papa after a squeeze of her hand in his before going to Reign.

"I do not want Tiya here," Papa said, glancing in the direction Tiya went in. "She raised her hand to slap your mother. She has *never* done such a thing before. What is wrong with her?"

"Where do you think she ran off to?"

"Tiya?" He peered down the hall. "Maybe the cafeteria. Hiran's always hungry."

Devesh aimed in the direction of the elevator.

"Devesh," Reign called after him. "Don't do anything that's going to require me to come up with bail money."

He paused, but only for a split second; didn't turn to face her as he said over his shoulder, "I can't promise that."

Then he took off in a sprint.

With a few seconds of careful thought, Reign pressed Leena into Anaya's arms and quickly ushered Kamran to Papa, then took off in the direction of her husband.

"Devesh, calm down," she warned, watching as he kept pressing the call button for the elevator to come.

"She tried to put her hands on my mother."

"What are you going to do?" she asked, angling so she was in his path when the silver doors opened.

"She has lost what little mind she had," he responded, pushing up his sleeves. "I'm going to help her find it."

"Devesh, you can't put your hands on your sister."

"I wouldn't dream of it," he said, taking out his cell and punching in a few keys before stepping onto the elevator. "I have something else entirely in mind."

❀ ❀ ❀

Tiya visibly paled when she looked up from her spot at a corner table in the brightly lit cafeteria. Devesh was barreling down on her. She shrank back, almost cowering, the contents of her drink nearly spilled on Hiran.

Devesh's movements were so frantic and out of sync that it caused others to look in their direction. Some quickly shifted to booths or tables that were much further away.

"Nebraska or Alaska?"

Tiya first looked to Reign, then back to Devesh before she grasped his meaning. "I don't know anyone there."

"And that's my point. There's no way for you to cause trouble for anyone there or here."

"You can't make me leave," she said in a false show of bravado that Hiran tried to mimic by puffing out his chest.

"Yes, he can," Reign said. "All it will take is having Mumma file a restraining order against you if you don't leave peacefully."

Tiya showed all thirty-two of her pearly whites. "She would *never* do that."

"Just like she would never believe you would hit her?"

"I didn't hit her," Tiya protested, but quickly averted her eyes.

"You came close enough," Devesh said through his teeth. "Too close to allow you to be near her again. First with my wife, then my daughter, and now with my mother. You're like the Energizer Bunny—you keep coming and don't know when to quit. But I know how to make it stop."

"We have that video," she said with a lift of her chin before locking a victorious gaze on Devesh. "That's a game-changer."

"Video?" Reign inquired. "What video?"

"Reign, go back upstairs."

"Absolutely not," she said, angling so that she was a mere three feet in front of Tiya. "What video?"

"The one that was recorded in his bedroom," Tiya taunted, with a wild laugh but she flickered a quick look in the direction of the security guard near the entrance.

"Tiya, I'm warning you," Devesh said, face darkening with anger.

"Awwwww, she doesn't know," she said in an innocent tone.

"Tiya, don't do it," Devesh warned and he moved forward trying to block her view of Reign.

She scoffed, putting her eyes on Reign. "The one that shows my brother screwing you—"

Reign flexed, and Tiya scrambled out of her chair and quickly took three steps back.

"I've never seen a rear end so wide in my life," Tiya taunted, ignoring Hiran's gesture for her to be quiet.

She should have listened to Devesh. Or her husband.

Reign snatched up the glass of soda on Tiya's tray and introduced the contents to his sister's face.

Tiya inhaled a mouthful of liquid and could barely breathe.

"There is no video," Devesh said, and his voice was deadly calm. He held Reign against him so she wouldn't give his sister the beat-down she'd been aiming for since Reign had set foot on California soil. As if nearly slicing her neck wasn't enough to show that Reign was not to be toyed with.

He leaned in closer so they were a breath apart and repeated. "There. Is. No. Video."

"You fool," she screeched, pounding a fist into her husband's chest. "You didn't get the master or a copy?"

"Howard was giving me a look at the master right then all those men came into the theatre. I told them to give us a few moments, but they came in before the right movie was queued up. He—" Hiran gestured to Devesh. "Destroyed the rest of them before Howard was picked up by the police."

"That's not an excuse. You had keys to his place," she snarled. "You could've went by and found something on his computer."

Devesh almost released his hold on Reign to let her finish teaching Tiya a valuable lesson. The depth of the couple's deception was unnerving. Did they know the levels of depravity that they found on that man's systems?

"We could've made millions!" Tiya shook her fist in her husband's face. "Like that Kardashian whore."

"The police took everything," Hiran admitted and took a step back from his infuriated wife.

"So *they* have all our money right now," she said, slamming her hand against his chest.

"Hey, we're going to need y'all to keep it down in here," a beefy security guard said, ambling over to where the four of them were standing.

They were silent for a moment as Reign put her focus on Devesh, waiting for an explanation that wasn't forthcoming.

Devesh passed his cell to Reign and said, "We'll talk about that later.

For now, could you finish these out for me?"

Reign studied the screen for a moment, then looked back to him. "Are you serious?"

"As fast as you can."

She nodded and put her focus on the task at hand.

"I'm going back to India," Hiran said to Devesh. "There's nothing for me here."

"I should've never married you," Tiya growled, punching him again. "You're weak. Spineless. Coward. You're a man. You're supposed to take care of me," she protested with a wry twist of her thin lips.

"Take care of you; not become a slave trying to do it." Hiran sighed, and the sound of it was sad and defeated. "It was never enough. It will *never* be enough."

"So you're just gonna leave me here with your little brats?"

"My brats? Not yours?" Hiran's laugh was brash. Something Devesh had never heard from the man before. "That's fine. They'll come with me. My family will help me. Can you say the same for yours?"

Devesh kept his focus on Reign, who was clicking away while his sister's marriage was imploding right before their eyes.

"That's how this works?" Tiya asked. "You're going to leave me with nothing?"

"And what's the reason you'll have nothing?" Devesh whispered. "Have you thought about that? No one in this family will help you after what you did." He flickered his look between the couple. "You ran through that money so quick it was as though you never had it. Now you need more. You can't even blame it on drugs or something tangible.

"Our parents indulged you way too much, and you feel the world owes you; that *everyone* owes you something. But you made the choices that brought you to this point in life. You'll have to live with that, little sister." Then he leveled a stony glare at Tiya. "Did you know Howard had a tape of Mumma and Papa?"

Tiya's hand went up to her mouth. Reign's head whipped upward to him.

"And he had several images of *your* little girl in a pedophile sharing network."

Reign gripped Devesh's shirt, "Did he—"

"No," he answered. "There weren't any pictures of Leena or Kamran. We made sure of it."

"We?" Reign shot back. "Who's the *we* you're talking about?"

"He wasn't supposed to do that," Tiya said with an angry look at her husband who shook his head. "He was only supposed to give us Devesh and Reign."

Reign slid the phone into Devesh's hand. He turned the screen to face Tiya.

"I have a one-way ticket to Omaha for both of you," Devesh explained. "And a single residence room waiting."

"You can't do this," she said, alarmed, probably because she realized that the opposite might be the case. "I'm going back to India, then."

"With what money?" Devesh challenged as Hiran seemed oblivious to the exchange since he was scrolling through his phone.

"The money that—"

Hiran coughed into his hand, ending Tiya's sentence. "Actually, I used the last of it to pay the movers, who charged us triple by the way," he said shooting a glare at Reign. "We've been living in a hotel suite. There isn't any money for a ticket for you to India. I can't even buy a bus ticket to Los Angeles."

"I'll pay for you both to get to Nebraska," Devesh offered. "But the children will remain here with us. Mumma would not do well without seeing her grandchildren. She'll be worrying about whether they're being taken care of. We can raise them right, here."

"We?" Reign asked, blinking her confusion. "What do you mean— *we*—Indian man?"

"I mean, that the children—my niece and nephew—are at the point where they can learn to be better. We can influence them and—"

"I need a plainer interpretation of that whole "we" thing, Mr. Maharaj. Because your mother and father are in no position to care for another set of children full-time."

"Alright," Devesh said facing her head on. "They will stay with us."

"And you're putting that out there without asking me first?" she snapped, moving so she was directly in his space. "You're just telling me that I'm going to have to accept the children of my known enemy into *my* house?" Now it was Reign pushing a hand into his chest. "I'm supposed to split my time with them and my own children?" She shook her head. "I didn't sign up for that. Hell, you'd better be glad *your* children made it here. I'm no spring chicken."

"And you're no old cluck, either," he shot back.

She blinked, absorbed that retort and tried, really tried, not to smile. "That was funny."

Devesh lifted his hand and gave himself a pat on the back, then pulled her away, whispering so only she could hear. "Honey, I know this isn't what either one of us wanted, but I'm thinking of the children. And it serves another purpose. It's less likely that she'll do something stupid if her children are under our care."

"Now, that's some Game of Thrones type stuff right there," she whispered back, then pulled away to look up to him. She parted her lips to speak, but Devesh kissed her instead.

"It's settled," he said to Hiran and Tiya. "The children remain here, and—"

"We get shipped off to some Podunk place where we don't know a soul."

"How would my wife say it?" Devesh replied, leaning in so there was only a breath between them. "You don't have to go, but you've got to get the hell up out of here."

chapter 42

Reign actually had to come up with that bail money. Howard Gaytan was arrested and charged with several counts of selling and disseminating child pornography. He was the gatekeeper for an underworld of pedophiles who entrusted him to keep their network, file-sharing catalogs, videos, and images of children they held in their possession and shared amongst each other. Though Devesh, Jay, and Anaya had altered the security tapes and had taken other precautions, Howard served up the three sleuths and others in order to get an immunity deal. The police brought charges of evidence tampering against them, but the case was weak because other than Howard's word there was nothing that connected the trio to any crime.

Those charges were immediately dropped against Jay and Anaya when Devesh confessed, despite his lawyer's advice, that he alone destroyed the tapes of his family. Devesh also made them aware that Howard was the one to drop the rest of the recordings in the mail to the women he had violated. And Brynn Weimer, the lawyer representing him, made a clear point that he had left all of the videos and photos of those exploited children fully intact for law enforcement to take care of things.

When Devesh stood before the judge, and the television cameras were situated in the back of the courtroom after Brynn put in a motion to bar any press, but it was denied. Some jail time seemed likely, so Devesh angered the prosecutor, Linda Rice, and ticked off his lawyer by asking, "May I have permission to speak freely, Your Honor?"

Linda immediately chimed in with, "Your honor, that is not appropriate. We have all the evidence and his own confession."

"Oh, I'm not trying to get out of that confession," Devesh countered smoothly. "But before he makes a determination or sentences me. I'd like to say something that says why I took the action that I did."

Brynn snapped a look at him that meant she really wished Devesh would let her do what he paid for.

Judge Roseboro said, "You have the floor, but only for a few minutes."

"Thank you, Your Honor."

Both Brynn and Linda took a seat.

"Your Honor," Devesh began with a quick glance over his shoulder at Jay before continuing with, "I had Howard mail those tapes to the women he had violated because he took their power away. I only wanted to give it back. They were women, too. Women just like my wife, my mother, my sister, my cousins—who he also violated that same way." He paused and looked toward Reign. "If you knew what my wife went through for her to even allow *me*—her own husband—to see her naked, when another man—actually men—had taken her power. For her to know that someone else had a video of her doing something only that her husband should see, and that Howard would spread it to the entire world ..." He shook his head. "I could not allow that to happen. So if I have to spend some time in jail because I did what it took to protect my wife and my family, I understand your position, because the law is the law. But when the law is that blind to punish *me* for doing what was right so that those images didn't fall into anyone else's hands? Not even the police—who are—wait for it—men and who have come under fire for misdeeds. That's not any kind of fair.

"I didn't kill anyone. I didn't stab anyone. I didn't hurt—well, I did put a hurting on Howard's behind, but he had that coming."

Chuckles abounded from every area of the courtroom, even not-so-discretely from the judge and bailiff.

"Devesh," Reign whispered, but it was loud enough that several people turned their heads toward her. "You might want to pull back on that honesty, thing—you're digging yourself deeper."

"No, the judge is allowing me to say something that needs to be said," Devesh answered. "My lawyer has to gloss over some things on my behalf, the prosecutor has her own agenda, but the only thing I have in my favor is the truth." Devesh turned back to the Judge whose chin was resting in his open palm.

"Now you all want me to spend time in the pokey when I gave law enforcement the full opening of what it would take to find each and every one of those children who is being held somewhere being abused and brutalized every day for men who only see them as property and a source of pleasure. Children who are alone and believe that pain is all the world has to offer them.

"I'll do my time," he said, pausing at Reign's choked cry. "I'll miss my wife, I'll miss my children," he said, looking at the twins and then to Jay, "I'll miss my friend." Then he took in all of the people on the rows behind Reign, Jay, Anaya, Aunt Kavya and the twins. "I'll miss my family and friends, but what I won't have is any regret over doing what was best to protect my wife from someone hurting her again."

Brynn sent a pleading look in Reign's direction.

"Your Honor," Reign said, getting to her feet. "If I may speak on my husband's behalf?"

"Yeah, we might as well hear from the entire courtroom," Linda said sourly as she stood.

The judge banged his gavel then pointed it toward Linda who instantly reclaimed her seat. "I will hear you," the judge said, "You have five minutes to wrap this up. The Lakers game is coming on and my wife's cooking Italian tonight. I love both. And her too." Then he grimaced and added, "Being here, not so much. But this is getting pretty interesting."

He gestured with the gavel for Reign to speak.

"Your Honor, he's right," she said. "I love him, but even now I struggle with allowing him to see me as I really am. There's a man who once told me that Black men don't like fat women and that I would have to pay him for sex."

The bailiff, who had to be at least two inches over six feet, scrunched up his face and snapped his attention to the judge, who also frowned.

"When he told me that, I didn't let a man touch me that way for almost twenty years," she said. "I allowed myself to believe him and I became a victim of a man who did not see me as anything worth anything except for what was between my thighs. The same way my sister was a victim and killed by my uncle who only valued her for the very same thing. He thought nothing of throwing her down the stairs to keep his dirty secrets. We didn't have a man in our lives who was willing to protect us. I didn't have a father in my life to protect me."

She focused on Devesh for a quick moment. "Only this year did I venture out to date someone. All these years, I thought I was so ugly that no man would ever love me for me. Now I have a husband that has gone to this degree to protect me. In this world where so many people only think of themselves, you can't know what that has done for me. My husband protected me, and those anonymous women who can press charges on their own. And it was done in a way that still gave the police and FBI the opportunity to find those children and bring those men to justice.

"Somewhere those children are with men who feel they are justified in doing the horrible things that they do. Please put the energy and effort into finding each and every one of them, and putting *those* men in jail. I pray for those children every single day. While we're in this courtroom, or when we're going about our everyday lives—working, eating and laughing and talking about things that don't really matter; those children know nothing but pain and fear and their souls are being drained of any life they may have. That, Your Honor, is a travesty that bears judgment, not what my husband has done."

The judge sighed, studied Reign, Devesh, and even the family members who took up five full rows. He also looked to the media who awaited his ruling.

"Though, I do not condone you taking matters into your own hands …" He focused on Linda table and asked, "How many women have come forward so far?"

"Ummmm," Linda hedged, looking at her more polished colleague who responded, "About thirty-five so far, but that wasn't—"

"Thirty five," the judge repeated and glanced at Devesh. "And how many envelopes did you send that night?"

"Did *Howard* send," Devesh corrected.

"Don't mince words with me, Mr. Maharaj," the judge warned.

"Seventy-three," he answered. "I wanted the women to decide if they would involve the police and have their lives ripped apart."

The judge peered at Linda. "And how many arrests have you made in the child sex trafficking case?"

"One hundred and …"

"Forty-seven," Linda's colleague supplied.

"One-hundred and forty-seven," the judge mused with a quick look at his watch.

"And how many children have you recovered so far?"

Linda flipped through a folder, found some notes, and said, "Approximately three hundred; give or take. But this case is spread across several states and even internationally. It might take a while."

Judge Roseboro banged the gavel. "I've made a decision."

"Wait! What?" Linda exclaimed, jumping up from the chair.

"You haven't even heard—"

"That you all have put away twice as many pedophiles as women who didn't decide to come forward," the judge finished. "That you've recovered nearly five times that amount in children who are safely back with their families."

Devesh leaned over and whispered to Reign. "Did he just split things down the middle?"

"In reverse," she replied.

Judge Roseboro narrowed his gaze at Devesh. "Did I hear you call it the pokey?"

Devesh gave him a sheepish smile and said, "That's what my wife told me."

"Haven't heard that word in years." Judge Roseboro banged his gavel and quickly got to his feet. "No sentence. All charges dismissed. I'm going home to my wife."

chapter 43

"Ms. Maharaj, I'm sorry to inform you that Leena was taken off the school grounds a few minutes ago."

Reign sat up on the lounger and ran those words from Ms. Addison, the director of the twin's school, back in her mind. She still couldn't process them quite right. *Leena was taken off the school grounds.* As in kidnapped?

"What?!" Reign shrieked, causing Devesh to leave his studio and came to her side. "Wait a minute."

She put the phone on speaker, trying to stay upright though her knees were ready to give out.

"A man and a woman shot three of our teachers, two security guards, and a teacher's aide before they snatched Leena and took off. Kamran fought that man off. But he had no choice but to stop when the man put the gun to Leena's head."

"Sweet Jesus," Reign cried.

Devesh caught her before she slipped to the carpet.

"The police are here," Ms. Addison confirmed.

"We're on the way," Devesh said, keeping a tight hold on his wife.

🪷 🪷 🪷

Uniformed and officers in plainclothes from Newport Coast Police, and a sprinkling of FBI agents were scattered over the school grounds. Traffic slowed to a crawl as drivers craned their heads around to check out all the commotion. Several detectives were surveying the scene and questioning the rest of the teary-eyed staff who were concerned for the others who had been wheeled off in a series of ambulances. One was dead at the scene; the other five were in critical condition.

"Ma'am do you know anyone who would do such a thing?" the lanky officer asked Reign.

"I have restraining orders against my sister-in-law and my ex," she admitted. "But I don't think he would stoop to such measures. He has a wife; he has children. He has a life."

"And some woman," Devesh added, looking to the office for answers. "They said there was some blonde who helped the kidnapper."

"My ex isn't into White women." She glanced at Devesh. "Maybe Tiya hired someone? She's still in contact with Amy. Both of them have hated me from day one."

"I personally put Tiya and Hiran on that plane to Nebraska," Devesh explained. "Kidnapping Leena? My sister wouldn't stoop that low."

"She went low enough to have us all recorded," she shot back. "And to have someone ready to sell it all over the world."

Devesh clamped down on his response.

The officer flipped open a notepad. "We checked into Dr. Newsome once the principal told us about the restraining order you had out on him. He doesn't have so much of that life anymore."

"What do you mean?" Devesh asked, placing his arm around Reign's shoulder

"His wife left him, took the kids and filed for divorce. He lost his tenured position at the university, and his speaking tour ended when sponsors pulled out after a televised confrontation with"—the officer looked up—"Devesh Maharaj."

"There's also the fact that you all helped take down a major child sex trafficking network," another officer said coming to stand next to the older one. "Those people are well connected and don't take too kindly to someone poking a hole in their beehive. Several high-profile men are on their way to prison behind that investigation. But they're not all behind bars just yet. One of them could have taken her as revenge."

chapter 44

"Oh, my God," Reign said, burying her face in Devesh's chest. "Those criminals have my baby."

Devesh embraced her as the sobs wracked her body. "Did you have to tell her that?" he growled at the officer, rocking with Reign in his arms, trying to give some comfort for the blow that statement had rendered.

"I'm just making you aware of all possibilities," officer Richards said, meeting Devesh's glowering look head-on.

"Richards, go back inside to the scene," one of the veteran officers commanded. "I'll keep the parents up to speed."

Richard shrugged and stalked off in the direction of his fellow officers milling about near the beginning of the taped off crime scene.

Jay pulled up in a silver Buick LaCrosse, tires screeching in protest. He barely parked it at the curb before scrambling from behind the driver's seat. Jay took off running, making his way past the throngs of people to where the detectives were speaking with Reign and Devesh. He was stopped by a set of officers who were camped out by the yellow tape. The Latino detective nearest Devesh gestured that it was alright to let Jay through.

"What happened?" Jay asked, placing his arms about his mother's shoulder.

Devesh filled him in because Reign was too choked up to speak.

"But one of the teachers gave a description, and our sketch artist should be here in a few hours," said a red-cheeked officer. "She'll get right on it."

"Give me a minute," Jay said and sprinted back to his car. When he returned, Jay flicked on his iPad Pro and said, "Let me take a stab at it."

The vet looked over to his slimmer partner who said, "I don't see why not. We can either wait a couple of hours for Latisha Dewalt to arrive or use what he has and get moving."

Jay took ten minutes to absorb the description the school secretary gave him. The elements that came as the woman gave details that were all too familiar caused Reign to barrel into Devesh's chest, trying to let the warmth of him sweep out the chill that had settled in her soul. By the end of the composite sketch, the image was clear.

"He has a daughter," Reign whispered. "Why? Why would he take my baby?"

"He wants money," Jay replied.

Devesh said, "We'll give him whatever he wants,"

"Sir, you'll have to work with us and the FBI," the detective warned.

"If it comes down to handling this on our own, we will," Jay said in a resolute tone, and Devesh nodded. "I know y'all want him. But what we want is my sister—*alive.*"

❀ ❀ ❀

The Maharaj home had a vibe of solemnity as all of the family sat in silent support while Devesh and Reign waited for the call. Tonight's dinner was still intact as though no one, not even the children, had an appetite. Kamran was practically inconsolable. He immediately went to the Puja the minute they made it into the house. Tiya's children were

by his side. A stark change from when they had first come to live with
Reign and Devesh. The first time Tiya's children got into some major
mischief, Kamran was the one to give his older cousins the new pecking
order. He told them, "Mama said when she was growing up, that if any
of her brothers or her sister got in trouble, they were *all* in trouble."
Kamran put a steely focus on his cousins. "That's not happening here.
Get with the program or it's not going to be happy times around this
camp."

Leena folded her little arms over her chest and nodded her simple,
And that's that.

Devesh's stunned expression as he watched from the threshold of
their den, was MasterCard priceless. Then his concern immediately
transformed into laughter so hard he had tears streaming down his face.

Reign had given her children a subtle head nod, and they both returned
it in kind. To say that the cousins quickly realized there was a new
sheriff and deputy in town, was putting it mildly. Having to care for
Tiya's children did not become the burden that Reign believed it would
be. More or less because the children actually took to boundaries and
also enjoyed the rewards that came with doing things right.

Reign situated herself next to Kamran on the floor as he went on and
on about what he should've done differently, then Leena wouldn't be
gone. Reign rocked him as he cried, and the normally less verbal of the
twins, talked himself straight into the point he passed out. Devesh took
him from her arms and settled him with Mumma and Aunt Kavya so
Reign could listen in on the plans the officers and agents, spread out
over their living and dining rooms, had come up with.

Up until the police and FBI arrived an hour ago, the men of the family,
and even a few women, had held bats and knives and looked more like
gang lords ready to go in search of Leena than a normal, loving family.
The scene of support would've been laughable if the moment weren't
so serious.

The FBI had set up camp and tons of devices in the dining room.
Devesh and Reign had placed their phones on the chargers so that they
were fully ready whenever Shawn made contact. Both because there

was a greater possibility that he would reach out to Devesh since Reign had him blocked on all fronts.

Five hours after they'd made it to the house, Devesh's cell rang and everyone tensed.

The robust FBI agent at the dining room table nodded, but reminded him, "Put the phone on speaker on my count."

"Try to keep them on the line as long as possible," a pretty brunette agent reminded them.

The agent with salt-and-pepper hair at the table in front of the laptop flashed his fingers for a count of 1-2-3-4.

"Where is my daughter?" Devesh demanded.

"You don't call the shots here," Shawn said, trying to mask his voice. "Put Reign on the phone. Right now."

Reign closed her eyes, trying to stem the tide of tears as she asked, "Shawn, why are you doing this?"

The officer grimaced at her mention of Shawn's name. Several of them groaned.

Reign flinched, realizing that she'd made a mistake she couldn't afford to make so early on.

Shawn paused for so long, Reign thought he had disconnected the call. Then he asked in his normal voice, "How did you know it was me?"

"Everyone saw you, Shawn. You shot *six* people. How did you think you were going to get away with it?" she asked. "What do you want from me?"

"All I want to do is talk."

"Then why take my daughter?"

A tall agent with sandy brown hair nodded toward the one sitting at the computer who shook his head. Not enough time had passed to get a lead on his location.

"Because you'll come for her."

Reign's shoulders slumped behind that admission. "How do I know she's alright?"

"You don't," he taunted. "And that's not my problem."

Reign righted herself quickly, a determined, calculating look in her eyes. "That means she's already dead," she whispered a choked cry. "Then there's no reason for me to come. Goodbye, Shawn. I'm hanging up now."

Agent Bateman's head snapped up. The brunette shook her head. Devesh gripped the edge of the dining room table, angling to send a frantic message to Reign. She held up a hand to ward him off.

"Wait," Shawn said, and a few seconds later, they heard, "Mama."

Reign exhaled a relieved breath, but several agents gestured for her to remain calm. "Hey, baby girl." She chanced a look at Devesh, who closed his eyes and whispered a prayer of thanks before opening them again.

"He hurt Kamran," she said, her voice clear and not whiny as though she was afraid.

Of course, that would be Leena's first concern. "Kamran's alright, sweetie."

"He gave me some peanut butter and jelly, but I wouldn't eat it. Mama, I don't like him. When are you coming for me?"

"Soon baby, real soon."

Papa pulled Mumma close to him. Tears were streaming down her face. Anaya laid her head on Pranav's chest whose expression was feral. Aunt Kavya, carrying Kamran, wound her way through the throng of family members and settled in the Puja.

Then Shawn was on the line again and gave an address. "Bring your passport and that smart ass Swami dude. I want to show him a thing or two." Then he paused before adding, "If I see the police, I will hurt her. Think I'm playing?"

He disconnected the call.

"The San Francisco Naval shipyards. The perfect hiding grounds," Agent Harper said, putting his focus on the rest of the team. "Part of it has been developed into condominiums."

"But most of it is closed by the EPA," Officer Mitchell said. "The site's been part of a superfund cleanup effort to remediate the leftovers of decades of industrial and radiological use."

The lead detective peered at the images of the area on the laptop. "We need to call the EPA to see if we need to be in Hazmat suits to go in that place."

"And it's still a ship yard, which means he's set up some way to get out of the country," Devesh said.

Jay frowned, pointing out, "He didn't ask for money."

"He wants something more valuable than money," Devesh mused. "He wants my wife."

A grey-eyed agent came forward with a pendant on a silver chain. We need you to wear this," he said, draping it around Reign's neck. "That way, we can hear everything and keep up with where you are."

"He asked you to bring your passport," Jay said, looking over his notes on the iPad. "So he plans on taking you out of the country and into another one somehow."

"He didn't ask me to bring hers," Reign mused, tightening her hold on Devesh's hand.

"Let's hope he plans on allowing Leena to go with her father," Agent Sturnham said. "You're his real target."

"No way in hell I'm letting him take my wife," Devesh said in a voice that was barely a growl.

Pranav retrieved a small gun that was strapped to his lower leg and slid it into the back Devesh's waistband, then untucked his shirt to cover it.

Reign turned to her husband and said, "If it comes down to her life or mine, you let me go. I can survive him. She cannot."

chapter 45

"You know you won't make it out of the country," Reign warned, cautiously maneuvering over the cold ground in the darkest part of the shipyard in Hunter's Point. They arrived at this spot twenty minutes ago, only to find that the Feds were right. The area was still closed off because the company contracted to handle the cleanup of massive radiation had falsified test results for the Navy to transfer the land to real estate developers. The EPA shut it down and the decontamination efforts were ongoing. This was definitely not a safe place for anyone to be right now.

"The police are aware of any place you might think about going," she said, and her voice echoed off the remaining shipping containers that were stacked five high. The air was cooler coming off the ocean and the chill was causing her to shiver. "Who is that blonde you had helping you?"

"Nobody you need to concern yourself with," he said, stepping out of the shadows with Leena right behind him.

"Mama!"

"Yes, baby girl," Reign said in the calmest tone she could manage, but her heart was hammering in her chest. "I'm here."

Shawn angled so he could look behind her. "Where's the Swami?"

"Don't call him that."

"I'll call him whatever I want," Shawn said, grinning with a gleam in his eyes that frightened Reign. "Where is he?"

"I'm the one you want," she replied, glancing at the gun he aimed toward her. "Powerful man now that you have a gun in your hand."

"A little firepower can get my point across." Shawn looked down at Leena whose expression was pure stone. "You wouldn't be here if I hadn't used it."

"So let's trade," she offered, inching forward a little. "Me for my daughter."

"Nah, we'll wait for muscle man to show up."

Disappointment flooded her soul. "Why?"

"I want him to see what I'm going to do to you."

"In front of my daughter?"

"Oh, please," he said, dismissing her with a wave of his gun. "He'll pass her off to someone out there who you think is going to save you. They won't get to you in time. I paid a lot of money for this kind of transport. The police can't stop us. We won't be in their jurisdiction."

Devesh appeared from behind Reign, where he'd been waiting until the agents were in place. "Give me my daughter."

"Give me your wife," Shawn countered, and the predatory glint in his eyes caused Reign's breath to hitch.

"I'm not giving you a damn thing. Earn her love and trust the same way I did." Then he snapped his fingers. "Oh, wait, you can't do *that*—which is why you're doing *this*."

"Devesh, please don't irritate the man," Reign warned.

"Yes Swami, don't irritate Shawn," he taunted, eyes glazing over with hatred. "Say my name, Reign. It's not *the man* or *that man*. You know my name. Say it."

She didn't respond.

He cocked the hammer.

"Shawn," she whispered.

"That's more like it," he said with a cocky tone, then stared at Devesh. "So we're supposed to do some type of exchange, right? Your daughter for your wife?"

"Send her over," Devesh commanded, his hands balled into tight fists.

"Now, now. Don't be so impatient," Shawn teased.

"Mama. Papa," Leena said, "Where are the police?"

"Don't worry about the police," Shawn said, with an evil grin. "We have plenty of time to get to where we're going. They won't be able to interfere. Reign, come here."

Devesh tensed, took a step forward the moment Leena started to shiver from the cool air.

"Devesh," Reign warned, and he froze, before putting his focus on his daughter who was glaring up at Shawn.

"Yeah, that's a good, good doggie."

A vein throbbed an angry pulse at Devesh's temple. She could tell it took everything within him to remain still.

"Let her go, and I'll come to you," Reign implored, trying to hold her gaze steady so she wouldn't give away the fact that shadows flickered behind him; a sure sign that more agents were moving closer.

"Come with me," he said, giving her a lustful once over. "I can't wait until you're screaming my name." Then his expression filled with disdain. "Letting some foreigner between your legs."

"I thought you said all you want to do is talk."

"Gonna be hard to do with your mouth full," he said, glancing at Leena, who glared openly at him, trying to tug her hand out of his. "Can't say more than that. We have little ones around."

Reign inched forward, saying, "Let her go."

"You know I didn't mean what I said that night," he confessed, and his voice had taken on a softer tone. "I was drunk. You could've given me a second chance. I actually begged you. More than once. I would've made it up to you."

"How? More sex?" she retorted, adjusting so she had a better stance on the uneven concrete. "That's all I was good for in your eyes. That's the only thing you wanted."

"I was young." He repositioned the gun, then lowered to pick up Leena, who struggled against him.

"You're only upset about me being with Devesh because you missed out on everything else I brought to the table." She paused when Leena reached for her. "Put her down. She's cold and hungry."

"I tried to feed her," he defended. "She wouldn't eat. Stubborn little thing."

"Put me down," Leena said, squirming in Shawn's arms.

"Be still, Leena," Reign said, fearing that any sudden movements would make his gun discharge. She complied, but her frown said she was not happy.

"Feisty, just like your mother." He flickered a gaze over Leena's face before putting his focus on Reign again. "Walk this way, and I'll release her."

"Easy, Reign," Devesh said, keeping a steady focus on Shawn. "Make sure he keeps his word."

"Make sure he keeps his word," Shawn taunted in a whiny voice.

"You sound like a little girl," Devesh shot back, ignoring Reign's warning look.

Leena's head snapped to her father as she frowned in a way that meant, *that's an insult to little girls everywhere.*

Shawn grinned, then proceeded in telling Devesh in the crassest way possible, exactly what he didn't do like a little kid, and how all of it would be done to his wife.

Leena covered her ears and scowled at Shawn. When she lowered her hands and balled them into fists, Reign could swear that her daughter was about to punch Shawn in the face. "That's nasty," Leena admonished. "I shouldn't hear that. Be a grown-up."

Shawn's eyes widened with shock as he looked at Leena and she glared right back.

"No class then," Reign said sourly, totally agreeing with her baby girl. "And none now. No matter how many degrees you have. Leena …"

Leena's eyes snapped to Reign, who said, "Be still for now, baby girl."

She grimaced and unclenched her fists, but the look in her eyes said forget whatever program the adults were on, she was ready to take him down by herself.

"All I wanted was your forgiveness," Shawn said.

"She forgave you a long time ago," Devesh countered. "You just believed that forgiving meant forgetting what you did, allowing you to pick up where you left off. There's no coming back after what you said to her. There's no kind of trust you can build after that. Sorry stud, get over yourself."

The glint of something flashed in her peripheral vision. Devesh had slide to one side, slowly removed a weapon—Pranav's gun—waiting for an opportune time to put it to use.

If only Shawn would put Leena down, Devesh could even the score. Permanently.

"You don't want me," Reign said to Shawn, realizing she needed to keep him engaged and distracted. "You want to win at something, since you've deliberately destroyed your own life. I'm just convenient. You don't have any respect for me. Never did."

"Yes, I did," he whispered, trying to steady Leena in his arms.

"Did you ever take me out to dinner?" she asked. "A movie? For a walk in the park? To the beach?" she roared. "For a whole year, you were afraid to be seen in public with me."

"That's not true," he countered, but his voice was weak.

"You don't respect any woman. Not even your wife." Reign pointed a finger at him. "You went on national television practically proclaiming that you still have a thing for me."

"I love you, Reign," he said softly. "I just wanted a second chance."

"But doing that told your wife that she wasn't enough," she said, in the most soothing tone she could manage. "That she was so lacking, you wanted to reach back into your past to get with the woman who clearly hadn't given you any indication that she wanted anything to do with you. She took vows with you, and you threw her away."

"I didn't want her," he yelled, and his voice echoed off the shipping containers. "I *never* wanted her. She was a substitute."

Devesh sighed and shook his head. Something that infuriated Shawn who growled, "Get over here."

She took a few steps forward, saying, "Release my daughter now."

Leena's expression turned serious as she studied Shawn's stance as though measuring him up for some reason.

"Leena, go to Papa," Reign instructed, moving just within Shawn's reach.

Shawn gingerly placed Leena on the ground. He put a grip on Reign's arms.

Four things happened simultaneously.

Devesh raised his gun.

Leena doubled back, sending a roundhouse kick to Shawn's genitals causing him to double over in pain.

Shawn's gun went off.

Leena fell to the ground.

chapter 46

The police were gathered around the entrance of the shipyard. Officers Mitchell and Gill were questioning Reign and Devesh for the third time but were interrupted when a pencil-thin detective came up and said, "We found the body of Amy Seran at the mouth of the yard that led away from the more developed areas. She was shot in the chest and temple, and died instantly."

"What did she have to do with him?" Reign asked, noticing that Devesh was trying to school his features into a mask of indifference, though she could tell he was affected by the news of his ex-girlfriend's murder. "Shawn was never into White girls."

"While that may be the case," Officer Mitchell said. "Evidently, from the records we pulled, they've been corresponding for a while now." He flipped a few pages of his notepad. "First contact was on Facebook Messenger after he posted an article about Reign and Devesh. Seems like she wanted you totally out of the picture, but Newsome had other plans."

"I guess she went in for that old saying, 'the enemy of my enemy is my friend,'" Officer Gill said.

"I can't believe we were both attracted to crazy," Reign said, causing Devesh to nudge her into silence.

"So," Officer Mitchell said, turning the conversation back to getting his questions answered. "Let me get this straight," he said, scratching his temple, as the paramedics wheeled a moaning Shawn to the waiting ambulance. "The little girl took him down?"

"Yes," Reign and Devesh said in unison, then glanced at each other.

The officer shook his head and looked at his partner, who shrugged but peered at Leena as she lifted her chin, staring back at him as though daring him to say something out of order.

"My daughter took martial arts in Chicago to learn how to protect herself," Reign explained, with a side-eye at Devesh.

"And she'll be starting new classes next week," Devesh offered, nodding as if that was now the end of the debate they'd had for nearly six months.

"Leena was supposed to go to her father the minute I was close enough for Shawn to grab me," Reign said with a pointed look at Jay and Pranav who came to stand next to Devesh. "Instead, she surprised him—and us—by landing what's called a roundhouse kick to his—"

"Softer parts," Devesh supplied, and Jay stifled a smile. "That would have been enough time for me to get a shot off and get both Reign and Leena to safety. But instead, Reign wrestled the gun from his hand, and it went off, shooting him in—"

"The softer parts," Reign said, glancing at Leena whose lips crooked into a smile.

"It's a penis, Mama," Leena said, causing the officers to grin. "Didn't you teach us that?"

"Good Lord," Devesh whispered, rubbing his forehead. Jay lowered his head. His shoulders shook, a sure sign he was failing at holding in his laughter. Same with Pranav.

"I've been on the force for almost twenty years, and I've never heard anything like it." Officer Mitchell lowered until he was eye level with Leena. "Little lady, you're going to be one powerful woman."

Leena beamed up at him. "That's what Papa says all the time."

epilogue

Three days after Leena was safely home with her family, Mumma arrived at Reign's home at daybreak. Several of the Maharaj women were gathered around her.

"Is something wrong, Mumma?" Reign asked, pulling her robe tighter about her body.

"Nothing is wrong," she replied. "We have a request."

Reign stood back to allow them in. The women, all nineteen of them, spread out in the living room. Their expressions were so serious that Reign believed Mumma had not been honest.

"We would like to give you and Devesh a proper wedding."

Reign blinked, trying to process that request, before taking a sweeping look at all of them. "So you're saying I'm not married, already?"

"No, not that," Mumma said, smiling. "Only that we would like to do it the proper way this time. A blend of your culture and ours."

Devesh sauntered into the parlor, leaned on the doorjamb and took a sip of coffee.

Reign explained what his mother had said.

"It's not every day a man gets to marry the woman he loves twice," he said, lifting his mug in a salute. "I'm game."

Mumma clasped her hands with glee. "The pandit is waiting at our home to talk with you."

"Just knew I'd say yes, eh?"

"We could hope," Mumma replied with a comedic lift of her eyebrows.

"Give us a few minutes," Devesh requested. He put his arm around Reign's waist and guided her to the cuddling chair in the living room. They sank down into its soft cushions. He placed a hand on her knee, his finger tracing the swirly design on her silky robe. "We can do this if it's what you want."

"I never saw myself in a white dress and walking down the aisle or anything like that," she said. "That 'til death do us part' thing does something to me." An involuntary shudder ran through her body.

Devesh let his chin fall to his chest for a moment, then looked up at the ceiling while drawing in a deep breath. "Honey, look at me."

She slowly let her eyes meet his.

"Are you saying you're still planning to leave me in eight years?" he asked. "After all we've been through together. You don't want a lifetime for us?"

She looked deep into his eyes while a montage of images from their life together ran through her mind. This man had been good to her. Better than good. He had proven to her that she was deserving of his love. He was a great father to their children, wonderful and loyal to her son.

"Devesh, we've had our struggles for sure. Most couples couldn't have lasted through half of what we've been through in this short amount of time."

He gave a cautious smile. "You have brought me more happiness than I ever dared dream a man could have."

He picked her hand up and gave it a gentle kiss.

"But ..." She bit her lip while she searched for the right words.

"No ifs, ands, or buts, my love." Devesh nodded toward the other room. Leena and Kamran, dressed in their pajamas, had gotten out of bed and were being greeted with hugs and kisses from Mumma, Aunt Kavya and the rest of the women. "You're buying an issue before it's been sold."

"You've been hanging out with Jay too long," she accused.

"Guilty." He stroked his fingers across her open palm. "I love your son. And I love you." He kissed her. "My family wants to show you how much they love you. Let's do this. Let's live, my love."

She leaned into him, returning his kiss. When she pulled away, she called out to the twins who came running to join them in the cuddle chair.

"Leena, Kamran," Devesh began. "Your Mama and Papa are getting married."

The twins shared a curious glance, before frowning up and asking, "Again?"

🪷 🪷 🪷

Several days before the wedding, they placed the traditional mehndi— henna markings—on Reign's hands and feet. The deeper the final color, the more the bride would be loved by her husband and mother-in-law. The bride was also forbidden from doing any housework as long as the color of the bridal mehndi remained on her hands.

"Hey, that works for me," she said to Devesh when Aunt Kayva explained everything. "You do know how to mop, right?"

Devesh could only shake his head.

Reign and her bridal party of Maharaj women, nieces Jennifer and Shakira, friends Renee, Debra, and Janice were treated to skin and spa treatments with her favorite team as well as private meals. The garments were all made by Aunt Kavya and her growing group of seamstresses. She alone, made each one of Reign's wedding dresses. None of them were white.

An Indian wedding is a three-day affair. The Maharaj family had traveled from places as far as New Delhi, Mumbai, Goa, and Africa and as close as New York City, Los Angeles, and Miami for the wedding.

On day one of Reign and Devesh's wedding, white tents were erected across the gardens outside of the Maharaj home. The array of food was sure to be pleasing to even the toughest palate. Champagne and liquor were free-flowing to keep spirits high.

Reign, Devesh, and the rest of their guests were dressed in emerald—the color of Reign's eyes.

On day two, everyone wore magnificent shades of red and gold, and the tents and their house were layered in flowers, sheers, and silks that transported the guests into a glorious rendition of an Indian palace for the ceremony and the reception.

On day three, one side had been done in rich shades of royal and electric blues, deep lavenders with silver accents, tiny pinpricks of light on the ceiling gave the impression of being under a moonlit sky.

The neighbors had also been invited, and the entire Shoreview area between the Maharaj place and Devesh and Reign's home had been blocked off. Devesh arrived on a white horse, followed by twenty groomsmen and bridesmaids—all sisters, cousins, and nieces of their respective families, most of whom wore magnificent blues. Pranav and Jay, the best men, were dressed in traditional hand-embroidered sherwanis of blue and silver silk. Reign, draped in a Kavya Patel royal blue and silver silk sari, wore jewelry given to her by the Maharaj family.

Devesh, Pranav, and Jay carried matching swords that made them look dashing and dangerous. Reign smiled, realizing they were three of the most handsome men there. When they walked into the area, traveling up the plush blue carpeting specifically laid for the event, and arrived in the specially crafted ballroom that had been created inside the formally designed tents, Devesh draped a blue floral garland around Reign's neck.

Reign started the first of Saat Phere, the seven vows that they were to repeat after the Pandit recited them.

When it came time for her to repeat Phera—the prayers to God for plenty of nourishing and pure food—she simply said, "I do," causing everyone to break out into laughter and for Devesh to nudge her a little.

Devesh leaned over to Reign and said, "You must say all of the words."

Reign lifted the silk scarf covering her hair and answered. "Sweetheart, he needs to hit the cliff notes of this whole thing. It's been an hour already. Come on, now."

Jay stepped to the podium, and leaned in to Devesh and asked, "What's the problem?"

"Indian marriages take about seven hours."

Jay blinked his confusion, looked first at Reign then Devesh. "Seven hours?

"As in 420 minutes?" Reign asked, and put her focus on the Pandit who nodded. "No one mentioned that. And Sesvalah still has to do her part of the ceremony."

The silence that ensued after that revelation was ample time for Jay to come up with a plan.

"Do you know the story of King Solomon?" he asked the Pandit.

"As a matter of fact, I do," the robust man answered with a lift of his bushy eyebrow.

"Great," Devesh replied, splaying his hand over Reign's back. "Then you'll understand if we ask that you split this one down the middle?"

Reign looked to Jay as they both laughed.

The family waited as the Pandit started with the second round of prayers to God for a healthy and prosperous life, for physical, spiritual and mental health. Round three—prayers to God that they could walk together to attain wealth, that they could share the happiness and the pain together. The fourth round—prayers to God to increase the love and respect for each other and their respective families. The fifth round—prayers for beautiful, heroic, and noble children was altered and shortened immensely as the couple already had that covered; and the sixth set of prayers, asking for a long peaceful life with each other.

By the final step, even though the pandit was rolling through the words at twice the normal speed, Reign was ready to slide into the front row, but she stayed true and asked God for companionship, togetherness, loyalty, and understanding. She asked God to make them friends and give her the maturity to carry out the friendship for a lifetime.

Devesh turned to her at the end of the ceremony and said, "We have now become friends. We will not break this friendship in life."

She beckoned for the twins to come forward. Bending down to eye-level with them, she smiled and said, "Yes, we're married, again."

❀ ❀ ❀

Reign moved to stand by Devesh's side, watching as the family-style dinner began. The servers brought out each dish to tables draped in colors that were complementary to the theme. They explained the contents and placed them on the table around the tall cylindrical glass centerpieces with candles and lotus floats. Music that complemented all tastes—Hindi, popular, dance, and even a few of Reign's favorite Jazz, House, Hip-Hop tunes, and songs from Devesh's new album releasing in two months—were part of the night's line up.

"I have never seen anything more beautiful," Devesh whispered to her, giving her a slow once-over.

That statement brought a smile to Reign's tear-stained face. Certainly tears of joy as he had never seen a smile so bright.

As both the Alvin Ailey Dancers and the Mahira Troupe began their respective African American and Hindi traditional dances, Reign took a seat in one of the elaborately silk-covered chaises that had been created for them. Reign joined in when the attendees were taught Punjabi folk songs and how to dance the bhangari. Reign looked Devesh's way and added a few extra hip movements for his benefit. Devesh nodded toward the twins and mouthed the words, "Behave, woman."

The final event was the "light-hearted" ritual called the ring of control. A ring and a few coins were put into a silver dish filled with milk and vermillion rice. The bride and groom dipped their hands into the bowl to search for the ring.

She took in the amused expression on Mumma's face and stared at the dish for the longest time before smiling. "Looks harmless. I'll give it a whirl."

Devesh and Reign placed their hands in the silver dish. They reached in. Both came up empty—no ring whatsoever.

The entire room went silent.

Reign took in the range of shocked, amused, and horrified expressions on everyone's faces and looked to Devesh for an explanation.

"The one who finds the ring four out of seven times is most likely to rule the roost."

"But I didn't feel any rings in there, did you?"

"No love, it's just proving something that's obvious," Devesh said with a nod to a place right behind her. "We know exactly who's in control."

The twins shared a mischievous glance with Jay, as all three of them held up the ring and coins and smiled back at them.

www.ingramcontent.com/pod-product-compliance
Lightning Source LLC
Chambersburg PA
CBHW030646260626
47157CB00007B/2521